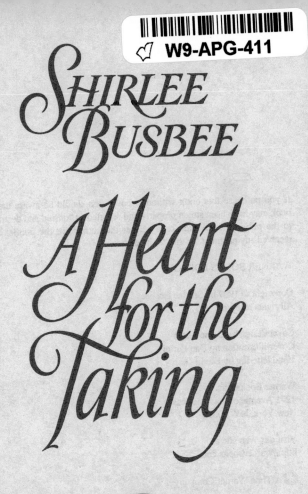

SHIRLEE BUSBEE

A Heart for the Taking

WARNER BOOKS

A Time Warner Company

WARNER BOOKS EDITION

Cover design by Diane Luger
Cover illustration by Dan Perini
Hand lettering by David Gatti

Warner Books, Inc.
1271 Avenue of the Americas
New York, NY 10020

Visit our Web site at
http://warnerbooks.com

Ⓦ A Time Warner Company

Printed in the United States of America

First Printing: September, 1997

10 9 8 7 6 5 4 3 2 1

FANCY NEVER KNEW WHAT IT WAS THAT HAD BROUGHT HER AWAKE, BUT SHE WAS SUDDENLY HEART-POUNDINGLY ALERT.

Something had disturbed her, and frantically her gaze scanned the little glen. A terrified gasp came from her lips as her eyes fell upon a pair of moccasins.

Panic twisting through her, Fancy scrambled upright, her gaze moving swiftly upon the tall, lean body in buckskins; another equally large buckskin-clad body just behind the first. The Thackers! But when her eyes finally rested on the dark, granite-hewn features of the man standing in front of her, her heart gave a great leap as she realized that it wasn't the Thackers who had found them. It was someone infinitely more dangerous to Fancy's peace of mind— Chance Walker.

"A NEW SHIRLEE BUSBEE BOOK IS ALWAYS A SPECIAL TREAT."
—*Romantic Times*

"ONE OF THE BEST ROMANCE WRITERS OF OUR TIME."
—*Affaire de Coeur*

"BUSBEE REAFFIRMS HER LONG-HELD PLACE AT THE TOP OF HER GENRE."
—*Publishers Weekly*

A Featured Alternate of the Doubleday Book Club®

Also by Shirlee Busbee

LOVERS FOREVER

Published by

WARNER BOOKS

To fine friends and good companions:

CARLA and SANDY REIMER, who feed us in moments of crisis and graciously share horse knowledge.

AND

BARBARA and LOREN MACK-FISHER, who delight with "dead dog" stories and lucid explanations of ancient text.

AND

HOWARD—who is still the best!

Prologue

Chance Meeting

Colony of Virginia
April 9, 1740

In the dead vast and middle of the night.

William Shakespeare,
Hamlet

The storm shrieked across the land like a furious banshee, the treetops tossing violently in the fierce wind and lashing rain. Lightning tore the utter blackness of the sky time and again, and the angry rumble of thunder rose above the fury of the storm, sometimes just a sharp crack that seemed to shake the very ground, other times merely a long, ominous grumble.

It was certainly not a night, if she had been given a choice, that Letty Walker would have chosen to give birth. But then, just as she had no control over the arrival of one of the most violent storms to strike the Colony of Virginia in a decade, so did she have no choice over the arrival of her own firstborn child. It was not an easy birthing.

Letty hadn't expected it to be. She had been married for

nearly twenty years to her beloved Sam Walker and had just celebrated her thirty-eighth birthday this past January in this year of our Lord, 1740. She was far too old to be having her first child, and her body made that clear with every spasm of pain that streaked through her. But, oh, dear God! She and Sam wanted this child so desperately. So *very* desperately.

The only children of only children, when they had married, they had planned to have a large, boisterous family. But as the years had passed, those desperately longed-for babies had never appeared. The one that was presently attempting to be born was the culmination of years of hope and yearning, and she would suffer this pain tenfold if it put a babe in her arms.

While Letty and Sam longed most urgently for this child, there was someone who did not. Constance Walker, Letty's ridiculously young stepmother-in-law. Constance had arrived in the Colonies from England two years ago as the bride of Letty's father-in-law, John, and had subsequently given birth to a baby boy. Until Letty's pregnancy, it had been understood by everyone that at some time in the future, Constance's son, Jonathan, would inherit all of the great Walker fortune.

In the normal course of events, it would have been Sam's children who would have inherited, but Sam and Letty had not been so blessed. John had been determined for his vast estate to flow into the hands of his own direct bloodline, and at the age of sixty-two he had gone to England in search of a suitable wife to bear him another child—or children, if the fates be kind. To his delight, he had found everything he had been searching for in Constance Wheeler. When Jonathan had been born, some ten months after their marriage in England, John had been ecstatic. Letty and Sam had been happy over the event, and they all doted on the infant, Jonathan. Tragically, John had not lived six weeks beyond the birth of his youngest son. His vast estate had been divided equally amongst his two sons, with Sam having total control of the entire fortune until Jonathan reached the age of thirty-five, when his portion would be turned over to him. Constance

d slipped easily into the role of beautiful young widow,
nfident, since Sam and Letty had no heirs, that in due
urse, Jonathan would inherit *everything*.

From the moment she had stepped into the New World,
onstance had viewed all the diverse wealth of the Walkers
her own, from the thousands of acres of untamed land, to
e rich tobacco fields and the elegant plantation house, to
alker Ridge, the palatial home in Williamsburg, to the
ips and the cargoes in their holds, to the cold hard cash
at John Walker, unlike most colonists, commanded. And it
as cold, calculating greed for her son's future that made
er view Letty's stunningly unexpected pregnancy with
ch great rage.

The Walkers were Virginian aristocracy. An ancestor had
en one of the early settlers at Jamestown in the last cen-
ry, and John Walker, as his forebears before him, had con-
nued to increase the family holdings. The Walkers
mmanded respect and prestige in the colony and con-
olled a great fortune. A fortune that had induced Constance
the age of nineteen to marry a man forty-four years her se-
or.

Not that John Walker had been a raddled old man. He had
t been. Like the majority of the Walkers, Sam and
nathan's father had been tall, broad-shouldered, and ro-
st, proud of the fact that he still had all his own teeth and
at he had no need of wigs and powder to give himself a
shionable head of hair. Despite his age, with the glinting
ue eyes and handsomely chiseled features of the Walkers,
hn could have taken his pick from any number of eager,
bile young women. He had traveled to England for the ex-
ess purpose of finding a bride to give him a son, but he
d taken one look at Constance's lovely green eyes and soft
ir hair and had fallen in love like a callow youth.

Possessing no fortune of her own and coming from a
ackground of genteel poverty, Constance had wasted little
me in debating the wisdom of marrying a man so much
lder and leaving behind all that she had ever known. There

was a fortune to be had, and she had every intention of se
curing it for herself . . . and her child.

For a moment her unfriendly gaze drifted to Letty, as sh
lay on the bed, her wan features twisted with pain as anothe
contraction knifed through her. Constance's lips tightene
She didn't hate Letty, she actually liked her; Letty was kin
to her and openly adored Jonathan. It was Letty's child wh
aroused all her resentment and antipathy. All her hatred wa
focused on the child who would supersede her own son an
who would one day inherit an enormous share of the Walke
wealth. It just wasn't *fair*, she thought bitterly. Jonathan wa
the heir! Jonathan was supposed to inherit *everything*!

Since Letty's ecstatic announcement of her impendin
motherhood, Constance had had seven long months to broo
over the injustice of it all, and she had come to view thi
child struggling so to be born as a rival, a usurper who ha
no right to take away her own child's inheritance. It didn
matter that as John's youngest son, and Sam's half-brothe
Jonathan would still be wealthy and have land and a fortun
of his own to order. All that mattered to Constance was tha
a major portion of the fortune she had considered her son'
would be given to someone else. If it weren't for Letty'
child, it would all be Jonathan's, which as far as Constanc
was concerned was how it should be.

A loud boom of thunder brought Constance's thought
back to the matter at hand. The babe was early—it wasn't t
be born until sometime in mid-May, and here it was not eve
the middle of April. Over a month too soon, and the birthin
was taking too long. Far too long. Hope suddenly sprang
into her breast. Perhaps the babe would die.

Slightly cheered, she bent over and, wiping Letty's damp
forehead, said kindly, "Push, dear. Try not to fight the pain
You must not struggle so—your babe will arrive soon
enough."

"Oh, Constance! Do you think so?" Letty whispere
tiredly. "It did not take you so long to bring forth Jonathan
as I recall." She smiled faintly. "It seemed that the servan
had barely entered our wing of the house when Father John

rrived almost on his heels to tell us that you had safely delivered a son."

Constance couldn't help the superior smile that curved her small mouth. "That is true, dear Letty, but you must remember that I am much younger." At the anxious look that flashed in Letty's beautiful gray-blue eyes, Constance said hastily, "Which should not concern you at all. You will do just fine. 'Tis just taking a trifle longer. Do not worry. All will be well."

"If only Sam were here," Letty murmured. "I know he *never* would have gone to Philadelphia if he had had the least notion that the baby would decide to come early."

"Shush. Sam's task is done and 'tis up to you to finish the deed."

Another contraction savagely clenched Letty's swollen body, and she gave a soft cry. It was now well over thirty-six hours since the first onslaught of pain had struck her, and she was growing very weak and exhausted. Anxiety about the safety of her child gnawed at her, and with every passing moment she feared that both she and her baby would die. Poor Sam. He would be devastated.

Thoughts of her dear husband's grief at the demise of both wife and child roused Letty from her dark musings, and she began to concentrate on the messages her body was sending her, pushing with renewed vigor with each contraction. For several moments there was just the sound of the raging storm outside the stout walls of the plantation house intermingled with Letty's harsh, panting breaths as she struggled to rid her body of the baby within it.

It was a spacious, richly furnished room in which Letty labored. The huge bed in which she lay was lavishly hung with pale green silken curtains, a carpet in hues of rose and cream lay upon the floor, and a fire leapt comfortingly on the hearth of the gray marble fireplace. Lamps holding the finest whale oil shed a gentle light over the remainder of the room, revealing the tall mahogany wardrobes on the far wall and a satinwood dressing table with its velvet-covered seat. A chair near the bed held several clean towels and the small blue-and-white blanket that Letty had knitted herself in anticipation of the coming child. Next to the chair, sitting on an elegant walnut table, was a china bowl and ewer, both filled with warm water.

Letty and Constance were not alone in the room. Anne Clemmons, Constance's companion-servant, who had accompanied her from England, was also present. It was Anne who carefully lifted the sheet and viewed the progress of the birthing. Intensely loyal to the mistress she had served for fifteen years, since she had been twelve and Constance only six, Anne had come to believe that her fortunes were firmly aligned with Constance's. It had been a maxim in Anne's life that whatever was good for Constance was good for her. Anne wanted this baby no more than her mistress did.

Pushing the sheet farther out of the way, Anne glanced up to meet Constance's eyes. "The head is there," she said flatly. "A few more strong pushes and the babe will be delivered."

Letty heard the words with a fearful joy. Her baby. In a matter of moments, her child would be laid in her arms. "Please, *dear* God, let all be well."

Caught up in the pain of the impending birth, Letty was hardly aware of the ugly look that crossed Constance's face or the manner in which her fists clenched at her sides. Filled with impotent rage, Constance could only stand by helplessly as the end to all her schemes was forcing its way into the world. Shattering her world.

Anne was very busy for the next several moments as Letty brought forth her child. As the worst of the contractions subsided and Letty fell back in exhaustion, Anne lifted the infant from the bed. "A boy," she said. "Stillborn."

A scream of anguish rose up from Letty. With tears streaming down her face, she demanded, "Give him to me! You must be wrong. He cannot be dead."

But he was. Even Letty could see that as Anne gently laid the blue-faced infant in her outstretched arms. The cord had twisted around his neck, and the long birth had stolen what chance he'd had of life. Weeping soundlessly, Letty clutched the small body to her bosom.

Releasing her pent-up breath, Constance shot Anne a look of triumph. To think she had worried. Letty was too old to have a *live* child.

Now that any threat to her happiness had been removed, Constance was able to offer comfort to the grieving mother. "Oh, Letty!" she cried, almost sincerely. "I am *so* sorry! I know how much this child meant to you and Sam."

Tenderly Letty's hands touched her dead baby, marveling at his perfection, too stunned by the tragedy to care very much for Constance's words of comfort. "He is so beautiful," she muttered. Instinctively she glanced at his tiny feet, noting the six toes on the right foot. "He even," she whispered painfully, "has the six toes of Sam's family—every Walker child since Sam's grandfather has been so marked." Her hand gently brushed that soft little foot, her gaze wandering over the small, still body. "Isn't he perfect? So very perfect?" A huge sob welled up inside of her. "And so very dead."

Anne and Constance moved quickly to soothe her, Anne eventually taking the dead child from her arms, Constance pressing a concoction of brandy and laudanum on her. "For the pain and to help you sleep," Constance said softly as she helped the older woman to sit up against the pile of pillows and swallow the liquid.

For several moments only the sound of the storm was heard in the room as the other two women worked quickly, wrapping the dead infant in one of the towels and clearing away the stained sheets. Grief-stricken and exhausted, Letty merely lay there, welcoming the black numbness offered by the laudanum.

More moments passed, Constance mentally composing the sad little letter she would have delivered to Sam in Philadelphia as she supervised the tidying up; Letty drifting slowly into a deep, drugged sleep; and Anne, pleased that her mistress was pleased, almost humming as she followed Constance's orders.

Suddenly, a sharp urgent pain lanced through Letty, and her eyes flew open. "Merciful heavens. What is happening?"

"The afterbirth," Anne said calmly. " 'Tis nothing to fret about, mistress."

But Anne was wrong, as she and Constance soon found out. Exhaustion and the laudanum had taken firm hold of Letty, and despite the pain that racked her body, she drifted deeper and deeper into unconsciousness as her body fought to relieve itself not of the afterbirth, but of a second child! Without waking up, Letty was unknowingly giving birth to *twins*. The second boy was as strong and lusty as the first had been weak and lifeless.

Her jaw set, Anne swiftly cut the cord and wrapped the second infant in the blue-and-white blanket his mother had knitted with such joyful anticipation. The boy had a powerful set of lungs, and Anne fitted the blanket securely over his head, hoping to muffle the cries.

She and Constance looked at each other. "What do we do?" Anne hissed, holding the child to her bosom. "This one is alive."

Constance bit her lip, fury at the trick fate had played on her giving her pretty face an ugly cast. It just wasn't *fair*! The baby had been born dead—no one expected twins! There was only supposed to be *one* baby.

Her gaze suddenly narrowed and she glanced at Letty. Letty, who was too deeply drugged to be aware of what was going on. Letty, who thought she had given birth to a dead son. And *only* a dead son.

Constance took but a moment to make her decision. This child stood between her son and a great fortune. Letty thought her son was dead. Why not let her go on thinking that?

Constance took a deep breath. "Get rid of it," she said sharply. "Everyone is asleep. You can slip out of the house and throw it in the river. No one will ever find out. Letty's stillborn son lies just over there. No one need ever know about this child."

Anne hesitated. She had taken care of Constance since the younger woman had been a mere child and she loved Constance dearly. Being Constance's companion had saved her from a life of drudgery and uncertainty. There was nothing she wouldn't do for her . . . but cold-blooded murder? The child wiggled against her bosom, and her reluctance grew. This was a babe they were talking about. A newborn.

"Well. What are you waiting for?" Constance demanded. "Get rid of it."

"Mistress, I . . ."

Constance's eyes narrowed, and reaching across the short distance that separated them, she slapped Anne hard across the cheek. "Do you hear me?" she snapped. "Get rid of it, I tell you."

"What harm has he done you—Master Jonathan will still be a rich young man—you are a rich young widow—far richer than you ever dreamed when we lived with your father in Surrey. You have so much now. Couldn't you—"

Constance's green eyes flashed angrily. "How *dare* you! You forget yourself! And you forget that I am your mistress and that you will do as I say or it will go ill for you." She stepped closer to Anne. "I could send you back to England without character. How would you like that? I could write Father and tell him that you were a lying, thieving wretch and that he was not under any circumstance to offer you employment and to tell all his friends what a terrible person you were. What would you do then? Penniless and without character?"

For a long moment, Anne stared at Constance. This was the way it had always been: Constance threatening her with some dire fate if she didn't do or obtain something that Constance desperately wanted. Once the objective had been gained, Constance would turn back immediately into the sweetly smiling creature most people knew. Only Anne knew of the greed and viciousness that lay behind that lovely face. Constance *would* do precisely as she had threatened.

Anne's slender shoulders drooped with defeat. "Very well."

"Oh, Annie, dear, I knew you would not let me down," Constance said softly, a pretty smile curving her mouth. "And I would never have really sent you back to England—how could I? You are the dearest creature. You never fail me."

When Anne remained unmoved by her words, Constance said quickly, "I'll make it up to you. Truly I shall."

Her heart heavy, Anne paid her no mind. The squirming baby clutched to her bosom, she slipped from the room. Moving swiftly down the long, wide hallway, her step faltering only as she came to the ornately framed portrait of Letty's grandmother, Charity, and her twin sister, Faith, she silently made her way through the darkened house. After finding her cloak in her room, she flung it on and, moving carefully, fearful that some servant might be awakened by the storm and find her, quickly departed from the house, the baby hidden beneath the folds of her cloak.

Outside, the full force of the storm hit her, the wind and rain clawing at her like a wild thing. Grimly Anne struggled forward, deliberately shutting out all thoughts but one. The river. She had to reach the river.

The river, a branch of the James, lay a good three-quarters of a mile from the main house and the last of the outbuildings. Usually it was a pleasant walk, several tree-lined lanes leading to a landing at the river's edge, but in the middle of a fierce storm, with no light to guide her but the brilliant and terrifying flashes of lightening, Anne took no pleasure in her journey. The horrible thought of what she would do at the end of it filled her with pain and sorrow.

The babe was quieter now, the soft, mewling sounds that he made muffled beneath the blanket and cloak. Anne tried not to think about him, tried not to respond to the warm weight of him in her arms, or the emotions that rose up within her as he instinctively rooted near her breasts.

The sound of the river rose above the wind and rain. Swollen by the storm, it roared and surged in wildly tossed waves, and Anne's steps grew even slower as she neared it. How could she do this thing? Even for Constance, whom she loved more than anything in the world? But what *was* she to do? She didn't doubt for a moment that Constance would do as she threatened—despite what she had said afterward. Anne knew Constance, and if she didn't obey her . . . Anne swallowed painfully. Well, it just didn't bear thinking about.

Reaching the river's edge, she sought out a small bluff. A streak of lightning snaked across the sky, revealing the dark, furiously churning water below, the current running hard and fast. Slowly she opened her cloak and brought forth the babe. She even got as far as lifting him in the air to toss his swaddled weight in the river. But she could not. A sob broke from her. What was she to do? She could not murder this innocent babe. And she could not return to Constance with the deed undone.

As she stood there indecisively, her desperate gaze suddenly caught sight of a tiny light moving through the woods in her direction. Someone was coming. But who? Who would be out in a storm like this? Her breath caught in her throat, and she clutched the baby tighter to her. She couldn't be discovered. Not here. Not now.

She glanced around frantically, utter blackness meeting her look. What was she to do? The small bobbing light drew nearer, and still Anne stood there undecided. The force of the storm seemed to lessen for a moment, the wind falling, the rain slacking, the thunder and lightning slowing in its intensity.

The sound of a man's voice carried to her, and to her astonishment she realized that the fellow was singing. Singing in the midst of a storm like this?

The baby gave a great lusty cry just then, and to Anne's horror the singing stopped and a voice called out, "Who goes there?"

Thoroughly terrorized, Anne did the first thing that occurred to her. She laid the baby gently on the ground near the edge of the bluff, and then, without a backward look, she plunged into the undergrowth. The infant's howl of outrage rang in her ears as she ran through the night toward the house. Please, dear God, she prayed silently, let him be safe—let whoever was singing find him and take him far, *far* away from Walker Ridge! Somewhere where he will be safe!

There was a moment when it appeared as if Anne's heart-felt prayer would go unheeded, as a long and loud rumble of thunder drowned out the infant's cries. Hearing nothing but the sounds of the storm, the man in the woods, Morely Walker, shrugged his broad shoulders and decided some-what foggily (he had consumed many pints of ale over the course of the evening) that he must have been hearing things. Rather unsteadily, Morely began to make his way once more toward his destination—the overseer's cottage at Walker Ridge.

Morely was a distant cousin of Sam's. Somewhere back on the Walker family tree they shared a great-grandfather, and while Sam and most of the Walkers were respectable, hardworking gentlemen, occasionally within the family someone like Morely would appear—a charming rapscallion, unable to keep a penny he earned. Not that Morely was a ne'er-do-well; he was simply a handsome, amiable young man who just preferred drinking and gambling and decid-edly *un*respectable feminine company to anything even faintly resembling work. Orphaned at the tender age of twelve when his parents had been killed in an Indian raid, Morely had grown up at Walker Ridge, and John and Sam had ably administered the tobacco plantation left to him by his father until Morely had reached his majority.

Unfortunately Morely had not the least head for business, and within two years he had managed to lose everything. Two years of riotous living and frankly bad management had left him deeply in debt at the age of twenty-three. Only Sam's intervention had saved Morley's plantation from the sale block. But while he could still claim he owned nine thousand fertile acres planted in tobacco and a charming little house, in actuality Sam controlled everything—the price Morley had had to pay to save the land.

It had always been clearly understood that this was a temporary arrangement, that when Morely had proven himself a responsible and prudent young man, Sam would return the reins of power to him. Regrettably, in the six months that had passed since the debacle, Morely had shown no indication of changing his dissolute ways. In fact, if Sam hadn't given him the overseer's cottage at Walker Ridge in which to live and provided him with a nominal sum—which Morely promptly spent on ale and women—Morely would have been homeless and penniless.

Since the family, with the exception of Sam, made no secret of the fact that they considered him a disgrace and a definite blot on the family honor, Morely saw no reason why he should make any attempt to change. And he hadn't. He lived in the overseer's cottage and spent most of his time drinking and wenching in a small, rough tavern about two miles away from Walker Ridge, where there was a tiny settlement nestled in the curve of the James River. This was where he had been this evening, and he had been making his wayward way home when he'd heard the infant's cry. Having decided that he had imagined the noise, he had just taken two steps forward when the sound of a howling baby came unpleasantly clear to him.

He froze, his ale-befuddled brain trying to make sense of what he had heard. Another angry scream galvanized him and had him stumbling in the direction from which the cry had come. As he left the patch of wood in which he had been traveling, the sky and landscape were suddenly lit up by a tremendous, jagged bolt of lightning. It was in that brief moment, as bright as midday, that, to his amazed horror, he spied the small, wiggling bundle lying near the edge of the bluff.

In that split-second flash of light, Morely saw not another soul. Clearly the baby had been abandoned! Instinct drove Morely forward. When he reached the now squalling infant, with the exaggerated care of a man who has had too much to drink, he set down his lantern and clumsily lifted up the swaddled form.

He'd been hoping that he'd been imagining this entire event, but the squirming, screaming baby in his arms promptly dashed that notion. Helplessly he glanced around, expecting a distraught parent to appear at any second. No one did. He was alone on the bluff in the middle of the night, in the midst of one of the worst storms he had ever experienced, with a very angry infant in his arms.

Any lingering effects of too many tankards of ale vanished, and in an instant Morely found himself stone, cold sober. His agile brain working furiously, he gazed uneasily at the dark, roiling water below him. There were only two reasons, he decided grimly, for him to have found a baby obviously abandoned on the bluff: the mother of the child had killed herself by leaping into the river, inexplicably leaving behind her infant, or the baby had been cold-bloodedly left to its fate. An even more grisly idea crossed his mind. Perhaps someone had intended the baby to disappear beneath those raging waters.

A chill snaked down his spine, and his grip on the infant tightened protectively. His young face set, he picked up his lantern and left the bluff in a swift, long-legged stride.

The baby's cries had lessened to a heartrending little hiccup, and Morely found himself crooning a nonsensical litany of reassurance as he hurried through the night. His voice seemed to soothe the baby, and by the time they reached his cottage a few minutes later, the infant had fallen into a fitful slumber.

Carefully setting the baby in a large black leather chair near the hearth, Morely coaxed the remaining coals into life and soon had a warm, leaping fire. He lit a whale-oil lamp on the mantel and then, gently laying aside the blue-and-white blanket, for the first time took a good look at the infant.

The baby was obviously newborn, the birthing blood barely dry on his tiny body, and Morely realized that his unexpected presence must have frightened off whoever had been on the bluff—whether a mother who had leaped to her death or someone with something far more sinister in mind.

His eyes traveled over the baby, and Morely caught his breath when his gaze fell upon the long right foot and the six perfect toes. Except for Sam's immediate family, he was the only one who knew the significance of those six toes. And he only knew because of his intimacy with the family.

He could remember clearly the night, some five years ago, when he and Sam had been out hunting and had been caught far from home when night—and a sudden rainstorm—had descended upon them. They had eventually taken refuge in an old hunting shack, and once they had a fire going, they had shucked aside their dripping boots and clothing. Their feet warming near the fire, Morely had noticed Sam's six toes and had exclaimed over them. Sam had half smiled and said, "I'm pleased you think them merely odd and not a mark of the devil—as some might, if it were common knowledge." Sam had stared ruefully at his right foot. "I suppose I should be gratified by that sixth toe. It first manifested itself with my grandfather, who by way of my father passed it on to me. You might say that it is proof of my parentage." He had glanced over to Morely and with a slight rising of his color had muttered, "I would appreciate it if you kept this to yourself. There are many superstitious folk about, and I would not want my father and me to become objects of fear and loathing."

Morely had ardently sworn to keep his silence. The Salem witch trials and all the horrors that had accompanied them were not so very long ago—less than fifty years—and there were still the occasional cries of "Witch!" or "Warlock!" to be heard in the Colonies. Sam and his family were wise to keep the oddity of the six toes to themselves.

His eyes still fastened on the baby's sixth toe, Morely nodded to himself. That toe more than anything else confirmed that this child *had* to be Sam's son. And Constance, he reminded himself uneasily, had *not* been happy about the baby that Letty was due to give birth to in a month or so. His throat grew tight. Sam was gone to Philadelphia on business, leaving Letty all alone with Constance. An ugly suspicion leaped to his mind.

He didn't want to credit the horrifying thought that curled through his brain. He considered briefly that the baby could be Sam's bastard, but he immediately shook that idea away. If Sam had a mistress, he'd have known about it. Sam's devotion to Letty was legendary, and it would be too much of a coincidence for Sam to have gotten both Letty *and* another woman pregnant almost simultaneously. No. As sure as he was that the sun would rise tomorrow, he knew that he was staring at Letty and Sam's son. A son someone had left to perish on that lonely bluff at the edge of the river.

His blue eyes anxious and undecided, Morely stared hard at the infant. What was he to do? If Constance *was* behind tonight's mischief, he dared not approach the big house with the baby. And there were Letty's feelings to consider—if this baby wasn't hers, if Sam *had* gotten another woman pregnant, Morely definitely didn't want to be the one to disillusion her about her husband. Constance's probable involvement worried him a great deal. If she had tried to dispose of the child once, what was to stop her from trying again? And who would believe his wild accusations? With his reputation? He swallowed painfully, for the first time regretting his lackadaisical ways.

He owed everything to Sam and his family. Could he betray their many kindnesses to him by giving voice to his dark suspicions about Constance? What if he were wrong? What if the baby's possession of six toes was just an incredible coincidence? What if Sam had had nothing to do with this child's conception? That it was just mere chance? The only problem with that thinking was that the nearest dwellings for several miles around were at Walker Ridge, indicating that someone on Sam's plantation had given birth. And why would anyone so callously abandon a newborn, unless there was a powerful reason—such as gaining an entire fortune?

The baby stirred and began to whimper, and Morely picked him up gently and began to rock him. He knew the baby needed sustenance, and putting aside his unpleasant thoughts, he glanced around his small quarters for something to feed an infant. His mind was blank, until he remembered the small jug of milk that a slave from the big house had left in his larder just this evening—that and some molasses would have to do.

Feeding the baby was difficult, but using a clean cotton rag soaked in the milky concoction, Morley managed to get quite a bit down the baby. It helped that the baby suckled strongly on the cotton rag each time it was put to his mouth. When the baby finally fell asleep again, Morely laid him once more in the big chair and began to consider his next step.

If Sam were here, he'd take the baby to him—Sam would know what to do. Sam would settle the business and get to the bottom of it. But Sam was in Philadelphia and wasn't expected back for another few weeks. Keeping the baby here in his own house was out of the question. Not only did he suspect that the child was in danger, but he had neither the knowledge nor the means to care for an infant.

Since Sam wasn't available, Morely needed a safe place to take the baby temporarily until he could talk to Sam. But where? Whom could he trust?

His brow furrowed in thought, Morely paced the confines of the room, mentally reviewing all his various friends and relatives. Eventually his choice came down to his cousin, Andrew Walker. Andrew owned his own private little school on the outskirts of the tiny hamlet of Petersburg at the point of the Appamattuck River. Andrew was a kind man and well respected in the small settlement. And Petersburg was a perfect place for the baby—far enough away from Walker Ridge for the infant's safety, but not so far that it would be difficult to retrieve the baby when the situation was resolved. If he were lucky, he could make it to Petersburg in under five days. *If* he were lucky.

Andrew and his wife, Martha, were perfect, too—Martha had suffered through several stillbirths, and after over ten years of marriage, they were beginning to become resigned to being childless. The latest generation of Walkers did not seem to be very prolific, Morely conceded with a wry twist to his mouth. At any rate, Andrew and Martha would be thrilled to take care of the baby for however long it was necessary.

I must swear them to secrecy about the toes, he reminded himself suddenly. If his suspicions were correct and Constance were to learn of this baby with the six toes, it could prove dangerous. And if he gave Andrew and Martha the same reasons that Sam had given him for keeping quiet about the odd feature, he was certain they would eagerly comply. They would, no doubt, be certain that the baby was his and that *he* was dismayed and ashamed of that sixth toe.

Morely glanced at the sleeping child, and his face softened. What did it matter what they thought of him, if the babe was safe? His reputation was already in tatters. What was one more black mark?

His mind made up, Morely set about preparing for his journey. Since his position as overseer was a courtesy at best and since there were many days during which he was too drunk to work, no one would think too much of the fact that he had taken himself off for a while. Morely winced. It would simply be assumed that he was sleeping off the effects of his latest drunken stupor in the arms of one of his many light-skirted wenches.

The decision to take the child to Andrew and Martha did not come lightly to him. A thousand doubts deviled him, and he worried that he was leaping to the wrong conclusions— that there was a reasonable explanation for the newborn baby's presence on that bluff. One fact, however, was inescapable: if he had not chanced along tonight, the infant sleeping so soundly just a few feet away from him would have died.

Grimly determined to make no mistakes with the young life placed so precipitously in his hands, Morely brooded through the remainder of the night, speculating, wondering, and worrying a great deal about the conclusions and decisions he had made. He fed the baby twice during that time,

eeling something stirring deep within his heart each moment he held that tiny, dependent life in his big hands.

When dawn came, the worst of the storm had passed, although there were still showers and a persistent drizzle to
make Morely view the coming journey with a jaundiced eye.
He'd been busy for the past hour or so; his horse was saddled, food for the trip and various items that he hoped would
take care of the baby's needs were packed safely in the saddlebags, and he was garbed in his greatcoat, ready to leave
for Petersburg. Shrugging his broad shoulders, he finally
turned away from the window where he had been contemplating the weather and crossed the room to pick up the
baby, which he had wrapped up securely. Lifting the flap
that covered the baby's face, he stared down into the wide
blue eyes that foggily met his.

A smile twisted Morely's lips. "Well, little fellow, I think
you have the devil's own luck! If I hadn't chanced along
when I did, you'd have had a mighty short life."

The baby gurgled and stuck a fist in his mouth. Morely
laughed and, walking from the cabin, muttered, "There is no
doubt in my mind that chance has played a large part in your
life so far. When you think about it, it was pure, simple,
God-given *chance* that I decided even to come home last
night. Most nights I don't! But for some reason, I did last
night—to your good fortune, I might add. And, just as important—it was plain old chance that I even heard you
squalling when I did. Even that big bolt of lightning that
struck just then was chance—a few minutes earlier or later
and I might not have seen you at all!"

Approaching his horse, a nice, sturdy bay, Morely prepared for the tricky part: mounting while holding the baby
in one arm. There were no mishaps, and once in the saddle,
he settled the baby more comfortably in the crook of his arm
and gently urged his mount forward.

They rode several moments in silence, then Morely murmured, "You know, you *do* owe a damn lot to chance, young
man. In fact, I don't know of anyone who owes more. When
you think of everything that could have gone wrong . . ."

Morely shook his head. "Doesn't bear thinking about. But I have been thinking—you need a name. Since there ain't anybody else about, and since you might say that I'm the nearest thing to a pa that you have right now, I get to name you."

Morely took a deep breath and eyed the baby uncertainly. "Now you might not agree, but I've decided that since chance *did* play such an important part in your continuing existence, you couldn't have a better name than that— *Chance!*"

The baby waved his arms exuberantly, and Morely grinned. "Like that notion, do you? Well, then, Chance it is! Chance Walker!"

Morely's grin faded. "We'll just have to hope that chance continues to smile on us, little fellow. We've an uncertain journey ahead of us, and I ain't at all sure that my cousin will be overjoyed to see us." He glanced down at the baby. "Reckon we'll just have to leave it to chance!"

Part One

———◆◆◆———

Fancy

Colony of Virginia
Summer 1774

A damsel of high lineage, and a brow
May-blossom, and cheek of apple-blossom,
Hawk-eyes; and lightly was her slender nose
Tip-tilted like the petal of a flower.

> Alfred, Lord Tennyson,
> *Idylls of the King*

Part One

Family

Colony of Virginia
Summer 1774

Chapter One

"Oh, Fancy, *do* come see! 'Tis the strangest creature I have ever seen in my life!" cried Ellen Merrivale as she leaned dangerously over the rails of the ship.

"Ellen! Please do be careful, dear—after we have managed to cross the ocean from England to the Colony of Virginia without a mishap, I would hate for us to start off our arrival with a tragedy," replied Frances "Fancy," as she strolled up to her younger sister's side at the railing. "Oh, my! I do see what you mean," she exclaimed, a sparkle suddenly gleaming in the long-lashed golden brown eyes.

"Is it an Indian?" Ellen asked, her cheeks rosily flushed with excitement. "A true savage?"

"Hmm, I think so. I've read that they do wear feathers in their hair, and with those long, black braids and that shockingly bright-colored blanket around his shoulders, I would say that he looks very much like what one would expect."

Ellen giggled, her blue eyes sparkling. "Oh, Fancy, must you be so stuffy? You sound like a blue-stocking."

Fancy laughed ruefully. "Mayhap I *am* a blue-stocking. Just like old Lady Wells in the village."

"Not you! Lady Wells would never have consented to coming to the Colonies—even just for a visit as we have done." Ellen shot her sister a sideways glance. "I still cannot believe that we are actually here. I was certain right up until the ship sailed that you would change your mind."

Fancy slipped an arm around her sister's slim waist. "Hmm, I almost did, poppet. A dozen times I have asked myself if I was doing the right thing, leaving England and coming for an extended stay at Walker Ridge. Jonathan Walker appears to be a proper sort of man and I'm sure he'll make you a fine husband, but . . ."

Her cheeks flushed a deeper hue, Ellen asked softly, "He has not actually offered for me, has he?"

"No," Fancy replied slowly, "but there is no use for us to pretend not to know why we are here—he has, without taking the final step, committed himself as far as an honorable man could." She sighed. "I just wish . . ."

Ellen leaned nearer her sister, her sweet features full of understanding. "What?" she asked softly. "Wish that he were not so much older? Or that I was not so young? Or that he lived in England and not in the New World?"

Fancy grimaced. "All of those things, I expect."

The sisters made a pretty pair as they stood there together at the side of the ship, Ellen as fair as Fancy was dark, both young women a bit above average height, both smallboned and slim, but nicely rounded in all the appropriate places. There was a facial resemblance between them, but it was not strong; Fancy's chocolate brown hair complemented her peach-kissed complexion and cat-shaped golden brown eyes, while Ellen's wheat-fair hair and bright blue eyes blended attractively with her creamy skin. Both possessed a delicate tip-tilted little nose, a rosy mouth just made for kissing, and a delightfully rounded chin with an unmistakably stubborn cast to it. Ellen's expression was open and sunny, Fancy's more reserved, her slightly slanted topaz eyes and slim, dark, almost haughtily arched brows giving her a faintly exotic air. Fancy, more properly called Lady Merrivale, was the widow of a baron and was ten years Ellen's senior, although anyone looking at them this fine, sunny morning in late June would have been hard-pressed to decide which one of the sisters was the eighteen-year-old and which one had just recently enjoyed her twenty-eighth birthday.

As Ellen said frequently, Fancy didn't *look* like a dowager baroness. And Fancy would be the first one to admit that she certainly didn't feel like one. But she had always been the more pragmatic of the two, having taken over the care of Ellen upon their mother's death, when Ellen had been six and she had been only sixteen.

Their father, Edward Merrivale, had been a charmingly careless rogue who had infrequently remembered that he was married and the father of two young daughters. He was content to leave his wife and children immured on his small estate in Surrey while he enjoyed himself in London, gaming and wenching as if there were no tomorrow. His wife's death had merely caused a faint ripple of dismay in his carefree existence. His reaction upon learning of his wife's demise had been only to comment how very inconvenient it had been for Sally to die and leave him the care of their daughters. Sally *knew* that he didn't have the least idea how to go on with children.

Edward had been thrilled when he had discovered that Fancy was extremely capable of stepping into her mother's position as chatelaine of Limewood, as his estate was known. Since Sally Merrivale had been an invalid for a number of years before her death, Fancy had been running the household for quite some time and she didn't think it the least bit strange that, after the funeral, her father had departed immediately for London. Of course, he had not been totally irresponsible; he had somewhat hastily installed an old aunt of his for appearances. But he had mainly left the true reins of control in Fancy's young hands.

Fancy didn't mind. The life she led was the only one she had ever known, and while she might have wished that her father were different, she and Ellen were quite happy in their home and old Aunt Mary had been both amiable and kind. As she grew older, Fancy sometimes longed for a more interesting life, something other than making the frugal amount of money her father sent (when he remembered) cover all their expenses or dealing with the recalcitrant Meg, the cook, or convincing the butcher that they truly would pay their bill next quarter, or figuring out how she could save enough money for Ellen to get a new gown. There were some compensations to be had, for sure, such as riding her fat old mare down the winding country lanes and sneaking into Lord Wells's prized and jealously guarded orchard to steal an apple or a pear.

But while Fancy prosaically took care of her small household, at night, as she had stared out at the starlit black sky she had frequently longed for something more—a social life, for instance, one that included balls and routs and had a great deal more to offer for amusement than having tea and cakes with Aunt Mary's friends or joining a family dinner party at the vicar's on Sundays. Sometimes she wondered what her future would hold. Not even in her wildest dreams would she have guessed that one day she would be married to a handsome, wealthy peer of the realm.

It wasn't a love-match, and if she'd had time to consider the situation, if her father hadn't pleaded so abjectly with her, Fancy didn't know, even today, if she would have married her father's cousin, Spencer, Baron Merrivale. But everything had happened so swiftly. Just turned eighteen, she had been stunned when her father had returned home unexpectedly . . . returned home to die. He had been wounded in a duel over a married woman, and his days on earth were few.

As Edward lay dying, he had considered for the first time what his daughters' fates might be without him. Creditors would swallow up his meager funds and estate, and his children would be thrown penniless upon the world. In desperation, he had written to the head of the family, Lord Merrivale, begging for help.

Lord Merrivale, of an age and much the same ilk as his dying cousin, moved by a whim that he never quite understood, came to call at Limewood. At the time, having parted from his latest mistress and bored with the sophisticated, fashionable ladies of London, Fancy's fresh young loveliness and exotic beauty aroused his jaded interest.

His wife, after dutifully presenting him with three sons in rapid succession, had died while attempting to deliver a fourth, and Spencer had been a widower for nearly two decades. He had his heirs, his eldest son already the proud father of a child of his own, and since he was a wealthy man able to indulge his every whim, there had been no need to cast about for another wife. Until Fancy. Seducing his own cousin's daughter was out of the question, although he did consider it briefly before deciding that not even he was that much of a cad.

It can't be said that Lord Merrivale fell in love with Fancy, but he came as close to that emotion as a man of his character was capable. When Edward explained his dilemma, Spencer astounded his cousin and himself as well, by offering for Fancy's hand in marriage.

Edward was overcome with gratitude, and since time was of the essence, with hardly two days' passing between the offer and the marriage, Fancy found herself wed to a man she didn't know. A handsome man, to be sure, charming and urbane, but also arrogant and spoiled and five years older than her own father!

Staring down sightlessly at the busy wharf at Richmond where their ship had finally ended its long journey from England, Fancy wondered at the twists and turns of fate that had brought her here. Her marriage to Spencer hadn't been *un*happy; in his way, he had been kind and generous, willingly taking on the care of Ellen and Aunt Mary, sheltering them at his country seat, Merrivale, with never a complaint or question about the money Fancy expended on them.

Fancy sighed. In many ways her life hadn't changed upon her marriage. Spencer saw no reason for his young and beautiful wife to follow him to London, and while she no longer had to worry over unpaid bills and could indulge herself with the latest fashions and lived in a grand house with servants at her beck and call, she was still buried in the country. Oh, every now and then the baron would allow

Fancy to give a ball or a soiree, but since he followed his own pursuits and was away most of the time, after the first few months of their marriage, Fancy, Ellen, and Aunt Mary were left to their own devices. Sometimes Fancy almost forgot that she was married.

Even now, having been married for nearly eight years and widowed for over two, a faint flush stained her cheeks when she thought of the intimacies her husband had pressed upon her. Raised in the country, Fancy hadn't been entirely without knowledge about what would happen when her husband came to her on their wedding night, but there was no denying that the act of lovemaking had come as a distinct shock to her.

Spencer had been gentle with her that first night, and the loss of her virginity had not been the dreadful event she had feared. Painful and embarrassing, but not dreadful. In the first days of their marriage, Spencer had been a demanding bridegroom, seeking her bed frequently to satisfy his needs, but as time passed, his fascination with her innocence had faded, and to Fancy's humiliation, he had gone on to seek compensation in the arms of more knowing and sophisticated women.

Which was just as well, she decided ruefully, unable to say that she had *enjoyed* her husband's lovemaking. She hadn't *dis*liked it, precisely, but . . . If she were honest, she had been just as glad that Spencer had spent so much time away from Merrivale and that she hadn't had to share her bed with him more than a dozen times in the last six years of their marriage.

His death two years ago in a hunting accident had saddened her. He had been an affable, generous man, and he had never treated her unkindly—indifferently, perhaps, but not unkindly. In fact, Fancy still felt almost guilty at the sense of release that had washed over her when she had realized some three months after his death that she was truly *free* for the first time in her life. For the first time ever, there was no man in the background ruling her life, and lack of money was no longer an issue. Spencer had been generous to her—she had jewels, servants, and expensive horses and carriages to call her own, and as his widow, she had the dowager house at Merrivale at her disposal, as well as a handsome jointure left to her by him. Her relationship with his sons, all of them older than herself, had been cool but cordial. Taking Ellen and the ailing Aunt Mary with her, without a backward glance, she had moved from the grand halls of Merrivale to the smaller, but equally elegant dowager house.

Fancy probably would have been content to spend the rest of her days living happily in the dowager house, enjoying her own small circle of friends and pursuits, if it hadn't been for Ellen . . . and Aunt Mary's death. . . . Fancy sighed more deeply. Oh, how she missed Aunt Mary's gentle guidance and blunt common sense. Aunt Mary had not lived for six months after they had moved into the dowager house, and her death hit both the young women hard. For years she had been a kindly presence in their lives, and they had not known how much they would miss her once she was gone. But grief is not forever, and when their year of mourning was finished, to Fancy's surprise she discovered that Ellen had grown up and had turned into an exquisitely lovely young woman.

Suddenly everything that she had been denied Fancy wanted for Ellen. She wanted her to have a grand London season, to go to balls and soirees, the theater and rides in Hyde Park, and to mingle with fashionable and sophisticated people. Fancy's tidy fortune and a title would ensure that no door would be shut to Lady Merrivale, and as her sister, Ellen would reap and enjoy the benefits.

If Fancy had dreamed of a grand match for Ellen, she had never given voice to it—she only wanted her sister to be happy—but she would have been less than human if her heart hadn't swelled with pride when, not a fortnight after their arrival in London this past January, the eldest son of the duke of Montrose began to pay marked attention to Ellen. Unfortunately, the duke's heir had been an unprepossessing young man, and while Ellen had viewed him kindly, her interest had been immediately sparked by a tall and decidedly handsome gentleman visiting from the Colonies, a Mister Jonathan Walker.

A little frown knitted Fancy's forehead. She should be overjoyed that Ellen seemed to have fallen in love with a man of Jonathan's stature. He was in many ways a maiden's dream: tall, handsome, wealthy, and charming. In fact, Fancy could not think of one thing wrong with him. Not even the fact that he was a colonial—privately, she thought *that* the most fascinating thing about him, and even more than Ellen she had hung spellbound on his words when he had spoken of the Colonies and the life that he lived there.

So why, she wondered vexedly, did she have this tiny niggle of discomfort in the back of her mind? Was it because she sometimes caught Jonathan looking at her with an expression in his deep blue eyes that shouldn't have been there? Did she really suspect that he would have preferred to pay court to her rather than her younger sister? Was it because it was only after she had gently made it known that she was *not* interested in a second husband that he had shown an interest in Ellen? Mayhap Ellen was right: though there was not nearly the wide gap between Ellen's eighteen and Jonathan's thirty-six as there had been between her and Spencer, Jonathan was many years older than Ellen. Fancy flushed guiltily, suddenly admitting to herself that some of her reservation lay in the fact that at times, she also found him just a little *too* charming. Almost as if he were presenting an attractive facade and hiding his true character.

Beside her, Ellen stirred and said gaily, "Oh, here come Jonathan and Simmons now!"

Fancy glanced over her shoulder and stared intently at the tall, strikingly handsome gentleman approaching them, a warm smile curving his lips. He was followed by his manservant, Simmons, a small, olive-skinned man who the few times she had been in his presence had made Fancy uneasy.

In deference to shipboard conditions, Jonathan was not wearing a powdered wig, but his dark hair had been pulled back into a queue, and in his deep blue double-breasted

jacket and buff breeches he looked very stylish. There were
clocks on his silk stockings and silver buckles on his shoes;
the ruffles on his fine linen shirt were profuse, and he carried an amber cane in his left hand. Reaching the two
women, with Simmons standing respectfully in the background, Jonathan bowed very low and said, "Ladies, a good
morrow to you! And I must say that when I escort you from
the ship, I shall be the envy of every man in our great
Colony of Virginia today."

Ellen blushed, and a reluctant smile tugged at the corners
of Fancy's mouth. Dryly she said, "And you, sir, are far too
fulsome with your compliments."

Jonathan's features assumed a wounded expression, but
his blue eyes were twinkling. "My lady! How can you say
so, when I but speak the truth?"

It certainly was true that the two women looked delightful in their simple traveling costumes. Ellen, her unpowdered fair hair arranged neatly in a tidy pompadour with two
long curls hanging down her neck, was wearing a pale blue
dimity gown over a yellow quilted petticoat. A dark gray
cloak was carried over one arm, and an embroidered etui,
which contained her favorite bottle of scent, hung from her
waist.

Beneath the wide brim of her beaver hat, Fancy's dark
hair had been simply tied at the nape of her neck with a wide
russet ribbon; a row of delicate blond lace framed the round
neck of her striped tobacco brown gown, which was worn
over a fawn-colored petticoat. With the knowledge that they
would be meeting Jonathan's mother and older brother for
the first time and that she *was* a widow, Fancy thought that
she had dressed soberly and sedately this morning. She was
happily unaware of how the saucy angle of her hat coupled
with her cat-shaped eyes gave her a flirtatious air, or of how
the color of her gown brought out the warm golden glow of
her skin and the expertly fitted bodice drew attention to her
narrow waist and firm little bosom.

Jonathan certainly wasn't blind to Fancy's charms, and he
blessed again the caution that had kept him from fully com-

mitting himself to Ellen. The idea of a long visit in the Colonies while the Merrivale ladies met his family and friends had been an excellent idea. The ladies intended to stay for several months, and who knew what would happen during that time? Fancy might come to realize that widowhood was not quite as appealing as she had first thought, and as for Ellen . . .

It was a dangerous line Jonathan trod, delicately wooing one sister while keeping an avaricious eye on the other. Not even to his family had he clarified *which* of the two ladies he intended to marry. His letter home had indicated that a wedding was *possibly* in the wind, but he had not named the lady of his choice. And since his letter had been rather full of details about the baroness, his family might be forgiven for assuming that it was Fancy who was his probable bride. But clever man that he was, he had also managed to cloud the waters by singing Ellen's praises to the skies. His family, he thought with a smug smile, was no doubt thoroughly confused. And until his actual betrothal, to either Ellen or Fancy, was announced, he intended to keep it that way.

That Ellen thought herself in love with him could prove a problem if his plans for Fancy came to fruition, but it didn't worry him overmuch. There were several nice eligible bachelors he could think of who could provide a distraction for her, especially if at the appropriate time, he oh so delicately hinted to Ellen that perhaps they had made a mistake in their feelings for one another.

His handsome face showing none of his thoughts, with a lovely Merrivale on either side of him, he gazed down at the bustle on the busy wharf below them and asked jovially, "Well, what do you think of the New World, my ladies?"

" 'Tis most exciting," exclaimed Ellen. "I saw an Indian a moment ago."

The wharf was busy; carts and wagons of all sizes were loading and unloading; horses neighed and dogs barked, and a babble of conversation and shouts floated on the warm morning air. Several scarlet-coated British soldiers strolled by, as did a plainly garbed Quaker couple, the gentleman wearing a surtout about his shoulders, his wife's gown dark and worn with a white bib. A pair of fishermen in knitted red caps and heavy leather sea boots walked jauntily behind the Quaker couple, followed by a water carrier in a speckled patterned waistcoat and an old black felt hat, his back bent under the weight of the heavy wooden buckets he carried on a rod across his shoulders. A shopkeeper, an apron of green baize around his ample waist, hurried busily down the center of the wharf, and here and there an Indian with feathers in his hair or a frontiersman in rough buckskins sauntered through the shifting colorful crowd.

An elegant carriage pulled by a pair of high-stepping bays suddenly swung onto the wide wharf and Jonathan said, "Ah, at last, there they are! My family have come to greet us."

A little knot of nervousness formed itself in Fancy's stomach. She knew it was silly. There was no reason in the world why she wasn't going to like Jonathan's family, or why they should take a dislike to her and Ellen. She took in a deep, steadying breath. She needed to remind herself that she wasn't just plain Miss Merrivale without fortune or in need of a guardian or husband anymore and hadn't been for a number of years. But old habits died hard, and fiercely she reminded herself that she was *Lady* Merrivale, the widow of a peer of the realm, and that she had a nice little fortune safely invested in the funds in England. If Jonathan's family proved obnoxious and inhospitable, well, so be it! She and Ellen would do just fine without them!

Ignoring the flutter in her chest, Fancy watched as a tall gentleman, his hair powdered and tied in a black silk bag under a black ribbon bow, politely helped a woman in a gorgeous creation of green figured silk from the carriage. She guessed that the gentleman in the tan cloth coat trimmed in silver braid was Jonathan's half brother, Samuel, and that the woman was Jonathan's mother.

Beside her, Jonathan quickly confirmed her guess as the pair made their way toward the ship. They made a distinguished couple. The gentleman, though over seventy, walked straight and tall, and even from a distance Fancy could see that in her youth Jonathan's mother had been quite lovely. Constance Walker was still an extremely attractive woman, even if she had celebrated her fifty-third birthday in May. Her figure was perhaps a trifle fuller than when she had been a young woman, but she moved with the grace of a maid. As was the fashion, her hair was curled and powdered beneath a charming calash of a darker green than her gown, her full skirts swaying gently as she walked beside her much older stepson.

Intent as she was on Jonathan's relatives, as the minutes passed, Fancy became aware of a prickling sensation, an unease that she couldn't explain, almost as if someone were watching her and not *kindly.* She glanced around, seeking the source of her discomfort, but saw nothing out of the ordinary. Surely Simmons's presence behind Jonathan didn't bother her? Of course not! She shrugged her slender shoulders, deciding that she must be letting the coming meeting with Jonathan's family disturb her, and she wondered with sudden amusement if for the first time in her life she was going to suffer a fit of the vapors.

A faint, rueful smile curved her generous mouth. What a ninny she was being! These people weren't going to bite her, for goodness' sake!

Still, the sensation persisted and, becoming irritated, she took another impatient look around her. It was then that she saw him. . . . He was on the wharf, standing almost directly in front of them, an expression of amused contempt on his handsome face as he stared boldly back at her.

Fancy's heart gave a funny little start. From his garb, fringed buckskins and calico shirt, she took him to be a rough frontiersman, and he was certainly staring at them, her, in the rudest manner! Her chin lifted, but she couldn't seem to stop staring at him, something about those fiercely chiseled features and that tall, powerful body holding her mesmerized. His thick black hair was unfettered and waved freely about his dark face and broad shoulders, giving him a feral, untamed air. A lion, she thought giddily, that's what he reminds me of, a black-maned lion. A lion, leashed but ready to spring on its hapless prey in an instant. Fancy gave herself a shake and with an effort tore her gaze from his. A lion indeed. She was definitely fanciful this morning.

Forcing a bright smile, she kept her head firmly averted from the disturbing creature on the wharf and stared determinedly at Jonathan's relatives as they started up the gangplank. Who did he think he was, looking at her in such a way? Why, she had half a mind to . . . What? Hit him with her reticule?

A giggle threatened to escape, and forgetting for the moment the annoying man on the wharf, she was able, a few minutes later, to greet Samuel Walker and Jonathan's mother, Constance, in her usual charming manner. She liked Sam Walker on sight, but the hard, assessing gleam in Constance's green eyes and the slightly petulant cast to her mouth gave Fancy pause. She'd seen, upon the rare occasion, just that same expression in Jonathan's eyes and had also idly noticed the tendency for his lips to curve in a petulant pout when events didn't go precisely as planned. It hadn't bothered her before now, but seeing those traits more obviously defined in his mother caused her to speculate about the true nature of the man Ellen wanted to marry.

After the introductions had been completed and questions about their journey from England had been answered, the conversation became even more general for several moments. Fancy and Ellen were both enthusiastic about their first sights of the New World and they spoke animatedly about the small settlements and the vast green wilderness they had seen on their journey up the James River to Richmond.

Sam Walker was obviously pleased by their reactions, and Fancy was drawn to him by his ready smile and the warm twinkle in his deep blue eyes. He might be over seventy, but he was still an extremely attractive man, his skin firm and dark, his nose straight and broad, and his mouth wide and full lipped.

Beaming at the two younger women, Sam murmured, "I

hope that you will find your stay at Walker Ridge even more pleasant and entertaining than your journey has been so far. My wife, Letty, has been in a tizzy since she first learned that you were coming to visit. She would have been here with us this morning, but there were a few final things that she wanted to oversee before your arrival at the house. We all want you to enjoy yourselves."

"Of course," Constance said airily, "you must not expect to find things as you would in England, my dear Lady Merrivale. We are *such* provincials! I only hope that during your stay we can provide you and your delightful sister with suitable amusements and that you will find things here in the colonies not *too* backward!"

"I am certain that my sister and I will be most happy," Fancy said gently. "Jonathan has told us a great deal about life in the Colonies and we have been looking forward to our visit at your home."

"Well, Walker Ridge is, even if I do say so myself, quite, quite exceptional," Constance said proudly. "I doubt you would find a finer home, even in England." A superior smile on her lips, she added, "The Viscount Darnley and his lovely wife came to visit us just last year and we had a prodigiously gay time. Do you know them? Oh, I suppose that you do. After all, your late husband was a baron, was he not?" She gave a titter of laughter. "My dear, I simply cannot tell you how *pleased* I have been since my darling Jonathan wrote and said that he was bringing home a baroness and her sister for a visit. I must tell you that all my friends have been positively *green* with envy. Of course, they will all want to meet you."

Fancy wasn't quite certain how it came about, but a few minutes later, as they all walked toward the gangplank, she found herself firmly anchored to Jonathan's arm, his mother on his other side as they followed behind an amiably chatting Sam and Ellen. Fancy was paying only half a mind to Constance's chatter, and while she didn't want to be too judgmental, she sincerely hoped that Letty Walker was more like Sam and less like Constance. If she wasn't, it was going to be a *very* long visit.

They had almost reached the gangplank and were just starting down, when there was a sudden gasp from Constance and she stopped dead in her tracks. Her face almost ugly with displeasure, she grasped Jonathan's arm even tighter and hissed, "What is *he* doing here?"

Fancy's gaze followed the direction of Constance's look, and her heart gave another of those funny little leaps. The frontiersman who had stared so boldly at her just a short while ago was standing at the base of the gangplank, a cool smile tugging at the corners of his long mouth. Unable to help herself, she whispered to Jonathan, "Who *is* that man?"

An unpleasant expression on his handsome face, Jonathan said grimly, "Why, only the bastard of the family. Chance. Chance Walker."

Chapter Two

————◆◆◆————

Sam Walker heard Jonathan's comment, and sending his half-brother a stern look over his shoulder, he said quietly, "Have you been away so long in England that you have forgotten that this is a New World and a man should be allowed to put his beginnings behind him? Because of an unfortunate set of circumstances—none, I might add, of his own making—is Chance to be forever branded?"

Jonathan stiffened at the note of reprimand in Sam's voice and muttered, "Have *you* forgotten that he cheated us out of thousands of acres?"

Sam's eyes narrowed. "No," he said softly, "I have not forgotten precisely how it was that Chance came to own that particular tract of our land. And now, I think we have said enough in front of our charming guests." He smiled down at Ellen's wide-eyed expression. "Forgive us! You have stumbled across a long-standing family disagreement and we have been rude enough to air it in front of you. Believe me, we are not always so impolite."

The moment was smoothed over, but the exchange between the brothers left Fancy with the decided impression that Chance Walker was not someone she would care to know any better. It also left all sorts of questions floating around in her head. What were the circumstances of his birth, and how *had* Chance Walker obtained that land? And why, if he was the blackguard that Jonathan indicated, did his brother seem to defend him? Remembering the contemptuous way Chance Walker had stared up at her earlier, Fancy decided that in this case, Jonathan probably had the correct understanding of the man. Chance Walker was obviously *not* a gentleman.

As they continued down the gangplank, the closer they came to the tall, buckskin-clad figure standing so arrogantly on the wharf, Fancy found herself tensing, and unconsciously she clung more tightly to Jonathan's arm. She was suddenly glad that she wasn't alone and that they were in a public place with several people nearby.

Why she felt that way, she couldn't have said, but there was something in the way Chance Walker was looking at her, some expression in those hooded eyes, that warned her he was no more impressed by her than she had been by him. Which, of course, naturally put her on her mettle and put an unusually haughty expression on her pretty face and had her little tip-tilted nose firmly in the air.

Avoiding even looking in the direction of the waiting figure at the base of the gangplank, she began to speak with great animation to Jonathan, talking airily about some ball they had attended together in London. She didn't even know what she was babbling on about, and despite her apparent lively conversation with Jonathan, she was unbearably aware of the other man. She could feel his gaze like a searing blade, boring into her.

They finally reached the wharf, where Sam Walker greeted Chance with a warm smile. "Good morning, Chance, I didn't expect to see you here in Richmond. The last I heard of you from Morely, you were somewhere out in the wilderness trading with the Indians. Was it a profitable trip, my boy?"

At thirty-four years of age, Chance hardly resembled a boy, standing nearly six feet three in his stockinged feet. Beneath the fringed buckskins that he wore with such careless elegance, his shoulders were broad, his body whipcord lean, and his dark face was hard and shuttered. An unforgettable face, Fancy thought in spite of herself, her gaze noting the swooping black brows, the startling cobalt blue eyes, and the long, mobile mouth.

Their eyes suddenly met, and Fancy felt her heart drop right down somewhere around her curling little toes. Mercy! No one had ever looked at her that way before! The cool contempt was plain to see, as was the inexplicable dislike, but it was the flash of something else deep in his eyes that made her pulse leap.

Ignoring a craven impulse to pick up her skirts and run back up the gangplank to the relative safety of the ship, Fancy lifted her chin even higher, and her lovely eyes held an angry sparkle. Who did he think he was, this backwoods buffoon, looking at her in *such* a manner?

Sam cleared his throat gently, breaking the odd spell between them, and Fancy's mouth nearly fell open in shock at the change of expression that swept over Chance's features as he glanced at the older man. A warm, stunningly attractive smile tugged at the corners of that long mouth and lit those blue, blue eyes as he said in a deep voice, "It is good to see you, sir. And as for my trip . . . well, it was not very successful—you know that Logan has joined with Cornstalk and that the Shawnees and other Indian tribes have banded together. They have been raiding and killing all along the Ohio since Logan's family was slaughtered in April. I went more at the governor's request to see if I could convince them to meet to talk peace, but . . ." Chance shrugged. "I was, I am unhappy to admit, no better a peace emissary than I was a trader."

It was too good an opportunity for Jonathan to pass up, and he drawled, "I say that I am surprised that Lord Dunmore sent someone of your ilk to deal with these warring savages. After all, your, er, skills are more in fleecing the unwary, aren't they?"

Chance smiled coolly in Jonathan's direction. "I have often wondered how you explained your losses that night."

Jonathan's face congealed with fury, and he took a threatening step forward. It was his mother who recalled him to his senses by saying sharply to Chance, "How dare you speak to my son in that manner!" She looked angrily over at Sam. "Are you going to just stand there and let him get away with insulting your only brother in that manner?"

Sam shook his head wearily. "I have told you a hundred times, Constance, that I am not going to be drawn into the middle of this senseless feud between the pair of them. And as for Chance insulting Jonathan, I believe," he said dryly, "that it was Jonathan who cast the first stone. Now then, before we subject our guests to any more of our inexcusable rudeness, I suggest that we bid Chance good-bye and continue on our way." Sam looked at Chance. "In view of the circumstances, I think it would be best if we postponed introductions to our guests to a later date, do you agree?"

Chance nodded curtly and, after one long, insolent glance at Fancy, turned on his heel and strode swiftly down the wharf. Feeling as if she had just survived a fall from a high cliff, Fancy let her breath out in a rush and only then became aware of how tightly she had been clinging to Jonathan's arm. Embarrassed and feeling a little silly, she loosened her hold instantly and said with an attempt at lightness, "Well! You did promise us some exciting moments in the Colonies, Jonathan—I just did not think that they would start the moment we stepped off the ship! I was fearful for one awful moment that you were going to come to the blows with that impertinent creature."

Jonathan laughed, his good humor restored now that Chance's tall figure was lost among the shifting crowd on the wharf. Taking Fancy's hand with a gleam in his eyes, he brushed his lips across her soft skin. "That was not exactly the kind of adventure I had in mind for you and your sister, but I am happy that you have been so kind as to make light of my deplorably bad manners. Chance is no friend of mine—there is a great deal of bad blood between us, and I am sorry that you and Ellen had to see such an ugly scene.

Will you forgive me?" He glanced meltingly over at Ellen. "And you, too, my dear?"

Ellen sent him an uncertain smile, her eyes very big and round in her face. "It was rather shocking, wasn't it?"

Straightening the folds of her skirts, Fancy said quietly, "Yes, it was, but we will not repine on it. And as for forgiving you . . . there is nothing to forgive, Jonathan, it was just an unfortunate occurrence." Looking at Sam, she flashed him a dimpled smile. "We shall talk no more of it. Instead, Mr. Walker shall escort us to the carriage and we shall all forget about Chance Walker! I doubt that after today he will be brazen enough to even show us his face again."

"Oh, he is brazen enough!" Jonathan said. "I doubt that there is anything that he would find *too* brazen to do."

Sam looked troubled, and ignoring Jonathan's comment, he muttered, "I am sorry that Chance has made such a bad impression on you. He is, perhaps, blunt and inclined to speak his mind, but there is no evil in him."

Jonathan's brow sketched upward. "So you say, but you will not find *me* in agreement with you, brother."

Sam opened his mouth to reply, but Constance rushed in with, "Oh, fiddle! I am sick to death of hearing that man's name. He has been nothing but a trial to this family since he was born. It grieves me to say it, Samuel, but he is just like that no-good drunken father of his. And it matters not to hear you say that Morely hasn't touched a drop in over thirty years. To me, Chance and Morely, too, will always be a blot on the Walker family name." Having done her part to further blacken Chance's character, Constance suddenly smiled charmingly and said, "Oh my, how I do run on! But, now, please, let us follow the baroness's lead and just forget about Chance Walker and his coarse ways."

Sam bowed to her wishes and, smiling ruefully, began to usher the ladies and his brother toward the waiting carriage. Regaling them with tales of how Richmond had begun in 1637 as a trading post because of its location at the head of navigation on the James River, Sam effortlessly put the unpleasant scene with Chance behind them. Fancy, her topaz eyes gleaming with interest, listened carefully as Sam explained that some years later Richmond had been the site of Byrd's Warehouse, but that the actual town hadn't been laid out until 1737 by Colonel William Byrd. Staring at the village, which was scattered over several hills on the north side of the James River, as the carriage moved smartly down the street, Fancy was thoroughly fascinated to think that this bustling port town had humbly started out merely as a place to trade furs and trinkets with the Indians.

Thinking of the Indians, she could not help but recall Chance Walker's earlier statements. A little uneasy, she asked suddenly, " 'Tis likely that those Indians which Mr. Walker spoke of would attack us?"

Jonathan snorted derisively, but it was Sam who answered slowly, "Living in the wilderness as we do, far away from any town, anything is possible, my dear Lady Merrivale. But I do not believe we have anything to fear. The raids are well over a hundred miles away from us, in the Ohio River Valley. I doubt that any of the Shawnees or Mingos would push very deep in our direction." He smiled reassuringly. "While we have suffered attacks in the past and have even lost members of our family to the Indians, the Walkers have long been known as friends to the Indian. You have little to fear at Walker Ridge. The plantation is large and well armed, and there are numerous slaves and indentured servants about, as well as several other men who work for me. We are too strong for any Indians to think seriously of attacking us."

"Not unless Chance Walker were to incite them against us," Jonathan said grimly.

Sam sighed. "I thought," he said quietly, "that we had decided to drop the subject of Chance Walker?"

Chance wouldn't have been surprised at the way Jonathan continued to defame his name. After all, bitter experience had taught him that vilifying and destroying another's character was simply Jonathan's way. Chance expected little else from the other man—lies, hints, and innuendo were the young Mr. Walker's stock-in-trade.

Chance tried not to dwell very often on his rancorous feud with the heir to the Walker fortune, but Jonathan, and his hatred of him, were never far from Chance's mind. Even the sight of the seductive little creature who had clung so confidingly to Jonathan's arm couldn't keep away the dark, ugly thoughts that deviled him as he left the wharf a few minutes after the Walker party had departed in their carriage.

He, like most of even the slightest acquaintances of the Walkers, had been aware that Jonathan was returning home from England and that he was bringing a baroness with him. Constance had trumpeted the news to all and sundry for days after she had received Jonathan's letter imparting the thrilling news. Her conversation had been full of "when the baroness arrives" or "the baroness and her younger sister will be staying with us . . . an extended visit, of course," or "The baroness is a widow, you know," which was followed with such an arch look that the listener was left with the impression that a betrothal would soon be in the offing.

Chance hadn't paid Constance much heed—he never did. His feelings for Jonathan's mother were only marginally less lethal than those he felt for her son. He had known that Jonathan had gone to England presumably to find a suitable bride, and he hadn't been surprised to learn that Jonathan had managed to snare the interest of a highborn lady. The fact that Jonathan was heir to one of the largest fortunes in Virginia certainly did not diminish his appeal. Jonathan was, Chance conceded grimly, a handsome man. He knew to his great and bitter cost *precisely* how charming the other man could be. So charming, in fact, he thought with a deadly glint in his blue eyes as he entered a small tavern near the wharf, that other men's wives forgot their vows and found him irresistible.

Scowling blackly at the inoffensive tavern maid who hurried to meet him as he selected a table in a dark corner of the smoke-filled room and slid into a battered oak chair, Chance jerked his thoughts away from the path they had inevitably followed. But having pushed Jonathan out of his mind, he discovered to his annoyance that he couldn't so easily erase the enchanting image of the slim woman in the saucily tilted beaver hat. The baroness, he thought, his upper lip curling into a sneer. No doubt Jonathan's bride-to-be.

She certainly had come as a shock to Chance. He had pictured an older woman, stiff-necked with pride and condescension. He still couldn't quite believe that the young and undeniably lovely creature Jonathan had been escorting ashore could be the baroness. She definitely hadn't *looked* like a widow, and the almost virginal air about her would make anyone, any *man*, Chance thought dryly, wonder if her late husband had been a monk.

Becoming aware of the hovering tavern maid, Chance smiled wryly at her and ordered some ale. Leaning back in the chair and stretching his long, buckskin-clad legs out in front of him, he attempted to focus on something else, but when the maid returned with a pewter tankard full of foaming ale a few minutes later, he was still speculating about Jonathan's baroness. The beguiling image she had made as she had leaned at the railing of the ship wouldn't leave his mind.

He'd known the instant he'd spied her who she had been. It had been no secret which ship Jonathan and his guests had taken from England, and Chance had known, from talking to Morely, that Sam and Constance would be meeting them this morning. He'd had his own reasons for being there at that time—the same ship that had brought the others to Virginia had been bringing him the start of what he hoped would be the foundation of an impressive Thoroughbred stud farm—a stud farm he had begun carving out of the same ten thousand acres he had won on the throw of the dice from Jonathan some eight years previously.

In the hold of the ship was a big bay stallion out of the brilliant and undefeated Flying Childers, as well as two mares that had been bred early that spring to Matchem, a grandson of the famous Godolphin Arabian. Their arrival in Virginia would be the culmination of a dream Chance had long held. He had been counting the days until he actually laid eyes on the animals that, after he had decided on the bloodlines he wanted, had been selected by his agent in London.

The meeting with Jonathan had left a sour taste in his mouth, dimming some of his pleasure at the arrival of his horses. The sight of the baroness smiling with Jonathan had aroused a whole host of emotions he found distinctly irritating. Chance envied no man, not even the heir to the great Walker fortune. But as he had stared up at the slim figure in the tobacco brown gown as she had leaned against the railing of the ship and watched the expressions that crossed her lively features as she had laughed and chatted with the other young woman (the younger sister, he had thought fleetingly), he had become aware of an odd pang deep in his gut. The idea of Jonathan having possession of all that fragile beauty woke the sleeping demons inside of him, and the bitter taste of bile had risen in his throat.

He was appalled by his emotions, furious to discover that for one brief moment he *did* envy his enemy, that he wished, to his furious astonishment, that this beguiling little creature had come all the way from England to be with *him*. He had been filled with contempt at himself and an equal amount of contempt for the young woman at the railing. Didn't she know what kind of man she was considering marrying? Or didn't she care? As long as he was rich enough, did it matter to her that Jonathan Walker was a scoundrel, a bald-faced liar, and a seducer of other men's wives? That there was blood on his hands?

Chance let out an angry breath. What the devil did it matter to him if she married a black-hearted villain? The baroness no doubt knew exactly what sort of man she was contemplating marrying, and if the haughty expression she had worn on that lovely face of hers had been any indication of her nature, she and Jonathan Walker deserved each other.

It took an effort, but eventually Chance was able to banish the baroness and Jonathan Walker from his mind. Let Satan take 'em! he thought contemptuously as he swallowed the last of his ale and rose from the table. They were two of a kind and he despised both of them.

Intent now on finally seeing his purchases, he left the tavern and walked with that long-legged stride of his back toward the ship. Shortly, after a brief exchange with the quartermaster, he learned that he had arrived just in time—his horses were being unloaded almost immediately.

Chance watched anxiously as each animal, wrapped securely in heavy webbing, was swung aloft and lowered carefully to the wooden dock. A pleased smile crossed his dark face at the first sight of his stallion. The animal had survived the crossing well, and though a little thin, his coat dull and coarse, the clean-limbed, long-bodied majesty of a well-bred Thoroughbred was plainly evident. The mares, a fine-boned chestnut and a tall black (a rare color for a Thoroughbred), seemed in much the same condition. They still had to make the journey to Devil's Own, his burgeoning plantation on the James River, but at least now he would be overseeing their feed and care.

The horses safely unloaded, Chance glanced around impatiently, wondering where Hugh and Morely could be—they had promised to be here to help him. The thought had hardly crossed his mind before he caught sight of two tall figures walking swiftly in his direction. The younger man was garbed much as he was, the older more soberly dressed in a dark gray suit of drab, a black stock tied neatly around his neck, and a three-cornered hat sitting on his unpowdered head. Both men wore their hair neatly clubbed in a queue at the nape of their necks.

At the sight of them, an easy smile curved Chance's lips. Hugh, the younger man, was his closest friend, while Morely, Hugh's father and more than likely his own, though he had never admitted it, had been guiding his steps and hovering over him for as long as he could remember. A faint shadow crossed Chance's dark features. He'd often heard the tale of how Morely had shown up at his adopted parents' home with a squalling infant in his arms. Morely had never admitted that he was Chance's father, but he had also never explained how *he* had come to have possession of the infant.

Nor had he ever offered any clue as to who the child's mother might be.

Despite some resemblance between them, a resemblance shared by most of the widespread Walker clan, Chance didn't honestly believe that Morely was his father. There was no reason for Morely to continue to remain silent about the issue. Everyone firmly believed, and had right from the beginning, that Chance was Morely's bastard son. It would have been much easier for Morely to admit to being Chance's father than to remain mysteriously close-mouthed about the matter, but that was precisely what he did. And while Chance had put away much of the speculation about his own birth years ago, he sometimes wondered, as now, what role Morely had really played in the events surrounding his entrance into the world. Was Morely his father? And if not, who was? And why had his father denied his existence all these years?

A teasing comment from Hugh jerked him from his musings. A wide smile creasing his handsome face, Hugh said merrily, "So these are the nags that you have commandeered us to help you deliver to Devil's Own!"

"Nags?" Chance questioned with a mocking lift of his brow. "Have you no shame, denigrating in that cruel manner some of the finest horseflesh to reach the Colonies in recent memory?"

His gaze fastened avidly on the bay stallion, Hugh let out a deep sigh of pure appreciation. "Pay me no heed. I am just envious. Even after six weeks at sea, his quality shows through. Next spring you shall have horsemen from miles around wanting to breed their mares to that fellow. And as for the mares"—his eyes moved knowledgeably over them—"I think you should send your agent in London a bonus. He did very well by you."

"Hugh is right," Morely said, his own gaze roaming over the restive horses, "they are a fine trio and I think in years to come will repay your initial investment handsomely."

There were now several silver strands in Morely's dark hair, and his face was attractively lined, the passing years gently revealed. He still moved easily with a quick, lithe stride, and while his middle had thickened slightly, time had treated him kindly.

Hugh looked very like him at the same age. There was not a half-an-inch difference in their heights, and Hugh had inherited his father's build, as well as his dark hair and the Walker blue eyes. At twenty-seven, Hugh was the eldest of Morely's four children, and he had long ago developed an unshakable case of hero worship for Chance. The fact that Chance might very well be his own half-brother only added to his allure to the younger man. Since Hugh was an extremely amiable and likable fellow, their friendship was long-standing.

"Hmm, I am glad that you approve," Chance replied to Morely, his own gaze resting pleasurably on the horses. "And I hope that your words prove prophetic."

After Chance had settled with the quartermaster, the three men, each leading one of the horses, walked swiftly from the wharf. They headed directly to the small livery stable that was situated on the western edge of the town and from whence they would depart on Friday. Adjoining the stable was a tidy little tavern, the Cock's Crow, where Chance often stayed when he had business in Richmond. This was their destination once the horses had been settled in their temporary quarters.

It wasn't until the three men were sprawled comfortably in the tiny private room at the side of the tavern that Chance spoke of the meeting with Jonathan. Each man had a large tankard filled with ale in front of him; Morely had lit his long-stemmed pipe, and the fragrant odor of fine Virginian tobacco drifted in the room.

Fiddling with the handle of his tankard, Chance said abruptly, "Had you arrived a few minutes earlier this morning, you would have had a chance to meet Jonathan's baroness."

Morely sat up straighter. "You saw her . . . and Jonathan?"

Chance nodded. "And Mrs. Constance Walker and Sam, too."

"What does she look like?" Hugh asked idly. "Long in the tooth and horse-faced, I trust?"

Staring at the scarred pine table in front of him, Chance said slowly, "Actually, no. She was, in fact, quite a tempting-looking little morsel. So tempting, in fact, that I have a mind to see if she tastes as sweet as she appears."

Morely looked alarmed. "Now, Chance, you would not be thinking of . . ."

A lethal gleam in his cobalt blue eyes, Chance glanced at the older man. "Of what? Of giving Jonathan a taste of his own medicine? You cannot deny that it would be fitting."

Morely blanched. "Chance, you cannot. I know what happened with Jenny was tragic, and God knows that I do not condone Jonathan's part in it, but you must put these thoughts of vengeance from your mind." A look of sadness crossed his face. "You cannot continue to torture yourself over what you cannot change or punish yourself for decisions that were made long ago. Let the past go—if you do not, it will destroy you, my boy."

As it nearly did me, Morely thought heavily. It cut through him painfully, the bitter knowledge that through cowardice and vacillation he had never told anyone how he had come to arrive at Andrew's home with a baby in his arms. The knowledge, too, that Sam and Letty were growing older, and that he himself was no longer a young man, filled him with a gnawing urgency. That and the fact that last winter he had suffered a debilitating inflammation of the lung that had left him weak and bedridden for several long, terrifying weeks and had brought home the fact of his own mortality. If he did not speak, and soon, Chance's history might die with him.

Ignoring Morely's heartfelt advice, Chance said flatly, "If I can destroy Jonathan Walker in the process, my own damnation will be worth it."

"Father is right," Hugh murmured. "I know you still mourn her, but Jenny has been dead seven years now. And while it would give me great pleasure to see Jonathan Walker get his comeuppance, I would not want to see it at cost to yourself."

Chance snorted. "So we are all to just pretend that he didn't seduce my wife, my bride of not even two years? Or get her with child and then coldly abandon her to face me alone upon my return from England? We are to forget that sweet, terrified Jenny didn't hang herself just hours before I arrived home? We are to forget that after being away for nearly eight months, eight very *long* months, I might add, I came home to find my beloved wife dishonored and dead?" Chance's eyes went almost black with suppressed rage. "Jonathan Walker killed her as surely as if he had hanged her himself."

"There was never any proof," Morely muttered. "Just because he called frequently at your home while you were gone—several neighbors and friends did the same, you must remember—or because a few gossipy old cats claimed to have seen them riding together about the countryside does not mean that he was her lover."

Chance flashed him a look. "Do you doubt the identity of her seducer? Do you think even for one moment that it was anyone else?" Staring blindly at his tankard, he said heavily, "Everyone knows that before Jenny fell in love with me, her father and Sam were considering a match between her and Jonathan. Just as everyone knows that Jonathan was furious when Jenny and I married and that he has always hated me."

Hugh shrugged. "That may be, but if you feel so strongly about it—after Jenny was buried, why did you not simply call him out and kill him and be done with it?"

A smile that sent a shiver down Hugh's spine curved Chance's mouth. "Kill him?" he drawled softly. "Oh no, I have no desire to kill Jonathan Walker—I only want to take something very precious from him . . . something he prizes highly. I do not want him dead, Hugh, I want him to live a long life, a very long life, aching and hurting, full of bitter regret and pining every day for that which he has lost." Chance's gaze narrowed. "And who knows. Perhaps this baroness of his will give me the weapon I have long searched for. . . ."

Chapter Three

———◆◆◆———

Fancy was glad to leave Richmond behind. When the Walker party finally departed on Thursday, after four days of being paraded through the town like a trophy by Constance, she was more than eager to leave. And if she were introduced by Constance just once more as "my friend the *baroness*, Lady Merrivale," she was going to do her hostess a violence. While she *was* the baroness, technically the dowager baroness, there was something so smug, so unhealthy, about the way Jonathan's mother lingered over her title that Fancy was repelled.

It wasn't just the harping on her title that bothered her, either: both Jonathan and his mother seemed to be totally preoccupied with *her*, not Ellen. Ellen, she had noticed with growing dismay, was always introduced almost as an afterthought. She was also deeply troubled that the possibility of a marriage between the two families seemed to be common knowledge and, worse, that *she* was the prospective bride!

The expression of bewildered hurt in Ellen's eyes tore at Fancy's heart. Determined to discover just what sort of game Jonathan was playing, on the eve of their departure for Walker Ridge, she had sought him out. Finding him alone in one of the private sitting rooms, a militant sparkle in her fine eyes, she had shut the door firmly behind her and said bluntly, "I find myself in an awkward position. . . . I fear that I must know precisely what your intentions are toward my sister."

"My intentions toward Ellen?" he asked slowly. A faint smile curved his mouth as he put down his newspaper. He crossed the room and reached for Fancy's hand. Dropping a brief kiss on the back of it, he said softly, "My intentions toward your sister are precisely the same as they were in England. Why do you ask? Is something amiss?"

Fancy searched his face. He seemed perfectly sincere. She would have sworn that those blue eyes were guileless and that his face wore only an expression of polite interest. So why did she doubt him? Biting her lip, she slipped her hand from his, unconsciously scrubbing at the spot where his lips had touched her skin. What did she do now? she wondered vexedly. She could hardly take him to task because he did not appear to be paying as much attention to Ellen as she thought appropriate. She felt deucedly awkward putting into words her feeling that he and his mother were deliberately misleading everyone about *which* of the two Merrivale sisters might become his bride. And she couldn't very well complain about the way his mother tossed her title about to all and sundry, either. It would seem petty and, well, rude.

Sighing, Fancy muttered, "I just wanted to be certain." She glanced over her shoulder at him. "If you have changed your mind, I would appreciate it if you told me now before we leave Richmond. It will be very awkward for all of us if you were to discover at Walker Ridge that you had made a mistake in your affections."

"I can assure you that my feelings have not changed. And if they do," he murmured, "you shall be the first to know of it." A quizzical expression on his face, he asked, "I do not know what you are worried about, my dear. After all, was that not the entire purpose of your visit to my home, for Ellen and me to have a chance to know our hearts? Was that not *precisely* the reason that there has been no formal announcement . . . nor any actual betrothal? If I remember correctly, it was understood that either of us *could* change our minds."

Fancy frowned. Of course he was right. That was exactly why she and Ellen were in the Colonies—and he had just stated that his feelings for Ellen had not changed. She should have been totally reassured, but she wasn't. Feeling no more at ease than she had before she had spoken to Jonathan, Fancy bade him good evening and departed.

Jonathan stared consideringly after Fancy, deciding grimly that he was going to have to tread more carefully— the baroness was far more astute than he had initially thought. If she suspicioned that she was his ultimate quarry, she would immediately whisk herself and Ellen away on the first ship sailing to England, leaving him without *any* bride.

Marriage had never been of particular interest to Jonathan, but he had always known that someday he would have need of a wife, if only to breed him sons. His problem these days was that it had become increasingly apparent to him that the generous allowance he had inherited under his father's will was not sufficient for his needs. He had a passion for gaming, and over the years, from time to time, he'd had some particularly bad luck such as the night he had lost those thousands of acres to Chance. His losses, however, did not deter him; if anything, they increased his compulsion for wagering large, very large, sums on the turn of a card, the speed of a horse, or a roll of the dice.

Sam had settled his enormous gambling debts several times, but his older brother had made it clear the previous spring that he had done it for the last time—and Jonathan was going to have to learn to live within his means. Which was when Jonathan had begun to consider other ways to increase his command of ready money. Controlling his gaming habits never occurred to him. Some highly dubious schemes and marriage did.

He had no real need of an heiress, but he did need to marry. His father's will had left the bulk of the estate in Sam's capable hands, including management of his portion of the Walker fortune, but there was a provision for a substantial settlement when he married. Despite a degree of reluctance, Jonathan had concluded that marriage was a simple and logical solution to his problem. After casting a critical eye over the available damsels in the colony, Jonathan had decided that a trip to England was in order. Not only would England give him a wider scope in which to search for a bride worthy of him, but it would also allow him to further along a scheme he had hit upon to increase his revenue.

Thinking of the muskets and shot safely hidden under the layers of legitimate goods, iron axes, knives, and trinkets for trading with the Indians that had come on the ship from England with him, Jonathan smiled. Those muskets would bring him a huge profit, especially since there was already trouble in the Ohio Valley. The savages would be willing to trade exorbitant amounts of pelts for those muskets.

His smile widened. Of course, no one would ever connect *him* with such a nefarious, deplorable practice as arming the savages. He was a *Walker.* But not being a fool, he had also taken the precaution of having nothing directly to do with it. His man, Simmons, had arranged it all; he had merely provided the money. And if, by chance, he was connected to the sale of arms to the Indians, well then, he could depend upon his staid older brother to move heaven and hearth to protect the Walker name from scandal.

A discreet tap on the door interrupted his musings, and at his command, Simmons walked into the room. Jonathan quirked a brow at him.

His dark face giving nothing away, Simmons bowed and murmured, "The arrangements have been made. The Thackers will rendezvous with me near Green Springs."

"They know that you will be following closely behind my party?"

Simmons nodded. "Yes. They think that I am doing this on my own, and they understand that under no circumstance are they to show themselves to your party, that our meeting must be completely secret."

Jonathan rubbed his chin. "Are you certain that they can be trusted? Their reputation is not, ah, commendable."

Simmons smiled coolly. "They are distantly related to me, and while they are knaves and scoundrels, they have a strong belief in the blood tie. They will not cheat *me*."

"And *you* will not cheat me, will you?" Jonathan asked silkily.

"Since you can have me hanged if you decide to tell what you know about me, I rather doubt that shall happen."

Jonathan chuckled. "My dear fellow, I confess that you are a perfect tool, and as long as you obey me, I see no reason to speak of the disappearance of your previous employer."

His black eyes inscrutable, Simmons asked quietly, "Does it not worry you that someday I may rebel and make you disappear as well?"

Jonathan shook his head. "No. You see, I know what you are capable of. Poor Ned Jenkins did not, and it was just your bad luck that I stumbled across you attempting to hide his body that night." Jonathan's eyes narrowed. "And of course we both know of the letter I've given to my solicitor in Williamsburg which is to be opened immediately should something untoward happen to me." Rising to his feet, Jonathan clapped his valet on the shoulder. "But let us not talk of unpleasantness. Let us think of all the filthy lucre which will be ours when the Thackers return next spring from trading with the Indians."

Fancy woke cross and out of sorts the next morning, but by the time they pulled away from the tavern just at daybreak, she had managed to push aside her misgivings and looked forward to the next phase of their journey.

It was quite a large party that made up the Walker contingent. In addition to the Walkers and Merrivales, there were a dozen slaves and three indentured servants who accompanied them, as well as several wagons—household goods and supplies that had been purchased in town. Simmons, busy with some errands for Jonathan, was going to follow them later, and it was planned for him to overtake them before they had traveled very many days.

The three women rode in an excellently sprung carriage, while the two gentlemen rode astride, Jonathan on a restive bay gelding, Sam atop a quiet chestnut mare. Uneasily Fancy noted that both gentlemen and the indentured servants were armed with long black rifles, and Jonathan and Sam each also wore a brace of pistols across their chests. The tales of treachery and danger in the wilderness that Jonathan had told her, of people who disappeared, of murdered husbands and raped wives and stolen goods and horses, suddenly took on a more personal meaning for Fancy.

Depending on the weather, the condition of the roads, what roads there were, and the state of the various rivers and streams they had to cross, the journey to Walker Ridge would take several days. Fancy was looking forward to her first taste of frontier living, as it were. She knew, from all the supplies and servants, that it wasn't going to be true frontier living, but it would be like nothing she and Ellen had ever experienced in their lives.

They soon left Richmond behind, and as the miles gradually passed, signs of settlement became fewer and fewer. By the time they stopped that first evening by a cheerful stream, Fancy had seen no sign of habitation for more than five or six hours.

Glad to escape the confines of the carriage, she and Ellen wandered about the camp, watching interestedly as tents were set up and fires were lit. The swarming, buzzing insects eventually drove them to take shelter in one of the newly erected tents. Sam had warned them not to wander far from camp and to watch where they stepped—copperheads and rattlesnakes were not uncommon. From the safety of their tent, the sisters stared at the green gloom of the forest that seem to close in on them as darkness fell and decided that they would have no trouble at all obeying Sam's words.

By the time they had been on the road for five days, Fancy's enchantment with camping out under the stars had faded somewhat, but she and Ellen were of good spirits. The journey and its attendant discomforts, as well as its simple pleasures, were a thrilling adventure for a pair of gently reared Englishwomen, and they were reveling in every moment of it.

Fancy had been enjoyably surprised by Constance as they had continued on their journey. Away from town, she had dropped her affected airs and become much more likable. During the long hours in the carriage, she gaily regaled them with tales of life at Walker Ridge. When those were exhausted, well then, it was time for Ellen and Fancy to talk of London. Constance was hungry for news of the latest fashions, the theater, and any bit of delicious scandal the Merrivales might have been privy to. She took such simple delight in the few scraps Fancy could give her that Fancy had to smile. Perhaps Jonathan's mother wasn't quite the social-climbing harridan she had first appeared.

To Fancy's quiet pleasure, she noticed that both Jonathan and his mother doted on Ellen. In the evenings, Jonathan took Ellen for walks along the creek banks. When they returned, Fancy noticed that frequently there was a starry-eyed expression on her sister's pretty face. The knot of uncertainty that had been in her chest lessened gradually, and Fancy decided that she really must have been just overwrought from the long sea journey to have thought that there was anything amiss in Jonathan's actions toward her sister. Just an odd humor, she conceded wryly as she prepared for bed that evening, only half listening to Ellen's happy prattle about Jonathan. But just before she drifted off to sleep, the unpleasant thought occurred to Fancy that the change of manner by Jonathan and Constance might only be because there was no one else around for them to impress. . . . She made a face. What a wicked creature she was!

The next day dawned bright and clear. The heat, even when they broke camp at seven o'clock in the morning, was already oppressive, the air muggy and cloying. After helping Fancy into the carriage, Sam cast his eyes skyward and said,

"Not a sign of a cloud, but I would not be surprised to find ourselves in a thunderstorm before evening."

Constance gave a heavy sigh. "Oh, dear. If it rains very much, the trail will turn into a quagmire. I only hope that you are mistaken, Sam, or that the storm holds off until we have made camp for the evening—even if we have to stop early."

Sam's prediction proved true. By four o'clock that afternoon the rain had been falling steadily for forty-five minutes, the sky lit by brilliant flashes of lightning, thunder booming frighteningly close, and the narrow trail they were following was turning into a morass of mud.

Water dripping from his hat, Jonathan finally pulled his horse alongside the carriage and, leaning down to the window, said, "Green Springs and good grazing for the animals is just a mile or two ahead. Rather than struggle on, we shall camp there tonight and give the storm a chance to move on." He smiled. "And the trail a chance to dry out."

The simple yellow dimity gown she had chosen to wear that day clinging uncomfortably to her skin, Fancy was very glad when the springs were reached and her tent was erected and she could leave the confines of the carriage. The storm had passed, and a short while later the slaves were busily preparing the evening meal. Constance was in her tent overseeing the setting up of her bed for the night, while Jonathan and Sam were inspecting their various goods to see that they had suffered no damage from the rain. Fancy and Ellen carefully made their way into the privacy of the forests. The necessity of relieving herself behind the nearest bush was one part of traveling in the Colonies that Fancy would be very happy to put behind her, thank you very much!

Nature taken care of, a few minutes later the two young women began to walk back toward the camp. They had wandered some distance in their search for an appropriate privy, but there was no fear of getting lost, as the sounds of the camp could be faintly heard through the concealing trees and vines.

Fancy was in the lead, concentrating on where she put her

feet, Sam's lecture on poisonous snakes having made an enormous impression on her, Ellen following closely on her heels. They had not taken three steps when Fancy heard a funny little sound behind her. Apprehensively she whirled around, her eyes widening at the sight of her sister held captive by a burly figure in tattered, stained buckskins.

A rifle was slung across his back, the barrel showing over his shoulder; a huge knife was strapped to his side, and his matted hair hung in greasy, lank strands around his bearded face. He towered over Ellen, his hand crushed against her mouth, preventing any sound from escaping.

Fancy didn't even think. With a muffled sound of rage, she flew across the short distance that separated them. Fists clenched at her sides, she stared up at Ellen's captor. "Unhand her this instant, you brute," she said furiously, "or it shall go very ill for you."

The sudden feel of cold steel in the middle of her back made Fancy stiffen, and a shiver of fear went through her as a coarse voice said low, "Now, ain't she just the most spirited little filly you ever seen, Clem?"

Her mouth dry, Fancy met Ellen's terrified stare, her mind racing. Fancy knew exactly who held them captive—these men had to be some of the ruthless outlaws and murderous bandits whom Sam and Jonathan had said often preyed on the unwary along the various trails in the wilderness. They had not feared them, because their party was large and well armed. What neither Sam nor Jonathan had considered was that they would be bold or desperate enough to pick off anyone who strayed beyond the confines of the camp.

"I wouldn't scream, purty lady, if I were you," the hateful voice breathed into Fancy's ear. "Not if you don't want ole Clem over there to break your little friend's neck . . . or me to put a hole through this fine yellar gown of yours."

Clem smiled mirthlessly, revealing a mouthful of stained and broken teeth, his hand cruelly forcing Ellen's head backward. Fancy's blood ran cold. Dear God! What were they to do?

She didn't have time to think. A hard prod with the barrel

of a rifle pushed her forward and her captor said, "You jest follow Clem and keep your mouth shut. Now move!"

Helplessly Fancy complied. Alone she might have risked a fight, but not with Ellen's life at stake. The image of her sister's white, frightened features danced before her eyes with every step she took.

Fancy didn't know how long they walked. It seemed forever, and with every minute that passed, with every stride that took them farther away from the camp, her heart sank lower. They would soon be missed, she knew, but dusk would be falling shortly and she doubted even in daylight that anyone would be able to find any trace of them in the tangled verdant wilderness through which they walked.

Knowing what fate awaited them when their captors did decide to stop, Fancy frantically turned over plan after plan for their escape. Not only would they be raped by these despicable creatures, she was certain that she and her sister would also not live to see very many more days—perhaps, she thought with a shiver, not even tomorrow's dawn. Once these beasts had satisfied themselves, she didn't doubt that she and Ellen would be summarily dealt with and that their ravaged dead bodies would lie undiscovered and moldering in the emerald gloom of the forest.

When their captors finally decided they were safe, they laughed and whooped and congratulated themselves on their coup. It was then that Fancy saw for the first time the features of the man who had abducted her. They were not reassuring.

Like his companion, his hair hung in long greasy strands around his face, a dark stubble hiding most of his features. It didn't hide, however, the cold, empty blackness of his eyes or the ugly scar that marred his right cheek. The white scar ran from his temple, just missed his eye, crossed his cheek, and ended just below his chin. Shabby moccasins were upon his feet, and he wore buckskins as filthy and tattered as his friend's. While not as tall, he was built like a bull, his chest massive, his arms bulging beneath the stained material of his clothes. Fancy's heart sank even lower. She and Ellen could never overcome these brutes. They were doomed.

Defeat did not come easily to her, and while she knew there was little chance of escape, she kept her senses alert for any possible advantage. Again, the problem was Ellen. A half a dozen times Fancy almost bolted into the woods, willing to take her chances in the unknown wilderness rather than face the fate she knew lay ahead, but she could not desert her sister. Ellen seemed to be utterly cowed and demoralized by their situation, her expression dull and empty.

The indigo-and-purple shadows of dusk had just begun to fall when their captors called a halt. Fancy had no idea where she was, but they had obviously reached the campsite of the two men. A pair of scrawny horses were tied nearby, and some saddlebags lay dumped on the ground near a small creek.

"Me and Clem been following yore party all afternoon," her captor said conversationally as he shoved her forward. "We left our things here and was jest going to reconnoiter a bit, to see what the pickings might be, when you two little pigeons crossed our paths."

A ray of hope sprang in Fancy's chest. "Are you going to ransom us?" she asked. "Mr. Jonathan Walker will pay handsomely for our return. Our *safe* return."

"Ransom?" her captor repeated acidly. "Now thet's a right fine idea! I should of thought of it myself." His gaze narrowed. "Think I'm a fool? Them Walkers don't bargain with no one. They'd jest as soon shoot us on sight as talk to us. We've had dealings with them in the past."

Clem spoke up. "Specially that damned Chance!" he said bitterly. "He hates us Thackers. Besides, Chance is the Walker bastard who gave Udell that scar." Clem spat out the side of his mouth. "We don't bargain with the likes of the Walkers."

In spite of the circumstances, Fancy felt a spurt of warmth spread through her at the mention of Chance Walker and the fact that he had been the one to mark her captor. Bravo! she thought savagely, wishing that Udell had died beneath Chance's blade.

Udell leered at the women. "Afraid you fancy pieces are jest going to have to git used to Clem and me." He stepped closer. "You treat us real special and we might jest let you go."

Fancy held her ground, unwilling to let him see how terrified she was. "You intend to let us go?" she asked warily, her flesh crawling at his nearness.

His gaze met Clem's. An ugly grin crossed his face. "Shore. You be nice to us and don't give us no trouble and we'll let you go."

Fancy knew he was lying. She and Ellen were going to die. The only question was when.

Clem let loose the cruel grip he'd had on Ellen's arm and she sank slowly to the ground, her head bowed, the skirts of her blue gown billowing out all around her as she began to cry in great tearing sobs. Fancy flew across the small space that divided them and, kneeling beside her sister, clasped her to her bosom. "Ellen! Are you all right, dear?"

Ellen hugged her convulsively, instantly angling her fair head so that her lips were almost touching Fancy's ear. "We must escape!" she breathed softly between her loud sobs. "They think that I am helpless with fear and don't pay me any heed . . . we can use that to our advantage."

Fancy nodded her head slightly, jubilation surging through her. Ellen was pretending! Thank God! Together they would find a way to escape. Arms about each other, they rocked together on the ground, renewed hope springing in Fancy's breast.

"Quit yore squalling," Udell growled, dragging Fancy away from Ellen. He raised his rifle in a threatening motion and, glaring at Ellen, said, "You shut thet noise up, woman, or—"

Ellen's eyes seemed to go blank with fear, but her cries ceased and she rocked mutely from side to side, her face deliberately blank and stupid. "Thet's better." He gave Fancy a shake and ordered, "Now gather up some wood and git us some supper. You'll find fixin's in them bags."

Closely guarded by the hulking Clem, in the dwindling twilight the two women scrambled around on the outskirts of the camp, gathering up fallen, dead wood. Clumsily using the flint her captor grudgingly handed her, Fancy soon had a blazing fire crackling in the ring of stones taken from the creek edge.

The saddlebags held meager goods, but Ellen and Fancy soon had coffee perking; some beans flavored with a bit of salt they found were bubbling in a battered iron pot over the fire; and an iron skillet with hot corn mush was cooling on the stones. The two men lounged on the ground nearby, drinking from a bottle of corn whisky, their hungry eyes never leaving the two women as they moved about the fire. From time to time one of the men would let out a snort of laughter, and with every second that passed Fancy could feel the tension building. From their crude comments and the way they were stripping her and Ellen with their eyes, Fancy knew that time had just about run out for them. They must escape soon, or escape would be impossible.

Despairingly she glanced around her. Darkness had fallen, and only the leaping flames of the dancing yellow-and-orange fire kept the utter blackness of the night at bay. The forest closed in on them, the trees near the edge of the camp swaying in weird and menacing shapes, the waiting silence full of portent.

"Them are shore purty wimmen," Clem said in a slurred voice. "What do you think, Udell? Is mine purtier than yores?"

Udell smiled, the scar on his face outlined grotesquely by the flickering flames. He licked his lips. "Can't tell for shore. Reckon we'll have to strip 'em to find out."

Fancy's jaw firmed, her eyes full of golden fire as she glared at him. He wasn't, she thought wrathfully, going to find it an easy task.

Ellen shrieked suddenly, and to Fancy's horror, she saw that Clem had grabbed her sister's ankle and was dragging her over to him, despite Ellen's frantic struggles to escape. Clem was chortling, enjoying Ellen's fright and attempts to evade him.

Blind, panicked rage exploded through Fancy. Grasping the big iron skillet in her hand, heedless of its searing heat, she brought it down on Clem's head with all her might. He gave an odd sigh and slumped forward, his hold on Ellen loosened.

Udell couldn't believe his eyes. In slack-jawed astonishment he stared at Clem's motionless body on the ground beside him. Those few stunned seconds were all Fancy needed. Wielding her skillet with desperate efficiency, she struck Udell a glancing blow on the side of his head, the mush that remained for dinner flying everywhere. He let out a yowl of outrage and staggered to his feet, murder in his eyes.

Freed from Clem's grasp, Ellen reached for the only other weapon available—the coffeepot—and hurled it unerringly into Udell's face. He screamed and clawed at his eyes as the boiling liquid splashed across his skin.

Fancy dropped the skillet and picked up her skirts; grabbing Ellen's hand, she said breathlessly, *"Run!"*

Ellen needed no urging. Together the two sisters plunged into the forest, running like fleet deer. They ran like does before hounds, mindless terror driving them. There was no direction to their flight; they simply ran and ran and *ran*.

Branches whipped at them; brambles clawed at their clothes and arms; and vines tangled and curled around their feet. Still they ran, their feet hardly touching the ground as they raced through the enveloping blackness.

Only when her lungs felt as if they would burst from her chest and the stitch in her side was almost unbearable did Fancy slow her breakneck pace. Ellen's hand was still clasped in a death-grip with hers, and with great gulping sobs, half laughter, half tears, the two sisters hugged each other.

They stood frozen in the darkness, their labored breathing calming gradually, their ears and eyes painfully alert for any sound or sight of their captors. Agonizing minutes, which seemed like hours, passed and nothing alarming greeted them.

"Do you think we lost them?" Ellen eventually whispered into Fancy's ear.

"I don't know. There is no sound of pursuit and Clem was unconscious—probably for a week. I certainly hit him hard enough." Her voice grim, Fancy added, "As for that horrid Udell creature, I'm quite hopeful that if the coffee you threw at him didn't do permanent damage to his eyes, it at least disabled him for some time."

A twig snapped nearby and the two women shrank together, visions of Clem and Udell flashing across their minds. Seconds passed and then they both heard the soft startled snort of a deer and the noise of a large body moving swiftly away from them through the brush.

"Oh, Fancy! I was *so* scared," Ellen finally said softly.

Fancy squeezed Ellen's shoulder. "My heart was in my mouth," she admitted.

They listened again, but only the lonely, haunting cry of an owl floated on the humid, dark air.

"We've truly lost them, haven't we?" Ellen asked a few minutes later.

In the darkness Fancy made a wry face. "I think so, but we've also managed to lose ourselves as well. I have no idea which direction camp may be, and until daylight we dare not move from here." Glumly she added, "And what use daylight will be to us, I have no idea. We are utterly lost."

Ellen gave a tearful giggle. "But we are having an adventure, are we not?"

Torn between laughter and tears, Fancy hugged her fiercely. "Indeed we are, miss!" she said in a shaky voice. "So don't you *dare* tell me that you are not enjoying yourself."

As more minutes passed, it became apparent that the two women *had* escaped. Putting aside the horrifying image of Clem and Udell stealthily creeping up on them, Fancy finally said, "We had better sleep here. We cannot continue to stumble about blindly in this impenetrable darkness. Come daylight, perhaps things will not appear quite as bleak for us."

Gingerly the two women arranged themselves on the ground, Fancy leaning against the trunk of a tall oak tree, Ellen's head resting in her lap. Determinedly Fancy pushed aside thoughts of rattlesnakes and copperheads . . . and bears and the mountain lions, or panthers, that Jonathan and Sam had said abounded all through the colonies. Wolves, too, she remembered tiredly. And raiding Indians. . . . Too exhausted by the terrible events that had overtaken them, she found that not even the thought of a red-skinned savage seeking her scalp could prevent her eyes from closing. She slept.

Daylight did not vastly improve their dangerous situation. Rising to her feet and stretching uncomfortably, Fancy glanced around her. A tangle of green forest, vines, and brambles met her gaze. She recognized nothing, and despair washed through her. Had they escaped the Thackers, only to perish in the wilderness?

Her spine stiffened. Not bloody likely! she told herself stoutly.

Ellen bit back a huge yawn and muttered, "I am so thirsty and oh, so very hungry. What are we to do, Fancy?"

Fancy wrinkled her nose. "I don't know, my dear, but we cannot stay here. The Thackers will no doubt be searching for us, and hopefully, Jonathan and his brother as well. We must move forward and pray that we find a trail or path which will lead us to some habitation." Fervently she added, "And pray merciful God that we cross the path of Jonathan and his brother *before* that of the Thackers."

During the next three harrowing days only part of Fancy's prayers were answered. They did not cross the path of the Thackers. Neither did they find any discernible trail to follow, or stumble across the Walker brothers. They did manage to find several cool running streams and creeks in which to quench their thirst and bathe their scratched and insect-bitten flesh. Fancy had discovered mosquitoes and chiggers with a vengeance, as well as the stray tick or two, and she was *not* enamored of them!

Since it was summer, they were able to quell the very worst of their constant gnawing hunger with berries and wild grapes and plums. Their stomachs seemed to growl continuously, and at night, as they slept restlessly wherever they stopped, they dreamed of rich mince pies, plump roast chickens, and Yorkshire puddings.

As daylight broke slowly across the land on the morning of their fourth day in the wilderness, Fancy stared bleary-eyed at the gold-streaked sky overhead, wondering dispiritedly if today would be any different from the previous ones. It *had* to be, she thought grimly, aware that she and Ellen were becoming weaker and more vulnerable with every passing day. They had heard the blood-freezing scream of a panther last night, and yesterday afternoon, as they had hungrily filled their mouths with ripe juicy berries, they had been frightened away by the sudden emergence of a huge brown bear from the middle of the brambles. It hadn't mattered that the bear had been as frightened as they had been. His menacing appearance had terrified both women, and they had run pell-mell into the concealing embrace of the forest.

Keeping their direction by the rising and setting of the sun, Fancy and Ellen had been heading in a generally easterly direction. They had decided that since they had absolutely no idea which direction their camp lay and since in all probability the majority, if not all, of the Walker party had moved on, there was no sense in trying to find it. Fancy's haphazard plan was simple. If they traveled east, eventually they should reach the shore of the Atlantic Ocean, if they did not come across some settlement first. Once they reached the ocean, by traveling north up the coast of Virginia, they *should* come to habitation. If they didn't die first, Fancy thought dully.

Before the sun climbed any higher, the two women rose and, ignoring their aching muscles and empty stomachs, doggedly continued through the wilderness. It was imperative that they travel as far as they could in the coolness of the morning; by afternoon the heat and humidity made exertion nearly impossible. It had become their habit to find a shady spot in the afternoon in which to rest and doze until the worst of the muggy warmth abated and then arise and continue on their way until dark.

This day proved no different from the days that had passed. Sometime around one o'clock in the afternoon, they chanced upon a shady glen edged by a small brook. After refreshing themselves in the water, the two sisters settled themselves beneath the spreading arms of a magnolia tree and fell into exhausted slumber.

Fancy never knew what it was that brought her awake, but she was suddenly heart-poundingly alert. Something had disturbed her, and frantically her gaze scanned their little glen. A terrified gasp came from her as her eyes fell upon a pair of moccasins . . . moccasins that encased a pair of rather large feet.

Panic and rage twisting through her, Fancy scrambled upright, her gaze moving swiftly up the tall, lean body in buckskins; another equally large, buckskin-clad body stood just behind the first. The Thackers! But when her eyes finally rested on the dark, granite-hewn features of the man standing in front of her, her heart gave a great leap as she realized that it wasn't the Thackers who had found them. It was someone infinitely more dangerous to Fancy's peace of mind—Chance Walker.

Chapter Four

———◆◆◆———

It was no accident or mere coincidence that had brought Chance Walker to this lonely little glade where the Merrivale ladies had stopped to rest. He and Hugh had been searching for them since noon of the day after Fancy and Ellen had disappeared.

Chance, Hugh, and Morely had left Richmond with the imported horses two days behind the Walker party. Chance had known that it was only a matter of time before they caught up with the others. In confirmation of that, they had come upon Jonathan's man, Simmons, driving a heavily laden wagon, the second day of their journey. They would have joined forces with him, but Simmons seemed oddly reluctant for their company. So, with a shrug, they had pushed onward. With no wagons and only themselves to worry about, Chance and his two companions could have overtaken the larger group quite rapidly, but the Thoroughbreds were not in as good condition as Chance would have preferred and he had not wanted to push them, especially the pregnant mares. It was obvious from the camp remains they found on the trail that his party was gaining on Sam's group.

From the very start of their journey Chance had known that he was looking forward to overtaking Sam's party. He had told himself that it was only because he enjoyed Sam's company enormously and that he could amuse himself endlessly by tweaking Jonathan's arrogant nose. But he knew in his heart that his eagerness to catch up with the others had nothing to do with any of those reasons. No, his anticipation had nothing to do with meeting the Walker men, but it had, he admitted reluctantly, everything to do with that haughty little creature with those great golden brown cat-eyes. . . .

To his intense annoyance, he had discovered that he could not get Jonathan's baroness out of his mind. Her image tantalized him every waking moment of the day, and at night . . . at night she drifted seductively through his dreams, her exotic-shaped eyes daring him nearer, her soft mouth taunting him.

Oh yes, he'd been quite eager to see the baroness again. When they had at last come across Sam's camp four days ago, he'd felt a sharp stab of elation. Elation that had swiftly turned to icy fear when he had learned why the party was still encamped at high noon: the baroness and her sister had disappeared.

It had taken him several minutes to get the full story from a hysterical Constance. Sam and Jonathan were not present; they were away from camp, searching frantically through the forest for any sign of the two young women.

In grim silence Chance had listened to Constance's terrifying tale, and he realized instantly that the ladies could not have simply wandered away. It was highly unlikely, with all the warnings Constance tearfully claimed they'd been given, that they would have willingly strayed out of earshot.

Everyone was convinced that the women were simply lost, but Chance didn't think so. In his brief glimpse of her, he'd seen lively intelligence in the face of the baroness. Chance was bone-deep certain that she wouldn't do something so foolish as to get herself lost in the middle of the wilderness. And if she hadn't gotten lost . . . His mouth had thinned.

There were several reasons why the women could have disappeared so inexplicably, and he didn't like any of them. And if his suspicions were correct, Sam and Jonathan were wasting their time looking for them in this area. By now, they would be, if still alive, miles from this spot.

After a hasty consultation among themselves, it was decided that Morely would stay with the Walker party and the horses and that Chance and Hugh would begin their own search. They would do so afoot, a common enough way of traveling through the vast untracked wilderness of the Colonies, carrying with them the supplies that they would need. A bow was slung across Chance's broad chest, and some arrows were in the quiver on his back; he'd be able to hunt silently and not betray their presence to others. Chance wasn't sorry to leave the horses behind; in the virgin wilderness through which they would travel, there were many places a man on foot could go that a horse couldn't.

Sam and Jonathan arrived back at camp just as Chance and Hugh were on the point of departing. Even under the circumstances, Jonathan was not happy to see Chance. Sam was delighted. And after listening to Chance's theory that there were only two explanations for the disappearance of the baroness and her sister, Indians or outlaws, Sam sadly concurred. Sam also agreed with Chance's plan: Chance and Hugh would undertake to pick up a trail and find the two women while the others continued on their journey to Walker Ridge.

Jonathan had been furious that he had been excluded from the search party. Bitterly conscious of the prearranged meeting between Simmons and the Thackers in this area, he had already surmised what had happened to the women, but his lips were sealed. Knowing the men involved, he was certain the women were dead—or worse. While he intended to take his vengeance, he had already decided if this whole farce was not to be a total failure he had to wait until he had received the profits from the trading venture to move against the Thackers. The loss of the women was a terrible blow to his ego, and his private rage against the Thackers was very great—perhaps even greater because he could not give vent to it.

Staring across at Chance, his emotions carefully hidden,

Jonathan had simply demanded that he be allowed to come with the other two.

Coolly, Chance had looked him up and down and said flatly, "You have spent too many months in London to be much help. You were never one for the wilderness anyway. I doubt you would last a day at the pace we will set. The last thing we need is a London dandy to worry over."

Jonathan's fists had clenched and he had taken a menacing step toward Chance. "By God!" he had exploded. "I ought to teach you some manners toward your betters."

Chance had smiled, a cold glitter in his blue eyes. "Any time," he had said softly. "Any time you think you are my *better*. . . ."

Jonathan had frozen, and with his mother crying and clinging to his arm, begging him not to risk his life in a brawl with Chance, he had spun on his heel and left the field to Chance. Once again Chance and Hugh prepared to leave.

Despite the scene with Jonathan, Sam had shaken Chance's hand and said, "I pray God that you are successful."

Chance had smiled. "I usually am, sir. If the women can be found, Hugh and I shall do so. Rest easy on that fact. Worry instead as to the state we will find them in."

Sam had nodded grimly, and then, with Hugh at his heel, Chance had melted into the forests. Picking up the trail was not easy. Sam and Jonathan had trampled over many of the signs of the passage by the two women and their abductors. It took the two men several hours of searching in ever-widening circles before they discovered what they were looking for: a scrap of pale yellow material clinging to a briar vine.

In the time that followed there were not many clues for them to find: a feminine footprint near a creek bed; a blue thread dangling from a branch; several strands of blond hair tangled in a bush. But with their keen eyes and extensive knowledge, slowly, methodically, and inevitably they followed the scant trail left behind by the women. Darkness was falling that first day when they stumbled across the camp where the women had made their escape. It was too dark for them to continue their search, and reluctantly they camped for the night at that same spot.

The next morning Chance's mouth had been grim as he and Hugh began to follow the obvious trail left by the women. The fact that their captors had abandoned the women seemed very ominous, and he feared that the pitiful trail he was following would end in tragedy.

But by the time they made camp that second night, Chance was hopeful again. It was apparent that the women had not been followed very far by their captors, and the painful thought of finding the baroness's lifeless, mutilated body in some shadowy glade gradually faded from his mind.

As he and Hugh continued to follow the traces left by the women, Chance was conscious of a grudging admiration for the baroness and her sister. They might be delicate, pampered Englishwomen, but they had shown pluck and great daring in managing to escape from their captors.

Despite his growing optimism that they would find the women alive, it wasn't until he and Hugh actually stood there looking down at the two exhausted ladies as they slept on the ground that the anguished knot deep in his belly finally loosened. They had found them, and they were alive.

And not, he thought with grim humor, exactly pleased to see them, either. The quickly masked expression on the baroness's face certainly suggested that she would have preferred to be rescued by just about anyone other than Chance Walker. His lips quirked. His baroness certainly wasn't a hypocrite; she didn't like him, and even the present circumstances weren't going to change anything.

Grudging admiration flickering in his eyes, he drawled, "My apologies that your charming host was not the one to have found you, Your Ladyship. But then if Jonathan had been looking for you, well, I fear you would never have been found."

"It does not matter who found us," Fancy said crisply, as she rose to her feet and shook out her tattered gown. "All that matters is that we *have* been found, and for that I thank

you with all my heart." Despite her sincere and deep gratitude, some imp of mischief made her add, "You *were* looking for us? You have not simply stumbled across us as did
those wretched Thacker creatures?"

The good cheer vanished from Chance's gaze, and Hugh
audibly sucked in his breath. "Udell Thacker? *He* was your
abductor?" Chance demanded roughly.

Unconcernedly helping Ellen to her feet, Fancy replied,
"Mmm, yes, that was his name, Udell Thacker. I believe that
the other cretin with him is called Clem." Smiling sweetly at
Chance over her shoulder, she asked, "Are they friends of
yours?"

Hugh choked and hastily looked away.

"Not exactly," Chance growled, not best pleased by her
manner. Under the circumstances, a little more gratitude
would have been expected and, he admitted ruefully, appreciated, but he should have known that his baroness would do
precisely the opposite—bait him instead of placating him.
And damned if he'd let her get the better of him.

Blue eyes suspiciously guileless, he inquired innocently,
"Did you enjoy your stay with them? Other, er, ladies, have
not found them, ah, polite."

Fancy glared at him, suddenly tired of the situation. "We
did not, as you know very well! From the moment that those
wretched beasts made their presence known, it has been
most, *most* disagreeable."

Hugh spoke up. Gravely he said, "You are very lucky to still
be alive, Your Ladyship. Few women who fall into the hands
of the Thackers live to tell about it. And those who do . . ." He
hesitated and then asked awkwardly, "They did not . . . ?" He
cleared his throat, not certain how to proceed. "You were
not . . . ?"

Fancy shook her head, knowing precisely what the young
man was attempting to ask. "No. They did not violate us, but
only because we managed to escape before they could."

Her big eyes fixed on Hugh, Ellen said shyly, "Fancy was
wonderful! She hit that awful Clem over the head with a
skillet!"

"And do not forget," Fancy added softly, hugging Ellen to her, "that you threw the coffeepot at Udell. Had you not done that, we might never have escaped."

"Resourceful of you," Chance murmured, again admiring the women despite himself, this time for the way they were attempting to make light of their frightening ordeal. It was obvious that they had been terrified and were now exhausted and, he suspected, extremely hungry. Their faces were thin and worn, remembered terror lurking in the depths of their eyes; their clothing was torn and stained, hanging in tatters on their slender forms; yet both acted as if nothing untoward had occurred. Gently he said, "You have been very brave. Not many women, even those raised in the wilderness and used to its dangers, could have survived."

Fancy sent him her first genuine smile. "Why, thank you," she said softly. "That was very handsome of you."

Chance was stunned by that smile, something warm and powerful unfurling within him. He stared bemused at her for a long moment, then seemed to shake himself and turned away. He glanced around the little glen and said gruffly, "We will camp here for tonight. You both are in need of rest and probably a good meal."

Ellen laughed and clapped her hands. "Oh, *yes*. We have talked and dreamed of nothing but food these past four days."

Chance smiled at her, liking the baroness's younger sister. "You may have to make do with cornmeal mush unless I can find some game."

"That sounds wonderful," Ellen exclaimed, her blue eyes bright with anticipation. "Anything other than berries."

Chance looked across at Hugh. "You stay here with the women. I'll see what I can find."

After placing his long black rifle against the trunk of a tree next to the large pack he carried, he unslung his bow and took a few arrows from a quiver, then disappeared into the forests.

Fancy almost cried out in protest as his tall form slipped into the green gloom. Something about Chance Walker seemed to bring out the worst in her, yet she had felt bereft when he left. Telling herself that she was being utterly irrational, she looked at the young man who remained and smiled brightly at him.

"You have rescued us and we don't even know your name," she said softly.

Hugh smiled. "Hugh Walker, Your Ladyship. Chance and I are cousins of a sort—at least that's what my father claims. Just about all Walkers in Virginia are cousins of some sort."

"Well, I am very glad to meet you, Hugh Walker," Fancy said warmly. "This is my sister, Ellen. Considering the circumstances, I think we can dispense with 'Your Ladyship.' My name is actually Frances, but all my friends call me simply Fancy. I hope that you will do so."

Hugh stared at her, admiration obvious in his blue eyes. The baroness was not as he expected. Neither haughty, nor demanding, nor very old, and despite the circumstances, extremely pretty.

A slow, lazy smile curved his long mouth. "I'd be honored to be counted as one of your friends, Fancy." He glanced at Ellen. "And I'm very happy to meet you, too, Ellen."

Ellen gave a little sniff and held her head high, muttering, "*Mistress* Ellen, if you don't mind!"

Fancy glanced at her in astonishment. Ellen never stood on ceremony and occasionally accused *her* of being stuffy. So why was she acting so stiffly to this very nice young man?

A gleam entered the nice young man's eyes as he looked, really looked, at Ellen for the first time. The knowledge that the baroness's young sister was also very, *very* pretty suddenly dawned on him. "Very well," he said with mocking amusement, "*Mistress* Ellen it shall be . . . and you may call me Master Hugh."

Ellen shrugged. Her nose at an imperious angle, she said, "Well, now that we have that settled, shouldn't you be *doing* something, *Master* Hugh? Or are you just going to stand around and chat with us?"

It didn't help Ellen's frame of mind when, not the least

put out by her haughty manner, Hugh asked affably, "And what would you wish me to do, Mistress Ellen? This is hardly the queen's drawing room."

Ellen took in an indignant breath, very much aware that this far-too-handsome young man was amused by her. Feeling bewildered and mortified by her contrary actions, she said crossly, "I am aware of that. But are you just going to stand around and wait until Chance returns?"

"Chance?" he asked with a quirked eyebrow, laughter dancing in his thickly lashed dark blue eyes. "Not Master Chance?"

Ellen gave a sound like a thwarted kitten and turned away, just as Fancy recovered her wits and entered the fray. "I am certain," she interjected hastily, "that Chance would not consider it impertinent. In fact," she added with a speaking look at Ellen, "I think that this is no time to stand on ceremony." Quietly she said, "These gentlemen have, no doubt, saved our lives. We owe them a great deal."

Ellen nodded her blond head, shame flashing through her. Contrition in her big blue eyes, she looked up at Hugh. "I do not know what was wrong with me. I am not usually so horrid. Please forgive me?" A beguiling smile teased the corner of her pink little mouth. "And call me Ellen? Please?"

Hugh stared down into Ellen's face. Even dirt stained and tired, she was undeniably lovely. And that smile of hers . . . His heart, normally the most reliable organ, seemed as if it would leap from his chest, and for a second he was struck dumb, his mind going curiously blank. It was Ellen's gentle touch on his hand that brought him back to the present.

She had stepped closer to him, and, concern on her pretty face, she asked, "Are you all right? You look . . . queer."

Huskily Hugh said, " 'Tis that smile of yours. You should not spring it on a man without warning, Ellen."

"Oh, what a handsome thing to say," she said happily, her smile deepening. "Now may I call you Hugh?"

He swept her a low, gallant bow. "I would be honored."

Amusement in her voice, Fancy murmured, "If you two

have worked out what you will be calling each other, could we please set up some sort of camp?"

Roses bloomed in Ellen's cheeks, and Hugh, his color a little high, glanced over at Fancy as if remembering for the first time that he and Ellen were not alone. "Our camp will not be very luxurious, I fear," he warned. "We had to carry everything with us. But if you ladies will sit down over there, I will see what I can do."

"We will help," Fancy said. "Ellen and I can gather firewood, while you unpack what we'll need for the night."

When Chance returned just as dusk was falling, with the hindquarters of a small deer slung across his back, he found a fire burning brightly near the stream, a pot of coffee burbling merrily near the edge, and the smell of baking johnny cakes wafting on the air. Hugh and the two women were absorbed in their conversation as they sat around the fire, and it wasn't until Chance was almost upon them that Hugh became aware of his presence.

After leaping to his feet, his hand going automatically to the long-bladed knife that hung at his side, Hugh grinned sheepishly when he finally recognized Chance in the fading light. "I did not hear you."

"And if I had been one of the Thackers, or an Indian seeking scalps, you would not be hearing anything ever again," Chance returned dryly.

Settling his knife once more in its accustomed position, Hugh grimaced. "You are right. I should have been paying more attention."

Chance merely grunted and, laying down the hindquarters, said, "This should still the worst of everyone's hunger. What we do not eat this evening, we can smoke through the night and finish it off in the morning."

The meal that followed was one of the most delicious Fancy could ever remember eating. The venison was sweet and succulent, the coffee strong and dark, and the johnny cakes, which Hugh explained had originally been called "journey" cakes, were crusty on the outside and tender in the middle. She and Ellen would have made pigs of themselves, but both men warned them not to subject their empty stomachs to too much food at one time. Fancy ate slowly, relishing the pleasing flavor of the deer, and only when Chance took her pewter plate from her and said quietly, "That's enough for now—in an hour or two you can have some more," did she realize that her hunger had abated.

Her stomach satisfied for the present, Fancy leaned back against the trunk of a nearby tree and sighed. They were, as Hugh had explained, a long distance from Walker Ridge and habitation, but the long and possibly dangerous journey ahead of them didn't worry her at the moment. The blackness of the night pressed close, but the fire was cozy, fear and hunger were no longer her constant companions, and she was aware of an odd contentment. For the first time since they had been captured by the Thackers, she felt safe.

Her gaze traveled over to the shadowy spot just beyond the fire, where Chance sat partially concealed. She didn't like him very much. When he wasn't irritating her, he was mocking her. But inexplicably, he also made her feel . . . protected. All her life, Fancy had been the one doing the protecting. It was a strange sensation for her to be on the receiving end. This feeling wouldn't last, of course, she told herself sternly. Once they were at Walker Ridge, she would seldom see him, and, she reminded herself grimly, she *really* didn't like him.

Chance stood up just then and walked over to the fire, carefully arranging the remaining strips of venison over a spit fashioned from a freshly cut maple branch. The fire was tamped down and green wood was added to the coals, so that drifts of smoke spiraled upward around the meat. Chance watched his handiwork for several moments, his tall, lean, buckskin-clad body clearly delineated by the firelight. When he was satisfied, he looked at Hugh and said, "That should last for several hours. When we change watches, one of us can add more." He cocked an eyebrow at his cousin. "Do you want to take the first watch or shall I?"

"Watch?" Fancy asked, puzzled. "What do you mean?"

Chance sent her a look. "I mean, Lady Merrivale, that one

of us has to stay awake and alert to ensure that someone like Udell Thacker does not surprise us with a visit."

"Oh!" she said in a small voice, thinking uncomfortably of the nights she and Ellen had slumbered in the forests, the idea of watching for any nocturnal visitors the furthest thing from their minds. "I had not thought of that." She glanced around at the suddenly threatening darkness and asked uneasily, "Do you think that they are still following us?"

Chance shook his head. "No, they have no doubt given you up for dead and gone in search of other prey." He grinned at her, the firelight flickering across his dark face, his teeth very white. "Easier prey."

For some reason, Fancy felt a hot flush surge into her cheeks. She was more aware of him than she had been of any man in her entire life. She was positive that she didn't like the odd little tingle deep in her belly when he looked at her in that mocking way of his. There was something about him, something in the way he spoke to her or acted around her that she found disconcerting. It wasn't anything that she could put her finger on, but there was a glitter now and then deep in those cobalt blue eyes of his that made her distinctly nervous. He looked, she decided warily, almost as if he were a hunting tiger considering one particular doe for dinner.

A yawn caught her by surprise. "Oh, my. I see that I am more tired than I realized." Prompted by some devil within her, she deliberately ignored Chance and looked admiringly over at Hugh, where he sat on the ground near the fire. "I shall sleep better tonight, knowing that you are watching over us."

Chance snorted and walked over to his place at the base of a towering magnolia tree, where he lowered himself to the ground. "The baroness seems to have made the choice, my friend. You take first watch," he said to Hugh. "Wake me whenever you're are ready to switch." Without another word, he pulled his blanket over him and went to sleep.

Annoyed with herself for her petty act, Fancy arranged herself next to Ellen on the ground. The smoke from the fire kept many of the insects at bay and, wrapped securely in one

of the blankets the men had brought with them, with Ellen
lying by her side, Fancy soon drifted off to sleep. But even
in her sleep she couldn't escape from him. Chance's dark,
mocking face and long, lean body drifted erotically through
her dreams.

It didn't help that the first face she saw upon waking the
next morning was Chance's. Especially not after some of the
astonishingly explicit dreams she had had about him during
the night. Feeling grubby and embarrassed, she sat up and
brushed back a tendril of dark hair. Trying to pretend he
wasn't there, she yawned, rubbed her eyes and face to fully
awaken, and finally let her gaze travel in his direction.

Chance was sitting not six feet away, his back resting
comfortably against a tree trunk, one knee bent and those
ridiculously long-lashed blue eyes fixed boldly on her.
Fancy's heart gave a painful thump. She'd had gentlemen
look at her before, but usually there was interest or polite admiration in their gaze. Such was not the case with Chance.
There was not one whit of admiration, polite or otherwise,
in his look. The expression on his face was downright hostile. He looked, Fancy decided uneasily, very much as if he
would like to wring her neck.

Fancy wasn't far wrong. Chance would very much have
liked to wring her neck all right, but only after he had spent
hours, days, perhaps months, making love to her. He wasn't
at *all* happy about his desires. Sternly reminding himself
that she was an English lady—a baroness, for God's sake!—
and Jonathan's intended bride at that did nothing to banish
the images of her naked body twisting beneath his. Nor did
it make him stop thinking about that lushly curved mouth of
hers and how her lips would feel and taste.

Chance had had several hours after Hugh had awakened
him to stare and study the slender woman in the dirty yellow
gown as she lay sleeping innocently near the fire. Unfortunately, watching the tempting rise and fall of her small
bosom, the way the ruined gown sloped lovingly over her
hip and outlined her shapely legs, none of his thoughts were
innocent. The smoldering firelight caressed her sleeping fea-

tures, making him unwillingly aware of the strength in her face, of the character revealed in the clean line of her jaw and the promise of passion in the curve of her bottom lip. The last thing he wanted was to be attracted in *any* manner to her, and yet, though he was aware of every rustle, every sound, made in the forest that surrounded them, his attention was firmly riveted by the woman lying on the ground in front of him. Despite his best efforts not to be, he was painfully aroused; his swollen, aching member reminding him of how long it had been since he'd had a woman. He cursed the Englishwoman, Jonathan, and himself most of all for his present state. All in all, it had been a *very* long night.

Hugh had awakened at first light, and Ellen not a half an hour previously. Despite Ellen's wry grimace, they had gone in search of some berries to add to their breakfast, leaving Chance and Fancy alone in camp. Chance hadn't been happy about *that* situation, either, and he had almost volunteered to go with Ellen instead of Hugh, until he had noticed the way Hugh was looking at Ellen.

His mouth had twisted. Hugh was aiming high. Too high, but it wasn't up to him to disillusion the younger man. At least that was the excuse he gave himself for remaining behind. But he knew that he was only avoiding the real reason he had stayed with the baroness. Ellen was sweet; Ellen was charming; but she didn't fascinate him the way her sister did—even when the lady in question was sound asleep. Damn her cat-eyes.

Those same golden brown cat-eyes had finally registered that they were alone. Fancy asked uneasily, "Where are Ellen and Hugh?"

Chance stood up. "They have gone to forage for some berries." He gave her a thin-lipped smile. "Do not worry, Duchess, you will not be left long in my tender clutches."

Fancy glared at him. "First of all, I am *not* a duchess! Second, my name is Merrivale. *You* may call me Lady Merrivale."

He flashed her a crooked grin that did queer things to her heart. "Not Fancy, as Hugh calls you?"

Suddenly realizing how Ellen had felt last night, Fancy bit her lip and said stiffly, "Of course you may call me Fancy."

Fancy got up and, studiously ignoring him, walked to the creek, where she splashed her face with water. Returning to the vicinity of the fire, she discovered that there was hot coffee in the pot, and she poured herself a cup. Her back to him, she looked at the forest and sipped her coffee. The silence between them was prickly and uncomfortable. Feeling that something more was required of her, she said abruptly, "Ellen and I are beholden to you for our very lives. I would not want you to think that I am ungrateful for what you have done for us. We are enormously obligated to you and Hugh, and I am aware that we owe you a tremendous debt of gratitude."

"Do you?" Chance asked from directly behind her, startling her.

Fancy whirled to face him, her eyes widening at the angry glitter in his. He took the cup from her and tossed it carelessly on the ground.

Jerking her into his arms, he pulled her hard against his chest. His mouth a fraction above hers, he growled, "Since there are just the two of us here alone . . . shall we see just how much of that *great* debt you're willing to pay?"

Chapter Five

————◆◆◆————

Fancy knew Chance was going to kiss her, and that he would not be gentle with her; what he intended was explicit in the hot glitter of his eyes. But she was too astonished, too aware of him, too *curious*, to offer even token resistance. As his hard mouth came down almost brutally on hers, her eyes clamped shut, and to her utter shame, she felt a bolt of erotic excitement shaft through her.

Dimly Fancy realized that for all her years as a wife, she was an innocent when it came to physical desire. She had never experienced anything even vaguely resembling Chance's embrace. Never. She was burningly aware of him in ways that she had never been with any other man. It was as if he simply *invaded* her very being. His strong arms crushed her to him, her breasts were flattened against his broad chest, her legs were pressed intimately against his muscled thighs, but his mouth . . . His mouth was pure sweet sin, hot and forbidden, thrilling and dangerous, seductive and treacherous, and oh, so, intoxicating.

There was no gentleness, no tenderness, in his kiss. His mouth upon hers was fierce and demanding, and Fancy was gallingly aware that while she should be insulted, she was not. At least not at the moment. At the moment, she was too battered by newly awakened sensations, too stunned by the frankly arousing sensation of his warm body against hers, of his lips consuming hers, of his hands suddenly cradling her head, angling her face up so that he could feed more deeply, to feel anything but plain, naked, carnal delight.

With something between a groan and curse, Chance forced his tongue into the dark, warm recesses of her mouth. The coffee she had just sipped still lingered on her tongue, and he knew that he had never tasted any brew so heady. She enflamed him, increased the urgent ache to bury his rigid manhood within her sweet body. To his fury, not only did she make him blind to anything but the demands of his own body, but she effortlessly aroused other, deeper, more powerful emotions. The sudden painful surging to life of feelings he had thought long dead and the violent need to suppress them nearly loosed what little control he still had of himself. Frantic to deny the burgeoning tenderness that flowed through him, Chance blocked out coherent thought and let passion and blind desire rule him. There was nothing in the world for him but her soft body and sweet mouth, no yesterday, no tomorrow, nothing, just Fancy in his arms. . . . It was the creeping awareness of how close he was to the edge, of how near he was to ripping back her skirts and taking her upright against the nearest tree, that abruptly brought him to his senses.

With something akin to loathing, he suddenly thrust her away from him. His chest heaving, his eyes nearly black with the powerful emotions that still raged within him, he said savagely, "Consider the debt paid! I find that having a woman respond to me out of gratitude"—his mouth twisted derisively—"even you, Duchess, is not quite as satisfying as I thought it would be."

Reeling from the cruel cessation of his embrace, Fancy could barely register his words; it took almost thirty seconds for her to realize what he had said. Then, as the full import of his words trickled into her brain, whatever remnants of that treacherous desire she had felt in his arms were totally eclipsed by the fury that suddenly shook her. "Why, you arrogant, presumptuous *barbarian*!" she spat, her eyes blazing with angry golden lights. "How *dare* you think for one moment that I *responded* to you or that I would allow myself to be mauled by a crude creature like you in order to show my gratitude!"

A smile, not a very nice one, curved his lips. "Would you like me to kiss you again and prove to both of us that you're spouting arrant nonsense, Duchess?"

"I am *not* a duchess," she said through gritted teeth, the palm of her hand itching to wipe that mocking expression off his face. "My husband was Baron Merrivale, which makes me the *Baroness* Merrivale." Her upper lip curled. "Even a backwoods lout like yourself should be able to understand something so simple." Pride made her add, "And as for kissing me again—it would simply prove that Jonathan was right—that you *are* a bastard. A cruel, black-hearted bastard who cannot be trusted not to take base advantage of any woman left in his care."

"Such language, Duchess! And here I thought that the English were so prim and proper," Chance drawled, suddenly enjoying himself and discovering that fighting with her was *almost* as pleasurable as kissing her—and certainly a lot less dangerous.

Fancy took in a deep, fortifying breath. The man was impossible! And it was obvious that she was not going to win this battle. Chance Walker was too arrogant even to realize when he was being insulted. Drawing herself up and putting on her most haughty air, she said dismissively, "We English speak our minds, and there is nothing *improper* in calling a knave a knave."

Chance's brow rose. Softly he taunted, "But you did not call me a knave, Duchess. You called me a bastard."

Rashly she snapped, "And would do so again a thousand times from the rooftops of every house in a thousand cities!"

Chance grinned, his blue eyes mocking her. "You truly dislike me very much, do you not, Duchess?"

"Dislike you?" Fancy murmured sweetly. "No, of course not. I do not dislike you; I *loathe* you."

Chance might have continued baiting her, but to Fancy's profound relief, Hugh and Ellen returned. That they had both heard her words was obvious from the wary expressions on their faces. Forcing a bright smile, Fancy said gaily, "Oh, there you are. You were gone so long that I was beginning to wonder if something had happened to you."

Ellen carried a small iron pot filled to the rim with dark, plump berries. Setting it down, she said, "We wanted to pick sufficient to take with us, and it took a while to find enough." She smiled over her shoulder at Hugh. "Hugh said it looked like a bear had beaten us to all the very best places."

The awkward moment passed, and for the next several minutes they were busy eating breakfast and then breaking camp. It didn't take long, and before the sun was very high in the sky, they were moving quietly through the forest.

Chance set a steady pace, but, mindful of the women, he called for frequent halts and unobtrusively gauged their degree of exhaustion. It was apparent that though they tried to conceal it, the days of near starvation had taken their toll and they tired easily. Again, Chance found himself admiring the two Englishwomen and was furious with himself for doing so. His mouth twisted. The *baroness* had certainly made her feelings about him crystal clear. She and Jonathan would, no doubt, spend the rest of their lives together discussing precisely how much of a bastard he really was.

Having allowed Hugh to take the lead for present, with Ellen following close on his heels, Chance eyed Fancy's stiffly held back as she walked in front of him. Like Ellen, her hair had been captured in a long, thick braid that hung almost to her waist. As they traveled through the green shadows of the forest, he found himself nearly mesmerized by its gentle sway. She was the most baffling, beguiling, *dangerous* creature he had ever come across, and for his sins—she utterly fascinated him.

To his deep disgust, he discovered that the memory of her soft mouth beneath his would not leave his brain, nor had her angry words and cool manner made her any less desirable to him. In fact, he found that her very dislike of him aroused the hunter in him. That, and the knowledge that she was to be Jonathan's bride. Jonathan had cuckolded him, had lain in his bridal bed and made love to his wife—what was wrong in paying his enemy back in kind?

It was difficult for Chance to push aside thoughts of revenge against Jonathan, especially if the revenge gave him something that he wanted very badly for himself. He didn't delude himself into believing that he *didn't* want the baroness. His problem was that he was having trouble separating the two—revenge against Jonathan and his desire to take the cat-eyed temptress in front of him to bed. The trouble, he conceded grimly, was that he wasn't certain that if he ever did get her into his bed, he'd be able to let her go.

He scowled, suddenly disliking her almost as much as she disliked him.

Perhaps only Hugh noticed that Chance seemed to wear a perpetual scowl in the days that followed and that he seemed unusually short-tempered. Fancy was very aware that he treated her with cool, barely concealed contempt. His attitude nettled her. What did *he* have to be upset about? She was the one who had been unceremoniously jerked into his arms and kissed so fiercely. He was everything Jonathan had implied, she told herself grimly. He was crude, rude, hateful, arrogant, and insulting. She shouldn't spare him a second's thought. But to her complete dismay, she couldn't stop thinking about him, and that cataclysmic kiss they had shared.

The situation wouldn't have been so bad if they could have simply avoided each other. Unfortunately, that was not possible. Day after day it was just the four of them. And Fancy's uneasy conscience couldn't forget that she was dependent upon Chance for her continued survival. It went very much against the grain to treat Chance as she did, and Fancy was deeply ashamed of her manner toward him every time he returned to camp with fresh meat or fish or every time he reached out a lean, warm hand and helped her over a nasty stretch of woods or water. Every night, as she lay on the ground, wrapped securely in one of the blankets provided by Chance, her belly full of food provided by Chance, she writhed with shame, knowing that somewhere in the darkness he was standing guard, *protecting* her even as she slept. Guilt smote her hard.

But worse than the guilt or shame that ate at her, much worse than having to put up with his disturbing presence all through the day, were the explicitly carnal dreams that tormented her at night. It was humiliating and infuriating that even in her dreams—dreams over which she had no control—he could tempt her and rouse her body in ways that even her husband's most intimate caresses had not. She longed most ardently for this wretched journey to be ended and for Chance Walker to disappear into the wilderness and never to darken her path again.

The journey would have been unendurable if it hadn't been for Hugh's and Ellen's presence. They were like a pair of merry puppies, full of enthusiasm, unflagging energy, and easy, lighthearted camaraderie despite the seriousness of their situation. Seeing them laughing and teasing together around the campfire at night, Hugh's dark head bent attentively near Ellen's blond one, Fancy was relieved that her sister's inexplicable, initial stiffness around him had abated.

Fancy smiled to herself. But then it would have been very hard for anyone to dislike Hugh Walker. Not only was he kind, considerate, and unfailingly polite, he was also handsome, charming, affable, and amusing. Something, she thought with a tightening of her fine jaw, his cousin was not. Well, she amended reluctantly, Chance *was* handsome, she wouldn't deny him that.

There was one other thing that made the journey bearable: by unspoken consent Fancy and Chance did not allow their differences to spill over onto the other pair. During the day, it was simple to conceal their animosity; there was seldom time for conversation, beyond the necessary and most mundane. But when they would stop and camp for the night . . .

Fancy dreaded the fall of darkness, dreaded those moments of enforced intimacy when they all gathered around the small fire to shut out the encroaching darkness. Invariably Chance sat directly across from her, and like one mesmerized, she would watch the dancing firelight caress his lean features, the broad forehead, the bold nose, and the hard mouth. Garbed in his buckskins, his face dark from the sun, the thick black hair falling carelessly to his broad shoulders, he could easily have been mistaken for an Indian, except for his growing beard and those eyes, eyes that could gleam with amusement at the others or become cold and bleak when they rested upon her.

Fancy learned much of the Walker history during those nights. Hugh and Chance, both being excellent raconteurs, were able to spin fascinating tales of the Walkers that kept the two women riveted. They told of an early Walker who had turned pirate, raiding and plundering the high seas at will. And of another who had reputedly loved an Indian princess but had given in to the demands of his family to marry a white woman. There had been the Walker who had killed a panther with his bare hands. And finally they spoke of the tragedy that had overtaken Sam and Letty when their only child, a son, had been born dead.

"Oh, how sad," Ellen exclaimed as Hugh finished the story this particular night, about eight days into their journey. "Mr. Walker seems like such a nice man, and I am sure that his wife is every bit as nice. It is so very tragic that after all those years of wishing for a child, the son they'd longed for so ardently should be born dead."

Dryly Chance replied, "Sadder still that Sam's heir is now his half-brother, our dear cousin Jonathan."

"Jonathan Walker is a fine man," Fancy said sharply. "And it would behoove you not to make disparaging remarks about him when he is not here to defend himself."

Chance's eyes glittered mockingly in the firelight as he looked at her. "What a wonderful bride you will make him, always loyally springing to his defense and putting the black-hearted villain who dares speak against him in his place."

"Um, I do not think that is what Fancy meant at all," Ellen

said, casting a nervous glance at her sister. "Jonathan is our host, and it is because of him that we are in Virginia. It would be terribly rude of us to repay his many kindnesses by talking about him in an impolite manner."

Fancy noted uneasily that Ellen did not correct Chance's mistaken impression about which one of them was here as Jonathan's prospective bride. This wasn't the first time her sister had done so, either. It had become increasingly clear that Ellen had no intention of enlightening either gentleman to the true state of affairs.

Which gives me just one more thing to wonder about and to brood over, Fancy thought wearily.

In marked contrast with the way he had greeted Fancy's rebuke, Chance merely grinned at Ellen. "I stand corrected, little one. On my honor, I swear that for the remainder of the journey you shall not hear one uncomplimentary word from me about your sterling host."

Ellen beamed at him. "Thank you. And now would you please tell us the story about how Hugh's father came to bring you to his cousin Andrew? It sounds so very mysterious and exciting."

Hugh nearly choked on the coffee he was drinking, and he shot his cousin a wary eye. "Er, I did not mean to tell her—it just sort of slipped out once when we were talking," he said to Chance apologetically.

"Just slipped out?" Chance repeated sardonically. "For having known the lady for barely a week, you seem to be on uncommonly friendly terms—especially if you have been regaling her with stories of old family scandal."

A blush suffused Ellen's cheeks, and, looking very embarrassed, she said defensively, "These have not been normal circumstances. We have all gotten to know each other much faster than we would have if we had met in a more conventional manner. And as for the other—Hugh meant nothing by it—he was just talking to entertain me and to take my mind off our situation. If it embarrasses you, I am sorry for it and we shall talk of something else."

"It does not embarrass me," Chance said levelly, "I just do

not believe that my antecedents, or lack thereof, is a suitable, or very interesting, subject." He sent Hugh a dark glance. "And I would suggest that something else be found to talk about in the future."

The topic was hastily dropped, but Chance's desire *not* to talk about it only aroused Fancy's curiosity. She was determined to wheedle everything she could about Chance's history out of Hugh at the first opportunity. An occasion arose the next afternoon, when they sought a shady area in which to rest from the worst of the heat. Chance decided to scout around and see if he could find something to add to their meager diet. Once everyone was settled, he glided away, leaving Hugh with the two women.

The conversation was desultory for several minutes until Fancy said idly, "You know, I am rather curious why Chance did not want you to speak of that incident between your father and his cousin." She sent him an arch look. "Was it so very disgraceful?"

Hugh moved uneasily, clearly torn about revealing more, after Chance's rebuke the previous night. "No, it was not," he finally said. "Chance is just sensitive about his background."

Ellen raised melting blue eyes to him. "Oh, Hugh, please tell us the tale. Please?" When Hugh hesitated, she asked eagerly, "Is it true that he really does not know who his parents are?" Her cheeks burned as she realized what she had said. "Oh, dear! That was terribly rude and forward of me."

Hugh smiled at her and shook his head. "Not at all. As you said last night, we have met under most unconventional circumstances, and I think that the normal rules of polite society do not apply to us." His smile faded. "And Chance's parentage has been fodder for the Walker family for years." He flushed and said awkwardly, "Most people believe that my father, Morley, is his father, that Chance is his bastard son, and that for reasons of his own he chooses not to acknowledge him."

Fancy gasped. "You mean Chance is your half-brother?"

Hugh hesitated, then said, "I am not certain. And since my father will not discuss the subject, it is a mystery."

"But that is impossible!" Fancy exclaimed. "Surely Chance has some idea who his parents are?"

Hugh made a face. "The only one who can answer that question, my father, steadfastly refuses to do so. The story is told that my father simply showed up one April morning at the home of his cousin Andrew, with Chance wrapped in a blanket. Andrew and his wife, Martha, were childless, and they did not ask too many questions when my father thrust him into their arms and asked that they care for him until he could make other arrangements."

"Other arrangements?" Fancy inquired with a little frown. "What did he mean by that?"

"No one knows, but the 'other' arrangements never came about. Chance grew up living with Andrew and Martha. From what I have heard, he could not have asked for better or more loving parents—for the short time that he had them."

"What happened to them?" Ellen asked.

Hugh sighed. "Martha died of fever the fall of his tenth year, and Andrew was killed by Indians the summer he turned sixteen. Immediately after that, Chance promptly set out on the trail to find the savages who had murdered Andrew." Proudly he added, "Alone, he tracked them down, and after he found them, he strode boldly into their camp and demanded to know which one had murdered Andrew." Hugh shook his head slightly, still amazed by the thought of what Chance had done. "The leader of the band was so impressed by Chance's bravery—foolhardy though it was—that he allowed him to meet Andrew's killer. Both of them were armed only with knives in a fight to the death." Hugh shot Fancy a half smile. "And since he is still here, it is obvious that he succeeded in his quest for revenge against Andrew's killer."

"He killed a fellow man in cold blood?" Fancy asked, revulsion clear on her face.

Hugh's eyes met hers. "You do not understand. After

Martha died, Andrew became both father and mother to him. Andrew became *everything* to him. My cousin Andrew was a gentle man. A scholar, a lover of books, a schoolmaster whose passion was imparting knowledge and shaping young minds—Chance's included. He was a compassionate man, a man who never denied food or shelter to anyone, not even an Indian." Hugh's voice hardened. "And they repaid his kindness by killing him one afternoon in his schoolhouse and setting it on fire. This savage you apparently feel so sorry for murdered and mutilated the man Chance called 'Father.' What did you expect him to do *but* kill him?"

Fancy looked away. No, she realized, Chance Walker could not have been expected to do anything other than what he had done. No one would ever strike at anything of his and not pay the penalty.

Her blue eyes full of wonder, Ellen stared at Hugh. "He was but sixteen years?"

Hugh nodded.

A little silence fell. Just at the point it was becoming uncomfortable, Fancy mused aloud, "I wonder why your father still refuses to disclose Chance's ancestry. After all these years I would not think that it would arouse much scandal—especially if your father *is* his father, since everyone already believes that to be true."

"And what about his mother? Is there no hint of who she might be?" Ellen asked softly.

Hugh shook his dark head. "Nothing. Not one word—in fact, for years now, whenever anyone has been so foolish as to bring up the subject, Morely simply leaves the room. He will *not* talk of it."

"And I could wish," Chance said dryly as he stepped from the shadows of the forest, "that you would do the same."

Fancy felt her cheeks redden, but it was Ellen who said guiltily, "Oh, do not be angry with Hugh. 'Tis our fault, but we did not mean to pry."

Chance muttered something, and the subject was once more dropped. But it wouldn't go away. Both Fancy and Ellen were utterly fascinated by the mystery of Chance's parentage. That night as the four of them sat around the fire, Ellen said shyly, "We are very sorry that we badgered poor Hugh this afternoon into telling us about your background—especially if it is painful for you."

Charmed as usual by Ellen, Chance said lightly, "It is not painful for me. I just consider the subject of little interest."

"But it is so very curious," Fancy said, her eyes full of speculation. "From what Hugh has told us, 'tis as if you had no beginning until his father placed you in Andrew's arms."

Chance shrugged. "That may be, but it all happened a long time ago and I do not dwell on it anymore—and most of the family does not, either. A man must make his own way." He sent Fancy a lopsided grin that did strange things to her heart. "It is many years since I have needed either a mother or a father to worry over me."

"And do not forget," Hugh said heartily, "had it not been for your arrival—whoever sired you—my father might still be the disgrace of the family. I—might not even be here had it not been for you."

Her eyes very round, Ellen looked from one man to the other. "Why, whatever do you mean?"

"Only that until Chance made his appearance, my father was well on his way to drinking and wenching himself to death—and losing everything he owned."

"I do not believe that Morely was ever quite as bad as some of the Walkers claim," Chance said bluntly.

"But he changed after you were born?" Fancy inquired, one slim brow raised questioningly.

Chance sighed and stirred the fire with a stick. "So many say. Aunt Millicent, Andrew's sister, maintains that after he left me with Andrew and Martha, he became a transformed person. He stopped frequenting low taverns and the company to be found there and, even to this day, will only partake occasionally of a small portion of spirits. 'Tis said that it was around this time that he also began to work for Sam Walker like the meanest slave—he still does." Chance frowned. "It is almost as if he is consumed with guilt and only by working himself to the bone for Sam that he can atone for some black sin."

Hugh laughed. "I know that Sam still talks of how stunned he was when he returned from England four years later and found this sober, reliable, hardworking young man in place of the drunken layabout he left behind when he took Mistress Letty to England after their son was born dead."

"Four years!" Fancy exclaimed. "Mr. Walker was gone to England for four years?"

Hugh nodded. "Family legend has it that Sam returned home unexpectedly two days after the tragedy and that once he had seen where his stillborn son was buried, he simply scooped up his grief-stricken wife and whisked her away to England on the first ship that sailed." Hugh glanced over at Ellen's rapt features. "Of course, Sam never meant to be gone for so long," he continued gravely, "but Cousin Jeremiah says that poor Mistress Letty just could not seem to bring herself to come back to the Colonies—to the place where her son had died. And so Sam simply placed his affairs in the hands of his business agents and played the English gentleman, until his wife was finally ready to return to Walker Ridge."

" 'Tis no secret that Morely has always relied on Sam's judgment," Chance said abruptly, "and I have wondered, having deposited me safely with Andrew and Martha, if he did not intend to return to Walker Ridge to discuss the situation with Sam."

Hugh shrugged. " 'Tis possible—but if that was his plan, it was unfortunate that during his absence Sam had returned to Walker Ridge and immediately departed for England—well beyond his reach. Since it is obvious that there is some mystery surrounding your birth, I doubt there was anything that he was willing to put in writing and trust that his letter would make its way into Sam's hands in England."

"And by the time Sam did return to Walker Ridge, four years had passed and there was nothing to discuss," Chance said flatly.

Fancy could think of nothing to say as her eyes rested on

Chance's dark, enigmatic features. Her heart ached a little for him, not for the hard man he had grown into, but for the bewildered boy he must have been. How terrible for him, she thought compassionately, not to have known who his parents were and as a young child to have been the object of the gossip and speculation that must have been rife amongst the Walkers.

Chance glanced up from his contemplation of the fire, and seeing the expression on her face, his lips thinned.

"I trust that your prurient interest in my antecedents, or lack thereof, is now satisfied," he drawled, his eyes cool and hard. "And Duchess . . . I would warn you not to let that icy heart of yours feel any sympathy for me. Pity from the likes of you is the last thing that I want."

Fancy glared at him, her compassion evaporating as the increasingly familiar desire to slap his mocking face rose within her. She stood up abruptly and shook out her ragged skirts. "Pity you?" she demanded disdainfully. "I think not. The ones I pity are Mr. Walker and his wife. Their son died and unfortunately you did not!"

Part Two

Chance

The easiest person to deceive is one's own self.

Edward Bulwer-Lytton
The Disowned

Chapter Six

It had been a terrible thing to say, and as she lay on the ground later that night, Fancy writhed with shame. Turning restlessly in her blanket, she cursed her wayward tongue a thousand times and desperately sought forgetfulness in sleep. Sleep would not come, however, and the memory of her awful words kept repeating themselves in her brain.

What was wrong with her? she wondered fretfully. In her entire life, she had never spoken to anyone in the hateful manner in which she had Chance. She had always considered herself a calm, dignified, serene, *polite* sort of woman, the type of woman who *never* lost her temper. Yet around Chance Walker . . . Just one mocking word from him, one infuriating lift of his brows, one quirk of that long, mobile mouth, and she became lost to all decorum and dignity and turned into a raging virago, hotly spewing out the most appalling things, uncaring in that burst of fury if her words hurt. She grimaced. Not that anything *she* said could dent Chance's thick, impenetrable hide! She sighed deeply. If only this wretched, interminable journey would end and she could be free of his obnoxiously disturbing presence. She could only hope that once they reached Walker Ridge she'd be able to put events in perspective and view Chance Walker in a more favorable light—and recover her own composure.

Hidden by the darkness, Chance lounged on the ground not five feet away from Fancy, his back resting comfortably against the trunk of a tree, his hand lightly clasping the long black rifle that stood upright beside him. This close to her he could hear every sound she made as she wiggled and tossed on the ground, but he could have been twenty feet away and he still would have been aware of every single thing about her. Too damned aware, he thought disgustedly, his mouth thinning.

He'd hoped that upon closer association his initial interest in the baroness would fade. More than that, he'd been certain that the journey to Walker Ridge and her subsequent actions would effectively put an end to his inexplicable preoccupation with her. But it hadn't. If anything, she now fascinated him more than she had in the beginning, and he was thoroughly annoyed by that fact.

It wasn't supposed to be this way. He was supposed to see her at her worst, and God knew this trek would bring out the devil in just about anyone. But so far she had confounded him. She had been helpful and pleasant, at least to Hugh and her sister; she had not slowed them down with unnecessary demands, and she had not complained, or whined, or made a nuisance of herself—except with respect to his peace of mind, he admitted grimly.

Their journey was almost at an end, and Chance discovered himself oddly reluctant for the moment when Walker Ridge finally came into sight and the baroness was no longer his responsibility. He'd grown used to her, he thought with a sardonic twist of his lips. Used to watching that graceful slender form move about the camp; used to that soft, silvery chuckle of hers; *very* used to the way her eyes would glow with that golden light when she was angry; and used to the way her smile could lift his spirits—not that she ever smiled at *him*!

She was going to waste that lovely smile and that slim, beautiful body on that bastard Jonathan, and there wasn't one bloody thing he could do about it, Chance thought disgustedly. That knowledge ate at him, and every time he remembered how she'd felt in his arms, the sweet fire of her kiss, his determination to deny Jonathan those charms grew.

Why should Jonathan have her? he asked himself bitterly. He sure as hell didn't deserve her.

The old, familiar feelings of hatred and revenge entwined in his heart whenever he let himself think of Jonathan, and tonight was no different. Jonathan had deliberately taken the only thing that had ever mattered to him and cruelly defiled it and, when through with it, had discarded it carelessly. The agony Chance had felt upon discovering that his wife had hanged herself and that she had been pregnant with another man's child rose up inside of him, nearly choking him. Bleakly he wondered if he'd ever be able to remember Jenny without this terrible ache, this savage urge to rip out Jonathan Walker's throat.

It had been months after Jenny's death before he'd even been able to consider what had happened—to think about Jenny dying alone and frightened, abandoned by the one man who should have stood by her side—without wanting to smash something. By the time he'd been cool-headed enough to think about it unemotionally, he'd realized that it hadn't been just lust for Jenny's lovely body that had motivated Jonathan, but also the desire to strike at him. Chance's lips tightened. Jonathan had been furious about the loss of those ten thousand acres in that card game, and he'd sworn vengeance. Chance didn't doubt for a moment that seducing Jenny had been Jonathan's way of paying him back. Whether Jonathan had known that Jenny would conceive a child and kill herself when he abandoned her or not was moot. She had, and for that reason alone—cuckolding him had little to do with his need for vengeance—Jonathan deserved to suffer. And what better way to revenge himself against the man who had destroyed his wife than to steal the one woman who meant everything to Jonathan?

Chance's eyes narrowed. Not seduce her. No, nothing so common. No, he'd not plant any horns on another man's

head. He would simply take her away from Jonathan and
marry her himself! Now *that* would be a fitting revenge.
Jonathan would have to live the rest of his days with the
knowledge that the man he hated most in the world had married the woman he had chosen for his bride—just as *he* lived
every day with the memory of Jenny's tragic death.

He'd enjoy taking the baroness away from Jonathan, he
suddenly realized, and not totally because of what had happened to Jenny. The memory of that torrid kiss rose up to
taunt him. Oh, yes. He would indeed enjoy taking that
golden-eyed little witch away from Jonathan. In fact, he
thought with a wicked smile, he was damn well looking forward to it.

If Fancy noticed that Chance seemed exceptionally cheerful the next morning, she assumed that it was because the
end of their journey was in sight. Over breakfast he casually
informed them that if all went well, tonight would be their
last night on the trail. Tomorrow night they would sleep
soundly in the finest feather-beds at Walker Ridge.

The news should have left everyone jubilant, but Fancy
was conscious of an odd heaviness in her heart. Of course,
she wanted this horrible journey to end. And naturally, she
would be absolutely delighted to see the last of the infuriating Chance Walker. But somehow she couldn't muster much
enthusiasm for the prospect.

She wasn't the only one not particularly overjoyed by
Chance's promise of finally reaching their destination. She
noticed that Ellen seemed to take the information rather indifferently. Her sister seemed subdued, not smiling and
laughing as much as the day progressed. All of them should
have been thrilled for this ordeal to end, but in fact, it was a
curiously quiet little group that made camp on the last
night—except for Chance, who had worn a suspiciously
pleased expression most of the day.

More than once Fancy had glanced at him, wondering
what went on behind those dark blue eyes. Of course, there
was no reason for him not to be pleased. After all, he *had*

found them and would be returning them safely to Jonathan's open arms.

Since they were, according to Chance, very close to their destination, but not close enough to make it tonight, they had stopped early to camp.

"There is no use exhausting ourselves," he had said.

"You will be at Walker Ridge by noon tomorrow. And this is as good as any place we have seen to camp for the night."

It was a lovely place. A wide, shallow stream ran through the edge of a small tree-dotted meadow. Wild grape and berry vines cascaded over several oak and willow trees near one side of the stream, and the grass was thick and soft beneath their feet. From the forest that surrounded the meadow, they quickly gathered downed wood for the evening fire. Once he had seen that they were situated, Chance had left Hugh on guard and disappeared into the forest in search of their evening meal.

To pass the time and also to add to their nearly exhausted larder, Fancy and Ellen began to gather the ever-present blackberries. Hugh remained at a distance, his keen eyes scanning the forest for the first sign of trouble—not that anyone really expected any danger this close to Walker Ridge.

The two women picked in silence for several moments before Ellen said tentatively, "I suppose you have wondered why I have not corrected the impression that it is *you* who is to become Jonathan's bride."

Fancy's busy fingers stilled. She glanced over at Ellen's face, noting that her sister seemed to be concentrating very hard on the simple task of plucking berries. "Well, yes, I have wondered," she said gently. "Do you want to tell me why?"

"Oh, Fancy," Ellen fairly wailed, "it is so hard to explain. I do not even know if I understand my actions myself."

They picked in silence a few minutes more, then Fancy asked quietly, "Have you changed your mind about marrying Jonathan Walker?"

Ellen grimaced. " 'Tis so hard to explain. When we left

London for the Colonies, there was no doubt in my mind that I was in love with Jonathan and that I wanted nothing more than to be his wife." She paused, her face troubled. "But once we reached Virginia, Jonathan seemed to change." She slanted Fancy a look. "He and his mother may have been treating me very well after we left Richmond, but *while* we were in Richmond, they both made me feel superfluous. You were the one, the Baroness Merrivale, whom they eagerly introduced to their friends. They brought me forth almost as an afterthought."

Fancy looked stricken. "Oh, Ellen, sweetheart, I am so sorry you were made to feel that way. I told myself that I must have been imagining things."

"Well, if you were imagining things—I was imagining the *same* things. You will not be able to convince me that Jonathan and his mother would not have been just as happy if I had stayed in our room at the tavern and never showed my face in Richmond."

"I am sure that is not true," Fancy protested. "I know that Jonathan and Constance may have inadvertently slighted you, but I am certain that is all it was. You know how some people are impressed by a title, and, while I did not expect it of Jonathan, perhaps he and his mother simply wanted to boast to their friends a little. They did not mean to ignore you. And besides, you cannot have fallen out of love with him just because of what happened in Richmond. He is, after all, a very nice man."

"And since when have you become Jonathan's champion?" Ellen asked sharply. "You have never wholeheartedly embraced the idea of my marrying him. You were the one who did not want me to marry him in England. You were the one who counseled me to wait—to be absolutely certain that I really loved him."

"I know," Fancy admitted with a sigh, "but what does all this have to do with you letting Hugh and Chance think that I am Jonathan's bride-to-be?"

Ellen didn't answer her right away. Her blond head bent, she concentrated fiercely on picking berries. Finally, in a small voice she said, "You are going to think that I am the greatest fool in nature, but I have fallen in love with Hugh Walker." She raised a tragic face to Fancy. "If he were to find out that I am Jonathan's bride-to-be, I know he would be utterly disgusted with me, not only because I concealed the truth, but because, like Chance, he does not think very much of Jonathan." Ellen's eyes filled with tears. "Oh, Fancy, what am I to do?"

Fancy's heart sank. She had noticed that Ellen and Hugh seemed to be getting along uncommonly well, but the idea of a romance between them had never occurred to her. She had been, she thought bitterly, too preoccupied with all the turbulent emotions aroused by Chance Walker to worry about what Hugh Walker might be doing to her sister's notoriously tender heart. And Ellen on the verge of announcing her betrothal to Jonathan Walker. Dear heavens! What an awkward thing to have happened. Hiding her own dismay, she put her arms around Ellen and said softly, "Now do not cry, dear. Things are not so very terrible. We escaped from that awful Clem and Udell, did we not? This situation is far less dire, and I am positive that if we think about it, we can come up with a solution."

Ellen gave a watery chuckle. "Oh, Fancy, you are always so calm and cool-headed. Do you *never* put a foot wrong?"

Fancy's mouth twisted. Would Ellen feel the same if she ever learned of that never-to-be-sufficiently-regretted kiss with Chance? Brushing her lips across Ellen's blond head, she murmured, "I am not quite the saint that you believe me, but for the moment, that is not the problem." She put Ellen from her and, looking into her sister's tearstained face, began uncomfortably, "Has Hugh, um . . . does Hugh . . . ? Have you discussed your feelings with him?"

"Oh, no! He has been everything that is proper and decorous." Ellen's lips curved ruefully. "I doubt he even sees me as a woman. He is forever teasing me, and he treats me much in the manner I suspect he would treat one of his younger sisters."

Fancy stared hard at Ellen. "Ellen, are you *sure* you are in love with him? It is not just because of the way you met? You have not romanticized our situation, have you? Imagined Hugh to be this wonderful hero and not looked beyond to see the man he really is?"

Ellen shook her head. "Fancy, there has been nothing *romantic* about this entire venture—you know that. While I will admit that for the first day or two I did look upon him, and Chance, too, as our noble rescuers, I think I began to see him as a real person the first time he helped me remove a tick from my ankle." Ellen wrinkled her nose at the memory. "And, as you know, there is nothing the least romantic about that."

"But what about Jonathan? You thought you were in love with him just a few weeks ago."

Ellen sighed. "I know, and you are right to be skeptical." A glow suddenly lit her face. "Oh, but Fancy, this is so different. What I feel for Hugh has made me see how shallow my feelings for Jonathan actually were. I was, I think, blinded by Jonathan. Here I was, this provincial little miss in the great City of London for the first time, and I was frightened and a little nervous. I did not *really* know anybody, and while the gentlemen were very kind to me, the young ladies acted so superior that I wanted to sink into the floor. Then, just when I was on the point of begging you to take us back to the country, this utterly divine gentleman, this tall, handsome, wealthy man who had been so much sought after by those same young ladies, suddenly began to pay attention to me." She made a wry face. "I am ashamed to admit it, but I felt so smug when Jonathan squired me around London and I saw all those young ladies who had turned up their noses at me, looking so envious, that I did not stop to think about what I was doing."

"And you are now?" Fancy inquired dryly.

Ellen nodded her head vigorously. "Yes, I am. I am in love with Hugh and I want to marry him. It does not matter to me what his prospects are, even if he is poor or that I will not have a grand home and expensive clothing." She laughed. "These past few weeks have taught me that there are many things I once thought I could not live without that I have not missed at all. Oh, Fancy, I love him so much! I cannot imagine life without him."

"Ellen, are sure? I mean really, *really* sure?"

Ellen smiled softly at Fancy's concerned features. "Yes, I am."

The words were said with such simple confidence that Fancy finally believed her. A part of Fancy rejoiced that Ellen had had the good sense to fall in love with a fine young man like Hugh Walker. But another part of her saw nothing but trouble ahead. At least, she told herself gloomily, there had never been any *formal* betrothal between Jonathan and Ellen. Oh my, but it was going to be very difficult. They were staying at Walker Ridge as Jonathan's guests, the entire purpose of their visit for Ellen and Jonathan to know their hearts. After the journey they had just finished, Fancy dreaded having to coolly announce to their host that Ellen had changed her mind and that they were leaving immediately. Leaving for . . . ?

Fancy's runaway thoughts ground to a halt. Where were they going to stay, anyway? And how was she going to solve the vexing problem of Ellen and Hugh?

"Ellen, you may be in love with Hugh, but what about him?" Fancy asked abruptly. "You say that he has not indicated to you how he feels . . . you mentioned that he treats you like a younger sister—has it occurred to you that he might be in love with someone else or even married?"

"He is not," Ellen replied sunnily. "I asked Chance."

"I see. But even if Hugh is not in love with anyone else— that does not mean that he will fall in love with you," Fancy pointed out as gently as she could.

"Oh, but he will," Ellen answered confidently. An imp of mischief danced in her blue eyes. "He has only seen me looking like a bedraggled hen. Once we are at Walker Ridge, I intend to make him understand that I *am not* his younger sister."

"And Jonathan? You expect to make another man fall in love with you while staying at the home of the man who thought to marry you?" Fancy inquired incredulously. She knew that Ellen was very young and, she admitted with a grimace, a little spoiled. But surely not even Ellen thought it was going to be *that* simple.

Ellen's face fell. "I had not considered it in quite that light. But what am I to do?" she almost wailed. She glanced over to where Hugh stood guard, and her face softened immediately. "I cannot leave him, Fancy. I just cannot." Her gaze swung back to her sister. Desperately she pleaded, "Oh, Fancy, help me! Think of something. You are the one who always has a plan. Help me."

"Ellen, I—"

"*Please!* I'll die if you don't help me. You *must* help me!"

Fancy took a deep breath. She had never seen Ellen so frantic, so determined on a course. Ellen was the sunny-natured one of the pair of them, the amiable, lighthearted one, and she was not normally given to any type of histrionics. Deeply troubled, Fancy stared at her sister, noting the ravages of their long trek in Ellen's sunken cheeks and the lank blond hair. Her heart ached. Ellen had suffered so much— and it was *her* fault that Ellen had been placed in danger. If she had not insisted upon this trip . . . She had always protected Ellen, shielded her from the unpleasant aspects of life; how could she turn her back on Ellen now, when it was most important?

Reluctantly Fancy asked, "What do you want me to do? We cannot just . . ."

Ellen hastily wiped away any trace of tears, but there was a quaver in her voice as she asked, "Could we not just leave things as they are for a little while? Could you perhaps just pretend that what Hugh and Chance already think is true? That you are the one who is going to be betrothed to Jonathan?"

"*Me?* Have you gone mad?" Fancy burst out in astonishment. "Ellen, you know that I would do just about anything in the world for you, but sweetheart, I do not think that you have thought this through. 'Tis one thing to carry this pretense out while it is only the four of us, but once we reach Walker Ridge—"

"Jonathan will not mind," Ellen muttered, "he always seems to be just as happy in your presence as mine."

"Oh, but that is not true. You know it is not."

Ellen sniffed. "No, I do not. Not anymore. Richmond opened my eyes to many things."

"But, Ellen, I cannot just . . . Can you not see that Jonathan will notice something is wrong? That he will notice you are avoiding him and are busily setting your cap for another man?" Fancy shot Ellen a look. "I mean, I am correct in assuming that you *are* going to avoid him—you are not going to try to hold both men captive to your charms, are you?"

"Of course not," Ellen replied, affronted. "This is not some new parlor game to me, Fancy. I love Hugh Walker and all I am asking is for a little bit of time in which to make him fall in love with me. Is that so very much to ask?"

"Well, yes, it is, under the circumstances," Fancy replied bluntly. "We are Jonathan's *guests;* he thinks that you are going to marry him."

Ellen shook her head. "No, if you remember correctly, you were the one who advised against any betrothal. The entire purpose of this trip was to make certain if we wanted to marry. And I, for one, have made up my mind. I do not want to marry Jonathan Walker."

"Then the honorable thing for us to do is to tell Jonathan that information and remove ourselves immediately to Richmond."

Ellen's little face crumpled. "Oh, do not say such a thing! I will never see Hugh again if we do that. Won't you please help me? Could you not just let things alone for a few days? Just let everyone believe what they want? Please?"

Fancy's heart twisted at Ellen's unhappy, pleading features. What harm would just a few days do? she asked herself reluctantly. And if it made Ellen happy? Eventually everything would have to be sorted out, and she was going to have to apologize profusely to Jonathan and his mother, but in the meantime . . .

With great misgivings, Fancy finally said, "Very well, I will, er, let things alone for a few days." She shook a finger at Ellen as her sister's face miraculously cleared. "But you, miss, are going to have to handle Jonathan, and eventually you are going to have to tell him that you have changed your mind."

Ellen flung her arms around Fancy's neck, nearly over-setting her. "Oh, Fancy! I *knew* you would not fail me. You are the kindest, sweetest, most wonderful sister in the world."

"And quite, quite mad, I am sure," Fancy said tartly.

When Chance returned some time later, he found the women busy about a small fire and the inevitable johnny-cakes, made from the last of their cornmeal and mixed with blackberries, baking in the ash at the edge of the flames. Lifting up the fat turkey he carried at his side, he said cheerfully, "Tonight we shall feast."

He spoke the truth. Although it took the turkey a few hours to roast on the spit Chance had fashioned, with her first bite of the smoke-flavored flesh, Fancy agreed that it had been well worth the wait. Since there was no reason to hoard any of the food, they all gorged themselves, and for the first time since she had been captured, Fancy's stomach was satisfyingly full.

Fancy was certain, after the stunning conversation with Ellen that afternoon, that she would spend the night tossing and turning. To her surprise, she did not. Her head had barely hit the ground before she fell into a deep sleep from which she did not stir until Ellen nudged her awake the next morning.

Everyone seemed in much higher spirits as they left the campsite; Chance even whistled merrily as they walked into the forests.

The terrain they now traversed was hilly in some places, gently rolling in others, all thickly wooded and alive with gurgling streams. They passed springs and little brooks shaded by the spreading leaves of great sycamore trees and walked through groves of magnificent oaks and locust trees, with pecan and laurel trees scattered throughout. Later, they followed wide streams edged with willow and poplar, the ubiquitous grape and blackberry everywhere. They had been walking for several hours, and the sun was high in the sky, when they suddenly left the forest and stepped out onto a narrow path at the side of a huge tobacco field. Fancy blinked at the sight of the green tobacco plants, so abrupt was the change from the forest to the cultivated area.

The tobacco field was the first sign of the human hand upon the land, and as they walked along the red-clay path, Fancy glanced over her shoulder at Chance and asked, "Where are we? Do you know?"

Chance snorted. "Obviously you do not have much faith in my abilities. But yes, I do know where we are. In just a few minutes, the James River will come into view, and Walker Ridge with it."

Chance was as true as his word. The tobacco field ended and there, on the small ridge that had given its name to the imposing house that sat upon it, was Walker Ridge. The James River, gleaming silver and blue, was in the distance. There were so many much smaller outbuildings near the main house and fanning out behind it that the area looked almost like a village. Fancy was startled by the unexpected sight of such a large community in the wilderness. As they approached the house, she could see beyond it to more huge tobacco fields, like the one they had crossed. To the left of the house, she spied an orchard, recognizing apple, plum, and pear trees. There was a formal garden in front of the tall H-shaped house of brick and wood in which roses bloomed wildly. A grand sloping lawn, thickly dotted with pecan, willow, and oak trees, ran all the way down to the James River.

Their pace increased until they left the narrow path behind and reached the wide curving carriageway that circled the front of the house. Their approach had been spotted, and from several of the smaller buildings, people ran out and pointed. Fancy could hear the shouts of excitement. The soaring doors of the main house were suddenly flung open and Jonathan and Sam Walker appeared, followed closely by Constance and an older lady who Fancy assumed was Sam's wife, Letty.

With a great whoop, his handsome face alight with joy, Jonathan bounded across the broad porch and down the wide brick steps. Meeting them in the middle of the formal garden, the air heavy with the scent of the roses, Jonathan reached Fancy and swung her up into the air, saying delightedly, "My dear Fancy! We have been unable to sleep or eat, so consumed with worry about your fate have we been."

Oblivious of the others, he pressed a kiss to Fancy's cheek. "We had no idea whether you were alive or dead. You cannot imagine the terror we have endured."

Embarrassed and uncomfortable, aware of Chance and Ellen on either side of her, Fancy was stiff in Jonathan's arms. She wished heartily that she had never given her word to Ellen. Jonathan's forward manner with her certainly lent credence to some of Ellen's comments, and despite knowing that Ellen's affections now lay in a different direction, she was angry for her sister. *If* Ellen had been in love with Jonathan, this unseemly display would have hurt her unbearably. Ruffled and out of sorts by the entire situation, Fancy stepped from Jonathan's embrace, her mouth tightening with displeasure. Subterfuge was not her nature, and if it hadn't been for Ellen . . . Jonathan was acting far, *far* too familiar! Sending him a cool look, she replied somewhat acidly, "Let me reassure you that your terror, while I am certain it was immense, was nothing, my dear man, to what Ellen and I experienced."

Chapter Seven

The suite of rooms that Fancy and Ellen were shown to, on the second floor of the house, were luxurious. If she hadn't known better, Fancy would have thought she was staying in a grand country estate in England. Both elegantly appointed bedchambers had their own lavishly furnished sitting rooms, as well as spacious dressing rooms. A door in each of the dressing rooms opened onto a short wide hall between the suites and gave the ladies private access to each other without having to traverse the main passageway of the house.

The summertime furnishings were evident, from the finely woven grass mat that lay upon the polished oak floor of the bedchamber, to the pale-yellow-and-white seersucker curtains that hung from the tall windows in the room Fancy had chosen for herself. The mahogany bed with its soaring post and canopy was swathed in a cream-colored filmy netting, and a silk coverlet printed with tiny yellow rosebuds lay atop the plump mattress. Ellen's bedchamber was similar, except that pink and cream seemed to be the predominant color of the cloth furnishings.

Letty Walker had escorted the two women to their suite and shown them the arrangement of the rooms. She had smiled at them and, a twinkle in her eyes, had said kindly, "I imagine that the very first thing both of you would like is a bath and a change of clothes."

Fancy and Ellen had glanced down at what remained of their stained and bedraggled gowns and burst out laughing.

"Mrs. Walker, how did you guess?" Fancy asked, her face alight.

"Well, my dears, it happened that once when I was much younger," Letty said easily, "Sam and I got lost in the forest. It was three days before we managed to find our way home again. I can tell you that the first thing I wanted was a bath and change of clothing. I assume the same would hold true for you. Am I correct?"

"Indeed you are," Fancy replied. "Ellen and I have had dreams of doing nothing but soaking in a hot tub of water for at least a fortnight."

Letty chuckled, a warm, inviting sound that added to her already charming manner. Fancy found her initial liking of Sam Walker's wife increasing with every moment. Letty's seventy-two years sat lightly upon her slim shoulders. Her sweet-natured face was framed by a cloud of soft white hair that owed nothing to powder. Her gray-blue eyes had been warm and welcoming when they had been introduced upon their unorthodox arrival several minutes ago. Fancy's gratitude toward Sam's wife had been immense when she had briskly swept the two younger women away from Constance's embarrassingly fulsome welcome, stating calmly, "Yes, yes, Constance, I am sure that all of that is true, but I think our guests might like to refresh themselves and have a few moments of privacy right now, is that not so?"

Constance's lips had thinned, but she had not demurred. They had then taken their leave from the gentlemen, and keeping up a gentle flow of conversation, Letty had graciously ushered Fancy and Ellen up the broad, curving staircase and shown them to their rooms.

"Well, I hope that we can persuade you not to linger in the tub quite *that* long," Letty said teasingly. "As soon as I leave you, I intend to have a counsel with Cook and plan on presenting you this evening with a meal to tempt even the most delicate appetite." She chuckled again. "An easy task, I would think, considering what you have been eating."

"Oh, Mrs. Walker, that sounds lovely, but please, *please*, nothing with blackberries," Ellen said with a shy smile.

"No blackberries, I promise you, child." Letty crossed to the dressing room in Fancy's quarters and opened the door. "All of your trunks and belongings have been unpacked and hung in the armoires," she said. "I do not know if we guessed correctly whose possessions were whose, but you will be able to sort things out. I have assigned a girl to each of you. Lady Merrivale, I believe that Ora will do very nicely for you." Sending a smile to Ellen, she added, "Clover is a little young, only sixteen, but I think, Miss Merrivale, you will find that she is very cheerful and willing. If there is a problem, please let me know and I shall take care of it." Letty took one more glance around the rooms, then said, "And now, before I make a nuisance of myself, I shall leave and see about getting those baths for you."

Sinking into the warm lavender-scented water in the big brass tub in her dressing room some time later, Fancy was certain that she never wanted to move again. The tub was unusually deep and large, specially manufactured to Sam Walker's measurements, she'd been told proudly by Ora. As she lay back and the soothing water lapped at her chin, Fancy gave a great sigh. After the fortnight or better that she had just spent, she would never again take for granted such a simple act as bathing.

Fortunately, the Walker household had more than one brass tub. Knowing that Ellen was experiencing the same pleasure she was and that there was no reason to rush, Fancy lingered over her bath, scrubbing her body and her hair numerous times. Only when the water, despite some hot additions by Ora, began to cool did she finally rise from the tub. After drying and a lavish use of some of her favorite dusting powder, she slipped into an amber-colored dressing gown and began idly to brush her long *clean* hair. Even this is a luxury, she thought ruefully, remembering the lank, untidy braid she had worn during their trek through the wilderness.

Setting down her silver-backed brush on the satinwood dressing table, she stifled a yawn, then wandered into the bedchamber. Ellen was just peeking her head around the connecting hallway door as Fancy entered the room.

Her face scrubbed and shining, her damp hair held back by a white silk ribbon, Ellen was wearing a pale blue dressing gown edged in blond Brussels lace. Her eyes meeting Fancy's, she cried gaily, "Oh, Fancy! Wasn't it bliss? Did you ever think a bath could feel so wonderful?"

Laughing, Fancy shook her head. "Never, my dear!" She looked over at the big bed. "And if that is as comfortable as it looks, I fear I shall never leave this room again." Her stomach gave an unladylike rumble just then, and she added wryly, "Except for food, of course."

As if in answer to her words, there was a tap on the door and a moment later Ora entered, carrying a huge silver tray covered with all sorts of appetizing offerings. The instant the tall, stately black woman placed the laden tray on a large mahogany table in the center of the room, Ellen and Fancy, unable to help themselves, crowded close to the tray, staring greedily at the contents—sliced chicken and veal, a plate of jellied asparagus, some creamed cauliflower, cucumbers and radishes fresh from the garden, and a bowl of thick, clotted cream and some slices of apricot, as well as hot coffee and a pan of biscuits still warm from the oven.

Ora grinned at their expressions, her teeth very white in her round black face. "Miz Letty said that you all might be jus' a bit hungry."

"Ora, you have no idea," Fancy exclaimed as she bit down on a red radish and began to fill a plate with chicken and some of the jellied asparagus. "Mrs. Walker is a saint, and you may tell her I said so."

Descending the staircase a few hours later, her dark hair piled artfully high, with one long dusky ringlet lying upon her white bosom, the silken skirts of her brocaded Spitafields gown and petticoat rustling around her feet, Fancy was conscious of a knot starting to form in her stomach. In a few minutes she would see Chance Walker again, and the prospect filled her with a volatile mixture of excitement and dread, emotions she felt frequently in his presence.

There was comfort to be gained from the knowledge that she was looking especially attractive for a woman who had just spent the past fortnight struggling through the verdant wilderness, but as she reached the bottom step of the stairs, her fingers tightened unconsciously on the fan of delicately painted chicken skin she carried in one hand. She had never once given a thought to her appearance during the entire time she and Ellen had been in the wilderness, but now she found herself wondering what Chance would think when he saw her garbed in her normal attire. It was the thought of his eyes upon her that made her suddenly aware of how low cut her bodice actually was and made her embarrassingly aware that of the tops of her small bosom were boldly displayed for anyone to see.

Angry with herself for caring, even fleetingly, what Chance Walker might think about anything, she lifted her head imperiously. Reminding herself that she *was* the baroness Merrivale and that she was wearing a perfectly respectable, *fashionable* gown and that no rude, country dolt was going to put her out of countenance, she swiftly crossed the passage to a pair of doors set in a graceful archway.

Fancy opened one door and entered the room. Letty had pointed out this particular room earlier when she had escorted the ladies up the stairs and had called it the red salon. It was a large, lofty chamber, with three lovely crystal chandeliers and an impressive bank of tall, narrow windows that overlooked a different part of the formal garden. A Caucasian carpet in vivid shades of red and gold lay upon the floor; elegantly draped curtains in the same shades hung at the windows; and there were small tables and chests of mahogany and walnut scattered attractively throughout the room. A trio of delicate settees covered in gold satin and several comfortable red leather chairs constituted the majority of the remaining furnishings.

It was here, Letty had explained, that the family usually assembled prior to the evening meal, the gentlemen to drink some rum punch, the ladies some ratafia. Feeling oddly restless, Fancy had left Ellen still primping at her dressing table and come ahead. Aware, again from her kind hostess, that they usually dined around seven o'clock in the evening, and knowing that it was not yet gone six o'clock, Fancy expected to find the room empty. It was not.

A tall, broad-shouldered man stood at the far end of the room; his back was to her as he stared out of one of the windows at the garden. Catching sight of him, of the fashionable cut of his claret-colored coat and breeches, his dark hair unpowdered and caught at the nape of his neck in a black silk bag that hung partway down his back, Fancy first thought he was Jonathan, and her heart sank. After his extremely forward greeting to her upon her arrival, and her promise to Ellen uppermost in her mind, the *last* thing Fancy wanted was a private tête-à-tête with Jonathan. Her initial instinct was to slip from the room, hoping that he had not noticed her entrance, but even as she started to back away, he turned and her heart began to thump madly. The gentleman was Chance Walker. But a Chance Walker she had never seen before.

He was garbed and groomed as fine as any lord she had met in England. His black hair was swept back from his hard face, the darkness of his skin intensified by the neatly tied white cravat at his neck. His waistcoat of stiff figured cream silk with a small, tasteful design in fawn and claret was as fashionable as the highest stickler in English Society could have wished. Silver buckles decorated his shoes, his stockings were of silk, and there was a profusion of lace at his wrists and down the front of his white linen shirt. He was, she thought breathlessly, magnificent, looking every inch a gentleman. But even as she acknowledged that thought, she was aware of a longing for the Chance she had grown used to, the teasing blue-eyed devil in the worn buckskins, his unruly mane of thick black hair falling over his shoulders and framing his lean, half-bearded features.

They stared wordlessly at each other for a long moment, then Chance shook his head as if coming from a trance. A derisive smile suddenly tugging at his lips, he bowed low and murmured, "Duchess."

Fancy's grip on her fan nearly broke the fragile thing, but, keeping her voice cool, she returned, "I see that fine clothes do not fine manners make."

A genuine grin crossed his face. "No, Duchess, I fear they do not. Buckskins or satin, you will find me just as obnoxious and objectionable as ever."

Something in his expression invited her to share the amusement she saw dancing in his eyes. To her astonishment, she laughed and walked farther into the room. Stopping a few feet from him, she said lightly, "Perhaps, if you did not *try* so hard to be so very provoking, I might not find you so obnoxious."

Chance's brow lifted. "I think you are confused about which one of us is provoking, Duchess."

Fancy looked startled. "Me?" she demanded. "Are you implying that I am provoking?"

Chance's amusement faded, some undefinable emotion glittering in his eyes. He stepped nearer to her and, running a caressing finger down her cheek, said huskily, "Oh, yes, you, Duchess. So very, *very* provoking."

The present faded away, and their eyes locked as they stared mesmerized at each other. It was quiet in the room, the faint scent of a spicy potpourri drifting on the air, a few dust motes floating lazily in the rays of the fading sunlight that pierced the interior. But Fancy wasn't really aware of anything but the tall man in front of her and her heart beating as if it would jump from her chest as Chance bent nearer, his mouth mere inches away from hers.

The sound of the door opening broke the spell between them. "Ah, here you are, my dear baroness," exclaimed Constance as she bustled into the room. Catching sight of Chance, who had swiftly swung away from Fancy, she faltered and said in a far less pleased voice, "Oh. Chance. I did not realize that there was anyone else here. I thought you had left with Hugh for Fairview."

Chance shrugged. "No. I decided to stay for the night."

He glanced obliquely in Fancy's direction. "I have some unfinished business to take care of before I follow Hugh to Devil's Own."

Constance wrinkled her nose. "I still think that is the oddest name to call one's own home. One would have thought that you could have chosen something far more appropriate."

"But it *is* appropriate, do you not think so?" Chance asked, a sardonic gleam in his eyes. "Did you not used to refer to me when I was younger as the devil's spawn?"

Constance took in a deep, calming breath. "I may have," she said stiffly. She forced a laugh. "Heaven knows that you were certainly a handful. I do not know why Sam and Letty put up with your presence as they did."

"As you very well know, my dear Constance, we put up with his presence," said Letty from the doorway, "because we enjoyed his antics and have a great fondness for him."

An openly affectionate smile on her face, Letty walked farther into the room, the skirt and petticoat of her elegant pale blue silken gown swaying gently as she moved. Approaching Chance, she put out her hand. In a surprisingly courtly gesture, Chance bowed, a far more sincere bow than he had given *her*, Fancy thought wryly, and gallantly brought Letty's hand to his lips. Pressing a kiss to the back of it, he said quietly, "Ever my champion, are you not, Cousin Letty?"

Letty patted his lean cheek affectionately. "And why not? You are not half as wicked or dangerous as you would lead one to believe."

Chance laughed. "Madame, I beg you not to destroy my reputation. I have worked very hard at it."

"Too hard, I think, sometimes," said Sam as he joined his wife, his own affection for Chance apparent in the fond smile he sent his way. He was garbed as fashionably as Chance, his coat of mulberry cloth and gray embroidered waistcoat fitting him superbly. Like Chance, he also wore his dark hair unpowdered and clubbed neatly into a black silk bag, the broad silver streaks at his temples increasing his aristocratic air. After greeting everyone, Sam smiled at Fancy and said, "I trust that you have found your rooms and everything to your satisfaction, Lady Merrivale. 'Tis our urgent desire that you and your sister be comfortable and enjoy your visit—*especially* so after your unfortunate introduction to the Thackers."

Constance gave an exaggerated shudder. "Oh, those terrible men. I do not know why someone has not *done* something about them before now. Why, I swear, sometimes I am afraid even to shut my eyes in my very own bed for fear one of those wicked creatures will suddenly appear here at Walker Ridge."

Fancy's eyes widened. "Is that possible?" she asked, glancing around uneasily.

"Of course not," Letty replied firmly. She sent her much younger mother-in-law a stern look. "And Constance is very well aware of that." Turning back to Fancy, she said kindly, "You have nothing to fear while staying here, my dear. Walker Ridge may be remote and we may be surrounded by wilderness, but there are a great many people on our plantation and we are very civilized here. I do not believe that the Thackers would ever be so foolish as to show their faces in our vicinity. Those sorts of cowardly creatures only prey on the weak and defenseless, something *we* are not."

The conversation turned to more general topics, and by the time Ellen, and then Jonathan, joined them, the subject of the Thackers had been left behind. Just before the group adjourned to the dining room, they were joined by another person, an older woman, with worn features and a timid air. Wearing a gray silk gown, long out of fashion, her mousy hair arranged in a haphazard pompadour, she was extremely deferential to Constance. When Jonathan casually introduced her as Anne Clemmons, Constance's old governess-cum-companion, Fancy was not surprised; she looked exactly as one would expect a governess to look.

"My mother is very fond of her," Jonathan said in a dismissing tone as he escorted Fancy down the wide passage. "She is actually retired and has a little house here on the plantation, but Mother likes her about, and sometimes she stays here in the main house to be near Mother. Anne has always adored her."

The dining room was long and large, the furnishings of the finest quality and beautifully arranged. The meal, which was served by black servants in dark blue jackets and breeches, was as delicious as any Fancy could ever remember eating, from the terrapin soup, to the haunch of roast beef and loin of veal, to the vast array of vegetables in various sauces. The final course consisted of delicate Shrewsbury cakes and dishes of preserved gooseberries and white heart cherries.

Despite the stiff civility between Jonathan and Chance, their dislike of each other barely contained, the entire meal had been most pleasant, Fancy thought as she pushed away her empty dessert plate. Ellen, looking thoroughly charming in her rich blue gown and cream satin petticoat, had disguised whatever disappointment she might have felt at the news that Hugh was no longer at Walker Ridge and had been her usual sweet self, conversing easily with the others at the table. It would have been one of the most enjoyable evenings Fancy had spent in many a month, had it not been for the fact that Chance had been sitting on the other side of the table, sardonically watching Jonathan hover at her side.

To give Jonathan his due, he had not neglected Ellen, seated to his left, but as the meal progressed, no one was left in any doubt that he was thoroughly fascinated by Fancy. He hung on her every word; offered her the choicest morsels; and smiled indulgently at her vivacious comments. That Ellen had met his few sallies in her direction with mere politeness didn't help matters, and Fancy could have stamped her foot in vexation at the entire situation. From the speculative looks and arch manner of Jonathan's family, it was obvious that they believed *she* was the lady he was courting, and Jonathan's actions around her only emphasized that misconception. Clearly he had not told his family that it was Ellen who was to be his bride, and she wondered again precisely what he was up to.

She frowned. If Ellen had still been in love with Jonathan, his actions would have wounded her deeply. Fancy wondered precisely what game he was playing. In England he had never acted thus. In England she had been positive that he was a fine, honorable gentleman, and it had been clear that his interest was held solely by Ellen, but ever since they had reached the Colonies . . . Fancy bit her lip. Try though she might, she no longer thought as highly of Jonathan as she once had, and she had begun to question her opinion of him. Had she totally misjudged him? Not only his character, but his intentions? Or, like Ellen, had he suffered a change of heart? Her spirits sank. She hoped that his actions toward her were only those of an overly solicitous host. It simply would not *do* if his affections had alighted upon *her.*

Fancy's frame of mind wasn't helped by Chance's unsettling presence across the table from her. He sat between Constance and Anne and, beyond the merest pleasantries, paid little attention to his companions—which was just as well, as poor Anne stared at him as if she fully expected him to turn into a monster. As well she might, Fancy thought uncharitably. Occasionally Chance replied to something Sam or Letty, seated at either end of the long table, sent his way, but primarily his focus seemed to be on Fancy and Jonathan. To her dismay, whenever Fancy glanced in his direction, she found his coolly appraising gaze fixed upon her. She tried to ignore him, but even with her eyes lowered and fixed on her plate, his dark arresting features danced behind her lids.

It was with relief that she joined the ladies as they rose from the table and returned to the red salon for coffee. Fancy didn't really want coffee—but anything that took her away from Chance's unnerving perusal was welcome. Her respite was short-lived. The ladies had barely seated themselves and Letty had just begun to pour from a silver pot when the gentlemen joined them.

There was a brief flurry of movement as the men sought their various places in the room. Sam joined Letty on one of the settees and Jonathan placed himself strategically between Fancy and Ellen, leaving Chance to rest one long arm on the black marble fireplace mantel and view the entire scene with a faintly cynical smile. Constance and Anne Clemmons shared another of the settees nearby.

Passing Fancy a cup of the strong dark brew, Letty said apologetically, "I am sorry that we don't serve tea. Many of us are refusing to buy or drink tea since those horrid taxes were imposed by Parliament." She looked a bit embarrassed. "Did you hear in London what happened in the Port of Boston this past December? I cannot say that I actually condone what was done, but I must confess to a certain amount of sympathy for the action."

"Are you talking about the incident where some of the colonists disguised themselves as Indians and boarded ships in the harbor and threw over the entire shipment of tea and goods?" Fancy asked with interest. In London there had been a good deal of outrage about what had happened, and she was aware of the growing estrangement between the Colonies and the mother country.

Sam nodded and said dryly, "They are calling it the Boston Tea Party, but it does not sound like any party *I* would like to attend. And your Lord North has not helped matters by closing the port. Tempers are very high. There are even rumbles of rebellion."

"Do you disagree with the notion of most colonists that only *we* can impose taxes upon ourselves?" Chance inquired quietly, his expression intent and serious as he stared at Sam.

"What utter nonsense," Jonathan interposed impatiently. "We are Englishmen, England is our mother country—of course she can tax us."

"Odd," Chance murmured, "but I consider myself a Virginian first . . . and an Englishman second."

"And I suppose you belong to that . . . oh, what the devil is it that those rabble-rousers are calling themselves?" Jonathan demanded with a sneer on his handsome face. "Ah, I have it—the Sons of Liberty. I suppose you are a member of that seditious group."

Gently Sam said, "It does not matter, Jonathan, whether he is or not. You have been away in England this past year and much has happened, and not just in Boston. Even here in Virginia there is friction with the officials of the Crown. In May, Governor Dunmore dissolved our House of Burgesses simply because we voted for a day of prayer and fasting on the first of June, the date set for the closing of Boston Harbor. There are many, honest businessmen and planters and troublemakers alike, who are chafing at English rule and feel that Lord North has gone too far."

"You?" Jonathan asked, incredulity on his face.

Sam shrugged but contented himself with saying merely, "Perhaps. But what you have to be aware of is that the Colonies are divided—feelings are running strong and hard. The possibility of a break with England is very real."

"Good God! I do not believe what I am hearing," exclaimed Jonathan. "Are you serious? You would support rebellion?"

"He did not say that," Chance interrupted smoothly. "He merely warned you that there is a growing faction, and not made up simply of malcontents and hotheaded miscreants, that is committed to independence from England."

"Oh, pooh," Constance said irritably. "I refuse to listen to any more of this nonsense. The Colonies are English and they will always be so. This latest unpleasantness is just some little family squabble that will be ended in a few months, and everything will go on as before. All Boston has to do is pay for the tea and make obeisance, something even Benjamin Franklin has advised them to do." She smiled at Fancy. "Do not pay any heed to them, my dear, this is just a fuss about nothing." She shot Chance an unfriendly glance. "To listen to *some* people, you would think that you were sitting on a hotbed of rebellion, and nothing could be further from the truth."

Fancy had found the discussion invigorating, and she was sorry when the gentlemen, recalled to their surroundings, changed the subject and began to talk of more mundane matters. The remainder of the evening progressed uneventfully, and Fancy was thankful when it ended.

She and Ellen were both very weary from their long trek

and were grateful when Letty, a kind light in her eyes, said firmly, "I think that is quite enough, Constance. Our guests have had a long, distressful journey and I suspect are longing for their beds. You can continue your interrogation of Lady Merrivale tomorrow when she is more rested and far more capable of dealing with you."

Barely concealing the huge yawn that threatened to escape her, Fancy smiled at her hostess and murmured, "I *am* very tired." Sending a polite glance over to Constance, who appeared vastly annoyed by Letty's blunt words, she said, "And I shall enjoy talking to you in the morning about the latest London fashions."

A few more pleasantries were exchanged with the group, and in a very few minutes Fancy and Ellen were slowly walking up the stairs toward their rooms. Noting that Ellen seemed in good spirits despite Hugh's absence, Fancy couldn't help asking, "Were you very disappointed that Hugh was not here this evening?"

Ellen nodded. "At first very much so, but then I was able to have a private word with Chance just before we went into the dining room, and he mentioned that Hugh would be returning sometime in the morning with his father. Apparently their plantation, Fairview, adjoins Walker Ridge and is just over ten miles from here."

Fancy digested this information, wondering, with a little spurt of temper, why Chance always seemed to be kind to Ellen, whereas with her . . . It didn't matter, she told herself grimly. He would be gone before long, and she would never have to lay eyes on his mocking face again. For some reason that thought did not give her as much pleasure as it should have, and she frowned. What was the matter with her? Wasn't he the most provoking, infuriating man she had ever met? The vivid memory of his kiss and the emotions it had aroused unexpectedly floated through her mind. Fancy was conscious of a thrill, but it was a curious thrill, one made up of equal parts excitement and fear.

"Er, did Chance happen to mention how long he would be

staying at Walker Ridge?" Fancy suddenly asked with a hint of constraint in her voice, her cheeks burning.

Caught up in her own thoughts of Hugh, Ellen noticed neither the faint color that pinkened Fancy's cheeks nor her sister's tone. As they reached the doors to their rooms, she said carelessly, "Hmm, he did say something about having some unfinished business here—but he did not actually say how long he thought it would take him. I suspect he will be gone in a day or two." A yawn suddenly took Ellen. Laughing slightly, she said, "I am so glad that Mrs. Walker ended the evening. I was terrified that Jonathan's mother was going to ask me something and I would answer her with a loud snore."

The sisters took their leave of each other, and Ellen disappeared into her suite. Ora was waiting when she entered the dressing room, and Fancy was grateful for her ministrations as the black woman helped her from her gown and undergarments and carefully put everything away. Dismissing Ora for the evening with a smile, Fancy brushed her long dark brown hair and then, wearing a demure night rail of finest cambric, sought out the big featherbed.

Under any circumstances the bed would have been sheer bliss, but after the days she had just spent sleeping on the ground, it was a great deal more. Snuggling her cheek against the lavender-scented, linen-cased pillow, Fancy sighed deeply. Oh, my. Perhaps she would sleep here for a week—at least. And not once, she vowed fiercely as sleep overtook her, would she dream of that blue-eyed devil Chance Walker.

Chapter Eight

Fancy may have slumbered deeply, but sleep did not come easily to Chance that night. Awake and restless, he prowled the large, handsomely furnished bedchamber that had been set aside years ago for his exclusive use during his visits to Walker Ridge. He kept a few personal belongings here, primarily a change or two of clothing, which had enabled him to dress as he had this evening, and one or two other odds and ends. Not that he stayed often these days, he thought with a twist of his lips. And when the sad time came that Walker Ridge fell into Jonathan's greedy hands, well, he damn sure wouldn't be staying here at all.

One end of the room was the sleeping area, with a huge four-poster bed in fine mahogany and swathed in burgundy silk hangings. The opposite end of the room had been arranged into a sitting area, with sturdily constructed chairs and a few marble-topped tables strategically placed nearby, a painted canvas rug in shades of gray and ebony upon the floor. Along one wall sat a massive oak sideboard that held an array of glasses and snifters and crystal decanters filled with various potent spirits. After helping himself to a snifter of brandy, Chance sprawled comfortably in an overstuffed chair of oxblood leather, his head resting on the high back, his long legs stretched in front of him. His unruly hair had been freed from the black silk bag and waved at his temples and along his jaw as he relaxed in the chair. Earlier he had tossed off the cravat, jacket, and waistcoat, leaving his white linen shirt half undone. He looked very much at ease. Sipping the brandy, he stared blankly at the floor, the events of the evening turning slowly in his mind.

He would have liked to convince himself that this evening had been no different from scores of other evenings he had spent at Walker Ridge, but he knew he would be lying to himself. Fancy's presence, and her presence alone, had made it distinctly memorable. Recalling the swift stab of pleasure that had knifed through him when he had turned and seen her in the soft, fading sunlight of the red salon, he grimaced. She had been utterly lovely as she had stood there in her silken gown, her thickly lashed topaz eyes wide and uncertain, the end of that one long, dark curl resting so provocatively just above her small, tempting bosom. His heart had seemed to stop at the first sight of her, and as he'd stared, he'd known a mad impulse to stride across the room, to brush aside that strand of hair, and to press his eager mouth to the soft flesh where it had lain.

He scowled. Damned silly romantic notion. And if there was one thing he was not, it was *romantic*, especially not after Jenny. No, Jenny had taught him in the cruelest possibly way that women did not want romantic fools. What they wanted were black-hearted scoundrels like Jonathan. Chance took another, larger sip of his brandy, his dark thoughts following a too-well-traveled path as he dwelled upon Jonathan's perfidies.

The enmity between Chance and Jonathan that had brought about Jenny's death was of long standing, so much so, in fact, that Chance could not remember a time when he had not viewed the heir to Walker Ridge as his enemy. He had been just four years old or so the first time he had come with his adoptive parents to visit at Walker Ridge, and right from the beginning, Jonathan, not quite six at the time, had been blatantly hostile.

Andrew and his wife had actually come to see Morely, but the overseer's house where Morely had been living in those days was very small. Sam and Letty, just returned from their prolonged stay in England a few weeks previously, had graciously encouraged Andrew and Martha to stay with them at the big house during their visit. They were, after all, family.

It had been assumed that Chance and Jonathan, so near each other in age, would become friends and enjoy playing together. Such had not been the case—and whether Jonathan, used to being the focal point and darling of the entire household, had merely been spoiled and had not appreciated the fact that he was now forced to share the attention of the adults with another child, or whether it had simply been a case of instinctive dislike, Chance was never certain. Not that it mattered. But from the moment they had first met, they had been at each other's throats, bloodying each other's noses often in childhood and then, as they had grown up, moving onto more dangerous ways of competing against each other.

It was fortunate that Chance and his adopted parents lived some distance away from Walker Ridge and its inhabitants and that visits between the two households were not frequent. Morely came often enough to stay with Andrew and Martha—three or four times a year to assure himself of Chance's continued health and well-being. Upon the rare occasion, Sam and Letty also stopped for a brief visit, usually on their way somewhere else. But never Constance and Jonathan.

When Chance grew older and, at Morely's request, spent more and more time at Walker Ridge and sometimes at Morely's own plantation, Fairview, the two young men did not always meet. Like many of the wealthy planters' sons, Jonathan had been educated in England and had been gone from the Colonies off and on for much of his youth. But they met often enough, and any hope that they would eventually outgrow their initial dislike of each other was finally abandoned by everyone by the time they had reached maturity.

The friction that existed between Chance and Jonathan,

and to a lesser extent between Chance and Constance, had not endangered the fond relationship that had sprung up between Chance and Sam and Letty. If anything, Jonathan's hostility and Constance's cool disdain had appeared to make Sam and Letty all the more determined to see that Chance felt welcome and comfortable at Walker Ridge whenever he came to visit. Over the years a warm and affectionate bond had formed between them. Morely had always been there, hovering uneasily in the background, but Chance had realized long ago that it was Sam and Letty to whom he owed so much. Sam had taught him a great deal, and it was their championship of him that had led everyone in the family to overlook his bastardy and accept him as a member of the sprawling Walker clan. Everyone, that was, except Jonathan.

Jonathan had always deeply resented Chance's sporadic appearances at Walker Ridge, and he had also been openly jealous of the easy relationship between Sam and Chance. Constance had not liked it, either, but she had objected more because she followed Jonathan's lead and thought it disgraceful that Morely had managed to insinuate his bastard son into the Walker Ridge household than from any deep-seated aversion of him.

It was odd, Chance mused, but in the beginning Jonathan's attitude had never really bothered him. In fact, he had often found it amusing—which naturally only infuriated Jonathan all the more. Goaded, Jonathan issued a series of petty challenges—a horse race, a shooting match, the charms of a tavern maid, or any other number of small competitions. The friction between them had not been of great import until Chance had begun to make his own fortune and had won that large tract of land from Jonathan. No, he conceded bitterly as he sat sipping his brandy, the rivalry and enmity between them had not turned so very ugly and vicious until after Chance's thorough trouncing of Jonathan in that card game. It was then that Jonathan's gaze had fallen upon Chance's wife, Jenny.

With a wrench Chance tore his thoughts away from that still-painful episode. He was not going to dwell on that portion of his past. No, he had a future to plan, and if that future, he decided grimly, had roots that led directly to the past, well, he wasn't going to think too deeply about it.

He tossed off the remainder of the brandy and, after generously refilling the snifter, stalked the confines of his room. The outrageous notion of seeking revenge by taking away Jonathan's proposed bride had proved not to be a fleeting one for Chance. He'd thought of little else since the idea had first occurred to him—that and how very much he would enjoy bedding the lady in question.

Chance had waited a long time to take revenge against Jonathan for Jenny's death, coldly eschewing other ways of vengeance, such as a duel, in favor of a method that would hurt Jonathan where he lived—in his overweening pride. A duel would be over in a matter of minutes, and while Chance would not have minded killing Jonathan outright and there was no question in his mind which one of them would be the victor, there was a burning need deep inside him to make Jonathan suffer, to suffer as no doubt poor Jenny had suffered during those anguish-filled days before she had killed herself. No, he did not want Jonathan dead. He wanted him very much alive. Alive and suffering the pangs of damnation for the rest of his life, knowing that his enemy had snatched from underneath his very nose the one woman he had wanted as his bride.

A wolfish smile crossed Chance's face as he prowled about the room. Oh, yes, he was definitely going to enjoy every minute of Jonathan's pain.

Aware that what he planned to do would have wide-ranging ramifications, Chance considered it carefully, wincing just a little when he realized that Jonathan was not going to be the only one affected. He grimaced. Sam and Letty weren't going to be very happy with him, and he could not say that he would blame them if they threw him from the house and commanded him never to return. He would be sorry if that happened, but he hoped that in time they would forgive him.

As for the duchess . . . He grinned. She would probably

never forgive him, but he was looking forward to teaching her that marriage to him would not be such a very bad thing. Of course, she was going to be furious and she wasn't going to like his methods one damned bit, but it could not be helped. He had to strike quickly and with such devastating effect that there would be no way she could escape the consequences—or Jonathan could figure out a way to snatch victory from defeat.

If his conscience pricked him at all at the calculating way he was rearranging Fancy's life for his own reasons, Chance coolly ignored it. He told himself that Fancy was not in love with Jonathan; he had been able to ascertain that interesting fact for himself as he had watched them together all evening. She had been married before; she was not a young maid with a head full of silly dreams. If she was not in love with Jonathan, then her reasons for marrying him had to be practical ones. While he might not be able to provide her with the stature and wealth that marriage to Jonathan Walker would have, she would not be destitute, either. He would be a good husband, faithful and kind and generous, he told himself, not only with his money, but with his body as well. For a second the memory of the kiss they had shared drifted tantalizingly through his mind, and a throbbing heaviness suddenly pooled between his legs. Oh, yes, he definitely would be extremely generous with his body. And he was offering her, well, not *offering*, Chance conceded dryly, but he was going to do the honorable thing and marry her—not just seduce her and abandon her to her fate as some bastards might. Jonathan was a self-centered, hard-hearted son of a bitch—he would never make Fancy happy. Someday she might even come to be grateful for having been saved from marriage to Jonathan.

Convinced that he would almost be doing Fancy a favor by cold-bloodedly compromising her and forcing her into marriage with him as a means of taking revenge against Jonathan, Chance tossed off the remains of his second snifter of brandy and glanced at the ormolu clock on the mantel of the fireplace in his room. After midnight. He had several more hours to wait. Deciding that a few hours of sleep would not be amiss, he lay down on the bed and closed his eyes.

Chance woke less than an hour before dawn, the candles guttering in their holders, spilling uncertain light into the room. After rising from his bed, he stretched and splashed some water into his face from the pitcher on the washstand, then dragged his fingers through his sleep-tumbled hair. He eyed the brandy, wishing fervently for a cup of hot coffee, but brandy would have to do. A couple of swallows burning a path to his stomach, he carefully set down the snifter and took a deep breath. And now to greet his bride-to-be and set events in motion.

The faintest hint of dawn was breaking as Chance stepped into Fancy's suite of rooms a few minutes later. A casual conversation with Ellen the previous evening had elicited the fact that she had chosen the rose suite, while Fancy had taken the yellow suite. It would not do, Chance thought with grim amusement, to find himself in the wrong bed. As he moved stealthily toward the bedchamber, it occurred unpleasantly to him that the notion of stealing Jonathan's bride might not have been half as appealing if Jonathan's choice had been Ellen. Not wishing to examine his motives too closely, Chance pushed those thoughts from his mind and silently entered the bedchamber.

Once he had reached the edge of the bed, he swiftly removed his clothing. Brushing aside the filmy hangings, with great care and stealth he slowly slid into the bed beside a sleeping Fancy.

Fancy stirred slightly as his weight dipped the mattress and tipped her next to him, but she didn't wake as he carefully settled himself beside her. Chance could feel the warmth of her body next to his naked skin, and the urge to touch and kiss her into wakefulness flooded through him. With an effort he stifled his base thoughts and forced his unruly body to behave. There was no need for an actual seduction. Just his presence in her bed would be enough to thoroughly compromise her. Until she came to the realization that her fate was sealed, he was willing to wait to discover all her charms.

Fancy wasn't certain when she first became aware that she was no longer the solitary occupant of the big bed. Waking slowly, she stretched luxuriously and blinked sleepily at the yellow sunlight shining into the room. She had slept deeply, dreams of Chance kissing her, touching her, making love to her, filling her mind and leaving her languid with imagined fulfillment. She was reveling in the softness of the mattress when she became conscious of the comforting, *solid* warmth that was pressed intimately against her backside.

Instantly awake, she jerked upright with a gasp, clutching the sheet protectively to her bosom. Her eyes widened in shocked horror as she looked in Chance's direction and became aware of his indolent pose in her bed, his arms behind his head as he watched her, the naked expanse of his broad chest rising above the sheets.

Fancy scrubbed her eyes and pinched herself, certain she must be dreaming. Chance Walker could not be in her bed.

"Morning, Duchess," he drawled, his blue eyes gleaming, a faint smile tugging at the corners of his mouth.

"What are you doing here?" she hissed. "Get out of my bed immediately. You have no right to be here. Oh, my God. What if someone were to find you here?"

Chance looked hurt. "You mean last night meant nothing to you?"

Fancy appeared uneasy. "What do mean, 'last night'?" she asked nervously, explicit memories of her dreams flashing through her mind. Her cheeks flushed. Surely he didn't know that she had dreamed of him? And she *had* merely been dreaming, hadn't she?

Chance watched with undisguised interest as the roses bloomed in her cheeks. Now, what the devil had brought that on? His eyes narrowed. "You do not remember?"

Fancy took a deep breath. This was ridiculous. She had done nothing wrong, and those dreams, well, those dreams had been just that—dreams. Fixing him with a glare, she said sharply, "Of course I do not remember—there *is* nothing to remember!"

"That is not exactly how I recall our time together, Duchess."

Fancy's eyes blazed. *"Don't call me Duchess."*

"Lady Merrivale? Are you awake?" called Constance as she came into the room carrying a large tray that held a silver coffeepot and some fine china cups.

Fancy paled, a look of blind panic crossing her face. "Oh, my God," she moaned. "Jonathan's mother. What is *she* doing here?"

"Probably making certain that she has you all to herself," Chance murmured, a satisfied grin on his face. He'd assumed that it would be Ora who first discovered his presence in Fancy's bed and spread the word, or even Ellen, but this was a stroke of pure luck. For a moment he almost thought kindly of Constance.

"I was hoping that you were awake," burbled Constance from the other side of filmy half-concealing bed curtains as she looked around for a place to set the tray. "I thought this would be a good time for us to have a little chat . . . without any interruptions." She gave a tinkling laugh. "I know it is very bold of me to just march into your bedchamber this way, but considering the situation between you and Jonathan . . . I don't feel that we need to stand on ceremony with each other, do you? Why, we are already practically *family*."

Her heart pounding in her breast, filled with a mixture of fury and sheer terror, Fancy shot Chance a blistering look. "Not a word out of you," she snapped. *"Not one word."*

"What was that?" Constance asked brightly. "Did you say something, my dear?"

"N-n-nothing," Fancy stammered as she sat there, inordinately grateful for the gauzy bed curtains that half-hid the interior of the bed. In horrified fascination she stared at Chance, willing him to disappear. Willing herself to wake up and discover that this was all a nightmare. The sheet was still clutched protectively to her bosom, and her thoughts tumbled chaotically through her brain. If Constance, if *anyone* were to discover Chance in her bed . . .

"I have brought some coffee and fresh-baked biscuits for us

to share. Oh, and some of Letty's strawberry jam. I am sure that you will enjoy it. Where would you like me to set the tray? In here or the setting room?"

"Is there enough for me to share?" asked Ellen as she wandered slowly into Fancy's bedchamber from the connecting hallway. She was wearing her blue dressing gown and, covering up a small yawn with one dainty hand, she said, "Oh, my, but I slept wonderfully last night. Did you, Fancy?"

"Well, did you?" Chance mouthed silently, one brow cocked, his eyes dancing.

"This is not amusing," Fancy muttered, frantic that at any moment Ellen was going to push back the bed curtains. She eyed Chance distrustfully, one part of her wishing that he didn't look quite so attractive as he lay there, his black hair wildly tousled, his hard jaw darkened by a hint of whiskers, another part of her aching to kill him. Painfully. Slowly. With *great* relish.

"You planned this, didn't you?" she accused in a low, furious voice, uncomfortably conscious of the other two women just beyond the bed curtains.

A puzzled note in her voice, Ellen asked, "Fancy? Are you talking to yourself?"

As Fancy watched in stunned horror, Chance suddenly sat up, the sheets resting dangerously low on his hips. Reaching across her, he flung back the bed curtain. "Why, no," he said calmly, "she was talking to me."

Constance gave a shriek and promptly dropped the silver tray with a loud clatter at the shocking sight of Chance Walker lounging confidently in the bed beside Lady Merrivale. A very naked Chance Walker, if his upper body was any indication of the rest of him. Ellen stared first at her sister and then at Chance, her eyes getting very big, her mouth forming a perfect O of surprise.

"Oh, my God," Fancy groaned. Pulling the sheet over her head, she fell back against the pillows, wishing she could just die. "I am ruined," she muttered. "Absolutely ruined."

"Actually, no," Chance said coolly. "I have every intention of marrying you, just as soon as it can be arranged."

Oblivious of her wide-eyed audience, Fancy jerked upright. Her eyes flashing with angry golden lights, she spat, "Marry you? Why, you unscrupulous, conceited buffoon. You are the *last* person I'd marry!"

Chance looked suitably wounded. "Duchess, how can you say that, after all we have been to each other . . . after last night. . . ."

Fancy's temper broke, and with a small shriek of rage, she flung herself at him, her hands clenched into fists. More furious than she could ever remember being in her life, she pummeled him wildly with all her might, smiling fiercely when he gave a grunt of pain as one of her fists landed smartly against his ear.

With a smothered oath, Chance caught her flailing fists in his hands and, falling back onto the mattress, pulled her across him. "Now, now, sweetheart, is this any way to greet your lover . . . your future husband?" he murmured, a thread of laughter running through his voice.

"What in the world is going on in here?" demanded Letty as she walked into the room, not a hair out of place and wearing a pale blue gown and striped bodice with a white apron. From where she stood, just inside the bedchamber, all she could see was Fancy's back. Staring at the scattered pot and cups all over the floor and the stunned expressions on Constance's and Ellen's faces, she grew concerned. "I was walking down the hall when I heard the strangest commotion coming from Lady Merrivale's rooms," she said slowly. "Is anything wrong?"

Fancy gasped and, abandoning her fight with Chance, glanced back over her shoulder. In guilty dismay she stared at Letty.

"Is anything wrong?" screeched Constance, finally recovering from her stunned stupor. "Not a thing, if you do not consider it to be out of the ordinary to discover that Lady Merrivale is a brazen hussy without morals or character and that Chance Walker has repaid your many kindnesses to him by defiling my poor Jonathan's bride-to-be." She shot Fancy an ugly look, her face twisted with hatred and disgust. "Just you wait until I tell Jonathan. He will *never* marry you now. Your title might grant you special privileges and licenses and allow you to act the part of slut in England, but not here." Constance drew in an angry, shaken breath. "I have never," she pronounced grandly, "been so disappointed and disillusioned in my life. Why, I will wager you are not even a real baroness." Her nose held high, Constance swept regally from the room.

Fancy slumped against Chance, all the fight going out of her. "I want to die," she muttered. "Please God strike me dead and let this farce be ended."

"I am sure," Chance murmured warmly against her ear, "that when you have had a moment to think about it, you will find marriage to me is preferable to death."

Fancy shot him a look of venomous dislike. "*Not* bloody likely."

Chance shrugged and, releasing her, sat up once more. Meeting Letty's shocked gaze, he said, "I am sorry that at least one thing Constance said is true. I *have* repaid your kindness in a most dastardly way, Cousin Letty, and for that I am very sorry. I have no excuse, and I will understand if you and Sam decide never to see me again. But if it will redeem me somewhat, I want you to know that I intend to take full responsibility for my actions. I intend to marry Lady Merrivale just as soon as it can be arranged."

Letty sent him a long, considering look. "I will not pretend that I am not hurt and disappointed in you, Chance," she said quietly. "There is no denying that you have abused our hospitality most grievously." She sighed. "But I suppose you could not help it—you have always been a wild, unorthodox boy. And I am aware that these things *do* happen, even in the best of circles." She shook her head and added, "I doubt that Sam will throw you out, though he might very well want to."

"And you?" Chance asked softly. "Do you want to throw me out?"

Letty made a face. "No, despite everything I have a fondness for you and would be saddened not to see you anymore. But this is really too bad of you, Chance. And offering to marry Lady Merrivale does not make it right. It was dishonorable of you to steal another man's bride, even if nothing has been formalized, and I am afraid Jonathan is going to be *most* displeased by what has transpired."

Chance gave an unamused chuckle. "Displeased is no doubt putting it mildly. I suspect that he is going to be wanting my liver."

"No doubt," Letty returned equably. "And in order to forestall bloodshed, I think I had better go and apprise Sam of what has happened. We will make certain that Jonathan is kept away from you for the moment."

Letty's steady gaze rested a moment on Fancy, who felt a hot, crimson blush rising from her chin to her forehead as she bravely met the older woman's eyes. This was the most humiliating moment of her life, and her powers of speech seemed to have deserted her, just when she needed them so desperately. Protesting her own innocence did not seem feasible, however, not when she had been caught in such damning circumstances. Would *anyone* believe her if she told her side of the story? She doubted it. Not, she thought viciously, with that scoundrel Chance Walker denying every word she spoke. Why was he doing this? He didn't want to marry her. And God knew she didn't want to marry *him*. But how was she going to get out of this?

"Well, I have things to do," Letty finally said. "I will send Ora to clean up this mess, and I would suggest that the pair of you get dressed and be prepared to meet Sam in his office within the hour." A puzzled expression on her face, she looked once again at Fancy. "I suspected that your heart was not given to Jonathan, but I never dreamed . . ." She shook herself. "It is none of my business, but I just wish that if you had changed your mind, you had let Jonathan down more gently. He is going to be shattered by this. Shattered and very, very angry."

Fancy's eyes met Ellen's, but she slowly shook her head. Explaining that it was Ellen who had actually been Jonathan's choice wouldn't change anything—Chance would still be sitting naked in her bed. Her throat feeling hot and rusty, she said painfully, "I am very sorry to have caused you and your family such distress." She flashed Chance a look of sheer venom before turning back to Letty. "If I could have avoided it, I would have." Lamely she ended, "Some things are just beyond one's control."

Letty nodded slowly, her face softening just a little. "Indeed they are, my dear. Now then, I shall leave you."

"Oh, me too," Ellen exclaimed hastily as Letty began to leave the room. Her eyes not meeting Fancy's, guiltily aware that her actions had compounded her sister's embarrassing predicament, she added, "I am certain that you two wish to be alone. Y-y-you must have a lot to discuss."

And before Fancy could say anything, she darted into the connecting hallway, slamming the door shut behind her.

Chance lay back down and, his arms once more behind his head, glanced at Fancy's stony profile. The lady was not happy. He sighed. He certainly hadn't expected her to be happy. He just hadn't planned on it mattering so damn much.

There was a tense silence in the room for several seconds before Fancy turned and looked at him. "Why?" she asked bluntly. "Why did you do this? And do you really think that I am going to marry you?"

"I do not," he said easily, "see how you can get out of it. Not if you want to be left with a shred of reputation."

"I can return to England immediately. It is unlikely the story will follow me there," Fancy said sharply.

"Ah, but can you be sure? I am positive that Jonathan or Constance will not keep quiet about how you disillusioned them—and he has friends in England. And how do you think this sordid tale will affect Ellen? It certainly will not be pleasant for her if the whispers about you follow her."

Fancy's eyes closed in pain and her hands clenched into fists. "Do you know that you are the most despicable creature it has ever been my misfortune to meet?" she said finally, glaring at him. "I hate you. I will make you a terrible wife."

"Will you really?" he said tightly, his hands suddenly grabbing her and dragging her down to him. He brushed his lips across hers and then crushed her soft mouth beneath his.

Too stunned to resist, Fancy felt her lips parting for him, and as his tongue surged hungrily into her mouth, she was shamefully conscious of her body's instant response to him: liquid warmth burning low in her belly, her breasts tingling, her breathing labored and constricted. When his hand cupped her breast, she gave a low moan and a shudder of pleasure went through her as he gently tweaked one throbbing nipple.

Breathing hard, his own body responding fiercely to hers, Chance suddenly pushed her away. It was clear that she was not as indifferent to him as she pretended. As he stared into her flushed features, the unacknowledged fear that he had made a disastrous mistake suddenly vanished. A faint, mocking smile on his long mouth, he brushed his lips against hers once more. "Now tell me again," he said huskily, "just how very much you hate me and what a terrible wife you are going to be."

Chapter Nine

Fancy had been incensed by his words. Flinging him a scathing look, she had scrambled away from him, vowing never, *never* to marry him, no matter what horrid future awaited her. It had taken all of Chance's enormous powers of persuasion to finally convince her that she was well and truly trapped; if she ever hoped to hold her head up again, either in the Colonies or in England, she was going to have to marry him. It was obvious that, as furious as she was, Fancy might have risked her own reputation, but Chance had coolly pointed out again and again that it wasn't just *her* reputation at stake—as her sister, Ellen, too, would be tarred with the same brush, if Fancy continued to refuse to marry him. By the time Chance left to dress for the meeting with Sam, Fancy wasn't precisely resigned to her fate, but it was evident she understood the enormity of the personal and social disaster that had befallen her. With daggers in her eyes and, no doubt, fury in her heart, she had silently watched him leave her bedchamber.

There had been several reasons why Chance had wanted to meet alone with Sam, and not the least of these was that he wanted no opportunity for Fancy to wiggle out of marriage to him. Sam was notoriously soft-hearted, and if Fancy threw herself on his mercy, well, he just might try to figure out a way for her to avoid Chance's trap. He might tell himself that revenge was motivating his actions, but he was uneasily aware that he desperately wanted to marry Fancy and that when he thought of her as his wife, revenge had very little to do with the emotions that filled him.

Sam was not at *all* pleased with what had transpired, but, like Letty, he took it in stride. What was done was done, and while he greatly deplored the situation and wished it had not happened, there was no use crying over spilt milk—it changed nothing.

Chance was glad that Fancy was not at the meeting. He had been the one who had transgressed, not Fancy, and, for reasons he didn't quite comprehend himself, he wanted to make certain that Sam understood that particular aspect of the situation. It mattered, and it shouldn't have, that Sam not think ill of Fancy. There was the fact, too, that it was Chance who was a member of the family, not Fancy. Sam exercised no authority over Chance, but he *was* the head of the large, tightly knit Walker clan, while Fancy was merely a guest. A guest who had been taken base advantage of by Chance, as Sam had unhappily pointed out to him.

Chance's avowed determination to marry the baroness did much to mollify Sam. But Chance was painfully conscious that the older man was very disappointed in him, and he wondered dully if striking back at Jonathan was going to be worth the cost. His bride-to-be hated him and thought him the blackest villain in nature, and his disgraceful actions had greatly strained the warm relationship he had with Sam and Letty. He had not realized until this moment how much their approval meant to him. Had he, driven by thoughts of revenge against Jonathan, forever destroyed their trust and liking for him?

"You realize," Sam said slowly, having already vented the worst of his anger and dismay at the situation, "that Jonathan is not going to simply let this rest? You have grievously insulted him."

The two men were in Sam's office, which was located in

a modest building a few hundred yards away from the main house. Sam was seated behind a huge walnut desk, his feet propped on a low wooden stool as he stared broodingly at Chance, who sat across from him in a brown leather chair.

Garbed casually in fine leather boots, buckskin breeches, and a white linen shirt, Chance was the very picture of a son of a wealthy Virginia planter. Looking at him, Sam felt a pang of sadness. With that hint of unconscious arrogance in his bearing and a reckless gleam in those Walker blue eyes, Chance looked very much as his son might have, Sam thought regretfully, if the boy had lived.

Chance shrugged. "Can you remember a time in which just the mere sight of me has *not* affronted your esteemed half-brother? For reasons known best to him, Jonathan seems to find the very fact of my birth insulting."

Sam grimaced wryly. "How well I know. It would help if that damned Morely would just acknowledge you and get it over with. Why he continues to deny you your rightful heritage is a mystery to me. It always has been."

"But 'tis not just my bastardy that eats at Jonathan," Chance said quietly. "You, Cousin Letty, the majority of the Walkers do not seem to pay it any heed anymore. Why should Jonathan?"

Sam shook his head. "I do not know. It pains me to admit it, but I suspect that even if you had been born legitimate, Jonathan would only have found another reason to dislike you." He shot Chance a dark look. "And you, young man, have not helped matters. For God's sake, Chance, what the devil were you thinking of?"

Not meeting Sam's eyes, his own gaze resting on his boots, Chance murmured, "She is very beautiful, Sam. I am afraid that I lost my head."

Sam gave an angry sigh. "Dash it all, Chance. Under different circumstances, I would be kicking my heels together for joy to hear that you had finally put Jenny's death behind you and had found someone else. But dear Lord. Did it have to be Lady Merrivale?" He didn't really expect an answer and went on wearily, "I suppose you know that this is a very delicate situation. I can only thank God that no formal announcement has been made. But smoothing this over is not going to be simple. Even before the Baroness arrived there was gossip and speculation aplenty about the purpose of her visit. Constance, while dropping broad hints—*extremely* broad hints, I might add—has been very coy about actually admitting that Jonathan intended to marry Lady Merrivale—for which, under the circumstances, I am grateful. Jonathan has not been very forthcoming, either, although, he has made it clear that marriage was in the wind. In fact, until last night, I was not even certain which of the Merrivale women he intended to marry. One moment he seemed to dangle after the baroness, the next after her sister. It had me baffled, I can tell you."

"Well, at least you can have no doubts about which Merrivale I intend to marry," Chance said dryly.

"Indeed I haven't. I just wish you had chosen a more orthodox way to make your intentions apparent," Sam retorted grimly. "The kidnapping of the ladies by those despicable Thackers was bad enough, but now we have the problem of keeping Jonathan from your throat and of making this sudden marriage between you and Lady Merrivale appear as if it were nothing out of the ordinary. No mean feat, I can tell you."

Chance looked thoughtful. "Could we not use the abduction by the Thackers and subsequent rescue by Hugh and me as an explanation for the sudden wedding?" He grinned. "The beautiful rescued damsel falls in love with the handsome, dashing hero who saved her from a fate worse than death?"

Sam stared narrowly at him. "Is that what happened?" he asked grimly.

Chance's grin slipped a little. "Perhaps."

Committed to keeping the gossip and scandal to a minimum, Sam began to discuss various plans to lend respectability to the coming nuptials. It would be a small, hasty affair, with only the nearest members of the Walker clan attending the actual ceremony. Morely and his family would naturally be there, as well as some of Chance's adopted father's brothers and sisters and their families. Many lived within a forty-mile radius of Walker Ridge and would flock eagerly to the plantation to see Chance Walker marry a real English lady—especially one rumored to have been Jonathan's choice of a bride. It was going to be a nine days' wonder, and gossip would race like wildfire through the colony, but if they kept their heads about them, they just might brush through without any serious damage. From those attending the wedding the news would trickle outward, and as Sam said, the least said by the principals, the better.

Jonathan and Constance were a great stumbling block to any plan to present a unified family front, and their absence from the wedding would create rampant speculation and fuel just the sort of gossip they were trying to avoid. They would simply have to be there when Chance took Lady Merrivale as his bride, and it would be up to Sam to make certain that bloody mayhem did not result.

Overall, Chance was feeling rather satisfied when he finally left Sam's office some time later. It was firmly established that he would indeed marry Lady Merrivale just as soon as it could be decently arranged and that Sam and Letty would help cloak the affair with decorum. Chance had reason to be pleased; he had accomplished what he had set out to do, claimed as his own the woman Jonathan had wanted. The fact that Sam and Letty had not blamed Fancy for what had happened, or thrown him out on his ear, intensified his satisfaction.

Sam had already gently requested that both Jonathan and his mother remove themselves temporarily to Foxfield, the upper plantation, some fifteen miles up the river, and for them to stay there, at the small but comfortable house that had been built by some long-deceased Walker relative, until plans were more settled. Chance had been surprised to learn that they had agreed to do so, and he had to admit that for the time being, their absence would make life simpler for everyone involved. Without them at the house, there would be far less tension and discord, and it was obvious that Sam did not want to run the risk of any confrontation between Chance and Jonathan—or Constance, for that matter. Jonathan and his mother would return well before any of the Walker cousins arrived for the wedding and would, hopefully, by that time have become resigned to Chance's marriage to the baroness. Chance doubted it, and he would have liked to know what sort of persuasion Sam had used to get Jonathan to agree to the move.

Deciding that it would be wise if he made himself scarce for a while, at least until Jonathan and Constance had left for Foxfield, Chance did not return immediately to the big house. Whistling softly to himself, he wandered past the rows of slave cabins and various outbuildings behind Sam's office and entered the small patch of woodland that lay beyond. He had no definite destination, he was merely wasting time until Jonathan and Constance had left Walker Ridge. But eventually he found himself walking along the river's edge where it looped backward and wound itself sinuously along one side of the wooded area. It was a private spot, a favorite of his where he'd come often as a boy.

Chance was standing on a small bluff overlooking the water; the green, dappled coolness of the woods lay behind him, and below him gently meandered the James River. From this point, beyond glimpses of the tobacco fields and the small winding path that led back toward the house and outbuildings, there was no sign of human habitation. There was an agreeable sense of isolation from Walker Ridge, almost as if he were all alone and miles away. No intrusive human sounds traveled his way; there was only the somnolent drone of the insects, the soft lap of the river against the bank, and the occasional lilting song of a bird. It was very peaceful.

A yawn escaped him, and after settling himself on a patch of wild grass, he leaned his head back against the trunk of a large willow tree. The day was warm, the yellow sunlight filtering gently through the narrow leaves of the willow, and as Chance lounged there, the tenseness that had been with him since he had first conceived his wild plan gradually waned. In less than two minutes his eyes closed and he slept.

He had no way of knowing how long he slept, but a whisper of sound snapped him into sudden wakefulness. He lay very still, all his senses straining to fix the point of the noise that had awakened him. A brief glance at the sky showed him the sun was no longer high, and from the lengthening shadows he knew it was late afternoon. The sound came again—from along the path—and he relaxed slightly. Probably one of the servants had been sent by Sam or Letty to look for him here.

It wasn't a servant, and a slow, appreciative smile crossed Chance's dark face as Fancy came into view. She looked very lovely wearing a simple green-striped skirt and lace-edged bodice of delicate jaconet over a pale yellow petticoat. A wide, saucy-brimmed straw hat that was tied with broad yellow ribbon sat upon her head, her dark brown hair falling in soft curls down her back, and in one hand she carried a large wicker basket. She did not look pleased to see him.

"Letty said that she thought you would be here," she muttered as she approached him. Motioning to the basket she held, she added coldly, "She said that you would be hungry by now, and that since I am your"—her voice hardened and an angry flush burned in her cheeks—"*fiancée* and we have already anticipated our wedding vows, there would be nothing amiss in my bringing it to you."

From beneath his thick dark lashes, Chance regarded her. "This is kind of you."

Fancy's eyes glittered. "I did not want to do it. But I had no choice with Letty and Ellen simpering and looking all calf-eyed. If it had been up to me, you could have stayed out here and starved."

Chance grinned, his white teeth flashing in his bronzed face. "Now, Duchess, is that any way to talk to your husband-to-be?"

Fancy gave a strangled sound, halfway between a shriek and a growl, and very nearly threw the basket at his mocking face. She absolutely hated him. And he had no right to look so damnably attractive as he lolled there on the ground before her, like a pasha surveying his favorite harem girl. His black hair fell rakishly across his forehead and around his shoulders, and his white linen shirt was half-undone, revealing an indecent expanse of smooth, tawny skin. The buckskin breeches faithfully outlined his long, strong legs, and, remembering those same *naked* legs brushing against her that morning in bed, Fancy fought a wave of giddiness. She would *not* be attracted to him. She would not. He was loathsome. Staring at him with open dislike, she thrust the basket at him. "Here. Take it. I have delivered you something to eat and I'm not doing one thing more."

Chance straightened from his indolent pose against the tree trunk, and leaning forward, he took the basket and set it on the ground nearby. Cocking an eyebrow at her, he murmured, "Are you sure that I cannot convince you to join me? If I know Letty, she has sent enough food for both of us."

"No, thank you," Fancy said stiffly. "I am not hungry. And the less I have to share with you the better."

"You know," he said thoughtfully, "our life together is not going to be very pleasant if you persist in this unfriendly attitude."

Fancy took in a great angry breath. "If you were worried about our life together, you should have thought of it before you stole into my bed."

She swung on her heels, intent upon putting as much distance as possible between herself and this wretched creature, when Chance suddenly caught a handful of her skirts and gave a hard yank. Off balance, Fancy gave a startled cry and fell backward . . . into his arms.

Her saucy bonnet askew and her skirt and petticoat frothing immodestly about her knees, Fancy glared up at him. "How *dare* you," she said in a withering, furious voice.

Chance smiled. He was rather pleased with his effort. That sweet mouth of hers was only inches from his; he had her firmly in his arms, and she was sprawled tantalizingly across his thighs, every wiggle, every squirm of her bottom, pressing against his rapidly hardening body.

Fancy became aware of the danger almost immediately. They were all alone—any sound she made would be swallowed up by the dense forest. And it was obvious, blatantly so, that Chance was thoroughly aroused. She swallowed nervously, knowing that it was highly unlikely they would be interrupted for quite some time—unlike this morning in her bedroom.

To her shame, she was conscious of the rapid increase in her heartbeat—an increase that had very little to do with anger or fear. The power and warmth of his body beneath her thighs sent a wave of languid heat through her, and her breasts were instantly full and heavy, her nipples straining against the fabric of her clothing. His scent, warm and male and slightly musky, drifted to her.

Fancy stilled her struggles almost immediately, and eyes wide and uncertain, lips half-parted, she stared at him. Her gaze wandered over his lean face, the heavy-lidded eyes, the bold nose, the splendidly sculpted cheeks, and the wide, mobile mouth. Bitterly she admitted that Chance Walker had fascinated her almost from the first moment she had laid eyes on him. While he infuriated her and mocked her, there was something between them, something that drew her to him—even when she was at her angriest. As she stared at him, his smile faded and he suddenly looked very fierce with his black hair flowing wildly about his face and shoulders. But it was the hot glitter in those cobalt blue eyes that made Fancy's pulse leap in her veins.

Chance muttered something—a curse, a plea—and his mouth came down hard on hers, his arms crushing her against him. Like a starving man, he fed upon her ripe mouth, his tongue plunging hungrily into the moist warmth behind her lips, his hands gripping her upper arms, holding her prisoner to his ravenous kiss.

All of Fancy's senses were violently assaulted by the sensations that erupted through her body at the impact of his hard lips on hers, his seeking tongue delving deep in her mouth. No man, not even her husband, had ever made her feel the frankly carnal sensations that were surging in her blood; no man had ever made her body ache for his touch, yearn to have his hands upon her, eager to feel his flesh sinking slowly into hers.

Frightened, excited, and half-dizzy with desire, Fancy was hardly aware of Chance sweeping her hat from her head and lowering her carefully to the sweet, soft grass. The sun beat lightly against her closed lids, and the scent of honeysuckle and magnolia wafted on the warm, humid air; but she was only peripherally aware of them, the welcoming weight of Chance's big body as he leaned over her, the blunt demand of his mouth on hers, nearly blotting out everything else.

He kissed her many times, long, drugging kisses that fed the fire deep in her belly and banished coherent thought. Fancy wasn't aware of her arms creeping around his neck, or of the faint encouraging sounds that came from her throat when Chance's hand slid slowly downward to cup her aching breast. When he touched her, when his fingers plucked at her nipple through the fabric of her clothing, a jolt of pure feminine arousal went streaking through her. Heat pooled low in her belly, and between her thighs there was an insistent, needy hunger—a hunger completely new to her.

Fancy had never wanted a man before, never wanted, truly wanted, to be possessed by any male, but with Chance ... With Chance, she seemed to have no control over her thoughts or her body. He had only to touch her and she became alive to emotions and sensations that were totally foreign to her. She had thought herself cold and indifferent to the elemental urges that bedeviled other people, but in Chance's arms she discovered that she was as helpless as anyone else to resist the demands of passion. She wanted his hands upon her, wanted his mouth against hers, and even more, she wanted to touch him, to feel his hard, warm flesh beneath her own hand, to feel his heartbeat, to explore at will the entire muscled length of him.

She was astounded, terrified, and oh, *so* curious by what was happening to her. She knew she should struggle, and for one moment she tried to remember precisely why, but then Chance's wandering hand slid to her thigh and began to travel lazily up under her skirts. Her breath caught and her hands clenched instinctively in his hair as his seeking fingers touched her there between her legs.

Sanity glimmered for a second as his mouth left hers and burned a trail down her neck. She stammered, "C-C-Chance, I d-d-don't think this is—"

His voice dark with desire, his lips brushed her lips: "Don't think, Fancy. Don't. Feel."

And she did, as his clever fingers brushed aside her undergarments to touch the naked flesh hidden by the thatch of curly hair between her thighs. Fire seemed to sear up through her, and as he caressed her, exploring between the soft folds, Fancy was lost, sweet sensation after sweet sensation crashing through her.

Need flooded her as his finger slipped into her moist depths, and she twisted wildly in his arms, her hands moving restlessly over his shoulders and back, plucking impatiently at his shirt. She wanted, *needed*, to touch him.

Feeling her response, feeling the damp warmth between her legs, the intoxicating taste of her on his lips, Chance lost whatever restraint he'd placed on himself. She had tormented his dreams for too long. Tempted him unbearably simply with her nearness. He had to have her. Now.

He fumbled with the fastening of his breeches, and when at last his swollen manhood sprang free, he gave a deep sigh of relief. With demanding hands, he pushed aside the delicate clothing that kept him from his goal and slipped between her legs. Cupping her hips, he raised her to him.

Fancy stiffened, the reality of what was happening suddenly bursting through the erotic fog that had clouded her thoughts. Her eyes snapped open. "No. Stop. Oh, I never meant to . . ."

His face fierce with desire, passion glittering in the blue eyes, Chance stared down at her, trying to comprehend what she was saying. Stop? Was she mad? Or simply trying to drive him mad? She was soft and pliant beneath him, he knew she was aroused, he could feel it. His body was hard and aching, one swift movement and he would find the urgent release he so desperately needed. And she wanted him to stop?

He closed his eyes in near pain. Fancy wiggled slightly, her thigh brushing against his solid shaft, and a shudder went through him. She was asking too much of him. Of any man. And yet . . .

Gulping in a breath, he opened his eyes and looked down into her passion-flushed face, at the softly swollen contours of her mouth. His hands tightened on her buttocks, and bending his head, he gently suckled her nipple through her bodice, feeling with savage satisfaction the excited ripple within her that his action caused. His lips hot against her breast, he said thickly, "Fancy, don't ask this of me. I want you—I am dying with hunger for you. Let me. . . ."

He kissed her, his mouth melding urgently with hers, his body rubbing provocatively against hers, his big hands caressing her buttocks. "Let me," he breathed into her mouth. "Let me."

Ensnared by his kiss and the warmth of his body on hers, the boldly carnal sensation of his flesh rubbing against hers, Fancy forgot all about propriety, decorum, sanity. *She wanted him.* Her body ached for him, yearned for him, and she wanted most desperately to find out if there was more to this dark spell Chance had woven about her. Not giving herself time to think, mesmerized by the hot demand singing in her blood, her arms fastened closely around his neck and her body moving in an invitation as old as time, Fancy offered herself to him.

Chance groaned, and his lips sought hers hungrily as he lifted her and positioned himself more solidly between her thighs, then slowly sank deep into her moist warmth. She was so tight. So snug. So perfect.

Hardly daring to breathe, Fancy felt weak and dizzy as he filled her, her body stretching and widening eagerly to accommodate his substantial bulk. *Nothing* had ever felt like this before, and she trembled with giddy pleasure when he began to move, his body pumping lazily into hers, his lips crushing hers.

As Chance made love to her, his mouth moving erotically against hers, his powerful body driving more and more frantically into hers, the ache that he had first aroused in Fancy grew more persistent, more needy. In mindless hunger she met each thrust of his hips, pleasure she had never even imagined rippling through her every time their bodies collided. In wanton abandon she writhed beneath him, her tongue curling provocatively around his, her hands moving almost desperately over his back and breeches-clad buttocks. Every thrust, every meeting of their flesh, sent shocks of delight through her, and Fancy was staggered by her own passionate response. Never, *never* had she even dreamed that lovemaking could be like this. Unexpectedly a wave of intense pleasure erupted through her, and she cried out in stunned ecstasy and clutched Chance even closer to her.

Feeling her body clench and convulse around him brought Chance instantly to the brink. With a soft, shaken groan, he exploded inside of her, such pleasure as he had never known in his life flooding him. His breathing ragged and labored, he slowed his movements and relished the last faint eddies that rippled through him. Then he lifted his head and, bracing himself on his elbows, looked down into Fancy's face.

There was a dazed, dreamy expression in her cat-shaped, topaz eyes as her lids lifted slowly, and Chance thought he had never seen anything so beautiful in his life. Fancy's cheeks were flushed, her mouth rosy and swollen from his kisses, and her gorgeous chocolate brown hair spread in wild disarray around her head. Staring down at her, at the innocently provocative sight she made beneath him, he felt something tighten in the region of his heart. To his astonishment, he felt his body, still buried within her, stir and begin to harden.

A look of startlement crossed Fancy's features as she became aware of what was happening to him. Her gaze flew to his, disbelief widening her eyes. "S-s-so soon?" she stammered, blushing.

Chance smiled ruefully. "Probably not to completion. 'Tis just merely letting us know that the beast is not completely dead. He will live to service you another day, m'lady."

Fancy had never shared any intimate teasing with her husband, and she was uncertain how to reply. She was also rapidly becoming aware of what had actually transpired, and embarrassment and guilt at her incredibly uncharacteristic actions were banishing any lingering pleasure. To her further embarrassment, she suddenly realized that Chance was still fully clothed—as was she. A burst of shame went through her. She, the Baroness Merrivale, had been tumbled in the grass like any common tavern slattern. And by a man she didn't even *like*.

Thoroughly mortified, her eyes looking anywhere but at Chance's dark face, she pushed forcefully against his shoulders. "Get off of me," she said raggedly.

Chance hesitated, but then, realizing that her mood had undergone one of those baffling feminine changes, he slid regretfully from her body. "Whatever pleases you, Duchess," he said lightly.

Fancy's jaw clenched, but she made no reply. Still avoiding looking at him, she sat up and with trembling hands rearranged her clothing. Out of the corner of her eye, she could see him lounging on the ground beside her, propped up with one elbow, his breeches still unfastened. Thankfully there was no sign of the "beast," but she was acutely uncomfortable and embarrassed. She was appalled by what had happened, hardly daring to believe what she had done. And she had done it. The small pleasurable ache between her thighs and the fuzziness of her lips plainly told her so. She had kissed him, caressed him, and allowed him to make love to her. Allowed him to seduce her. Allowed him to make the reason for their hasty marriage a fact.

Suspicion suddenly darkened her eyes, and glaring at him, she said accusingly, "You did that deliberately, didn't you?"

Unaware of her meaning, and assuming she referred to the way he had made love to her, Chance merely grinned at her and drawled teasingly, "Oh, indeed I did, Duchess. I deliberately enjoyed it, too, and after we are married, I intend to *deliberately* make love to you as often as I can."

Already angry and resentful at the entire morning's events, Fancy lost her temper. Before she had time to think, she had twisted around and slapped him—hard. Eyes blazing, she spat, "You are the most aggravating, *horrid* man I have ever met in my life. And I cannot imagine how I will survive being married to you."

Chance's grin vanished the instant her hand connected to his face. Sitting up, he thoughtfully rubbed his smarting cheek. "You want to tell me what brought that on? A moment ago, you were willing in my arms and you gained as much pleasure from our coupling as I did—do not try to deny it. And I should warn you"—his eyes narrowed—"strike me again like that and you will not appreciate my reaction—that I can promise you."

Fancy was outraged. "What brought it on?" she almost shrieked. "You deliberately compromised me by being found *uninvited* in my bed." She took in a deep, furious breath. "And just now, you calculatingly set out to make this morning's ugly farce the truth. And then you make light of it. And if that was not bad enough, you have the audacity to *threaten* me."

"I did not threaten you," Chance said carefully. "I warned you."

Fancy surged to her feet and snatched up her bonnet. Jamming it on her head, she snapped, "And I am warning you: marry me and I shall make your life a living hell."

Chance leaned back on his elbow and smiled up at her.

" 'Tis an odd thing, Duchess, but I've always enjoyed playing with fire."

Fancy's teeth ground together, and with a sound halfway between a snarl and a snort, she spun on her heels and stalked furiously away.

Chance stared after her, his grin widening. Marriage to his duchess was going to be most interesting. *Most* interesting indeed.

Chapter Ten

The marriage between Frances Anne Merrivale and Chance Walker took place on August 26, 1774. It was a hot, humid day, the threat of a thunderstorm looming on the horizon, but no one seemed to pay the dark, ominous clouds any heed as Fancy and Chance exchanged their vows. Only Fancy, her face outwardly serene, felt that the weather was clearly indicative of her future as Chance Walker's wife.

They were married in the late afternoon by a traveling preacher whom Sam had sent for and who regularly made a circuit through this sparsely settled area. Preacher Parker was a bluff, jovial fellow, and he was very happy to do a favor for his generous benefactor, Sam Walker.

Everyone, it seemed, was very happy to do anything that Sam asked of them. Staring moodily at the throng of laughing, lighthearted guests who crowded around the long tables that had been arranged outside under a stand of towering oaks and were filled to overflowing with all manner of delicious food and drink, Fancy scowled. The Walker men seemed to have a definite knack for getting their own way, she thought sourly.

All during the previous fortnight, Fancy had hoped and prayed fervently that something would go wrong, that some-

how she could escape from the trap Chance had set for her.
A trap she had helped spring when she had fallen into his
arms like a disgustingly eager light-skirted trollop.

Even now she couldn't believe that she had allowed
Chance to make love to her—or that she was married to him.
Uneasily her gaze moved to where he was standing just six
feet away from her, talking easily to a group of men that included Morely, Hugh, and Sam. Chance looked very handsome, incredibly so, with a froth of lace falling down the
front of his shirt, his rose-colored silk jacket and breeches
and heavily embroidered white satin waistcoat fitting him
superbly. In honor of the occasion, his thick black hair was
powdered and tied back with a long black silk ribbon. It
made him look very different, almost a stranger.

Fancy's mouth twisted. He *was* a stranger. And God help
her, she had married him.

She was no longer the dowager baroness, Lady Merrivale.
From this day forward she would be known simply as Mrs.
Walker. The loss of her title didn't worry her; it had never
meant that much to her anyway. But the loss of her independence, the knowledge that her entire future lay in the
powerful hands of a man she barely knew—a man with a
dangerous, unsavory reputation (if Jonathan was to be believed) and a man who had proven, at least to her, that he
was a blackguard and a scoundrel—filled her with something approaching terror. That she also found this same man
devastatingly attractive, that with a simple glance from his
blue eyes he could set her pulse pounding, that his slightest
touch made her heart race, only added to her terror.

It had been a long time since Fancy had felt so helpless,
so vulnerable, and she was angry and resentful at the way
Chance had manipulated her. Even her marriage to Spencer,
though she had been young and innocent, had not created
the furor inside of her that this wedding to Chance did. And
the worst of it was that there was no one with whom she
could share her emotional disturbance. Everyone else was so
pleased by the marriage. Even Ellen. In fact, Fancy thought
grimly, Ellen was thrilled by the marriage. There was no

question of them returning to England now, at least not any time soon. Ellen would have plenty of time to work her wiles on Hugh.

Knowing she was being unfair, Fancy was annoyed with herself. None of this was Ellen's fault. And she should be happy that a terrible scandal had been avoided.

She grimaced. Sam and Letty, Morely and his wife, Prudence, had done their work well. Carefully selected Walker cousins had arrived for the wedding, and while there were the occasional flickers of speculation in the eyes of the people she was introduced to, Fancy knew that the family was closing ranks behind Sam and Letty. There would be no scandal.

The story concocted by Chance—that they had fallen in love after she had escaped from the Thackers and he had rescued her—was happily accepted. Most thought it very romantic. And if someone was slow-witted enough to mention that it was Jonathan's name that had been connected with Fancy's, a sharp look and quick jab in the ribs put all to rights.

Fancy supposed she should have been grateful that all had gone well. Unfortunately, she wasn't. She seemed to be the only one who viewed Chance with a jaundiced eye, the only one who knew to what depraved depths he would sink to get his own way. Except perhaps Jonathan. . . .

He and Constance had returned to Walker Ridge just three days ago, and the atmosphere in the house had been fraught with seething undercurrents the moment they had stepped inside. There was much about the situation between Chance and Jonathan that troubled Fancy. She knew of the long-standing hostility between them, and the uneasy suspicion had crossed her mind that the sole reason Chance had acted so unscrupulously toward her had been simply to steal her away from Jonathan. Which was ridiculous, she thought wearily, since she had never really been the woman Jonathan had planned to marry in the first place. But Chance didn't know that interesting little fact. No one did. And

Jonathan's actions, as well as Ellen's, both prior and afterward, had not helped to clarify things.

As she stood there sipping a glass of punch, her gaze traveled across the wide expanse of lawn to where Jonathan was standing between Constance and Letty, his lean face giving away nothing of what he was thinking. She knew that Sam and Letty had been fearful that Jonathan and Chance would come to blows over what had happened, which was why Jonathan had been temporarily banished to Foxfield. Certainly the reactions of the two men when in each other's company gave credence to those fears. Even having had several days in which to calm down and accept the situation had not done Jonathan much good; it was plain from the set of his mouth and the ugly glitter in his eyes that he was furious at the turn of events. There was an almost palpable hint of violence in the air whenever he and Chance were anywhere near each other.

Jonathan's reaction had puzzled Fancy. Certainly he had a right to be outraged at the black mark on the family honor that Chance's actions had caused, but not to the extent that he seemed to be. There was something very personal about his fury, almost as if he felt that Chance had deliberately insulted him, which had led Fancy to her suspicion that perhaps Chance had compromised her in order to thwart Jonathan.

It was an unpleasant thought, and it did nothing to soothe the angry, resentful emotions roiling in her breast. Fancy would have been much more resigned to her fate if she could have believed that Chance, as he had led everyone else to think, really had been thoroughly bedazzled by her and that he had been unable to stop himself from pursuing her so ardently. She didn't believe it for one moment—not when he mocked her, taunted her, and went out of his way to infuriate her at every turn. No one could have convinced *her* that there wasn't an ulterior motive behind his every act. Every time he was in Jonathan's presence, every time he smiled derisively at Jonathan or his eyes rested mockingly on the other man's closed features, her suspicions deepened that she had merely been a pawn in some duel between them.

Across the space that divided them, Jonathan's gaze suddenly met hers. He smiled without amusement and then deliberately turned away to speak to Ellen, who had just wandered up.

Fancy watched them as Jonathan began to pay extravagant court to a surprisingly willing Ellen, and her puzzlement with the entire situation grew. Had Jonathan, like the swine she had been compelled to marry, had a secret strategy that included a change of brides? Herself, instead of Ellen? His behavior since they had reached the Colonies would certainly have led one to believe that scenario. And now that she had been taken out of the running, had he fallen back onto Ellen? Or had he always intended to marry Ellen?

Fancy frowned as she continued to stare at the pair of them, watching as Ellen smiled winningly up at something Jonathan had said. What the devil was Ellen playing at? She had been very aloof and cool toward Hugh recently—after practically hanging on his every word for the past several days. Had Ellen changed her mind *again* and decided that perhaps she had been mistaken in her love for Hugh?

It was all very confusing, and Fancy wished she knew precisely how it would end. Her fate, of course, was already sealed, and she was *not* looking forward to the future as Mrs. Chance Walker.

Her gaze met Jonathan's again, and something in the way he looked at her made her wonder suddenly how he had felt when he had watched her marry Chance. He shouldn't have felt anything but relief that disgrace and dishonor had not been brought upon the proud Walker name. After all, despite the misunderstanding, a misunderstanding that still had not been corrected, it was Ellen who was to have been his bride, not her.

"Regretting your choice already?" drawled Chance from behind her.

Fancy stiffened and turned to glance at him, her heart thumping as she met his hard blue eyes. "Why, whatever do you mean?" she asked crisply. "I do not remember that I had much of a choice in the matter."

Chance's eyes narrowed, and for one moment she thought that he was going to answer her taunt; but instead he merely cocked a brow and nodded in Jonathan's direction. A cool, unamused smile on his mouth, he said softly, "Did you think that I would not notice the exchange of melting looks between the pair of you?"

She had thought him immersed in his conversation with the other gentlemen, but obviously he had been watching her and had seen that she had been looking at Jonathan. There had been nothing the least "melting" in the looks she had exchanged with him, and a little spurt of anger kicked through her. "I think," she said stiffly, "that you are imagining things."

"Am I?" he asked softly, his gaze intent upon her face. He reached out and ran a caressing hand down her arm. "I think I should warn you that I am a possessive man. What is mine I keep, and I do not share, or allow others to use what belongs to me. You should remember that fact in the future—especially with any dealings you may have with my beloved cousin Jonathan."

Fancy drew in a furious breath at the implication of his words, and it was all she could do to keep herself from tossing the remains of her punch into his handsome face. If they had been alone, she would have given in to the angry impulse, but as it was, she only tightened her grip on the delicate crystal and said in a low, enraged voice, "You insult me. And you insult yourself by implying you married a woman who would forsake her vows so easily that she would be looking for ways to cuckold you on your wedding day."

Heedless of who might be watching, she would have stormed off, but Chance's hand fastened around her upper arm. She glared up at him, and he smiled wryly at her. "Forgive me. I *was* insulting, and I did not mean to be so."

He hesitated, as if uncertain how to continue, and then he sighed and muttered, "Fancy, I know that none of this has been easy for you, and I am sorry for it. But whatever reasons may lie behind our marriage today, we *are* married. You are my wife, and I would only warn you that Jonathan means me no good. Be careful of him."

Too angry and resentful by what had befallen her at his hands, Fancy was in no mood to listen to him. "Do you know," she said tightly, "that he warned me against you? And considering that you have shown yourself to be without scruples or honor, I am far more likely to heed his warning than yours."

She carefully extricated her arm and then, sending him a smile as false as it was dazzling, walked across the lawn toward the group that contained Jonathan and Ellen. Chance watched her go, a faint frown creasing his brow.

Chance didn't know what he had expected to happen over the previous fortnight, but he certainly hadn't planned on being treated by his bride-to-be with the frostiest manner he had ever encountered from anyone in his life. He had known that after he had made love to her, Fancy would be a trifle skittish around him. But he had been confident that he could eventually win her 'round. A deprecating smile curved his mouth. Such had not been the case. She avoided him as though he carried leprosy in the very air around him. Any moment he contrived for them to be alone, she had neatly managed to escape. Since that afternoon on the bluff he had not been able to exchange more than a half a dozen words with her, and he was beginning to be just a little annoyed. She was his wife, dammit!

A surge of satisfaction went through him at that thought, and he grinned. Despite all his fears that she would escape him, he had managed to well and truly shackle her to him. Duchess was *his*. And tonight she would lie in his arms, and for all the other nights of their lives she would be there beside him.

Watching through narrowed eyes as Fancy gaily laughed and chatted with great animation with Jonathan and the others gathered around him, Chance was conscious of a faint unease. He had managed to marry Fancy, but was he going to be able to keep history from repeating itself? His jaw clenched. Fancy was no Jenny, but if Jenny, who had professed to love him, could be seduced, what was to stop Fancy, who obviously did *not* love him, from following in her footsteps—if for no other reason than to pay him back for forcing her into marriage?

Not liking the train of his thoughts, Chance scowled and reminded himself again that Fancy was not Jenny. And this time, he vowed grimly, his gaze boring into Fancy's back, he would make damn certain that his wife did not stray, that his arms and bed were the only ones in which she found satisfaction.

"Displeased with your bride so soon?" teased Hugh as he came up to stand beside Chance.

Chance made a face. "Rather my bride is displeased with me," he replied dryly, glancing at Hugh.

Hugh looked rueful. His gaze resting in perplexity on Ellen's lively features, he admitted, "You are not the only male to displease one of the Merrivale sisters. Ellen has treated me with unaccustomed coolness these past few days, and I cannot imagine what I have done to deserve her displeasure."

"Ah, now there I think I can help you," Chance answered lightly. At Hugh's look of inquiry, he went on, "Haven't you been treating Ellen much like one of your younger sisters? I saw you teasing her on Tuesday, pinching her cheek and ruffling her hair as if she were ten years old." Hugh opened his mouth to protest, but Chance went on, "And the other day, did you not sweep up Melly Sinclair in your arms when she sprained her ankle and carry her to the house?"

"Well, yes," Hugh replied, obviously mystified. "But dash it all, Chance, Ellen *is* just a child." Hugh flushed at the look Chance sent him. Pulling at his neatly tied cravat above his lace-covered shirt, he admitted awkwardly, "Oh, very well, perhaps I have been playing the older, wiser companion a little too assiduously. And as for Melly, why, Melly is a cousin. I have known her since she was a babe."

"It may have escaped your attention, but Melly is no longer an infant. She is sixteen and turning into a very beautiful young lady. And after gallantly carrying her to the house, didn't you spend the remainder of the afternoon sitting by her side, amusing her, instead of escorting Ellen, along with several other cousins, on a picnic near the river, as had been planned?"

"Well, yes, but Melly could not go," protested Hugh, his blue eyes worried. "I could not just leave her all alone at the house while the rest of us went and had a merry time of it."

Chance smiled pityingly at Hugh. "Not only are you not letting Ellen know that she is no more to you than a charming brat, but you have been paying a great deal of attention to a little minx who learned how to flirt in the cradle and who happens to be *younger* than Ellen." Chance laughed at the expression on Hugh's face. "Dear fellow, I am not at all surprised that Ellen is displeased with you. I think that if you want to win the fair maiden, you will at least have to let her know that you don't view her as a mere nuisance."

Hugh gazed across the lawn just as Ellen dimpled at something Jonathan said. His jaw hardened. He took a long swallow from the tankard of ale he held in his hand. "I believe you are right," he said grimly, and with a determined stride began to walk across the expanse that separated him from his goal.

Joining the small group that contained Ellen and Fancy, after a few moments of polite conversation, Hugh said abruptly to Ellen, "I believe that I promised to show you Cousin Letty's solarium, where she grows some of her rare plants and flowers. Would you care to see it now?"

Ellen looked at him, her heart beating a little faster. After the way he had been treating her, it was on the tip of her tongue to refuse. But something in his eyes, something that she had not seen before, made her shrug and say carelessly, "Oh, I suppose so."

Jonathan stared hard after the departing couple. "Dear me," he drawled with contemptuous amusement in a low undertone to Fancy, "do I scent a rival?"

They had moved to where they were standing a little distance from the original group. Over the rim of her punch glass, Fancy looked at him and asked dryly, "Does it matter anymore?"

Jonathan's eyes glittered fiercely as he returned her look. "Oh yes, dear lady, it still matters."

Fancy regarded him uneasily, but he suddenly smiled with great charm and said gaily, "Obviously I must look to my laurels. I think it behooves me to remind Ellen of her original suitor before she becomes too enamored of the dull, stalwart Hugh. I have been very remiss of late, something I shall have to correct."

His words should have reassured Fancy, should have made her feel that she had thoroughly misread the situation, that Jonathan had always intended to marry Ellen, and that she had been totally mistaken in his excessively fawning attitude toward her; but there was a note in his voice, an ugly expression in his eyes, that made her extremely anxious. Which was the real Jonathan? The charming gentleman she had known in England? Or the dangerous creature she glimpsed occasionally in his eyes?

Deciding to settle at least some of her worries, Fancy took a deep breath and, a little frown between her eyes, demanded, "Jonathan, what game are you playing at? From time to time you have acted, much to my confusion, as if I were your choice of a bride, which we both know was never true. Yet now you seem to imply that it was Ellen you intended all along to marry. . . ." Her words trailed off at the look of haughty astonishment that crossed his face.

"My dear lady! I am appalled that you have mistaken my sincere regard for you as something else. I would not have had something so embarrassing happen for the world." He smiled at Fancy, a smile that was not reflected in his hard eyes. "There was never any doubt whom I intended to marry. Let us just say that there have been a few unexpected obstacles along the way. My plans are the same as they were in the beginning. *Exactly* the same."

Even less reassured by his words than she had been previously, Fancy said mendaciously, "Well, I am pleased that there is no misunderstanding between us."

Jonathan brought her hand to his lips. "Oh, there is no misunderstanding, believe me. None whatsoever."

Wishing she could banish the feeling of unease that had lodged in her chest, Fancy smiled brightly at him and made some excuse to go join the others. For reasons she couldn't explain, she suddenly wanted to put as much distance between Jonathan Walker and herself as she could.

Smiling distractedly at Letty's light comment that Hugh seemed very smitten with Ellen, Fancy watched with growing trepidation as Jonathan began to stroll in the direction Hugh and Ellen had taken. Feeling that it would not be a good thing for Jonathan to find Hugh and Ellen alone, she said quickly, "I think that I would like to see the solarium, too." She glanced at Letty. "Would you mind if I saw it now?"

If Letty was surprised at Fancy's request, she gave no sign. She just smiled and said graciously, "Why, of course." Looking at Constance, Letty inquired, "Would you care to join us?"

Constance pursed her lips, but she nodded and said, "Oh, I suppose, although I cannot fathom what could possibly be so interesting about a room full of plants."

Feeling some of her tension easing as the three of them began to walk toward the solarium, Fancy wondered how this whole convoluted situation was going to end. She certainly hoped that Ellen's eventual marriage, whoever her sister married, would start out much more auspiciously than her own.

At the moment, marriage was the furthest thing from Ellen's mind. Hurt and bewildered by Hugh's behavior toward her since their arrival at Walker Ridge, as well as his pandering to that saucy-eyed hoyden Melly Sinclair, Ellen had finally given up on him. She had worked her wiles on him for better than a fortnight, and all she had to show for it was an avuncular pat on the shoulder and a jovially pinched cheek. Consequently she was very much on her high horse and determined not to weaken in her resolve to put Hugh Walker from her heart even if just his mere presence made her feel as if she had swallowed a crock of butterflies and even if he did look oh so *very* handsome in his close-fitting dark blue satin jacket and breeches, his bronzed face appearing even darker and more exciting above the pristine whiteness of his lace-covered shirt.

Airily brushing back one long powdered curl from where it lay nestled in the crook of her neck, Ellen said tartly as they entered the large solarium, "Are you certain you can spare the time from dancing attendance on poor, dear, *dear* Melly?"

A pleased smile quirked at the corner of Hugh's mouth. Was that a note of jealousy he detected? Greatly encouraged, he felt his heart lighten. Mayhap Chance was right. Mayhap it was time to let Ellen know exactly how he viewed her.

"Oh, Melly don't mind if I don't pay her any heed," he said easily. "She is just a child. I have known her since she was in swaddling clothes, and I felt sorry for her." His voice deepened, and he carried Ellen's hand to his lips. His blue eyes gazing warmly into hers, he murmured, "I would much rather have been with you than spent my time with a child like Melly."

Ellen's breath caught and her eyes widened. "Oh," she said stupidly, wishing her heart wouldn't pound quite so fast in her breast.

Hugh smiled tenderly into her upturned face. "Did you really think that someone like Melly could blind me to your charms, sweetheart?" And he swept her into his arms and kissed her soundly.

Drowning in the sweet sensation of finally having Hugh's lips on hers, Ellen let herself drift, let herself be caught up in the tide of emotions that swept through her. This was where she had dreamed of being, this was what she had dreamed of for weeks, Hugh's strong arms about her, his warm, knowing mouth moving softly against hers.

Ellen's senses were swimming when Hugh finally lifted his mouth from hers. At the dazed expression on her face, he smiled with blatant satisfaction, which proved to be an extremely unfortunate tactical error.

Seeing that almost smug smile on his face and recalling how very miserable she had been when he had paid such marked attention to Melly and all the unhappy days during which he had treated her only to brotherly kindness, Ellen stiffened, and her temper, normally remarkably even, suddenly sparked. An angry flush bloomed in her cheeks, and with a decidedly Ellen-unlike fury, she slapped him smartly on one lean cheek. "How dare you, sir. Unhand me this instant."

Bewildered, Hugh dropped his arms instantly, and in utter confusion he stammered, "E-E-Ellen, sweetheart, what is wrong?"

Her eyes flashing like blue diamonds, Ellen said hotly, "Do not call me *sweetheart*. And I will tell you what is wrong, you, you, *cretin*." Shaking a finger under his very handsome nose, she went on, "You have ignored me for weeks; you abandoned me so that you could sit at Melly's feet; and you have treated me as if I were your slightly addled younger sister. Now, when it suits you, you sweep me into your arms and expect me to fall into your hands like a ripe plum. Well, sir, you are mistaken."

Too angry to be moved by the stricken expression on his face, she lifted up the skirts to her amber silk gown, spun on her heels, and began to march out of the solarium. She had almost reached the door when Jonathan opened it and stepped in.

"Ah, here you are, my dear," he said urbanely as he swiftly took in the situation. The flags flying in Ellen's cheeks and the interesting outline on Hugh's cheek gave him a fair idea of what had transpired, and something snapped inside him.

Jonathan had not liked being banished to Foxfield, and only Sam's threat to name another heir to his own personal fortune had made him give in to his half brother's request. The morning he had been informed of what had happened, he'd been so enraged that for one frenzied second he had almost stormed down the hall and slain both Chance and Fancy with his bare hands. For Chance to steal the woman he had planned to marry! It was an outrage. The most grievous insult he had ever suffered in his life.

That Fancy had never agreed to become his wife was completely forgotten. He had become obsessed by the notion of making her his wife, convincing himself that he did indeed love her and that she was fated to be his . . . someday . . . soon. His initial rage against Fancy had eventually disappeared—after all, she was only a frail female and Chance a practiced seducer; what else could he have expected? He was a man of the world and he was prepared to magnanimously forgive her fall from grace.

But if his half-mad rage with Fancy had faded, he'd had an entire fortnight in which to feed his fury and hatred of Chance and to consider different ways in which to take his revenge against his enemy. A waiting game had seemed the most logical move. He could not stop the wedding, and from Foxfield, it was difficult—nay, impossible—to set in motion any plan for revenge.

Today had been agony for him, and keeping his savage rage in check had tried him sorely. He'd been forced to watch Fancy marry Chance, and he'd had to endure the bitter knowledge that she had already lain in that bastard's arms and that tonight, and until he could do something about it, she would be possessed by the man he hated most in the world. The thought of Fancy in Chance's embrace ate at him like an acid. Even knowing that one day Chance would die by his hand and that he planned finally to claim Fancy as his own bride did nothing to cool his raging fury.

Despite all his eventual plans for Fancy, finding Ellen in this intimate situation with Hugh was the final straw. It was bad enough that Chance had managed to steal Fancy, but he'd be damned if he was going to allow another of Morely's sons to take a woman from him.

Letting fury rule him, Jonathan tucked Ellen's hand possessively under his arm. Smiling warmly down at her, he said softly, "I have been looking for you, darling."

Confused by Jonathan's actions, Ellen stared up him. There had been nothing loverlike about him since they had finally arrived at Walker Ridge, and for him to act now as if there were something between them had her utterly baffled. Sensing that something was not right, but aware that Hugh was watching them, Ellen smiled up at him and asked, "Was there some particular reason you wished to find me?"

"My goodness," Letty exclaimed teasingly as she entered the solarium, followed by Fancy and Constance, "I do not believe that I have ever had so many people at one time so interested in my botanical efforts."

"But Cousin Letty," said Chance as he strolled up, having seen the women follow Jonathan and deciding to see for himself what they all found so fascinating, "your green thumb is known far and wide. Did not Tom Jefferson from Monticello get some plant cuttings from you this spring?"

Letty blushed with pleasure. "Indeed he did—such a nice young man and so interested in some of my rare plants."

Jonathan laid a hand over Ellen's, and at the sight of his enemy, his fingers bit viciously into her soft skin. Ellen gave a small cry and stared dazedly down at the faint bruise already showing.

Jonathan lifted her hand to his lips and pressed an ardent kiss onto the back of it. "Forgive me, sweetheart. I did not mean to clasp your little hand so tightly—but now that I have you, I do not want to ever let you go."

Viewing them, their closeness and Hugh's perplexed expression as he stood just beyond them, Chance frowned. "Is everything all right?" he asked slowly.

Jonathan smiled, a way to snatch victory from defeat suddenly occurring to him. Looking at Ellen, he said softly, "Nothing has happened as yet, but I think that this would be an excellent time to announce our own news, don't you, sweetheart?"

Unbearably conscious of Hugh's startled gaze upon her, Ellen froze, her heart sinking to her satin slippers in fearful anticipation. "Wh-what do you mean?" she stammered, and cast a frantic, imploring glance to Fancy.

There was nothing Fancy could do to help her, even though she did take an instinctive step forward as Jonathan, an ugly triumphant glitter in his eyes, said smoothly, "Why, only that I think now is a very good time to let everyone know of our own coming nuptials, don't you? That was the reason you and your dear sister traveled all the way from England to Walker Ridge, wasn't it? So that you and I could know each other better before we publicly proclaimed our betrothal?" He looked across at Fancy. "Isn't that right, Fancy? Though I am very fond of you, there was never any doubt that I always intended to marry Ellen, was there?"

Chapter Eleven

At Jonathan's words, Chance stiffened and his eyes narrowed as his gaze traveled slowly from Jonathan's smug face to Fancy's dismayed features. Ellen simply stared up at Jonathan, as if she could not believe what he had said. Hugh's breath sucked in audibly, while a startled exclamation came from Letty and a vexed gasp from Constance. Only Chance, beyond that narrowing of his eyes, apparently remained unmoved in the face of Jonathan's explosive statement, yet there was something ominous, something almost dangerous, about his very stillness.

But Fancy had no time to think of him or what Jonathan's news might mean to her own future. Faced with a direct assault, she could do nothing to protect her sister. She met Ellen's despairing glance before looking at Jonathan and saying quietly, "Yes, that's true."

Chance's features revealed none of the numbing shock he felt at Fancy's confirmation, but his eyes traveled even more intently across the faces of those gathered in the solarium. No one appeared particularly thrilled with Jonathan's announcement—except, perhaps, Jonathan. Which meant the bastard was up to something. "Let me see if I understand this situation correctly," Chance began levelly. "Despite your actions to the contrary—and you must admit that you've paid a damn lot of attention to Fancy—there was never any idea of an engagement between you and Fancy? Ellen was your choice of a bride right from the beginning?"

Jonathan's eyes glittered. "Why, yes, of course," he drawled insolently. "Though what business any of my actions are of yours, I fail to see. I have always been very fond of Fancy, and I have always looked forward to the day she would be my dearest sister-in-law." Sneering, he added, "If you, and other gossipy fools, tended to misinterpret my affection for her, well, that is your misfortune. I am just relieved that it was Fancy who caught your, er, fancy, and not my own sweet Ellen." He smiled, a bare showing of teeth. "If it had been Ellen you had trifled with, I might have been forced to kill you."

"You might have *tried* to kill me," Chance corrected him grimly, still reeling from what had been revealed. "And refer to me again as a 'gossipy fool' and I am afraid I might have to rip out your tongue."

"Oh, stop it, you two, right this instant," Fancy said sharply. "This is not the time for your silly masculine posturings."

Ignoring the tense exchanges, Letty suddenly posed the question uppermost in everyone's mind. In obvious bewilderment she asked, "Do you mean that it is *Ellen* whom you intended to marry?" At Jonathan's nod, she said in astonishment, "Why, we all thought— Even your mother . . . But Jonathan, you acted as if—" She stopped, plainly at sea.

Jonathan laughed easily, relishing the reaction his words had caused. Claiming Ellen as his bride was an added complication to his ultimate plans for Fancy, but one that didn't worry him at the moment. It was worth all the additional schemes he would have to devise to reach his goal just to see the dawning awareness in Chance's eyes. It was also rather amusing to be able to put an end to the silly calf love that seemed to have sprung up between Hugh and Ellen.

Hugh seemed to shake himself as if coming out of a bad dream. His gaze, hard and angry, was fixed on Ellen's averted features. "Doesn't Ellen have anything to say?" he demanded harshly, his hands clenching into fists at his sides.

Ellen risked a glance in Hugh's direction, and at the sight of his accusing, contemptuous expression, her spirit quaked. Oh, dear. What was she to do? She did not want to marry Jonathan. But she was not quite bold enough to refute his words, either, or face the certain censure that would come at being labeled a jilt. Besides, she was still furious at Hugh. Who did he think he was, grabbing her and kissing her that way, after coolly ignoring all her shockingly forward ploys to catch his attention this past fortnight? What right did he have to condemn her? There was nothing between them; *he* had seen to that. Her chin lifted. How dare he look at her with that bitterly censorious expression!

Clasping Jonathan's arm even more tightly, Ellen muttered, "Of course I have something to say." She flashed Hugh a dark look, and then, hiding her fears and dismay, she smiled blindingly up at Jonathan. "I would be honored to become your wife. 'Tis what I have always wanted." There! See what Mr. Hugh Walker thought of that.

Hugh's mouth thinned, and brushing past Ellen and Jonathan, he snapped, "My congratulations. And now if you will excuse me, I will leave you all to your happy plans for the future. There is nothing here to interest me any longer."

With that he stormed from the solarium, leaving behind a small silence. Before it became too awkward, Letty blinked and said brightly, "Well. This has certainly been a momentous day." She beamed at Chance and Fancy. "Your marriage and now"—her warm gaze went to Jonathan and Ellen—"Jonathan's engagement to Ellen. How very thrilling. Don't you think so, Constance?"

Constance forced a smile. "Yes, of course it is." She glanced pettishly at her son. "I just wish that you had waited, Jonathan dear, before bursting out with this news," she muttered, her tight features revealing her displeasure. "You know that I like to discuss all your decisions with you before you make them public. And really, dear, it is too bad of you not to have let me plan a special ball where you could have made your announcement."

"Well, I see nothing wrong with keeping the news amongst ourselves for the time being . . . and I doubt Hugh will say anything about it. I am certain that if I have a word with him and explain that our betrothal is meant to be kept, er, secret, for just a little while longer, he will keep his mouth closed," Jonathan said smoothly. He glanced at Fancy and Chance and smiled wolfishly. "I think everyone who needed to know my choice of a bride knows it now. You may still plan your ball and invite your guests. The news that Ellen and I are to be married should definitely have its own festive occasion. Believe me," he went on nastily, "I want no hasty hole-in-the-corner affair such as we have seen today when *I* marry."

"Jonathan," Letty exclaimed disapprovingly. "How rude of you. Chance's marriage to Fancy may have been hasty, but it has certainly *not* been a 'hole-in-the-corner' affair. I think you owe all of us an apology."

Jonathan's eyes flashed angrily at Letty's rebuke, but he bowed low in her direction and said glibly, "As you say, my esteemed sister-in-law, it was rude of me. Forgive me."

Chance noted derisively that Jonathan had apologized only to Letty, and he said smoothly, "It was rude of you, indeed, and I am sure that my wife is waiting to hear your sincere regrets for having implied that there was something improper about her wedding."

Jonathan threw him a lethal glance, but Chance only smiled, albeit without amusement, his hard blue eyes cold and commanding. Under the interested gazes of the ladies, Jonathan had no choice. Swallowing the rage that clogged his throat, he bowed in Fancy's direction and said thickly, "I deeply regret any distress my comment may have caused you."

"Very prettily said," murmured Fancy, wishing this uncomfortable scene would end. Ellen looked as if she were going to burst into tears at any moment, and the distinct possibility of Chance and Jonathan erupting into violence could not be ignored. Casting Letty an apologetic look, Fancy said hastily, "After all this excitement, I think it would be best if we postponed the tour of your solarium, don't you?"

Letty beamed at her. Patting her hand fondly, she said, "Of course, my dear. I understand." Plainly oblivious of the dark undercurrents, she turned back to Constance and said, "Come along, Constance, dear. I am sure that the young people have things they want to talk about."

Dismay filled Fancy, and she barely controlled the impulse to grab Letty's arm and plead with her to stay. Being left alone with Chance and the newly engaged couple was *not* what she'd had in mind. Somewhat desperately, she said, "Oh, you need not leave us. We will come with you, won't we, Chance?"

"In a moment," Chance said perversely. "There are some things I would like to discuss privately with my bride, and the solarium seems like a perfect place to do it." He glanced pointedly at Jonathan. "I am sure that you and Ellen can explore here some other time, but Fancy and I will be leaving in a few days for Devil's Own, so I know you will not mind leaving us in sole occupancy."

Even less did Fancy want to be alone with Chance. Uneasily she said, "Oh, there is no need for that—there will be plenty of time for us to have private discussions later. I do not think we should desert our guests."

"Do not worry about the guests," Letty said with a twinkle in her eyes. "They are all too busy eating and drinking and enjoying themselves to be concerned with your absence. And no one will be surprised if the newlyweds choose to absent themselves from the festivities this late in the afternoon. I shall make your excuses for you." Before Fancy could utter further protest, Letty, with Constance following reluctantly behind her, disappeared through the doorway of the solarium.

"Well, my love," Jonathan said with false heartiness to Ellen, "it appears that you and I have been given our marching orders. The newlyweds wish to be alone." He smiled tightly. "And of course, for today, at least, their wish is our command."

With Ellen clinging numbly to his arm, Jonathan moved forward a few steps to stop in front of Fancy. Sending Chance a mocking look, he reached for her hand and lifted it gallantly to his lips. Brushing a polite kiss on the back of it, he murmured, "Congratulations on your marriage, my dear. I always knew that you were too young and too beautiful to remain a widow forever."

Still holding Fancy's hand, Jonathan met Chance's eyes. "You are a fortunate man, and you should guard her well. Wives, as you know, can be such fickle creatures."

His gaze never wavering, Chance coolly removed Fancy's hand from Jonathan's clasp and kept it firmly imprisoned in his own. "Perhaps some wives," he said silkily, "but not *this* wife."

Jonathan merely smiled. "Only time will tell, won't it?"

Looking down at Ellen, Jonathan caressed her small hand where it lay on his arm. "And now, my sweet, I think we shall see if my mother has managed to keep our exciting news to herself." Supremely confident, he strolled out of the solarium; Ellen sent one last despairing look in Fancy's direction before she was swept along with him.

It was very quiet in the solarium after they had departed. Fancy glared up into Chance's dark face and wiggled her hand in his grip. "You may release me now. There is no longer any need to impress anyone with your possessiveness," she said tartly.

A faint smile quirked at the corners of his lips. "Is that what I was doing?" he asked sweetly. "I thought I was merely holding my wife's hand."

"Do not take me for a fool!" Fancy said grimly. "There is something very ugly going on between you and Jonathan. In each other's presence you are seldom more than one word away from daggers' drawing. I do not enjoy being the source of contention between you."

Chance's eyes rested on their hands as Fancy tried futilely

to free herself from his grip. "What do you mean by that?" he asked quietly.

Fancy made an impatient sound. "Precisely what sort of a game Jonathan was, or is, playing I have no idea. I do know, though, that his actions have led several people to the very wrong conclusion that *I* was to be his bride instead of my sister." She took a deep breath and, unable to keep silent about her suspicions, burst out impulsively, "Are you going to deny that you thought that I was Jonathan's choice of a bride? And that because you thought so, you went to the outrageous lengths that you have to marry me?"

Fancy's reading of the situation was far too accurate, her words cutting far too close to the bone for Chance not to give some sign, and he winced—noticeably. Her breath caught angrily at his reaction. "My God," she said in a fury. "It is true. I had hoped that I was wrong, that you were not that monstrous."

Her words rankled, and Chance's temper rose. "What about you?" he asked coolly. "There were any number of occasions in which you could have clarified the situation between you and Jonathan. You did not. You let everyone think that you were his choice . . . or are you going to pretend that you did not?"

Some of Fancy's rage abated. She would have liked to deny the truth of Chance's accusations, but she could not, and not for the first time, she regretted her promise to Ellen. Glancing away from him, she said uncomfortably, "No, I will not pretend that I did not prevaricate. There were reasons for my actions . . . compelling reasons."

Chance's lips twisted wryly. The lady, it seemed, was painfully truthful, and he would have had to be blind not to guess the reason behind her actions. "You did it for Ellen, didn't you?" he asked softly. "Ellen did not want Hugh to know, did she?"

"She thinks she is in love with him," Fancy answered simply, suddenly very weary. "She was afraid he would think ill of her if he knew that she was encouraging him while near-as-makes-no-never-mind engaged to Jonathan.

And Jonathan's actions made it seem . . ." Fancy stopped, then added tiredly, "The way Jonathan acted around me led her to believe that he had lost interest in her. I am sure she meant to explain everything to Hugh, eventually."

"Instead, Cousin Jonathan, with his usual penchant for creating discord and antipathy, gleefully trod right into the middle of the situation," Chance said thoughtfully.

Fancy sighed, the memory of Ellen's woeful little face and Hugh's frozen expression flashing through her mind. "For once, I have to agree with you. Jonathan could not have timed his announcement more badly. I cannot help but think that he did it deliberately—to warn Hugh off and"—her gaze settled accusingly on him—"to let you know that you had married the wrong woman."

Chance stared at her for a long moment, noting not for the first time today how achingly lovely she looked. The formally powdered hair and soft curls framed her delicate features, making her brows and lashes appear darker and her eyes a deeper shade of topaz. Against her pale skin her lushly curved mouth looked rosier and even more tempting to him than usual—if that were possible. For their wedding, she had chosen to wear a gown of pale amber silk over a cream-colored petticoat, heavily embroidered with gold thread. Chance's breath had caught sharply in his chest when he had gotten his first glimpse of her as Sam had proudly led her toward him and the preacher this afternoon. Staring keenly down at her, aware of the sudden thudding of his heart, he said slowly, "But I do not think that I married the wrong woman."

With astonishment, he realized that it was true. The idea of taking Fancy away from Jonathan might have started him thinking of marrying her, but he knew with paralyzing certainty that if, on some elemental level, Fancy hadn't appealed irresistibly to him, he never would have compromised her and forced her into marriage. He couldn't deny that Jonathan had fooled him and that he hadn't wanted Jonathan to marry her, but neither could he pretend that the reason for his aversion to the idea of Fancy being Jonathan's wife had more to do with wanting her for his own than with any notion of revenge.

The knowledge of his own self-deception did not please him, and a muscle jumped in his jaw. He had sworn, after Jenny, that no woman would ever mean anything to him again. By heaven, he intended to keep that bitter vow. His reasons for marrying Fancy Merrivale might not have been the ones he'd originally thought, but that didn't mean he *cared* for her. He simply wanted her. He wanted that soft mouth and sweet body for his own, and *that* was why he had married her. There was simply no other reason.

Fancy smiled acidly at his words. "You married exactly the woman you wanted, is that what you are saying?" she asked dryly. At his curt nod, she murmured, "How very interesting. Does this mean that if you had known Ellen was really Jonathan's choice you would not have insinuated yourself in her bed?"

A dull red burned on his cheekbones. He didn't blame her for treating his statement so derisively. He'd certainly done nothing to make her take his words at face value, but her open contempt nettled him. "Yes, that is exactly what I am saying," he muttered. At Fancy's skeptical expression, he added tightly, "I would not have married Ellen simply to take her away from Jonathan." He suddenly needed to make her understand what he didn't understand himself, and he grasped her shoulders in his hands to pull her closer to him. As always, whenever he was near her, desire, stark and powerful, rose up within him. He could feel the heat in his loins, feel his staff hardening. Looking down into her face, he said thickly, "I do not want Ellen—for any reason. I want you— in my arms and in my bed."

Fancy searched his dark features, aware, and furiously not wanting to be, that they were alone and that his warm body was only inches from hers. His blunt words conjured up the memory of the way he had made love to her on the bluff — something she'd been trying desperately to forget, to pretend hadn't happened. Recalling vividly the giddy sensation of his body merging with hers, she trembled. No one had

ever made her feel that way, never made her lose control of
herself that way. Until Chance, she had never guessed the
pleasures that could be shared between a man and a woman.
The knowledge she had gained in his arms was both heady
and frightening. She didn't want to feel anything for him but
contempt and fury, but to her great shame she admitted that
she had never been so unbearably aware of another person
as she was of him, never been conscious of the primitive,
magnetic pull between two people—even when she was at
her angriest with him.

But it didn't change anything, she thought bitterly. He had
still compromised her for his own selfish reasons, and she
only partially believed him when he said that he wouldn't
have done the same to Ellen if he had known the truth. And
it didn't change the fact that he *had* thought she was to
marry Jonathan and it was that mistaken knowledge that had
brought about their marriage.

Burningly aware of his hands on her shoulders, Fancy
fixed her gaze on the heavy fall of lace on the front of his
shirt. Painfully she said, "You want me. Is that supposed to
comfort me for having my life destroyed?"

"Is your life truly destroyed, Duchess?" he asked softly,
his hands caressing her shoulders. "Or has it merely taken a
path you had not expected?"

Fancy swallowed, trying very hard to whip up her resentment and outrage against him. It was exceedingly difficult to
remember how despicable he was when he was standing this
close to her and touching her in that mesmerizing fashion.
Even harder to remember all the reasons why she should not
let him beguile her, harder still not to give in to the mad impulse to see if in his arms, she could savor again the carnal
joys he had shown her.

A gust of anger went through her, and she hated him again
for being able to breach her defenses so easily. Glaring up at
him, she said, "Tell me one thing. Did you marry me because you thought to thwart Jonathan?"

Chance's mouth tightened. Trust her to put her finger on
the one thing he didn't want to discuss. He hesitated, un-

willing to explain that thwarting Jonathan might have been his original plan, but . . . What? he demanded angrily of himself. That I do not understand my own motivations anymore? That I simply had to have you? That I could *not* bear the thought of your being Jonathan's wife? And that I was willing to go to any lengths to make you mine?

His hesitation confirmed her worst fears, and Fancy jerked angrily out of his arms. The sheen of unshed tears sparkling in her topaz eyes, she held out a warning hand to stop him when he surged toward her. "Don't," she said thickly. "Do not touch me and do not answer. I do not want to hear any lies."

"What do you want to hear?" he demanded harshly, suddenly furious with the trap he had made for himself. "Bedtime fables for children? Shall I swear that ruining Jonathan's chances of marrying you did not make me do what I did? Or perhaps you would prefer to hear that I lost my head? That I took one look at your lovely face and fell head over heels in love with you? That I could not stop myself from wanting you or arranging, however unprincipled it might have been, for us to be married?" His jaw clenched. "Is that what you want to hear? That I am half-mad with love for you?"

Fancy bit back a sob. That was *exactly* what she wanted to hear, she realized despairingly. But she wanted it to be the truth, not the obviously angry lies that they were. Hurt and furious, she spat, "No. I want nothing from you—not even your love."

Heedless of the anguished expression on Chance's face, aware only of her own aching heart, she picked up her silken skirts and fled. Like a wounded animal, she sought sanctuary, grateful that she passed no one as she slipped unnoticed through a side door of the house and swiftly made her way to her rooms.

I will not cry over him! I will not! she told herself fiercely as she ran into her bedchamber and threw herself on the welcoming bed. He's a disgusting, manipulative monster! And I hate him! I do! I absolutely do!

Having vented the worst of her hurt and anger, Fancy sat up and brushed back a strand of hair that had come loose from her elegant coiffeur. Scrubbing away any signs of tears that may have fallen, she stared glumly around her bedroom—a bedroom she was to share with Chance tonight.

She couldn't, she thought with a shudder, not knowing that he had married her simply to take her away from Jonathan. She had known that Chance had not loved her, known that he'd had some perverted reason of his own for compromising her, but she had hoped . . . Her lips twisted sadly. Had she really thought that there was some way he could explain his actions? She sighed. There was only one explanation, she realized miserably, that would have satisfied her, that would have made the heaviness in her heart go away—if he confessed to loving her. . . . She shook her head at her own folly. Love had obviously not played a part in any of his plans. Lust certainly had, she thought waspishly, he had brazenly admitted that much, lust and the desire to best Jonathan.

How had her calm, well-ordered life come to this? she wondered unhappily. How had she found herself thousands of miles from home and married to a man who at turns fascinated, beguiled, and enraged her? A man whose touch woke passions and turbulent emotions she hadn't known she possessed? A man whose mere smile made her heart thunder in her breast and whose presence filled her with both rapture and fury?

Fancy knew the answers to some of her questions, but she couldn't answer the most important one of all: she was married to Chance Walker, tonight was her wedding night, and what was she going to do about it?

She sat there for several minutes, her miserable thoughts chasing themselves around in her head. She had made a total disaster of her life. And she was honest enough with herself to realize that she couldn't lay the entire blame for the fiasco of their marriage at Chance's feet.

She had *let* herself be pressured into the marriage; she could not pretend otherwise. She could have run away, back to England, instead of marrying him. Of course, there would have been a prodigious scandal, and of course, it would not have been very pleasant for Ellen, but it would have passed. She was, after all, a widow, and everyone knew that widows had far more license than wives or maidens. Yes, some whispers might have followed her, but what did she care? She was dependent on no one. She had her own fortune, and in England, if the whispers persisted, it would have only made her appear a more sophisticated, dashing figure.

I should have packed up my things and returned immediately to Richmond and taken the first ship back to England, she thought grimly. No one could have stopped me, and it is what I should have done. *But you did not,* murmured a small, sly voice in her brain. *You stayed and married a man you claim to despise. Why did you do that, do you think?* Her jaw clenched. I do not know why, she answered herself harshly. I have no idea. I must have been mad. *Mad? Or half in love with Chance Walker?* taunted that sly voice.

Fancy clapped her hands over her ears. This was insanity. She would not listen. She would not allow herself to entertain for a second the absurd notion that she loved Chance. That she felt anything for him but disgust. She had allowed herself to be coerced into this marriage, but she would not, she vowed fiercely, convince herself that she felt any deep emotion for her new husband. Yet she had allowed herself to be married to him.

It suddenly occurred to her that all the things she could have done to escape marriage to Chance in the first place were still true. At this point an annulment was possible. If she acted quickly, she could return to England and, in time, live down the embarrassment and scandal. It wouldn't be easy. But it could be done. But was she going to do it?

Fancy sat there for a long time, a very long time, her thoughts not very pleasant. She would have been less than human if the idea of the terrible scandal and gossip an annulment would cause didn't give her pause, but at some point in her musings, she admitted that if she hated Chance as much as she pretended, if she truly loathed him, nothing, not scandal, not even outright ostracism by all and sundry, would stop her from seeking an end to her marriage.

She took a deep breath. So. She wasn't going to run away. She was going to stay. And be a good wife to Chance? Her mouth twisted. Perhaps. And perhaps not.

It seemed like endless moments that Chance had stood staring at the doorway through which Fancy had disappeared, but it was probably no more than a few minutes. Berating himself for being all kinds of a fool, he finally left the solarium and went in search of more congenial company—anything to take his thoughts away from Fancy's stricken face. He had thought to find Hugh and to try to smooth over the misunderstanding created by Jonathan, but it was Morely, staring off morosely into the distance, whom he found just a few paces away from the solarium.

Smiling faintly, Chance asked, "All alone, Morely?"

Morely jumped as if he had been stabbed. "Chance!" he exclaimed in obvious startlement. "What are you doing here?"

"Well, it is my wedding day, you know. Where else would I be?" Chance replied, looking speculatively at the older man. Morely had been acting damned odd of late, and Chance had the curious impression that something was preying on his mind.

"Is something the matter?" Chance asked quietly. "You seem more than usually distracted these days."

Morely sighed and looked away. "I had hoped it was not noticeable. I have had much on my mind."

"Anything I could help you with, sir?"

Morely looked at him strangely, almost, Chance would have sworn, guiltily. "No, no, I do not think so," Morely said heartily. "'Tis something I must do by myself." He sent Chance a sickly smile. "You know how I procrastinate and am forever putting things off—always waiting for a better time in which to do this or that. But I am afraid that I cannot put this particular thing off much longer. I should have spoken of it, oh, years ago." He sighed heavily. "Somehow the opportunity just never seemed to present itself."

The two men had begun to walk along the edge of the encroaching forest where the shade was thickest. For the first time in his life, Chance sensed that Morely was uncomfortable in his presence, and he frowned. What was troubling him?

Chance was on the point of asking that question when a sudden buzzing near Morely's left foot caught his attention. Chance swiftly jerked Morely to the side. "A rattlesnake," Chance said flatly as they stared at the large, coiled reptile directly in Morely's path. "Another step and my wedding day might have had a tragic end for you, sir," he said grimly as the snake uncoiled and slowly retreated deeper into the forest.

Deeply shaken, Morely seemed unable to take his horrified gaze off the disappearing snake. Finally, though, he looked at Chance and stammered, "W-w-why, I might have been killed. I might have died and no one would have . . ." He swallowed, his eyes fixed painfully on Chance's face. "If I had died," he said softly, almost to himself, "what I know would have died with me. No one would know the truth."

Puzzled, Chance said, "The truth about what, sir?"

Morely seemed to recover himself, and glancing back at the throng, he said swiftly, "Oh, nothing, my dear boy. Just the comments of a silly old man. Pay me no heed."

Under other circumstances, Chance would have demanded an explanation. But since he had troubles enough of his own, he was more than happy to follow Morely's lead. A few minutes later they rejoined the wedding party. Morely's odd words left his mind almost immediately, the memory of the way he and Fancy had parted driving all other thoughts from his brain. Now where, he wondered warily, had his prickly duchess hidden herself?

Part Three

Stormy Horizon

There is no gathering the rose
without being pricked by the thorns.

Pilpay
The Two Travelers

Chapter Twelve

The sound of a door slamming in Ellen's room jerked Fancy from her unhappy thoughts. After a quick glance at herself in the cheval glass, she pinched her cheeks to bring some color back into them and then, putting on a pleasant face, she walked through the connecting hallway to see who had entered Ellen's room.

As Fancy had suspected, it was Ellen herself, a very distraught Ellen. She was pacing agitatedly around the room, and at the sight of Fancy she gave a small sob. "Oh, Fancy! What am I to do? Hugh hates me now and, and, I *definitely* do not want to marry Jonathan." Her beautiful blue eyes filled with tears. "My life is ruined. I might as well throw myself into the river and end it all."

In spite of the drama of Ellen's words, Fancy smiled faintly. "Do you really think that would solve anything?" she asked gently.

"Probably not," Ellen admitted miserably. "But I feel so wretched and unhappy that I want to die."

Wearing a charming pale lavender silk gown, her normally blond locks formally arranged and powdered to a soft, silky white, she looked very young and desperate, and Fancy's heart went out to her. Her little sister might be a bit flighty and, perhaps, even silly at times, but Ellen wasn't entirely to blame for the situation in which she found herself. Fancy had no doubt that Ellen would have been honest with both Hugh and Jonathan—if she'd been given the chance. Unfortunately, Jonathan's actions had prevented her from explaining anything, and Fancy wondered precisely what Jonathan had been thinking of when he had made his surprise announcement. Especially since he'd followed it almost immediately with the statement that they should keep the betrothal more or less secret. Somehow Fancy did not believe his desire for secrecy had anything to do with saving the news for his mother's ball. Jonathan was still conniving, though what he eventually planned she could not even begin to fathom.

Putting aside her own troubles and further speculation about Jonathan's motives, she walked over to Ellen and put her arms around her sister's slender shoulders. Brushing a soft kiss against Ellen's temple, Fancy said, "I know that things look rather bleak right now, darling, but I am sure it is not so bad that you have to think, even for a moment, about such a final solution."

Ellen gave a watery chuckle. "I know you are right, Fancy, but, oh, it hurts so much."

"I know, dear. I know."

Ellen sighed heavily and reluctantly left Fancy's comforting embrace. "What am I going to do?" she asked forlornly as she wandered around the room. Her eyes met Fancy's. "I cannot marry Jonathan," she said quietly. "Even if I did not love Hugh, I still could not marry him. He is not what he pretended to be in England, is he?"

Fancy made a face. "No, I do not think so. And I cannot help but feel that he has some devious plan in mind." She frowned. "I do not think that he really means to marry you. I think Jonathan enjoyed the situation he created, but once his announcement had the desired effect—Hugh did leave in a temper—he wanted to make certain that no one else hears of the engagement."

Her face troubled, Ellen sat on the edge of the bed. " 'Tis

all a horrible tangle, isn't it? And my fault. All my fault. I should never have asked you to keep silent. I should have admitted right away that *I* was to be Jonathan's bride, then none of this would have happened." She grimaced. "At least Hugh would not think that I am an unscrupulous jade."

Fancy sat on the bed beside her. Taking Ellen's hand in hers, she said softly, "If he cares for you, he is not going to think of you as an unscrupulous jade forever. He was hurt and, no doubt, disappointed in you, and I am sure he was very angry. But I think that if you give him time to deal with the situation and then try to explain it to him, he will understand."

Ellen looked sulky. "I think you are wrong. I do not think Hugh Walker cares one whit for me." She sniffed disdainfully. "He has certainly given no sign of it this past fortnight—and you know that I have made a fool of myself trying to catch his attention." Her eyes sparkled angrily. "Do you know that he pinched my cheek? Just as though I were an infant."

"You *are* very young," Fancy said with a twinkle.

Ellen sent her a look. "Not *that* young."

"I agree, but did it occur to you that Hugh might be hiding his own feelings and that by treating you like a child, he is able to keep you at a distance?"

Ellen appeared entranced by that idea. "Really?" she asked hopefully, her earlier anger with Hugh suddenly forgotten. "Do you really think so?"

"I do not know. But I do know that until you untangle yourself from Jonathan, you are not in any position to find out, are you?"

Ellen's pretty face fell. "Oh, Fancy," she wailed again. "What am I going to do?"

"Well, if I were in your position," Fancy answered carefully, "I think that I would seek a private audience with Jonathan just as soon as I could. Tell him the truth—that you have changed your mind about marrying him."

An apprehensive look flitted across Ellen's young face.

"He is going to be very angry. And hurt if you are wrong and he really does want to marry me."

"That is a possibility. But, Ellen, what other alternative do you have? Will you let yourself simply drift into marriage with him because you are afraid to tell him the truth?"

Ellen shook her head vehemently. "No. Never." She cast Fancy an appealing glance. "I do not suppose . . ." she began tentatively.

It was Fancy's turn to shake her head. "No. I will not intercede for you in this case. You *must* do it yourself—if not for yourself, for Hugh—if you love him and truly want to marry him."

"Oh, I do," Ellen averred passionately, an ardent light shining in her blue eyes. "More than anything in the world."

"Then your course is clear. Talk to Jonathan. Tell him the truth."

Ellen stood up from the bed and took a deep breath. "Very well. I shall. Right now." A rueful little smile dimpled her cheeks. "Before I become too frightened to do otherwise."

Fancy rose from the bed and hugged Ellen. "He cannot eat you, love."

Ellen didn't look very convinced, but her small jaw firmly set, she gave her silken skirts a pat and then, her head held high, walked from the room.

It was very hard for Fancy not to call her back, not to weaken and intercede for her as she had done most of Ellen's life. She had always fought Ellen's battles for her, but she realized that it was time for Ellen to take charge of her own life. But perhaps I should have gone with her, she thought uneasily. Given her moral support in case Jonathan takes the news badly. Then she shook her head. No. This was Ellen's fight.

Ellen would have been very happy to have Fancy by her side when she finally found Jonathan and asked him quietly for a moment alone. Her heart was quaking in her breast, but he only looked at her for a long, unnerving minute and then courteously took her hand and, placing it on his wine-colored sleeve, began to walk toward the house with her.

Showing her into the large, comfortable study at the rear of the house, Jonathan shut the door behind them. After seeing her seated in a russet leather chair, he quirked a smile and, leaning his hips back against a large cherrywood desk, asked, "Now what was it that you wished to talk to me about, sweetheart?"

Her blue eyes huge in her little face, Ellen blurted out, "Jonathan, do you really want to marry me?"

Jonathan stilled, and one heavy black brow flicked upward in obvious surprise at her question. "I believe that not more than a few hours ago, I announced our betrothal. That should give you some idea how I feel about you," he answered evasively, his mind racing.

"But that does not answer my question," Ellen persevered bravely, her fingernails digging into the palms of her hands. He looked very large and almost threatening as he lounged against the desk. Staring at his face, seeing for the first time the selfish cast to his lips, the faint lines of dissipation on his face, and the cold calculation in the dark blue eyes, Ellen wondered how she had ever convinced herself that she was in love with him.

Jonathan let a small, intimidating silence grow as he considered the situation. It was fairly obvious that Ellen was working herself up to breaking off their engagement, the engagement that was still known only to the family. The question for him was whether he was going to let her do it or not. He'd accomplished what he'd set out to do with his sudden announcement—broken up the budding romance between Hugh and Ellen and made it clear to Chance which of the two Merrivale sisters had been his prospective bride. Jonathan smiled grimly at that knowledge. So why not let Ellen break off their engagement? It had served its purpose, and it would certainly make his plans less complicated. Jonathan's eyes narrowed as he stared at Ellen's lovely face. But it rankled a great deal, damaged his abundant pride, to realize that Ellen no longer wanted to marry him.

Staring down at the green-and-gold painted canvas rug on

the floor, stalling for time, Jonathan asked carefully, "Why is this so important to you now?"

Ellen sought desperately for a way to soften her words, but there was none. Her face unhappy, she said huskily, "Because I am afraid that I have made a terrible mistake. I do not love you and I do not want to marry you."

Jonathan's jaw clenched and rage rose up inside him. Despite the fact that he had no intention of marrying her, he was furious that she was actually turning him down. Throwing away the great honor that he, Jonathan Walker of Walker Ridge, had bestowed upon her. Stupid little chit. If it wasn't to his advantage to let her have her way, he'd hold her to their betrothal, force her to marry him.

Jonathan gave a twisted smile. "Well, my dear, I am hurt that you feel this way. But if it is your wish for our betrothal to end, I see no point in trying to dissuade you."

"R-r-really?" Ellen stammered out, hardly daring to believe that it could be this easy.

"Of course," he said blandly. "I have no desire to marry a woman who does not want me."

"Are you v-v-very disappointed?" she asked softly. "I do not want to hurt you."

Jonathan straightened and grasped one of her small hands, then pressed his lips against the back of it. "I am wounded, I cannot deny, but your happiness means more to me than anything. If you do not want to marry me, then there is nothing else for us to say."

Ellen stood up, and stepping away from him, she said, "You are being very kind." She walked quickly to the door, then stopped and looked back at him. Uncomfortably she said, "Fancy already knows of my decision. Will you tell your family?"

Jonathan nodded slowly. "Yes, of course," he said coolly. " 'Tis fortunate, is it not, that we decided not to make the announcement public?" A cutting note crept into his voice. "It would have been extremely awkward for us to explain to the guests such a short time later that we had made a mistake, is that not so?"

Ellen flushed. "I—I—I would have w-w-waited to tell you, if that had been the c-c-case. I would not have w-w-wanted to embarrass you or your f-f-family."

Another uncomfortable silence fell, and when Ellen still stood there uncertainly, he waved a dismissing hand. "Run along, dear, you have done what you came to do."

Ellen's flush deepened, but without another word she fled from the room.

His lips thin with anger, Jonathan stalked around the pleasant room, the urge to smash something very strong. Little bitch. He should have seduced her when he'd had the chance and then tossed her aside. It would be highly unlikely that Hugh would want his leavings.

A thought occurred to him. Suppose he told Hugh. . . . Some of his rage lessened, and a little smile suddenly quirked at the corners of his mouth. Yes, suppose he told Hugh that Ellen had broken their engagement and his heart in the process . . . and, most important of all, that they had been lovers? Wouldn't that put the wind up dear, old, honorable Hugh? Jonathan's smile grew. When Ellen came shyly tripping up to tell him of the broken engagement, Hugh would be in no mood to listen to her soft words. Jonathan laughed softly to himself as he pictured the scene. Hugh would be livid, and he would no doubt send sweet Miss Ellen away with her ears stinging. Ah, yes, he thought happily, he really should find Hugh and let him be the first to know of the broken engagement.

Unaware of Jonathan's malicious plans, Ellen hurried back up the stairs to her room. Once inside, she shut the door behind her and leaned back against it. Her eyes very bright, she looked at Fancy, who had remained in the room, waiting for her return.

"I did it," Ellen exclaimed on a note of disbelief. "I asked to see him alone and I told him that I did not want to marry him."

"And what was his response?" Fancy asked anxiously.

Her expression slightly dazed, Ellen replied, "He was very good about it. He said that if I did not want to marry him, then our engagement was at an end. He said my happiness meant more to him than anything."

Fancy rather doubted that, but she was relieved the confrontation had gone so smoothly. Yet the fact that Jonathan had agreed to the termination, within less than two hours of the engagement being announced, worried her. "Was he at all angry or distressed?" she asked curiously.

Ellen shook her head. "No. He seemed . . . thoughtful."

A frown crossed Fancy's forehead. "Thoughtful," she repeated slowly to herself. "I do not know that I like the sound of that. I believe that Jonathan has spent a little too much time thinking, and that when he does, it bodes no good for us."

Ellen appeared puzzled. "Why? What could he do to us? And why would he want to do anything to us, anyway? I do not think he really wanted to marry me. Otherwise he would not have acted as he has these past weeks." Crossing the room and seating herself on the bed, Ellen continued slowly, "You cannot deny that he has blown hot and cold on both of us ever since we reached the Colonies. If you want to know what I think, I think that during the journey from England, he changed his mind about which one of us he really wanted to marry."

"I have wondered about that myself," Fancy admitted grimly. "From time to time, he has certainly given everyone the wrong impression about which one of us was to be his bride."

"Well, I do not want to talk about *him* anymore," Ellen said firmly. "You are married to Chance and I am no longer engaged to Jonathan."

"That makes our present situation a little, um, awkward, don't you think?"

"What do you mean?" Ellen asked, her eyes very big.

"Ellen, stop and think," Fancy said with affectionate exasperation. "The embarrassing circumstances under which I married Chance are bad enough, but have you forgotten that we are *guests* of the Walkers?" She made a face. "We certainly do not seem to have been very good ambassadors for our country. Our behavior has been most scandalous, and I wonder how I will ever hold my head up again. First I allow myself to be caught in a most shockingly compromising position, and now you have broken your engagement to the family heir. I think that Sam and Letty Walker will be most pleased to see the last of us."

"Oh. I had not thought of that," Ellen said uneasily. "It is going to be extremely uncomfortable, isn't it? Whatever shall we do?"

"Just as we always have," Fancy replied gloomily, "muddle on through and make the best of the situation." She smiled faintly at Ellen. "You, of course, will come to Devil's Own with me." Patting Ellen's hand comfortingly, she added, "I shall be happy of your company in my new home."

"But what about your husband? Do you think Chance will feel the same?"

Fancy's smile faltered. "Quite frankly, my dear, I really do not care whether Chance feels the same or not. You are my sister, my only living relative, not to mention my ward and my responsibility. Of course you shall accompany me to my new home." She forced a light note into her voice. "Besides, it is obvious that Chance has a fondness for you." A genuine smile curved her mouth. "Have you forgotten that Chance has no love for Jonathan? I think the news of your broken engagement will probably please him a great deal and he will *demand* that you accompany us."

Ellen gave a big sigh. "I hope so. I had not really thought about how very uncomfortable it would be for the family with our being guests in their very own home." She fiddled with a scrape of lace that trimmed the sleeves of her lavender gown. "I shall be sorry to say good-bye to Jonathan's brother and his wife. They have been so very kind to us. We have treated them rather shabbily, haven't we?"

"Not deliberately, my dear. And we shall try to do better in the future and make them see that we are not the sort of rude, scandalous hoydens that we have appeared to be of late," Fancy said with a smile. "And now I think that we should rejoin the guests before our absence causes just the sort of speculation we neither one would like."

Arm in arm, the two sisters descended the great, curving staircase of Walker Ridge. Each hiding their inner trepidations behind a dazzling smile, they rejoined the assembled throng. Nearly everyone except the immediate family and Hugh and Morely were strangers to them, but the greetings and smiles sent their way were warm and friendly, and after a few minutes Fancy felt some of the tension knotting her stomach begin to dissipate.

Spying Letty and Constance standing near the huge crystal punch bowl that had been set up on one of the long, linen-covered tables, Fancy and Ellen made their way over to them. One look at Constance's tight features and the scathing glance she sent toward Ellen told its own story, and Fancy's heart sank. Obviously Jonathan had already told his mother of the broken engagement.

Letty appeared slightly stunned, and when Fancy and Ellen came up, she stepped over to the pair of them and asked in a low voice, "Is it true, Ellen? You and Jonathan are not . . . ? Hugh does not yet know, but Jonathan came to the rest of us, Sam and Chance, too, just a few minutes ago and told us that you have broken your engagement."

Ellen flushed bright red. Her pretty face unhappy, she admitted, "Yes, it is true. Jonathan and I have decided that we do not suit." Her eyes pleading for understanding, she muttered, "He is a fine man and you must think me a terrible jilt. But I—I cannot marry him."

Constance's lips thinned even more, and making her distaste for their company plain, she picked up her skirts and sailed away. Letty sighed heavily, watching her go. She turned back to Ellen and smiled wistfully. "I would have liked having you in the family, dear, but I understand. It is much better that you made a clean breast of your feelings now, rather than let things go any further. It was very brave of you and I am certain very hard for you to tell Jonathan that you did not want to marry him."

Ellen's eyes filled at Letty's kindness. "You are n-n-not disgusted with me?" she asked uncertainly.

Letty shook her head. "No, dear. How could I be? Nor do Sam or Chance think ill of you for your actions. My husband was a little startled; he had barely heard the original news from me when Jonathan came up to tell us that you were *not* engaged." She smiled. "From Chance's reaction, I gather that he thinks that you displayed wonderful good sense. He is very pleased with you." A twinkle in her eyes, she continued, "Now that I have had a chance to consider the situation, I think perhaps that Jonathan rushed his fences in making his announcement. Am I correct?"

Earnestly Ellen answered, "It is true that the entire purpose of our trip to visit you was for Jonathan and me to be certain of our feelings for each other. But he had said nothing to me, given me no indication of what he was planing to do, prior to telling you that we were to be married. I was as shocked as everyone else."

Letty patted her arm. "Yes, I rather imagine that you were." She made a pained face. "And just like my young brother-in-law to confound us with his theatrics."

Fancy's eyes strayed to where Constance was talking to a group of friends. "Is she very angry?"

Letty sighed again. "Yes, I am afraid that she is. Ellen did, after all, turn down her son, and she dotes on him, sometimes Sam and I think too much. But do not pay her any heed. Constance is always in a fret about something, and I am sure that shortly she will be able to look on the bright side of things." She glanced at Ellen. "But do not let her actions make you feel uncomfortable. Sam and I do not hold it against you for setting Jonathan straight." Letty shook her head. "He should never have presumed so much, and you were right to do as you did." Forcing a smile, she said on a lighter note, "And now we will have no more unpleasantness. It is your sister's wedding day, and that is all we should think about. Come along now and let us join the others."

Although she had troubles of her own, one part of Fancy's mind stayed on Ellen's broken engagement. She was relieved that everyone, with the exception of Constance, had taken it so well. But the information that Hugh hadn't yet been told worried her a trifle. While Jonathan seemed to be acting honorably and handling an awkward situation with great tact and aplomb, Fancy was vaguely uneasy with the notion that he might take it upon himself to explain the situation to Hugh. She couldn't shake the feeling that finding Hugh alone with Ellen had precipitated Jonathan's sudden declaration, and if that had been the case, she was positive that Jonathan's smarting pride—and she had no doubt that his pride *was* smarting—would lead him to cause more dissension between Hugh and Ellen.

She glanced around, looking for Hugh, and her heart sank when she saw him some distance away from the festivities, talking alone with Jonathan. The arrogant tilt to Jonathan's head and the slightly malicious smile on his lips told her everything she needed to know—that and the stunned, ashen expression on Hugh's face. Her jaw clenched in helpless anger. It was clear that Jonathan had just told Hugh some sort of shocking, ugly thing, and it didn't take Fancy very long to guess what that might have been.

Her eyes hard and bright, she glared across the distance that separated her from the two men and wondered sickly how she and Ellen could have been so fooled by Jonathan's outwardly kind and courteous manner. The man was a snake. He was manipulative and unscrupulous, and she intended to tell him so.

Fancy had even taken an impetuous step forward, when she brought herself up short, remembering where she was. A swift look around revealed that no one had noticed her preoccupation with the two men half-hidden now among the stand of oaks in which they stood. Murmuring an excuse to the group she was with, she left.

Pasting a serene smile on her face to hide the rage in her heart, Fancy began slowly to work her way toward the two men. She was almost at the fringes of the crowd when she saw Hugh, his features tortured and pale, turn on his heels and fling himself deeper into the stand of oaks.

The smile on Jonathan's face as he turned back in the direction of the guests and began to stroll toward them made Fancy's blood run cold. His gaze caught hers, and for a second a dismayed and slightly furtive look crossed his handsome features. It was gone so swiftly, Fancy almost thought she had imagined it. By the time Jonathan stopped in front of her, he was smiling once more, but a smile, she noticed, that didn't reach his dark blue eyes.

Taking her politely by the arm, he deftly detached her from the merry guests and murmured low, "You look angry with me, my dear. What have I done to displease you?"

Fancy's mouth nearly dropped open at his brazenness. She jerked her arm out of his grasp, not really caring who saw them, and asked tightly, "I was watching you with Hugh. What did you say to him to make him look like that?"

Jonathan's smile deepened. He was feeling very pleased with himself, and Hugh's reaction had been everything that he had hoped for. Looking at his soft white hand and the perfectly buffed nails, he said carelessly, "Oh, nothing very much. I just explained to him that Ellen had thrown me over. Why do you ask?"

Fancy's teeth gritted together. "You're lying. He would not have looked as he did if *all* you had told him was that you were no longer engaged to Ellen. What did you tell him? I demand to know."

Jonathan looked haughtily down his nose at her, annoyed that she had seen him with Hugh—and Hugh's great distress. "I am afraid that the excitement of the day has been too much for you, and that you are overwrought and misinterpreted what you saw," he said calmly. "Now, if you will excuse me?"

Fancy did not remember much of the remainder of the day. She knew she smiled and talked with many people, catching a glimpse of Chance, Ellen, and the others here and there, although she never did spy Hugh again. By the time the last guest had left and she was finally alone in her bedchamber once more, she was utterly exhausted—and miserable.

Tonight was her wedding night, and in just a few minutes she very much feared that her husband—her darkly charming, conniving, unprincipled, and utterly fascinating husband—was going to walk through the doorway and demand his conjugal rights. She prayed that for once Chance would show some restraint and consideration and *not* attempt to consummate their marriage tonight. She was hurt and angry; her spirits were in complete disarray and her defenses were in shambles; but worst of all, just the thought of Chance, of his intoxicating kisses and passionate possession, made her blood race and her heart, normally a very reliable organ, pound with excitement. She was thoroughly unnerved by her reaction just to the thought of making love with him. Attempting to shore up her crumbling defenses, she reminded herself angrily of every sin he had committed against her, deliberately fueling her rage and resentment.

Unaware of the passing time, she paced restlessly around her bedchamber, and the frothy confection of blond lace and pale gold silk that constituted her nightgown surged and billowed around her ankles with every step she took. Her hair had been brushed free of all powder and fell in soft coffee brown waves halfway down her back, the flickering candlelight glinting on the occasional red-gold strand among the dark mass.

Watching her agitated perambulations from his position in the doorway that led to the sitting room, Chance sighed. From her tense expression, it was apparent that his bride was not eagerly anticipating his arrival, and his mouth tightened.

Chance was half in shadow as he leaned casually against the doorjamb, his eyes fixed on Fancy's slender form. His arms were crossed over his chest, and while he had abandoned his jacket and waistcoat, he was still wearing the remainder of his wedding clothes. Like Fancy, he had rid himself of any sign of powder in his thick black locks.

After the way they had parted, Chance had not been certain of his welcome. He had fully expected her bedroom door to be barred and locked, and the fact that it was not gave him a tiny glimmer of hope that she had decided to be

... *reasonable* about their situation. That hope vanished when Fancy caught sight of him and, with a voice full of loathing, spat, "*You.* How dare you show your face to me?"

Suddenly relishing the battle to come—and the sweet victory he was determined would be his—Chance pushed himself away from the doorjamb. A crooked and far too appealing smile, as far as Fancy was concerned, curved his lips. "Ah, well, unfortunately, the face comes with the rest of me," he drawled. His smile widened into a full-fledged grin. Suggestively he added, "And it really was not my, er, face that I had planned on showing you this evening."

Chapter Thirteen

At his words, a shocking urge to burst out laughing suddenly whipped through Fancy. Only by biting the inside of her cheek, and reminding herself what an irrepressible rascal Chance could be, was she able to keep command of herself. From the gleam that leaped instantly into his dark blue eyes, she suspected that he had guessed her amusement. Speaking in her most disdainful tones, she said, "I presume that is some of your common colonial humor? You will forgive me if I do not find it amusing."

"Sweetheart, when a woman looks as you do, I would be willing to forgive her anything," Chance murmured, closing the distance between them, "even a lack of humor."

Her amusement fading, Fancy tried to summon up all the anguish and anger she had felt as she had fled the solarium earlier, but it was a futile endeavor. She had faced some hard, unpleasant facts during the time since that dreadful scene between them, and there was no use pretending otherwise. She was married to this infuriating creature with the teasing blue eyes. And despite all the reasons to the contrary for it not to have happened, she very much feared that, if she were not already, she was perilously close to being in love with him.

And yet, loving him or not, she was not about to fall tamely into his arms. He had hurt her and had had things too much his own way for far too long. For her own pride it was important that she make a stand, and she stiffened when his arms slipped around her and he pulled her next to his steel-honed body.

Deftly she avoided his kiss, twisting her head slightly so that his lips grazed her cheek instead of her mouth. "Don't," she said breathlessly, hating the little surge of excitement that went through her as soon as his arms had closed around her. Keeping her eyes locked on the luxurious fall of lace at the front of his shirt, she said swiftly, "We do not know each other very well . . . and I think it would be a good idea for us to become more, more c-c-comfortable with each other before we become i-i-intimate."

Chance snorted. "And I think that is the silliest damn nonsense I have ever heard come out of your mouth, Duchess. In case you have forgotten—we were married this afternoon. And unless my memory has completely deserted me, we have already *been* intimate." A sensual smile curved his lips and his voice grew husky. "*Very* intimate."

Fancy's head jerked up. "And you are no gentleman to remind me of that horrid incident. You took base advantage of me."

Chance grinned. "Duchess, I never claimed to be a gentleman. And as for the other, you were willing; you knew what I was and precisely what I was capable of when you came looking for me on that bluff." His hands tightened ever so slightly on her shoulders. "Deny it if you will, but you wanted me as badly as I wanted you. No one took advantage of anyone."

Fancy took in a deep, angry breath. "You do not have to tell *me* that you are no gentleman. I will tell you what you really are: you are the most arrogant, provoking, conceited, rude, aggravating . . ." Words failed her, and her topaz eyes snapping with temper, she attempted to break free of his hold. "Let me go," she said furiously a second later when her efforts had proved futile.

"Let you go?" Chance repeated with an odd look on his face. "Let you go, Duchess, when I have gone to such great lengths to bind you to me?" He gave her a gentle shake and, his eyes holding hers, said softly, "You are mine. Do not ever forget it, and I will never, in this lifetime, let you go. You are my *wife*."

Fancy continued her struggle to escape him, grimly ignoring the sudden leap in her pulse at his words. Angry at her reaction, damning him for having the power to disturb and, yes, unfortunately, delight her, she fought against the nearly overpowering pull of attraction that existed between them.

She most definitely did not want to want him—did not want to acknowledge the spark of desire that fairly crackled in the air between them. Even more, she did not want him to be able to cloud her mind, to make her forget his trickery that had led to their marriage. She certainly did not want to *like* him, much less love him. She wanted to be able to view him coldly and impersonally, to hug all his deceits and faults tightly to her bosom. And when she was away from him, it was a relatively easy task to accomplish. But when he was near . . . when those glittering blue eyes were fixed on her and that long, mobile mouth was curved in that mesmerizing smile of his and his arms were holding her near to the seductive warmth of his lean body . . .

It did not help Fancy's thinking process when Chance's mouth moved warmly over the soft, responsive skin at the side of her neck and nuzzled the small lobe of her ear or when the close proximity of their bodies made her aware of his rampant readiness to make love to her. To her great dismay, her blood seemed to thicken, she felt flushed, a deplorable weakness spread slowly through her entire system, and she knew that if she didn't take decisive action, her body would betray her.

With more desperation than anger, she suddenly pummeled wildly against his chest and managed to kick him on one knee. The kick caught him by surprise, and his leg half crumpled beneath him, which loosened his hold on her. Fancy sprang free.

Bosom heaving beneath the gold silk and blond lace, her hands clenched into fists, she stared back at him defiantly as he slowly straightened. His smile was gone, and the gleam in the blue eyes made her decidedly uneasy.

"Stay away from me," she said, half commanding, half pleading, as he advanced toward her. She began to edge backward away from him.

"No," he said softly, his eyes fixed intently on hers, "I will not." A bitter smile flitted across his dark face. "I cannot. I want you, Duchess. You have haunted my dreams for too long, and I will not be denied what is rightfully mine."

Fancy's back came up against the wall; there was nowhere else for her to retreat. The topaz eyes almost golden from the conflicting emotions rioting through her, she said desperately, "I will hate you, if you force me."

Chance shook his head slowly, a frankly carnal curve to his lower lip. "I have no intention of forcing you. By the time I take you, you will be willing, *that* I promise you."

"I want no promises from you," she spat as he stepped nearer.

"And I did not want it to be this way between us," he said gruffly, "but I am afraid you leave me no choice."

Before Fancy realized his intent, he ducked, and to her humiliation and astonishment, she found herself slung over his shoulder like a sack of grain.

"What are you doing?" she cried, her fists beating against his broad back.

"Taking my wife to our marriage bed," he said calmly as he strode from her bedchamber and through the sitting room.

Carried ignominiously over his shoulder, her fists and feet flailing with great energy, if little impact upon him, Fancy was helpless to stop his progress. Coolly ignoring her furious actions, Chance threw open the door to her rooms and began to walk down the wide hallway that led to his own.

Her face red, and not just from being carried upside

down, Fancy hissed, "Put me down, you great lout. Someone is going to see us."

"No doubt," Chance replied imperturbably, never slowing
his stride. "And if you had behaved yourself, you would not
have driven me to these, ah, indecorous lengths."

Stunned by his provoking words, she ceased her struggles
momentarily and gasped with sheer outrage. "I *drove you?*"

"Yes," he said with a smothered laugh, "you drove me to
this desperate action, so it is all your own fault."

Fancy fought an urge to shriek. Of all the unprincipled . . . !
How dare he make this her fault. So angry she could barely
see straight, she gathered herself to continue the attack. But
the scathing words she was ready to hurl at him died instantly when, to her utter horror, she heard a door open
nearby.

A wave of scarlet deepened the already rosy hue of her
face, and her heart sank to her little toes as she heard Sam
say, "Oh. 'Tis you. I heard some, er, noise and thought . . ."

"Sorry to disturb you, sir," Chance answered politely, just
as if he did not have a night-clad female slung over his
shoulder. "Fancy and I were just on our way to bed."

"Ah. I see," murmured Sam, amusement obvious in his
voice. "Well, good night, then." And he closed the door.

The hall seemed strangely silent after Sam had shut the
door. Certain that she had never been so thoroughly embarrassed in her entire life, Fancy hung there limply over
Chance's shoulder, wishing she could just disappear into
thin air and awaken in her familiar, comfortable bedchamber
in England. How was she ever going to look Sam Walker in
the eye again?

Apparently not the least abashed to have been found
strolling down the hall with his bride carried like a piece of
booty over his shoulder, Chance once again continued on his
way toward his room. The silence continued for a few more
minutes, Fancy having evidently given up her fight to escape from him—if her passive weight was anything to go
by. Chance found to his annoyance that he preferred her furious and struggling with him than quiet and defeated.

Clearing his throat, he said gently, "Unlike me, you will find that Sam is a true gentleman. Gallant and considerate. Tactful, too. I would not let his having seen us prey on your mind."

"Of course I am not letting the *most* humiliating moment of my life prey on my mind," Fancy said through gritted teeth. "I am far too busy concentrating on all the ugly and *painful* ways that I might kill you to worry about it."

Chance smiled, pleased that he had lightened her mood. He gave a hearty slap on the tempting buttocks near his cheek and said, "Excellent! I would not want you to have been brooding."

He thought she snarled something exceedingly unladylike, but as he was occupied with opening the door to his room, he couldn't be positive. Once inside the room, he shut the door behind them and locked it. Heedful of Fancy's state of mind, he carefully removed the key and slipped it into a small pocket of his waistcoat.

Fancy wiggled uncomfortably on his shoulder, and after taking a few more steps into the room, he shifted her weight and carefully stood her upright. The instant her feet hit the ground, she sprang away from him, brushing back the tangle of wavy brown hair that had fallen over her face. A wary expression on her face, she said stiffly, "Well, here I am in your room. I hope that you are satisfied." As soon as the words left her mouth, she knew she had chosen unwisely.

The infuriating smile that quirked at the corners of his mouth made her long to slap it from his handsome face. She was shocked at the violence of her emotions. She had never been given to such unmaidenly and rude impulses. Yet Chance, by just the flick of an eyebrow, a twist of his lips, a gleam in the cobalt blue eyes, could rouse her to stunning fury.

Leaning against one of the tall mahogany posts of his bed, Chance regarded her as she stood in the center of his room. "Satisfied?" he asked mockingly. "Hardly, my dear. I suspect that it will take several decades, perhaps a lifetime, before I am fully satisfied with you."

"If you find me so *unsatisfactory*," Fancy shot back hotly, "I am astonished that you went to such deplorable effort to coerce me into marrying you."

"Ah, now, Duchess," he replied softly, his eyes warm and caressing on her, "I did not say that I found you unsatisfactory. I merely said that it would be a while before I was satisfied with you. That is something far different."

"More colonial wit?" she sneered.

He shook his head. "No, merely the truth." He looked thoughtful. "You are very angry with me at the moment, and perhaps it is justified, but I think it is time for some plain speaking between us."

Fancy's chin lifted at his tone. "What do you mean?"

A thick black brow flicked upward. "I think you know exactly what I mean, but if you wish me to elaborate, I shall." When Fancy remained stubbornly silent, he sighed. "Very well, Duchess, we shall play this farce out. You are my wife. I intend to be your husband in every sense of the word. This is my bed. I intend to have you in it, and I have every intention of sharing it with you. Now you can come willingly to me, or—"

"You do not really expect me to *willingly* . . ." Words failed her and she glared at him.

He smiled. "Yes, sweetheart, I do."

Lounging negligently against the tall bedpost, his arms folded casually over his chest, Chance looked far too confident, far too handsome, for Fancy's peace of mind. The curve of that chiseled mouth and the glitter in those blue eyes as they roamed appreciatively over her aroused curious sensations deep within her. Sensations she wanted desperately to deny. There was something thrillingly feral and vastly appealing about him as he regarded her steadily across the all-too-brief distance that separated them.

The flickering candlelight from the pewter sconces on the wall caressed his compelling features, making her breathlessly aware of the strength and rugged character inherent in his face. His thick black hair was brushing his shoulders, a lock falling carelessly across one brow. Staring at him, she admitted helplessly that he was the most fascinating, beguiling, *infuriating* male animal she had ever met.

Her emotions in chaos, Fancy remained silent, her hands clenching and unclenching at her sides. To her alarm and shame, she was conscious that underneath all her anger was a growing sense of excitement—that she was actually *enjoying* this confrontation between them. Appalled by that admission, she tried to tell herself that it was mere rage making her heart pound and her blood race, but with a sinking feeling in her chest, she realized that she was lying to herself.

"But suppose you are wrong?" she finally said in a small voice. "Suppose I refuse to fall tamely in with your wishes?"

Chance pushed away from the bedpost and approached her, pulling her easily into his arms. Fancy stood warily in his embrace, and he brushed his lips against her temple as he said quietly, "Fancy, I know that you want to continue fighting me, and a part of me applauds your spirit and determination. But, sweetheart, you cannot win against me."

If his words were meant to soothe her, they did not, and feeling her stiffen, he cursed his clumsy tongue. Wryly he admitted, "That was not quite what I meant to say, even if it is true." He pulled her closer to him, and against her mouth, he murmured, "Fight me all you want to. I look forward to it. But not here and not now."

With his mouth brushing hers, his scent, clean and male, drifting in her nostrils, his arms strong and hard about her, Fancy was finding it difficult to concentrate. Worse, everything within her was urging capitulation.

"A truce for tonight?" she asked cautiously. Dare she risk it? He held the winning hand, even she realized that, but his unexpected offer gave her a way of accepting the inevitable while yet allowing her to have at least some control over the situation. There was much about his suggestion that she abhorred, and under different circumstances, she would have thrown it contemptuously back into his handsome face. But at the moment, it seemed very tempting.

"For all our nights, sweetheart," he promised against her tingling lips. "All our nights."

Toying with the lace at the front of his shirt, she said carefully, "You realize that a truce for the night will change nothing. You have *still* taken gross advantage of me, and I shall probably hate you for the rest of my life."

His lips traveling in a burning path down her throat, he said thickly, "Of course, Duchess. We both understand how you feel about me. What an unprincipled cad I am." Nipping lightly at that tender spot where her neck joined her shoulder, his hands cupping her buttocks to lift her against him, he muttered, "I shall always respect your feelings for me . . . even your hatred."

Fancy's arms slid slowly around his neck, her fingers tangling in the rough black hair, her mouth shyly following the outline of his ear, and Chance's breath caught in his throat. At the touch of her soft mouth, desire thrummed through his veins and his fingers tightened on her firm little bottom.

"As long as you understand my feelings," Fancy breathed huskily, "I suppose that a truce for the hours of darkness would be . . . acceptable."

A great weight, a weight that he hadn't even been aware of, suddenly slid off Chance. With a low sound, half growl, half laugh, he swung her into his arms and carried her to the bed. He instantly followed her slim form into the welcoming softness of the feather mattress, his mouth greedily finding hers, the desire that had been barely held in check bursting free as he lay beside her and dragged her into his arms.

He had sworn to himself that this would be no swift coupling, such as the one they had shared on the bluff overlooking the river. Yet when Fancy's lips hesitantly opened for him and he tasted the moist, inviting depths, he wondered dazedly if he had set too vast a goal for himself. Repressing the urge to fall upon her like a ravening wolf, Chance wooed her with kisses and lingering caresses, his hands moving warmly over her as he reacquainted himself with the soft, seductive curves that had taunted him unmercifully through several long, lonely nights.

Fancy was silk and fire in his arms, her mouth unbelievably sweet as he drank deeply, the curves and hollows of her slender body a tactile delight for his questing hands. He groaned when her tongue innocently traced the shape of his. His breathing was labored, and desire, hot and fierce as a dragon, coiled and twisted deep in his loins as she moved against him, her breasts burning into his chest, her belly pressing against the rigid, aching shaft of his manhood.

Fancy was no more immune to Chance's proximity than he was to hers, and a shudder went through her when his hand fondled her breast and he gently squeezed the yielding flesh. She had told herself that what had happened between them on the bluff had been an aberration, that her memory had been befuddled, that she had only imagined the exquisite pleasures of his mouth and hands on her. But she was giddily aware as his lips slid from her mouth to her breast that in this, too, she had deluded herself.

Until Chance had come into her life, she hadn't known that one could ache for another's touch, that one could burn for the brush of a certain pair of lips, or that one's body could come stingingly alive from the caress of just one particular person.

Chance's lips closed around her breast, and Fancy arched up off the bed, the tug and pull of his mouth on her plump nipple, even through the fabric of her gown, sending a spiral of hot sensation streaking through her body. She clutched at his shoulders, anxious and unbearably pleasured at the same time, wanting more and yet frightened of losing control of herself, of becoming that shameless creature who had writhed beneath him on the bluff.

But Chance didn't give her time to think. His blue eyes full of a primitive hunger, he reared up suddenly and, leaving the bed, began to tear at his clothing. In bemusement she stared at the powerful body being revealed to her, her breath catching in her throat at the sight of his sheer male beauty.

Despite her years of marriage, Fancy had never seen a fully naked man before; her husband had always come to her in the darkness. Watching as each piece of Chance's clothing fell to the floor, she was utterly fascinated by what was revealed. The candlelight flickered and danced over his body as he stripped off his garments in feverish haste, the soft light casting a golden glow here, a dark shadow there. Mesmerized, she stared at the broad shoulders, the play of the strong muscles revealed in his arms and chest with every movement he made.

Chance turned away briefly to dispense with the remainder of his clothing, and when he swung back toward her, Fancy's breath froze. Unable to help herself, she stared intently at the springy thatch of black hair between his thighs, most particularly at the hard rod of flesh that jutted outward from the center. Despite having little to compare him with, she knew that Chance was generously and magnificently endowed everywhere and that he was . . . oh, utterly *beautiful*.

Aware of Fancy's fascinated gaze upon him, Chance felt his body respond, desire tightening its carnal grip on him. The expression on her face made it clear that she found the sight of his naked body not unattractive, and a frisson of pleasure went through him.

As Fancy continued to look at him, Chance did some looking of his own, enjoying the picture she made as she lay on the bed, her pale gold gown in appealing disarray around her, one shapely calf and half a thigh revealed. His hungry gaze reluctantly left that sweetly formed thigh and traveled upward, past the tantalizing junction of her legs and flat stomach, to linger on her breasts, the dampness from his earlier caresses making the material cling revealingly to the firm flesh, the nipple hard and thrusting against the fabric. His eyes could not seem to move from that spot, the need to see her bosom bared to his gaze suddenly very strong.

Rejoining her on the bed, he reached for her and murmured, "I believe, Madame Wife, that you are wearing too many clothes." And he proceeded swiftly to divest her of the hampering garment.

When he had completed his task, his breath sucked in audibly at the loveliness that lay before him. Not even his most erotic imaginings had prepared him for Fancy's fine-limbed beauty. She was delicately made, her bones small and fragile, yet her shape was utterly feminine, from the small, gently rounded breasts to the flare of her slim hips and long, shapely legs. She was the color of palest cream, the tips of her small breasts a rosebud pink and the triangular patch of silky hair between her thighs almost black. Chance found her enchanting.

Shy beneath his gaze, Fancy sought instinctively to conceal herself, one leg shifting to hide that most feminine part of her, her hands coming up to cover her breasts.

"Nay, nay, sweetheart," Chance breathed softly, his hands gently pushing hers aside. His dark head bent, his lips caressed her nipples. "Your loveliness should never be hidden from me. You are undoubtedly the most beautiful creature I have ever seen . . . *ever*."

His warm lips on her breasts, as much as his words, lessened her self-consciousness, and, trying for a light note, she murmured, "Then everything is, um, acceptable?"

"Dear God, yes," Chance averred passionately, his mouth leaving her tingling nipples to trail a path to her lips. "I find you *most* acceptable," he murmured, then kissed her passionately.

Fancy sought for another light retort, but she couldn't think. The heat of Chance's naked body against hers, the feel of his hard lips moving on hers, his tongue plundering her mouth at will, left her flustered and at the mercy of her awakening sensuality. Hazy memories of Spencer's lovemaking, his cool, practiced passion, flickered through her mind. He had never made her feel like this. Never made her burn and yearn for that ultimate joining between lovers, never made her pulse pound and her heart thump, never caused fire to race through her veins.

Lovemaking with Chance was an all-new, wondrous experience. Fancy was becoming aware, for the first time in her life, of the pleasure to be derived simply from touching, her fingers trailing over Chance's back and daringly down to explore his hard buttocks. She was thrilled when he groaned at her naive caresses, elated when her actions seemed to arouse him even further, and thoroughly bedazzled by his unstinting pleasure in her body. He could not seem to stop touching her, first with his hands and then with his lips. Every place in which he touched her, her flesh came to life, wickedly pleasurable sensations flowing over and through her, making it harder and harder to concentrate on anything but the intoxicating magic between them.

"You are a witch, sweetheart," Chance muttered suddenly, his lips traveling from her mouth to her cheek and then her brow. "Such a sweet, *sweet* witch. So very sweet and so utterly irresistible that I fear you have me completely in your power."

Fancy's eyes were wide and luminous as she stared up at him, her mouth softly swollen from his passionate kisses. He felt something stir within him, something more than just desire.

Fancy couldn't breathe, couldn't think straight, with him looking at her that way, his blue eyes hot and intent upon her face. Her gaze fixed helplessly on his mouth, she said thickly, "If I am a witch, then, sir, you must surely be a warlock."

A twisted smile crossed his face. "If that be true—shall we see what sorcery we can find in each other's arms?"

Her eyes locked on his, Fancy nodded slowly, and with a low growl Chance fell upon her, his lips capturing hers in an urgent kiss. Snared by the age-old spell he evoked between them, she returned his kiss with equal fervor, the fire in her loins flaring higher and hotter with every second.

He kissed her a long time, his lips hard and hungry on hers, his tongue bold and plundering. She gloried in her body's wild response to him, the trembling of her limbs, the swelling of her nipples, and the melting ache between her thighs. When his mouth, hot and demanding, settled on her breast and his teeth lightly scraped the tender flesh, an arrow of sharp delight speared through her, making her gasp and arch up under his caress. She was dazed at her reaction, the ache in her belly and between her legs becoming fiercer, more demanding, the need to have it assuaged dominating her thoughts.

Helplessly she twisted against him, her hands gripping his hair as he fed at her breast, her legs moving erratically on the mattress. She wanted . . . she wanted him to take her again to that exquisite pinnacle they had shared on the bluff.

As his hand slid slowly down her body, her breathing quickened, and when he touched her, when his fingers parted that secret flesh between her thighs and began to probe the damp heat he found there, Fancy moaned aloud her pleasure. She had no thought of denying him, no thoughts of shyness or modesty. The feelings, the dizzying sensations, he created as he effortlessly brought her to the peak made her oblivious of all but what he was doing to her and how very much she wanted it to continue.

It was a powerful storm he brewed within her with every caress and kiss he lavished upon her welcoming flesh. Her entire body was taut with longing, every nerve yearning for the final phase of these sweet teasings. Fancy's hands roamed over him with increasing wantonness. She grazed the tiny hard buds of his nipples with her fingertips, explored the lean length of his back and the shape of his buttocks, his ragged, encouraging sounds driving her to finally seek and touch the rigid bar of flesh that so fascinated her.

Her caress was light, almost shy, but it sent Chance to the edge. There was a wildness, a feral demand, in his movements as his mouth crushed hers, his fingers delving deeper and more urgently into her. Lost in her own erotic world, Fancy reveled in his reaction, welcomed the frantic stoking of the fire that raged within her, her thighs instinctively splaying farther apart and her tongue meeting the warm invasion of his.

Unable to bear her gentle, uncertain touches a second longer, afraid he was going to shame himself, Chance muttered something—an imprecation, a warning, and slid swiftly between the heat of her thighs. He lifted her and with a muffled groan buried himself in her softness. Wedged tightly in her silken sheath, he trembled, the pleasure so sweet, so fierce, that he thought he would explode into a million pieces of ecstatically satiated flesh. His mouth found hers, and crushing her lips to his, he began to move upon her, the elemental need for completion of this act overpowering.

Mated with her husband, Fancy clung to him, her senses reeling, her body ardently dilated and filled with him. Dazed by the voluptuous sweetness of this joining, she arched and writhed beneath his driving body, matching his increasingly frantic rhythm, and, oh, the pleasure. Everything—Chance's scent, the deeply erotic sensation of skin sliding against skin, the hungry, almost desperate kisses—was so wonderful, so exciting, so thrilling, that the sudden clenching and wild throbbing deep within her tore a soft, surprised scream of ecstasy from her.

Chance fought to prolong the pleasure, fought to avoid that final burst, but at the sound of Fancy's cry, and the violent clasping of her flesh around his, he lost the battle with himself and plunged blissfully into that waiting cloud of scarlet delight.

Chapter Fourteen

At that particular moment, just down the hall from Fancy and Chance, there was nothing blissful for Morely Walker as he sat in Sam's sitting room, enjoying a last snifter of brandy before seeking his own quarters in another wing of the house.

For more than thirty years Morely had wrestled with his terrible suspicions about the circumstances surrounding Chance's birth, and his conscience bit at him every time he saw Sam and Letty with Chance. But he'd allowed his uncertainties to seal his lips—that and the fear of unnecessarily ringing down a nasty, *nasty* scandal. Today's incident with the rattlesnake, coupled with his illness last winter, had changed all that. It had suddenly become clear to him that if he were to die, there would be no one else who knew that Chance was more than likely the legitimate son of Sam and Letty Walker and that Constance had tried to kill their infant son. If he died, that knowledge went to the grave with him, and this he could not allow to happen. His own mortality had stared him in the face this afternoon, and he knew that no matter what Sam and Letty might think of him for holding his tongue all these years, he had to speak out or damn himself as the blackest coward in the colony of Virginia.

It wasn't supposed to have worked out this way, he thought glumly. When he had first picked up the infant Chance on the bluff all those years ago, he had known exactly what he was going to do: get the baby to a place of safety and the instant Sam returned from Philadelphia to Walker Ridge lay the whole affair in Sam's lap. He would not even have had to give voice to his uneasy conviction that Sam's stepmother had conspired to murder an innocent babe; he would have been able to recite the bare facts of what he knew and what he'd done, give Sam the knitted blue-and-white blanket the baby had been wrapped in, and then leave everything in Sam's capable hands. Sam would have known what to do. But all unknowingly Sam had confounded his simple plan by returning to Walker Ridge before him and leaving immediately for England with Letty . . . for four long, interminable years. Years in which Morely had uneasily watched Andrew and Martha grow inordinately fond of the baby they were only supposed to have had the care of for a few weeks, a month at the most. Years in which Chance had grown from a squalling infant to a chubby-legged charmer who adored his "Papa Andrew" and "Mama Martha," while Morely had wrestled constantly with himself, wondering if his suspicions were true or just precisely that—suspicions.

Morely had many times considered writing to Sam, but whenever he had finally brought himself to the mark and sat down to actually commit to paper the distinct possibility that this child whom Sam and Letty had no idea even existed was their very own offspring, his courage had failed. His convoluted conjectures weren't something he felt comfortable attempting to put on paper, and there was the fact that letters continually went astray. Who knew whose hands the possibly damning information might fall into? If the letter even reached its destination. Besides, with every month that had passed he had told himself that surely the next ship from England would bring word of Sam's planned return to Virginia and then he'd be able to tell Sam in person. But months had become years, and Morely's dilemma had only increased. He'd told himself that he was doing the right thing, waiting for Sam's return. It was best, he had consoled himself, for there not to be anything put on paper about the ugly crime he suspected had taken place. What if he were wrong? What if Chance *was* simply a by-blow of Sam's? Sam wouldn't take kindly to Morely throwing proof of his infidelity in his face. And Morely owed everything to Sam.

Morely was a good man, a simple man, but he wasn't a strong one. He was, unfortunately, indecisive, inclined to vacillation and easily swayed, and all of those traits had combined to create his current, painful dilemma.

Staring across at Sam, as the other man sat relaxed in a comfortable chair covered in a plum-and-gray canvas-stitch embroidery, Morely grew even glummer. Sam was his best friend in the world. Because of Sam and Sam's belief in him, he was now a wealthy planter in his own right; he had a loving wife and a family any man would be proud of, and he owed it all to Sam. And how have I repaid him? he mused bitterly. By taking the coward's way out and keeping silent about my certainty that Chance is a twin to the infant buried in the family graveyard.

What he suspected about Chance was never far from Morely's mind, especially when he was with Chance or at Walker Ridge with Sam and Letty. Today had been no different; he had been happy to see Chance marry the Englishwoman, but his happiness had been tinged by regret and uneasiness. Bitter, bitter regret that in the beginning he had not been bold enough to write Sam in England about finding the infant on the bluff and great uneasiness about the future. His own death aside, the situation was becoming even more complicated; no doubt Chance and Fancy would have children. He had struggled with this same question when Chance had married Jenny, but he had convinced himself to wait until a child was actually on the way. He considered doing the same now, simply waiting to see what the future held, but after the incident with the snake, his conscience nagged at him unbearably. The knowledge that Sam and Letty were both growing older with every passing day lent a new urgency to his dilemma. Was he willing to keep his mouth shut forever? Deny not only Sam and Letty the knowledge that Chance might be their son, but also the joy of watching their grandchildren grow?

I did my best, Morely told himself unhappily. Didn't I make certain that Sam and Letty were a large part of Chance's life? Didn't I foster a relationship between them? And haven't I always denied that Chance was mine? Didn't I pray that Sam or Letty would demand to know more about Chance? Haven't I longed and looked for a clear opportunity to arise for me to tell what I knew? And haven't I always done my best for the boy? Convinced Sam to take an interest in the fine young man Chance has become? And scrupulously told what I could of the truth about Chance's parentage? Have I ever denied that he was a Walker?

Morely's thoughts gave him little comfort, and again he reminded himself that he'd never planned for this to happen, but somehow . . . somehow events had conspired against him and, he admitted wearily, he had often found it easier to drift than to speak up, especially when to speak up was going to cause a great rift in the family—no matter what the truth was.

Morely took a deep draft of his brandy, getting up his courage. He had to speak. And now, when he and Sam were alone, and Sam was in a mellow mood, was the perfect time. Several minutes ago, when Sam had heard the noise in the hall and had returned laughing, explaining about seeing Chance carrying his new bride off like a piece of booty, Morely had known he must seize the moment. It had been a sign. An omen. Just like the snake. He had been seeking a way to gently introduce the subject ever since.

Smiling fondly across at Morely, Sam said suddenly, "You are looking most solemn, my friend. Is something troubling you?"

Morely took a deep breath. He *must* speak. "Yes, there is"—he swallowed nervously—"and it concerns Chance."

Sam chuckled. "If memory serves, it seems as if that young devil is always in trouble or on the verge of it. Full of spirit he is, and I am quite certain that his new wife is going to find life with him an adventure of no mean order."

Some of Sam's amusement faded, and he sent Morely a thoughtful look. "You should be proud of him, you know. He is a fine son, a son any man would be most proud to acknowledge. Don't you think 'tis time that he knows his true parentage?"

Morely met Sam's gaze squarely. "You think that Chance is my son?"

Sam shrugged. "If he is not your son, I would be hard-pressed to fathom a reason why you have never told anyone who his parents are."

Morely took another gulp of brandy. "Suppose there was a reason? And suppose there were *other* reasons why I held my tongue?"

"My dear fellow, you are not making a great deal of sense."

Morely surged to his feet and took several agitated steps around the room. Swinging back to face Sam, he said gruffly, "I have got something to tell you, something that is going to shock you and make you think ill of me. But Sam, I swear on my mother's breast, I never meant for it to turn out this way. I have wanted to tell you, but . . ."

It was obvious that Morely was laboring under great stress. Deeply concerned for his friend, Sam leaned forward in his seat. "What is it? You know that there is nothing you could tell me that would make me think less of you."

Morely gave a bitter laugh. "Oh, I think there is, and I can only say in my defense that I have been guilty, most grievously guilty, of forever waiting for the 'right' time to tell you. I realize now that there is never going to be a right time and that with my cowardly procrastination, I have made a bad situation much, *much* worse."

Alarmed now, Sam stood up. "What is it, Morely? What has you in such a fret?"

Before Morely could answer, there was a flurry of sudden rapid knocks on the door. An impatient look on his face,

Sam walked to the door and flung it open. "What is it?" he snapped.

Standing before him was a young man; Sam vaguely recognized him as one of the Sinclair branch of the Walker family. His young face worried, he blurted out, "S-s-sorry to disturb you, sir, but Jeffers Walker is determined to call out my brother, Nathan—despite all our efforts to stop him. Jeffers is at present waving his sword about and threatening to run through anyone who attempts to interfere." He gulped and added, "They have both been drinking, but Nathan was still enough in command of himself to whisper for me to get you." He fixed big, pleading eyes on Sam's face. "Jeffers will listen to you, sir."

"I am certain of *that*," Sam growled. Glancing back over his shoulder at Morely, he said, "Come along, Morely, I may need your help. We can continue this conversation later. For the present we need to stop a hothead from needlessly spilling blood."

With a sinking heart, Morely followed Sam out of the room. The opportunity was lost—for now. But at least he had started to tell Sam. Telling himself gamely that he would not let his courage fail him again, that he would demand an interview with Sam at the earliest convenience, Morely, as he had done so often in his life, pushed away again the words that had been locked in his heart for over three decades.

It was nearly an hour later before the two men were able to return upstairs. Jeffers, so drunk he could barely stand, had been singularly bent on killing Nathan, and it had taken all of Sam's considerable persuasion to convince him that Nathan, also a bit the worse for liquor, had meant no grievous insult by having foolishly mentioned that he thought Jeffers's sister, Lucy, possessed as Roman a nose as he had ever seen—except, of course, on a horse.

His hand resting on Morely's shoulder as they walked slowly up the staircase, Sam said tiredly, "My God, I am grateful that those days of false pride and quick temper are behind me. And while I have enjoyed all the hubbub surrounding Chance's marriage, I tell you frankly that I shall be most grateful when my house is empty of guests once more." He smiled and shook his head. "Every room is filled, and I cannot deny that I shall be glad to see them all go."

As they reached the landing on the second floor, Sam looked at Morely. "You realize that I do not include you and Prudence in that statement. You are always welcome." Sam sighed. "It seems that we do not often have a chance to visit these days."

Morely smiled faintly. "Pru has already informed me that she and Letty intend to have a nice long cozy visit once everyone has left."

Sam nodded, pleased. "Capital! Most of the others plan on leaving in the morning, and while one or two may linger a few days longer, I think by Wednesday we shall have the house to ourselves again." His face grew grim. "Definitely young Jeffers and Nathan will be sent on their way at first light—with well-deserved aching heads."

A yawn suddenly stretched Sam's mouth. Patting his lips with the back of his hand, he murmured, "I think 'tis bed for me, my friend."

Morely nodded, half-relieved to have lost the opportunity to bring up that stormy night when he had found Chance. But whipping up his faltering resolve, he said stoutly, "Sam, after all the guests are gone, I would like to have a private word with you . . . about Chance." He swallowed painfully. "It is very important that I finish our earlier conversation."

Biting back another yawn, Sam muttered, "Of course. Of course. We will see to it, just as soon as things quiet down. And now, if you do not mind, old friend, I really must seek my bed before I fall asleep standing here talking to you."

The two men parted, and as he wandered down the long hallway toward the room he shared with his wife, Morely told himself that this time he would not falter, this time he would let nothing dissuade him from speaking of those long-ago events. Sam *would* be told, and scandal be damned.

* * *

Lost in the wonder and delight of Fancy's sweet body, Chance would have been utterly indifferent to learn how close Morely had come to revealing his parentage. At present Chance had other things on his mind than the facts surrounding his birth. Pulling Fancy once more into his arms, he proceeded to take full advantage of the truce they had made. Dawn would come too soon, and with it, he was certain, Fancy would erect a formidable barrier between them. A barrier, he thought dizzily as he again sank his aching manhood into her soft, tight channel, he would take delight in demolishing when darkness fell again.

The darkness was too brief for Fancy. Everything was too wondrously new, too exciting, for her to think of anything but Chance and what he was doing to her. He was ravenous for her, and no matter how many times during that long, intoxicating night he took her to the heights of pleasure, he could not seem to get his fill of her . . . or she of him. Lost in the magic she found in his arms, she had had no time to think of the chasm between them, no moment to consider what she would do once daylight arrived and the devastating intimacy they shared was to end.

Despite her first marriage, despite having shared another man's bed, Fancy had never known, never guessed, never *dreamed*, of the physical pleasures to be shared between a man and a woman. Every time Chance touched her, every time his hungry mouth found hers and he delved slowly into her, she was stunned by the powerful emotions, the drugging, honeyed ecstasy, that flooded her. The pink-and-gold dawn was streaking against the brightening sky before Chance finally let her fall into a sweetly exhausted slumber. Her body ached in a way she had never before experienced, yet it was such a delicious ache, such a delightfully wicked ache, that she smiled as her eyes closed.

But daylight brought a whole host of problems for her, and as Fancy slipped deeper and deeper into sleep she was conscious of a niggling unease. Even in sleep a little frown formed on her forehead. What was it? What could possibly disturb her feeling of blissful satisfaction? Her bemused fascination with her new husband? What could dare shatter her thrill of anticipation for the future that shimmered beneath all the other emotions Chance had aroused?

Chance watched her as she slept, a sated, silly smile on his handsome face. She was everything he had ever dreamed of, everything he had ever wanted in a woman, in a wife. At that moment, he didn't care a farthing that he had gained her hand by outright trickery and blunt coercion. She was *his*.

Gently he brushed back a strand of gleaming dark brown hair that cascaded across her face, marveling at how lovely she was to him, even in sleep. Her long, curly lashes lay like great dark fans upon her cheeks; the faintest hint of pink tinted those same delicate cheekbones, and her mouth was slightly swollen and still rosy from his passionate kisses. As he stared at her, memorizing her every feature, something piercingly sweet knifed through the region of his heart and Chance's breath caught in his throat.

He was, he realized, happier than at any other time in his life—and his happiness, his future, his entire world, seemed to have come down to this one slim woman. Not even when he had married Jenny had he felt this wild delight, this lazy contentment, this powerful, eager anticipation for what life would hold for him, married to Fancy. And it worried him. A great deal.

Some of his pleasure faded and a scowl began to form on his face. It was dangerous, damnably so, what he was feeling for Fancy. He had sworn after Jenny's death never to let another woman have power over him. Time and again in the years since those pain-filled terrible days following the discovery of Jenny's infidelity and suicide, he had reminded himself of the agony she had inflicted upon him, and had fiercely renewed his vow never to love again, never to give his heart to a little pair of careless feminine hands—no matter how tempting.

He took a deep breath. It wasn't love that he felt for his new bride, he told himself stoutly. Of course, he had a *fondness* for her—he wasn't without feelings—and she did delight him. And please him. And satisfy him—utterly. And she would continue to do so, he decided grimly, as long as he kept his heart safe from her destructive grasp.

Mollified by his reasoning, Chance settled one long arm possessively over Fancy, a smile lurking at the corners of his mouth, and dozed contentedly.

Though she slept deeply, Fancy's frown did not abate, nor did that feeling of unease go away. It hovered just at the edges of her mind, never quite showing itself yet making its uncomfortable presence felt. Only some hours later, as she was slowly waking, did the nameless, relentless niggle reveal itself, and everything that she had pushed away, all those volatile, hurtful emotions and dark suspicions she had deliberately ignored when she had agreed to Chance's truce the night before, suddenly came rushing back.

Still half-asleep, she gave a little moan, shaking her head in vehement denial. Oh, she couldn't have been so stupid. Surely she had not agreed to that ridiculous truce of his? It would be, she realized sickly, impossible to keep. What had she been thinking of? Her mouth curved bitterly. Oh, she knew what she had been thinking of—she'd been foolishly thinking of Chance's kisses, his embrace, the wild, wondrous feelings he evoked within her . . . and just look where it had led her.

She buried her head deeper into the pillows, trying to escape from the unpleasant thoughts that were racing through her brain. But it was useless. Like stinging wasps, they bedeviled her until she conceded painfully that it was folly to think she would be able to hold Chance at a distance and revile him during the day and then at night come sweetly into his arms—no matter how very much she wanted to be in his embrace. And she admitted not very happily that she *did* want to be clasped passionately in those strong arms. She squirmed with shame at that admission. How *could* she be so base? So at the mercy of emotions she hadn't even known she possessed?

Attempting to keep Chance's vile truce, even for a short while, was fraught with all sorts of pitfalls. Continuing this farce of daytime hostility and nighttime loving belittled and made a mockery of her deepest emotions. And she had been a fool to think otherwise.

Ashamed of her own weakness, resentful that she had allowed Chance to brush aside her very real reservations, and thoroughly miserable at the trap she had dug for herself, Fancy finally opened her eyes. It didn't help that the first thing she saw was her despicable husband grinning down at her.

"Good morning, Duchess," Chance said softly, his eyes resting warmly on her face.

Fancy jerked upright and, clutching the sheet protectively across her bosom, scooted as far away from him as the bed would allow. Brushing back a swath of tumbled curls, she snarled, "Do not call me *Duchess*. In case you have forgotten, we were married yesterday and I no longer have *any* title."

He cocked a brow. "That is not precisely true, you know. You now have the title of 'Mrs.,' as in Mrs. Chance Walker."

Fancy flashed him a look of loathing. "Do not remind me."

Chance sighed. "When I suggested that ridiculous truce last night, I had hoped that by daylight you would realize just how ridiculous it was." He grimaced and, heedless of his nakedness, swung out of bed. Dragging on a burgundy Chinese silk robe and tying the sash, he said over his shoulder, "If we are going to fight, I at least would like some breakfast." He nodded toward a marble-topped washstand in one corner. "And I am certain that you will feel much better once you've thrown some cold water into your face and brushed your hair." His mouth twisted. "Women usually do."

"You know so very much about women?" Fancy asked sarcastically. "Strange, I would never have guessed it."

Chance shrugged. Ignoring her, he walked over to a velvet rope and gave it a sharp yank.

Reluctantly deciding that there was much sense in what Chance had said, Fancy found her wrapper and gown and hastily slipped into the garments. The clothing made her feel better, and just as her infuriating husband had suggested, she felt even better once she had washed her face and ruthlessly applied his brush to her tangled curls.

Chance, his broad shoulders propped against one of the bedposts, had watched her in silence and, once she was done, had given her a mocking little bow and proceeded with his own morning ablutions. Staring resentfully as he vigorously splashed water all over the marble top and then ran the brush swiftly through his black hair, Fancy decided that it was palpably unfair for him to look so handsome with such little effort. She was certain she looked a perfect hag, while he . . . Reminding herself fiercely that it was Chance's dark charms that had gotten her into this situation in the first place, Fancy resolutely dragged her gaze away from his handsome form.

Her chin set at a pugnacious angle, she said stiffly, "I realize that last night was entirely my fault. I should never have allowed myself to—"

"Be swept off your feet by my wicked charm?" Chance drawled with a wicked gleam in his dark blue eyes.

Fancy threw him a look. "Precisely," she said through gritted teeth. "It shan't happen again."

"How can you be so certain?" he asked softly as he approached her.

Fancy threw out a commanding hand. "Stop. Right where you stand." When he obeyed, she took a deep breath and said tightly, "It will not happen again, because you are going to give me your word as, as a gentleman, that until *I* feel easy in my mind about our marriage, you will not take unfair advantage me."

Chance stared at her, thunderstruck. "You want *my* word that I will not attempt to make love to you again?" he asked in tones of stupefaction.

Fancy nodded. "Your word as a gentleman."

"And if I do not give it?" There was a decided edge to his voice.

Fancy swallowed. "There is nothing I can do to stop you from forcing me into your bed—whether you use brute strength or, or . . ." She hesitated, and a blush stained her cheeks. "Or the powers of persuasion you subjected me to last night. But the result would be the same. I would grow to hate you, and any hope of our marriage eventually being anything other than a living hell for both of us would be lost."

"I see," Chance said slowly, his eyes narrowed as he stared at her. "You are telling me that I can take you to bed, but that if I do, you will hate me."

Fancy nodded again.

He smiled grimly. "Then tell me what is different from our present situation? Haven't you already stated that you hate me? What will I gain—other than sleepless nights and a lonely bed?"

She regarded him uncertainly. "My respect?"

"It is not your damned respect, Madame Wife, that I am particularly interested in."

"Well, you should be," Fancy flashed back, an angry sparkle in her eyes. "You forced me into this marriage by knavery and trickery. How can I have any other feeling for you but disgust and hatred? And now, all I am asking is that you give us time to learn to respect and care for each other."

Her words were not what Chance wanted to hear, but there was enough logic in them to give him pause. The last thing he wanted, especially after last night, was to sleep alone, but he was aware that Fancy had a certain amount of right on her side and that, except for those sleepless nights and a lonely bed, he had nothing to lose by giving her the promise she wanted, and perhaps much to gain.

"How long would you hold me to my promise?" he asked abruptly.

"How long?"

He shot her an impatient look. "Yes. If I agree to your terms, how long am I to be denied my conjugal rights. A week? A month? A year?"

Fancy swallowed nervously, hardly daring to believe that he was actually considering doing what she wanted. "I do not know," she answered. "It would depend upon—"

"Upon your deciding *not* to hate me anymore?" he asked dryly. At her nod, he added, "Considering your oft-stated opinion of me, I doubt a decade would be long enough for you to change your mind. Unfortunately for you, I am not willing to wait that long. A month. I will give you my promise that I will not compel you to suffer my lovemaking for one month." His voice hardened. "But you *will* share my bed."

Fancy opened her mouth to hotly refute his words, but Chance said harshly, "No. There is no further argument. I agree to abide by your absurd terms for one month. Do not, Madame Wife, push me for more or I may change my mind and not grant you even that."

Fancy fought back her anger at his high-handed manner, but she realized unhappily that she had gained as much as she was going to—at least for now.

"Very well," she said stiffly. "A month."

"And you will sleep in my bed during this blasted month of abstinence."

It was not a question. While Fancy would have liked to eliminate that particular provision, she knew from the expression on his face that it would not be wise to carry the discussion any further.

"And I will sleep in your bed."

He gave her a curt nod, his face grim and set. "Then we agree. You have your damn month and—"

A timid knock on the door interrupted him. Muttering a curse under his breath, he strode in that direction. After fumbling for the key, he unlocked the door and, flinging it wide, snarled, "What?"

Annie Clemmons, pressed into light service because of the influx of so many guests for the wedding, stood warily in the hallway, a large silver tray with morning refreshments held in her hands. At Chance's gruff words, her expression of wariness increased and she said uncertainly, "I believe that you rang, sir?"

Chance let his features relax. Stepping back, he said in

more normal tones, "Oh, I am sorry. I had forgotten. Please, come in. You can put the tray on that table over there."

Precisely what it was that made Annie glance down at Chance's bare feet, she never knew, but glance down she did.

Her gaze widened in mute terror at the sight of those six toes on Chance's right foot, and with a muffled shriek she dropped the tray.

Staring at him as if he were the Devil incarnate, she muttered, "Dear merciful God! It is as I feared—you *are* alive!"

Chapter Fifteen

As Chance stared at her in amazement, Annie, a fist to her mouth, eyes wide and fearful, suddenly spun on her heel and disappeared down the hall. His gaze dropped to the mess on the floor in front of him, and shaking his head, he stepped back inside his room and shut the door.

Glancing over at Fancy, he muttered, "Not only does my wife object to me, but it seems that I now have the remarkable ability to terrify elderly women simply by speaking to them." His mouth twisted. "Although in Annie's case, she has *always* looked at me as if she expected me to sprout a second head."

"Do not be silly," Fancy said, still ruffled by the outcome of their discussion—if it could be called that. "You fairly shouted at her when you first opened the door. No wonder you startled her."

Chance frowned. "She was not startled," he said slowly. "She was terrified ... but not until she looked ..." He glanced downward. Now what the devil had disturbed her so? He opened the door and stood there studying the floor. Nothing out of the ordinary, except for the scattered items from the tray, met his eye. His frown deepened. Something had certainly frightened her. But what? His wandering gaze suddenly fell on his feet.

The odd fact of having been born with six toes on his right foot had never bothered Chance, and since it was extremely rare for anyone to see him barefoot, he never gave his extra digit any thought. Could it have been that sixth toe that bothered her? There were, he knew, many deeply superstitious people who were terrified of any physical oddity, certain it was a sign of the devil. He grimaced, nodding to himself. In Annie's case, seeing that extra toe had no doubt set the seal on her belief that he really was a devil's spawn.

Satisfied that he had solved the mystery of Annie's strange behavior, he shut the door once more and walked over to the velvet rope. Giving it another pull, he said to Fancy, "Hopefully this time we shall have more luck getting our morning's refreshment."

"Unless you terrify the next servant."

Chance grinned at her. "It is not a habit of mine, but to ensure that it does not happen again, I think that I shall conceal the probable cause of Annie's fear."

Fancy looked puzzled, even more so when Chance found a pair of leather slippers near the bed and started to put them on. "Your feet?" she demanded, incredulous. "Annie was frightened by your feet?"

"Considering what a splendid figure of manhood I am, I know that you find such a thought shocking. But yes, I very much suspect that it was my feet, specifically my sixth toe, that overset her."

"A sixth toe?" Fancy asked, lively curiosity banishing some of her bad mood. "You have six toes?"

With an expression of long suffering, Chance sat on the bed and, after taking off one slipper, lifted his right leg and wiggled the six toes for her.

"Oh my," Fancy exclaimed with a gurgle of laughter. "You really do have six toes. I never noticed."

"Perhaps," Chance purred, "that is because you have generally been interested in another part of my anatomy?"

* * *

While Fancy and Chance were sparring in his bedchamber, Annie had reached her destination: Constance's suite of rooms. Constance had woken some time ago and was sitting up in her bed, enjoying a second cup of coffee, when Annie burst into the room.

Her eyes dilated, her face a pasty white, Annie exclaimed, "It is as I always feared: *he is alive*."

Still feeling rather disgruntled over Fancy's marriage to Chance, Constance was not in a pleasant mood. Sending her longtime companion an impatient look, she snapped, "Oh, Annie, do make sense. Who is alive?"

Annie gulped. "Chance Walker."

"Well, of course he is," Constance replied irritably. "We watched him get married yesterday."

"No, I mean—" Annie stopped, suddenly seeing the ground open up before her. She had never told the truth about the night Letty's twins had been born. Never said a word to a living soul. After leaving the squalling baby on the bluff overlooking the river that night, she had run back to the house. To Constance's anxious demand to know if she had taken care of disposing of the infant, Annie had only nodded, too scared and distressed to do anything else, certainly unwilling to admit that she had been frightened off by someone approaching or that she had merely left the baby on the ground and fled back to the house.

All through that stormy night and the next day, Annie had been positive that her crime would be discovered, and she had lived in guilty terror. Certain that whoever had been coming through the woods that night would have discovered the baby and would present it at any moment to the big house, she started and blanched at every sound.

When her worst fears were not realized, she was relieved, if still filled with guilt and curiosity about the baby's fate. Sam's unexpectedly early return and the sudden trip by the entire family to England had been a blessing for Annie. With an ocean between her and the abandoned infant, the time in

England had made her feel safe and had dulled her feelings of culpability over her part in the ugly events of that night.

When she saw Chance for the first time, he was nearly five years old, and the suspicion that he might be the infant she had abandoned on the bluff did not cross her mind. It was only much later, as he grew, in Annie's fearful imaginings, to look more like Sam every day, that the horrifying idea that he might indeed be Letty's child began to take hold on her mind. The fact that Morely Walker was considered to be his father did not calm her growing anxiety. If anything, that knowledge increased her fears, as Morely had been living at Walker Ridge the night of her crime.

For some time now, she had been worried that Chance was indeed the abandoned infant, but it wasn't until this morning, until she had seen those six toes, that she knew all her fears were true. The infant lived. Not only lived, but right under their very noses.

Constance, of course, had never given the infant another thought. But then, she hadn't known the truth.

Apprehensively Annie stared at Constance, who, still waiting with increasing impatience for an explanation, asked curtly, "Well, you mean what?"

Annie's hands twisted together helplessly. She was terrified of speaking and equally terrified of keeping quiet. Her secret had been safe for over thirty years. Why reveal it now? But if she didn't and by some wicked fate Chance's real identity were discovered, Constance would be caught totally off guard. All her life Annie had been blindly loyal to her less than lovable mistress, and all she could think of was that Constance must be warned of the danger.

As quickly and concisely as she could, Annie unburdened herself, ending only after she told of seeing this morning those six toes on Chance's right foot. All through her recital Constance had sat frozen, her face growing whiter by the moment, her eyes darkening with pure rage.

When Annie's voice finally faded away, there was silence for ten seconds. Then, furiously tossing her entire tray and its contents on the floor, Constance sprang out of bed. Wrath evident in her every movement, she approached Annie and, stopping in front of her, viciously slapped the older woman.

"You stupid, stupid fool! I give you one simple task to do and you bungle it. Having failed me, you then have the audacity to lie to me about it! And to think that all these years I had confidence in you." Her face contorted by rage, Constance demanded, "What else have you failed to do? I knew I should have dismissed you and left you in England. I *knew* it!" She took several angry steps around the room. "Now what are we to do?"

Her face smarting from Constance's slap, Annie said timidly, "No one knows but us."

Constance flashed her a look. "You are a fool. 'Tis obvious that Morely Walker found the baby. He *knows* who Chance Walker is." Her face twisted. "And wouldn't he take great pleasure in seeing me brought down."

"But why didn't he tell Master Sam as soon as he found the baby? The master came home not two days later."

Constance stopped her wild pacing and looked thoughtful. "Yes, but we left for Richmond almost immediately," she said slowly. "Don't you remember?" She paused, then thinking aloud, she murmured, "And while Sam was hustling us all to Richmond, to catch a ship sailing for England, Morely must have been traveling to his cousin Andrew's home with the baby." She smiled maliciously. "Sam and Morely must have just missed each other. What a piece of good fortune for us that they did."

Thankful that the worst of Constance's rage seemed to be over, Annie ventured uneasily, "But why did not Morely write to Sam? Telling him of finding the baby?"

Constance waved an impatient hand. "Knowing Morely, probably because he was not positive and because he has an inbred mistrust of putting anything in writing. He no doubt *suspected* what had happened, but he had no proof. Besides, he owes Sam everything. He would not have wanted to jeopardize his own standing by pouring out his incredible suspicions." Constance tapped a finger against her lips. "Yes, knowing Morely and how he vacillates, I am certain that is what happened. He wanted to tell Sam personally, but Sam was far away in England, and while you and I came back with Jonathan the following summer, Sam and Letty stayed in England for several more years." An expression of contempt crossed her face. "After burying her only son, Letty was far too distraught to face Walker Ridge. And Sam, the besotted fool, was willing to indulge her, even if it meant banishing himself to England indefinitely."

Annie nodded. "I can understand Morely not wanting to put such a shocking thing on paper, but why hold his tongue all these years? Why did he not say something as soon as Master Sam did return?"

Constance shrugged. "Four years is a long time to wait to reveal the sort of secret he thought he knew. Perhaps, by the time Sam returned, he was not quite so certain." She suddenly looked more cheerful. "Actually, what does Morely really know? He found an abandoned baby on a river bluff at Walker Ridge, who coincidentally just happened to have been born the same night as Letty's child. Of course, the fact that the baby has six toes on his right foot makes it a bit ticklish for us. There is no denying that the circumstances would be considered suspicious, I will grant you that, but it does not *prove* anything. Besides, who is going to believe that *I* would stoop to such a vile act? No one would credit me with doing such a thing. And Morely knows it. *That* is why he has kept his tongue between his teeth. He suspects, but he does not know for certain."

"So we should not worry?" Annie asked nervously, her expression anxious.

"Of course we should worry, you stupid slut. While Chance's birth date and toes do not prove anything, there is too much coincidence. It would certainly cause talk and speculation if Morely ever did nerve himself to speak."

"But what are we going to do?"

Constance's jaw hardened. "We are going to do what you should have done years ago: get rid of Chance Walker."

"Oh, Constance, no. Can we not just let it be? We have been safe this long . . . and you just said nothing can be proved. Mayhap Morely intends to keep his suspicions to himself."

"You *are* a fool," Constance said disparagingly. "I do not intend to run the risk of the truth ever coming out, or even just the fact that Morely found a newborn baby in the vicinity of Walker Ridge the same night Letty gave birth to a stillborn son. Morely has never fully explained where he got the child—now we know why. But even though most of the family believes that Chance is his own by-blow, if Morely were to start talking . . ." Constance's face grew grim. "Well, it just does not bear thinking about. Getting rid of Chance is the only solution." She looked pensive. "And possibly Morely, too."

Annie's heart sank. Leaving that small baby on the bluff had been hard enough, but to contemplate the murder—and there was no use calling it anything else—of two grown men, two innocent men, who merely had the misfortune to stand between Constance and what she wanted, made Annie feel sick. It was true that they also constituted a possible danger, but Annie did not care. Murder was murder. The merciful Lord had heard her prayers that long-ago night and had allowed the baby to be saved, and at this late date she was not going to undo the Lord's work.

Annie looked over at Constance's set features and amended her thoughts. She might not be able to completely wash their blood from her hands, but she was not *actively* going to take part in the murder of Chance and Morely. Constance would have to find someone else to do the deed.

Almost as if she read Annie's mind, Constance said, "This is not something that we can do ourselves. They are two strong men. We will need help." She took another turn around her spacious bedroom. "Jonathan will have to know," she finally said. "He will know how to handle things."

Not much comforted by Constance's words, Annie said miserably, "He is not going to be very pleased to learn what we did—and you do not know that he will agree to murder."

"When he learns the danger that Chance Walker constitutes for him, I know that my son will not hesitate." She smiled smugly. "He *is*, after all, *my* son. He will not let the major portion of the Walker fortune slip through his fingers. Especially not to Chance."

It was early evening before Constance could contrive a private moment with Jonathan. Because the house was still overflowing with wedding guests, and Sam had wanted to avoid any confrontation between Chance and Jonathan, Jonathan had spent the night at Foxfield. It had been late in the afternoon before he had finally returned to Walker Ridge. Many of the guests had departed that morning, and with the exception of the continued presence of Morely and Pru, the household was almost back to normal.

Constance had sent a note to her son earlier in the day, demanding his company, but since Jonathan was still seething over Ellen's defection and the bitter knowledge that Fancy had spent the night in Chance's arms, he was in no mood for his mother's antics and had ignored her message. His mood had not been helped by the sight of the newly wedded pair walking about the grounds with Sam, Letty, Morely, and Pru, Chance's arm resting possessively around Fancy's waist. He knew that Chance and Fancy would be leaving tomorrow sometime for Devil's Own and his banishment to Foxfield would be at end ... and his plans for Chance's demise could begin to take shape.

Somewhat buoyed by that thought, he eventually went in search of his mother. He found her in her sitting room with Annie, and from their expressions when he entered the chamber it was apparent that Constance's summons had been more important than he had imagined.

"I thought," he said dryly as he settled himself comfortably in a pale blue channel-back chair, "that I was the only one suffering from the megrims. You both look as if you have eaten bad fish. What is it?"

The telling didn't take long, with Constance doing most of the talking. When she finished speaking both women looked expectantly at Jonathan.

Except for a twitch at his temple and the clawlike grip of

his hands on the arms of the chair, he displayed none of his inward fury and rage. Not only had Chance stolen his bride, but now the bastard could very well steal his heritage, his fortune, as well.

Fighting down his rage, he tried to view the situation coolly and methodically. Like his mother, Jonathan saw immediately that not only Chance but Morely, too, would have to be eliminated and as soon as possible—and without raising any suspicions or any finger of guilt pointing in his direction—or his mother's. But unlike his mother, he also realized that there was another source of danger, and his gaze fell thoughtfully on Annie.

Annie had helped raise Jonathan from an infant, and she knew his moods and ways, perhaps better than even his mother. She was not as blind to his faults as Constance, and when he turned that cool blue gaze on her, a quiver of fear went through her and her heart thumped painfully in her breast. She had never, before this very moment, considered herself in any danger, but catching a glimpse of the icy implacability in the depths of Jonathan's eyes, Annie knew that her own life was in peril.

Frozen with terror, Annie watched him as he rose to his feet and, after walking across the room, stopped in front of her. His expression was carefully bland, no sign of what he was feeling evident in his features. But Annie *knew.* Still, if she hadn't seen that one frightening glimpse into what he was really thinking, she would have been utterly disarmed.

A polite smile on his handsome face, Jonathan put out a hand to help her rise from her chair and said, "If you please, Annie dear, I think that this is something that Mother and I must discuss privately."

Knowing it was her death that he wished to discuss with Constance, Annie hesitated, sending Constance a pitiful glance. But Constance, unaware of the currents flowing through the room, waved her away. "Go on. I can tell you what you need to know later."

If she was correct and Jonathan did plan to kill her, there was no use appealing to Constance, Annie realized sickly. If a choice had to be made between herself and Jonathan, there was no question which one of them Constance would choose. Not willing, not *wanting*, to believe that Constance would agree to her murder, Annie reluctantly allowed herself to be ushered from the room.

Light-headed with terror, Annie stood swaying in the hall as the door shut firmly behind her. She might have been wrong about the expression in Jonathan's eyes, she told herself weakly. Why, she had raised him! Surely he would never hurt her. And she had been Constance's faithful companion for nearly fifty years. Constance wouldn't let Jonathan murder her. But Annie sensed that she was only trying to reassure herself, as she slowly, painfully, moved down the hall. If Jonathan wanted her out of the way, then her death warrant had been signed.

And inside Constance's pretty blue-and-cream sitting room, that was precisely what Jonathan was suggesting.

"Annie?" Constance said incredulously, her eyes very wide. "You think that she would betray us? Oh, do not be silly. Annie adores me. And you, too, for that matter. She would never do anything to hurt us."

His hands steepled in front of him, Jonathan said simply, "Mother, you are letting your affection for her blind you to the very real danger she represents. What is the use of getting rid of Morely and Chance and then allowing Annie, a *servant*, to live, knowing that she could expose us? She would know not only about the original, er, incident, but also about the murder of two men. You told me you have already discussed it with her. Do you really want to live the rest of your life wondering if you are truly safe?"

Constance looked uncomfortable. "Well, no, but you are talking about *Annie*."

"And?"

"Well, she is . . . she has been with me for so many years," Constance finished lamely. "She has never given me a moment's alarm."

"Yes, and if it were not for Annie's foolishness, we would

not now be in the position of having to dispose of two grown men."

Constance made a face. "I realize that you are right, but I just cannot bring myself to . . . Let me think about it?"

"Very well," he said grimly. "But do not waste a great deal of time in doing so."

He rose to his feet and started toward the door.

"Wait!" Constance cried. "What about Morely and Chance?"

Jonathan turned and looked back at her, a bone-chilling smile on his face. "Oh, I would not worry about them. I shall take care of that particular problem. You may rest easy on that fact."

The hall was empty when Jonathan stepped into it. His expression introspective, he made his way downstairs, grateful that he met no one else. He needed privacy and time to think, and knowing that Foxfield was where he would have both, he was suddenly glad that he had been banished to the smaller plantation until Chance and Fancy had left Walker Ridge.

Tossing the reins of his lathered horse to a waiting black boy some time later, he hurried up the broad steps of the pleasant, if unimpressive, house at Foxfield. Shortly, alone in the small, comfortable study at the side of the house, a freshly poured snifter of brandy in one hand, a thick cigar of fine Virginia tobacco in the other, he sat in a black leather chair and stared into space.

Planning to murder two men, with no wind of blame blowing in his direction, was not, he decided, going to be too difficult. Though everyone knew of the enmity between him and Chance, it was highly unlikely that he would be suspected if Chance were suddenly to have a fatal accident. Life was hard in the Colonies; there were tragedies every day.

However, Morely's death either just preceding Chance's or very soon thereafter was going to cause a certain amount of talk. Still, Jonathan did not think it would create any danger for him. Everyone liked Morely, and since he and

Morely were on good terms, there would be no reason for anyone even to cast a curious eye toward him. Two accidents were risky, but accidents *did* happen all the time, even in the same family. Perhaps it could be arranged that the *same* accident killed both men? A distinct possibility. He would have to consider it.

It was, Jonathan thought idly as he sipped his brandy, more a case of deciding when and where and how than anything else. It really was too bad that Morely and Pru were not going to travel with Chance and Fancy to Devil's Own. A mishap along the trail would be a simple and swift solution to the problem.

Getting rid of Chance was imperative. Not only because of the danger that he represented, but every time Chance lay with Fancy, there was the possibility that she would conceive a child. An angry white line appeared around Jonathan's lips. If he did marry Fancy, and he had begun to have a few doubts about that, it was going to be difficult enough living with the knowledge that Chance had known Fancy's charms. But he would be damned if he would live with Chance's spawn growing up under his very nose.

Jonathan took in a deep lungful of smoke and slowly let it out. Watching the blue wisps rise in the air, he considered his position. Once Chance was dead, the greatest threat was over. What would Morely gain by telling of his suspicions then? There was no denying that Morely was a soft-headed, vacillating fool—but he knew which side his bread was buttered on. With Chance dead, there would be no point in making a scandal or attempting to implicate Constance. Killing Morely might not be necessary, but Jonathan decided to take no chances. With Chance, Morely, and Annie dead, he and his mother would be the only ones who knew the truth.

He grimaced. Except that he did not plan to do the actual deeds himself. Well, in Annie's case, it shouldn't be too difficult. An evening stroll along the river's edge, a tap on the head, and into the water she would go. By the time her body was found, it would be assumed that she'd slipped, fallen, and drowned. Any marks upon her body would be thought to have happened in the river. No, Annie would not be a problem, and he could take care of her quite easily himself. The two men, however, were something different.

Jonathan sighed. It was obvious that he'd have to employ someone else, and he'd have to do it with extreme delicacy and great discretion. For several long moments he sat there savoring the cigar and the fine brandy, turning over various schemes in his mind.

Suddenly he smiled. Of course, the Thackers! Their hatred of Chance was well-known, and their reputations as brutal, dangerous men, capable of any wicked deed, were also notorious in this part of the colony. All he would have to do would be to, anonymously, naturally, give them the slightest nudge in Chance's direction and everything would take care of itself.

A frown curved his forehead. Except using the Thackers might put Fancy in jeopardy. To himself Jonathan finally admitted that he was having trouble dealing with Fancy's marriage to Chance, specifically the knowledge that Chance had lain with her. The fact that she had been a widow and not a virgin had not bothered him, but to know that *Chance* had touched her intimately galled him, and his blind determination to marry her once Chance was dead wavered. Perhaps the use of the Thackers would make up his mind for him? If Fancy fell into their hands and suffered an unfortunate fate, rape or death, well, then, that would be a clear sign that she was not, after all, the bride for him.

Satisfied with his decision, he rang for his valet. When Simmons entered the room and shut the door behind him, Jonathan motioned him nearer.

"How difficult," Jonathan drawled, "would it be for you to arrange a private meeting for me with those, er, Thacker fellows?"

Beyond a slight lifting of one slim brow, Simmons gave no other sign that he was surprised by Jonathan's request. But he was. Very. All communication between Jonathan and the Thackers had been carried out by a carefully disguised Simmons. Now Simmons was extremely curious as to why his master wanted personally to talk with the two men he had frequently called a pair of noxious vermin.

But it was not a servant's place to question the master. Dropping his lids to hide the rampant speculation in his dark eyes, Simmons said, "It might take me a little while to find where they are currently abiding, but I am certain that I can do as you have asked."

"Do so," Jonathan said almost jovially. "I have a little, ah, chore for them."

Simmons cleared his throat and, unable to help himself, asked delicately, "Chore, sir? Is it something that I might be able to help you with?"

Jonathan smiled grimly. "No, this is something a trifle more complicated than transferring goods and gold."

Aware that he would learn nothing more, Simmons bowed and murmured, "Very well, sir. I shall find the Thackers for you just as soon as possible."

Pleased that he had set events in motion, Jonathan relaxed in his chair. He trusted Simmons, but not with something this important. Since secrecy was of the utmost importance, it would be folly to involve someone else too deeply. Unfortunately, he needed Simmons to find the Thackers for him, but beyond the curious fact that his master had requested to meet with the two men, Simmons would know nothing. When Chance died, it was possible that Simmons might guess the truth, but it was unlikely.

Taking a long drink of his brandy, Jonathan smiled to himself. Simmons was a good man. He knew to keep his mouth shut. Since it was Simmons who had made all the arrangements in the gun-smuggling endeavor and was the person the Thackers had always dealt with, Jonathan had no fear of ever being connected to the sale of illegal weapons to the Indians. And if Simmons did decide to talk? Jonathan shrugged. It would be Simmons's word against his, and he never doubted that his valet would be the one who suffered if the weapons smuggling came to light. All the evidence pointed clearly to Simmons; he'd arranged it that way.

Jonathan's smile deepened. After all, why would the heir

to the great Walker fortune sully his hands in such a sordid manner? *He* was a Walker of Walker Ridge—not some whining weasel. And as for Simmons speaking of arranging a meeting with the Thackers for him? Piffle. It would be dismissed as a desperate man's attempt to create whole cloth out of a pack of lies.

Feeling rather smug and satisfied with the situation, Jonathan poured himself another snifter of brandy. Seated once more, an ugly smile on his lips, he lifted the snifter in a silent toast. To Chance . . . and his numbered days.

Chapter Sixteen

————— ◆◆◆ —————

Jonathan's idea to murder Annie worried Constance. She was truly fond of her longtime servant, and despite Annie's dismal failure to get rid of Letty's son all those years ago, Constance trusted her implicitly. Annie would *never* betray her! But Constance also knew that, at present, Jonathan could not be convinced of that fact, so she was going to have to come up with a plan to keep Annie out of her son's murderous path for the near future.

Alone in her spacious rooms, she wandered about irritably. It really was too bad of Annie not to have carried out her orders all those years before, but she certainly did not deserve to die for an attack of conscience. While Constance did not have much of a conscience herself, she recognized it in other people and had often manipulated it. As long as Annie's conscience didn't cause any harm, she was willing to put up with it. But Jonathan . . .

Constance sighed. Jonathan would not be swayed. So how was she going to protect Annie, without causing a great deal of bother and discomfort to herself?

A loud thumping noise in the hallway caught her attention. A frown on her face, she threw open the door and glared at the offending source. Two young black boys had obviously been struggling with a large trunk, and it had slipped from their hands and clattered to the floor.

"What do you think you are doing?" demanded Constance. Before the frightened youths could answer, Fancy suddenly appeared, a look of dismay on her pretty face. "I knew that trunk of mine was too heavy for you," she said kindly to the servants. "Now run along and find someone else to help you take it downstairs."

Smiling faintly at Constance, she said, "I hope they did not disturb you. We are trying very hard to get everything loaded today so that there will not be such a rush tomorrow."

Constance's frown vanished as a solution to her problem instantly occurred to her. "Oh, it was no bother at all. I was just curious about what had caused the noise," she said lightly. Her earlier displeasure with Fancy vanishing, she asked warmly, "Are you rather excited to see Devil's Own? I have heard it is a handsome place. Of course," she couldn't help adding, "nothing as grand as Walker Ridge."

"I imagine that few places in the Colonies are," Fancy replied politely. "You have a most beautiful home. But I am sure that I shall be quite happy with the house that Chance is providing for me."

"Well, yes, naturally you would be," Constance answered quickly. "But will you not find it somewhat lonely? Your nearest neighbor is several hours away. Except for yourself and Chance and"—her voice hardened a trifle—"your sister, your only discourse will be with servants and the like. It is too bad that you have no older experienced woman to keep you company and help you adjust to life here. You may not find Devil's Own as genteel as Walker Ridge."

"I am certain that there will be times when I would wish for the advice of other women," Fancy said, "but I am confident that there will not be many problems that Ellen and I together cannot solve." A dimple appeared in her cheek. "We grew up in the country, and we are quite resourceful when we have to be."

"Er, yes, but I still think . . ." As if suddenly struck by a marvelous idea, Constance said happily, "Oh, silly me! I

have the perfect solution: Annie shall go with you. A change
of scenery would be nice for her, and she can help and guide
you for the first few months in your new home." Beaming at
Fancy's stunned expression, she prattled on, "Oh, it shall be
perfect. Why, just the other day Annie was saying that she
would like to go away for a while. She gets so bored here at
home month after month. And staying with you would be
just exactly what she needs; she would feel useful and yet
she would be away from the same humdrum surroundings.
A new setting would be like a tonic for her. I shall tell her
immediately." Shooing Fanny away, she said gaily, "You do
not have to thank me, my dear. You will be doing me a favor.
Now go along with you. I have to see Annie and tell her the
wonderful news and get her busy packing. After all, you are
leaving tomorrow. Oh my, how convenient this is going to
be for all of us. Run along, dear—we both have many things
to do."

Leaving Fancy standing there staring at her as if she had
been pole-axed, Constance shut the door and walked over to
the velvet pull rope that would summon Annie. A few minutes later, when Annie appeared in her rooms, Constance
met her with a wide smile.

"My dear, I have such news for you: you are going to stay
with Chance and Fancy for a few weeks. It will be like a
pleasure trip for you, and you will be doing the newlyweds
a great favor. Fancy is so very new to the Colonies; you will
be able to guide her and teach her our ways. Won't that be
nice? Just think, you will not have to put up with my grumpy
moods for the next several weeks, and you will have a much
needed change of scenery. I hear that Chance's plantation is
very pleasant. Besides, it has been nearly a year since you
have been away from Walker Ridge. 'Tis time for you to
shake all those nasty old cobwebs from your mind."

If Fancy had been pole-axed, Annie was dumbstruck. For
several long moments she stared dazedly at Constance's
smiling features. "Go to Devil's Own?" she finally croaked
out when she found her voice.

Constance nodded happily. "Yes, you shall act as, ah, mentor to dear Fancy."

Her eyes locked painfully on Constance's face, her hands clasped tightly together, she asked disbelievingly, "They have agreed to this?"

"Oh, yes, Fancy and I discussed it just a few minutes before I rang you. She thinks it is a marvelous idea."

Gathering up all her courage, Annie blurted out, "Why are you doing this? Why are you sending me away?"

Not meeting her eyes, Constance turned around and fiddled with a bottle of scent on the top of her dressing table. "Oh, there is no reason. I just think it might be for the best if you were *safely* away from Walker Ridge for the time being." Their eyes met. "Do you understand me?"

Annie nodded slowly. She did indeed. And she did not know whether to be grateful or terrified.

Fancy was not certain how she was going to explain to Chance the addition to their party of Annie. She was not certain herself how it had come about. She only knew that there was no way of getting out of Constance's stunning offer without appearing ungracious. She pitied Annie's plight in having to work for someone as demanding as Constance, but she wished there was a way that she could refuse Annie's presence in her own household without causing even more dissension. A rueful smile curved her mouth. She and Ellen had lived all of their lives with hardly a ripple of contention stirring their day-to-day affairs, yet look at what had happened to them since they had arrived in the Colonies. Abduction. Misunderstandings. Broken relationships. She shook her head. Perhaps it was something in the air?

She went in search of Chance and found him overseeing the loading of one of the wagons that was to accompany them to Devil's Own. Requesting a word in private with him brought a surprised flick of one brow, but he politely escorted her some distance away, guiding her down a pleasant walk edged with roses.

He suddenly looked very formidable to her, this tall,

broad-shouldered man who was her husband. To her annoyance, she found herself asking diffidently, "Would you mind if there was to be another addition to our household for a few weeks?"

Warily, Chance eyed her, something in her voice alerting him to the fact that he was not going to like what she had to say. And he didn't.

At first he thought that he had misheard her, but when she repeated Annie's name and somewhat haltingly, in the face of his growing scowl, relayed the entire tale, he realized that there was nothing wrong with his hearing. A stinging reply hovered on the tip of his tongue, but something in the expression on Fancy's face stilled it.

"Do you actually want that old crone to come with us?" he demanded with astonishment.

"Not exactly," Fancy admitted, "but the more I thought about it, the more I decided that it might not be such a bad idea."

Chance snorted.

"I feel sorry for her," Fancy said quietly, "always at the beck and call of that woman. And there is much in what Constance said: there may be times when Ellen and I would be grateful for her knowledge and company."

Chance made a face. "I doubt that Annie Clemmons will be of much help to you. But if you want her to stay with us for a while, I have no serious objections." He smiled charmingly at her. "You see what an amiable bridegroom you have?"

Fancy gave him a look over her shoulder as she walked toward the house. "Amiable? No indeed, sir, I see a man plotting to win his way into my good graces."

Chance grinned, and after watching for a few minutes the enticing sway of her skirts as she walked away, he returned to his task. But he was troubled by Annie's addition to their party. What was that scheming witch Constance up to? Not for a moment did he believe that she was showing a kindness to her old servant—or Fancy, for that matter. There was some reason she wanted Annie to go with them, but damned if he could think of what it was.

The rest of the day passed swiftly, and there was no time for a private moment between the newlyweds until they prepared for bed that night. Alone in their room together, Fancy again brought up the subject of their expanded household.

"You really do not mind that Ellen . . . and Annie are coming with us?" Fancy asked uncertainly.

Seated in one of the chairs, his long legs sprawled in front of him, Chance shrugged. "I cannot say that I am overly pleased to have that prune-faced Annie coming with us or that the prospect of having my sister-in-law following my every step is precisely how I envisioned my first few weeks of marriage, but under the circumstances, I do not see that their presence is going to cause any difficulties." A teasing gleam suddenly lit his blue eyes. "And of course, if I am very kind to Ellen, mayhap it will soften your hard heart against me."

Fancy snorted. "Now why would it do that? Especially since you have just told me that the only reason you would be so accommodating is for your own means."

"I did not say it was the *only* reason," Chance murmured, enjoying watching her temper rise. Fancy sent him a speaking glance, and he grinned before adding, "I like your sister. She is a sweet child, and even if I had hoped to have all of your attention to myself, I would never deny a member of your family the hospitality of our house. Ellen has a home with us for as long as she wants."

"That is very generous of you," Fancy said softly, wishing she understood him better. Used to her first husband's cold, supercilious manner when she had displeased him, she found Chance's easy acceptance of the situation between them confusing. Spencer had been a generous man, but she could not imagine him agreeing to terms that were not to his benefit without a great deal of open displeasure. Yet no one seeing Chance with her would have guessed of the bargain they had struck. He was as considerate and attentive as any bride could have wished. Perversely Fancy wished that he had been an utter beast. She would certainly feel more justified in the stance she had taken. Her eyes narrowed. Perhaps that was why he had been so agreeable?

Seeing the expression on her face, Chance cocked a brow. "What? What have I done now to vex you? I thought you would be pleased that Ellen will be coming with us to Devil's Own and that I have not been bloody difficult about Annie's sudden inclusion."

"I am," she admitted slowly. "I just do not understand you." At Chance's look of inquiry, she muttered, "I thought you would be angry about what we agreed this morning, but you have been most pleasant all day."

Chance shrugged again. "I cannot pretend that I will not find the next month a burden, or that it will be easy for me *not* to avail myself of your many charms. But I did agree to your terms. Having agreed to them, why should I act in a disagreeable manner?"

Fancy sent him a perplexed smile. "Not all men are so."

Chance smiled angelically. "I am not 'all' men."

Fancy walked restlessly around the room. A hopeful light in her eyes, she finally stopped before Chance and asked, "Since you have been so generous to me about Ellen and Annie, are you certain that you will not change your mind and allow me to sleep in my own bed?"

"Will you change your mind and allow me to make love to you?" he asked dryly. The light died in her eyes, and she shook her head vehemently. Chance yawned and stretched, making her aware of all that lean, exciting masculinity. "Then, sweetheart," he drawled, "don't expect me to change mine."

Fancy made a face. She had not thought that he would allow her to escape so easily, but she'd had to try. Not so certain of her own ability to resist him if he attempted to break the terms of their bargain, she was not looking forward to the night ahead.

Chance was not, either, being rather uncertain about his own powers of self-restraint. His bride was a very tempting morsel, and the knowledge that he could force his attentions upon her and slake the carnal demons that rode him was never very far from his mind. But to the surprise of both of them, they managed to share that big bed together with neither one of them having any reason for despair when they woke in the morning.

Fancy was not very pleased, however, to find herself snuggled up to his broad chest, one of her arms thrown across his shoulder and one of his legs nestled snugly between her thighs. She had lain there content and half awake for several seconds, listening to the steady beat of his heart, until she realized her position and had instantly jerked away to her side of the bed.

And of course, Chance did not have the decency to be asleep—or at least to pretend that he was. He was wide awake and had been for quite some time, enjoying the feel of Fancy's yielding body lying so intimately against his. A gleam in his blue eyes, Chance said softly, "I wonder which one of us is going to find this coming month the most difficult?"

Ignoring him, Fancy slid from the bed and hastily donned a wrapper over her nightgown. Tightening the sash firmly around her slender waist, a spot of color burning in each cheek, she said loftily, "It certainly will not be me. I was sound asleep and not responsible for my actions."

"Ah. So if one night I find myself making love to you, it will be because I am asleep and not responsible?"

Fancy's lips thinned. Pushing back a strand of hair, she said, "You know very well what I meant. Must you tease me all the time?"

"But, sweetheart, you have denied me the delights of your body. Must you deny me even this small pleasure?"

Fancy strangled an urge to stamp her foot with vexation and proceeded to wash her face. Several of her personal items had been moved down to Chance's room the previous evening, and studiously ignoring the provoking creature on the bed, she picked up her own brush and began to bring her tangled locks into order.

His hands behind his head, Chance watched her with ob-

vious pleasure. There was something both innocent and seductive about the way she brushed her hair, the sensuous
flow of her thick dark brown curls over the bristles almost
mesmerizing him.

Fancy was very aware of him, and putting down her brush
with a sharp thud, she turned to glare at him. "Will you *stop*
staring at me that way?"

The teasing gleam in his eyes pronounced, Chance sighed
heavily and murmured, "Do not tell me, sweetheart, that you
are adding *another* thing I am not to do to our bargain."

Hands on her hips, she said, "Has anyone ever told you
that you are the most aggravating, provoking creature in the
world?"

At her words, he assumed a look of such wounded innocence that Fancy felt her lips twitch with laughter. Knowing
that he was incorrigible and that she could not win in this situation, she turned away to hide her growing amusement and
said, "Oh, never mind. What time did you say that you
wanted to leave this morning?"

"No later than the noon hour, if Ellen and Annie can be
ready by then. We have several hours' ride ahead of us, but
rather than delaying until tomorrow morning, when it would
be cooler, I would like to be at Devil's Own tonight—even
if we have to travel the last few hours in darkness."

By midmorning there was much bustling about and a feeling of anticipation in the air as the servants scurried in and
out of the big house with trunks and bulky packages for
loading in the two small wagons that were to accompany the
newlyweds. To Chance's surprise, by ten-thirty that morning
everything was loaded and all the good-byes and good
wishes had been said and they were ready to depart.

Prior to the disastrous scene between Ellen and Hugh in
the conservatory, it had been arranged for Hugh to accompany the newlyweds on their journey to Devil's Own.
Though Hugh treated Ellen's presence with a cool disdain,
he kept his word and grimly joined the small party. Chance
and Hugh rode astride on tall Thoroughbreds that had been
ridden over the day before the wedding from Devil's Own

by two of Chance's men. The heavily laden wagons were pulled by pairs of stout draft horses—a wedding gift from Morely and his family. The two men from Devil's Own were each driving one of the wagons; the three women were all in the larger vehicle, where a canvas hood had been hastily rigged to give them some relief from the hot, brilliant yellow sunlight. Amidst smiles and good wishes the little cavalcade slowly pulled away.

A forced smile on his face, Morely, along with the others, watched them leave from the steps of the house. When everyone else went inside, he remained staring in the direction Chance had ridden until only the red dust lingered in the air from their passage. Then, sighing heavily, he turned and entered the house.

He had wanted to tell Sam about the night he had found the newborn infant before Chance left for Devil's Own, but with one thing and another it had been easy to put off the meeting with Sam—something he had been doing for over thirty years! But he knew now that he could put off the evil hour no longer. There were no more excuses. All the guests, except for himself and Pru, had left, the newlyweds were safely on their way, and quiet and tranquillity had once more descended upon Walker Ridge. At least until I open my mouth, Morely thought glumly as he went in search of Sam.

He found Sam several minutes later in his office. Sam was halfheartedly looking over some papers when Morely knocked and entered the building. A welcoming smile on his face, Sam waved him to a comfortable black leather chair, offering him some ale from a pitcher that rested on a long table against one wall.

Only after refreshments were taken care of and Sam had settled casually into the leather chair behind his desk, his booted feet propped on a corner of the desk, did Morely gather his thoughts and begin the difficult task of trying to explain why he had waited over three decades to speak.

It was not easy. He made several false starts before he finally said, "Do you remember Chance's wedding night, when we spoke of his parentage?"

Looking perplexed, Sam answered slowly, "I remember that you were laboring under some great emotion. I have remained curious, but waited until you wanted to speak again of it."

Morely drank nervously of his ale. The moment had come, and he knew a craven desire to once more avoid the subject. But he could not. He must speak, and he could put it off no longer, no matter what havoc it might wreak in his own life. He took a deep breath and then blurted out, "I swear to you on all that I hold dear that Chance Walker is not my son. I found him!"

"You found him?" Sam said in astonishment. "What the devil do you mean by that?"

Determinedly meeting Sam's gaze, he said, "Exactly that. I found him still wet with the birthing blood, wrapped in a blanket and lying on that big bluff out there in front of your house."

Sam looked incredulous. "In front of my house? Is this some Canterbury tale you have concocted?" When Morely shook his head vehemently, Sam added quietly, "Why are you doing this to yourself? If Chance is not your son, then simply say so and have done with it. You do not need to invent some wildly outlandish tale to convince me."

"I wish it were merely an outlandish tale," Morely muttered, "but it is the Lord's own truth. I found him." He took another drink of ale. A pleading note in his voice, he said, "Let me tell you how it was." At Sam's reluctant nod, he began slowly, "There was a terrible storm the night I found him. Slashing rain and rolling thunder filled the heavens, and I was struggling home in the midst of it all from an evening of deep drinking, singing to myself, if I remember correctly, when to my amazement I heard a baby crying. I could not believe it! Thought the liquor had fuddled my wits and that I was hearing things, but there was a lull in the storm just then and I could hear him squalling plain as day."

Morely gulped some more ale. "I was still in the woods when I first heard him—I could not see anything. Except for the lightning it was black as Hades and the brush hid the bluff from view. But it did not make sense to me, even as drunk as I was, for anyone to be out on a night like that with a baby. I figured that someone was in bad trouble. Thinking I could be of help, I stumbled toward the bluff."

Unable to sustain Sam's fascinated gaze, Morely stood up and took a turn around the room. His back to Sam, he stared blankly out of one of the many windows that lined one wall of the room. "I might not have seen him if it had not been for the lightning," he said softly. "I had finally gotten out into the open and was making my way toward the sound of the crying when there was a tremendous bolt—lit up the area just like high noon—and that is when I spied him. He was one angry little fellow, squalling and kicking in the blanket he had been wrapped in . . . and lying there all alone—just mere inches from the edge of the bluff."

Sam sucked in his breath. "Are you telling me that some-one had just *abandoned* a newborn infant? There was no one around? No one?"

Still not looking at Sam, Morely answered, "No one. It was as if the baby had just miraculously appeared there at the edge of the bluff. I called and called, but no one an-swered me. After a while, I decided that no one *was* going to answer, so I picked up the baby and took him to my place—your overseer's house—you were letting me stay there in those days, remember?"

His face grave, Sam nodded. "Yes, of course I remember. But Morely, I find this tale hard to believe. If it is true, why did you not tell me right away?"

Morely smiled bitterly. "Oh, 'tis a true tale, and I would have told you—that is precisely what I planned to do once I had seen that the baby was safely settled. Only you left for England before I could talk to you."

Sam's face went white. "Are you telling me that this hap-pened then? I knew Chance was born around that time, but I never realized . . ."

Morely nodded. "I found the baby the night Letty deliv-ered her stillborn son." He swallowed painfully. "Of course, I did not know that at the time, I only knew that there was this tiny infant wailing loudly in my arms and that someone had abandoned him to the fates in the middle of a raging storm. I wondered if his mother might have jumped into the river herself, but that was not something I could discover right then. I had to see to the needs of the newborn first." Morely ran an agitated hand through his hair. " 'Tis hard to explain, Sam, all the emotions that went through me that night." He sent him a wry smile. "You do not know how badly I wanted your presence, how very much I wanted to lay the babe in your arms and wash my hands of him. But you were in Philadelphia and I had no one I could turn to . . . no one I trusted. It may sound farfetched and nonsensical now, but I felt strongly that I had to see that he came to no harm, that whoever had left him on that bluff did not come back to finish the ugly deed I had interrupted."

A spasm of horror crossed Sam's face, but it was obvious that he hadn't taken in all the implications of the tale. Sighing heavily, Morely said quietly, "Sam, I found Chance right here at Walker Ridge, the same night Letty brought forth your stillborn son. Most coincidental of all, Chance has six toes on his right foot, the same as every man in your family for the last three generations."

Their eyes locked and a dark silence fell. "Are you saying," Sam finally managed, "what I think you are saying?"

Morely shrugged. "Letty was all alone with Constance. You were away in Philadelphia. Constance had good reason to want you to have no heir but her own precious son, Jonathan." Morely glanced away from the sudden anguish in Sam's face. "Twins run in Letty's family, don't they?"

"Yes," Sam said thickly, "they do."

Seating himself in the chair in front of Sam's desk, Morely said tiredly, "I had no proof. I still have none. I wanted to tell you, I had *planned* on telling you as soon as I got back from leaving Chance with Andrew and Martha. Only while I was doing that, you returned and swept Letty away to England." Haltingly he added, "What I suspected . . . it was not something . . . I just did not know how to put the words on paper . . . and if what I suspected was true, I feared that any letter I wrote to you might fall into the wrong hands."

"But when we came back, why in God's name did you not say something then? Why have you never before breathed a word of this incredible tale to anyone?" Sam demanded, his blue eyes bright with suppressed emotion.

"You were gone four years, Sam. Four years in which Andrew and Martha raised Chance as their own. That is also why there is the discrepancy of his date of birthing; they chose the date I left him with them as his birthday. He was nearly a week old by then. You were gone for years, and during that time they were the only parents he knew. He loved them as they loved him. They were a family." Morely sighed again. "I had no proof, beyond coincidence. Even the six toes is not irrefutable proof of his heritage. The only thing I do know is that Chance is not *my* son. But he does share the exact date of birth of your dead son, and he has the six toes. 'Tis obvious that he is a Walker bred in the bone. And that he looks enough like you to be your son."

Unable to bear Sam's painful scrutiny any longer, Morely dropped his gaze to the floor. "I am a coward, Sam. I should have spoken to you about this years ago, but I could not. 'Tis a terrible thing that I am suggesting, and with only coincidence to give it any credence, I was afraid that you would not believe me. That you would think I was simply trying to cause trouble for Constance. I always kept thinking that there would be a better time, that one day the good Lord would send me a sign that it was time to speak or something would happen that would make my telling of that night imperative." He smiled sadly. "But somehow the years just went by. I was busy with my own family, Chance was growing up strong and happy with Andrew and Martha, and you and Letty seemed to have dealt with your grief. I did not want to open old wounds or cause new ones."

"And now?" Sam asked, his voice thick and rusty. "Why do you speak now?"

"Because I am an old man now. I know I am not immortal. Chance saved my life the day of his wedding. It was like a sign, and I realized I had waited so long, I risked dying without having told anyone what I knew." His eyes lifted to Sam's hard blue eyes. "I owed it to Chance," he said simply.

Silence fell, both men lost in their own thoughts. After a long time, Sam said heavily, "Tell no one what you have told me. I will not have Letty learn of this until we know the truth. I do not want her overset."

Morely nodded. "Do you believe me?" he asked painfully.

"I believe you," Sam said harshly. "This is too wild and improbable a tale not to be true. The question is, who is Chance Walker? Was his birth that night and physical aspects some incredible coincidence?" His voice grew icy. "Or did my wife give birth to twins that night, one alive and one dead? And did my stepmother, or someone following her directions, deliberately abandon the living infant to die in the elements? They would not have left the baby there to be found the next day. It must have been planned to throw the child in the river, only your approach frightened them off."

"I wondered from time to time," Morely began hesitantly, "if some other woman had given birth that night, too. And if she disappeared, jumping into the river but leaving behind her child."

Sam smiled mirthlessly. "You think that Chance might be my bastard? That I sought solace in another's bed? That I made a mockery of my wedding vows to my beloved Letty and drove another woman to such despair that she took her own life? For shame, my friend—you know me better than that."

Morely flushed. "I doubted it, but it seemed as likely as the other." He took a deep breath. "Are you very angry with me?"

Sam sent him a level glance from beneath his brows. "Angry? Angry does not begin to explain the emotions I feel right now. You have just told me that Chance could very well be my son and that you have suspected it for years. From everything you have said, I agree with your suspicions: Chance Walker is my son!" Sam's fist hit his desk with a loud crash. "Yes, I am angry with you, furious and deeply wounded. And yet . . ." He brought his emotions back under control and muttered, "Despite everything, I would not willingly destroy a lifetime of friendship." Bleakly he added, "I could have wished you had spoken decades ago, but I understand many things now, such as why you managed to keep Chance always under our noses and were always enlisting my help in his behalf. I am thankful for that."

A weight slid off Morely's shoulders. Uncertainly he asked, "But what are we to do now? We still have no proof."

Sam smiled like a tiger, his resemblance to Chance very pronounced. "Then it is up to us to find proof, isn't it?"

Part Four

Devil's Own

There is something in the wind.

William Shakespeare,
The Comedy of Errors

Chapter Seventeen

Darkness had fallen an hour previous to the arrival of the newlyweds and their party at Devil's Own, so Fancy was denied her first eager glimpse of the place that was now to be her home. Lanterns, both on the wagons and carried by Chance and Hugh, had lit their way through the night, and only occasionally did she catch a hint of the changing landscape. From her swaying perch in the wagon, she gradually became aware of a feeling of openness. That sensation, coupled with the sight of fewer and fewer trees and brush outlined by the wavering lantern light, made her certain they had left the woodland behind. When she spied the tobacco plants growing at the edge of the narrow path they followed and, shortly after that, a strip of rail fencing, she knew that their destination could not be far ahead, and a sense of excitement swept through her.

The wagons began a slight ascent, and ahead of them, through the darkness, Fancy saw flickering lights and the vague outline of a building. A few minutes later the wagons halted in front of the house, the light from inside spilling outside: the wide covered front porch was lit on either side with an ornate pair of lanterns. A half dozen broad steps led to the porch, and just as Chance helped Fancy from the wagon, the double doors of the house were thrown open and a neatly garbed gentleman came outside.

A merry smile wreathing his weathered face, the man exclaimed, "Welcome! Welcome to Devil's Own, Mistress Walker. We have been eagerly awaiting your arrival." He sent Chance a look. "The house has been too long without a woman's touch."

Leaving Hugh to see to Ellen and Annie, Chance led Fancy up the steps, saying dryly, "That is strange coming from you, Jed, considering that your excellent wife, Martha, keeps the house in exemplary condition." Glancing down at Fancy, he said, "This is Jed Thompson. He and his wife came to me as indentured servants over ten years ago. By the time they had fulfilled the terms of our contract, I had discovered that my house could not be without them, and they had decided that working for me was not such a terrible fate."

Reaching the porch with Fancy at his side, Chance stopped in front of Jed. "My wife, Fancy," he said simply. "I trust that you and everyone at Devil's Own will serve her with the same diligence and care that you have shown me."

Jed bowed to Fancy. His hazel eyes twinkling, he said, "Mistress. It will be our pleasure to serve you, and I hope that we will always give satisfaction."

Fancy murmured a warm reply, instantly liking this small red-haired man, and allowed him to usher her inside.

Because of the darkness she had not been able to tell a great deal about the house from the outside, but entering the spacious hall, with its elegant spiral staircase disappearing into the upper reaches of the house, she was able instantly to set to rest whatever doubts she might have had about her new home. The heart-pine floors gleamed with polish, crystal and brass wall sconces held expensive bee's wax candles, and a delicate candelabra hung from the high ceiling, its golden light dancing across the tall gilt mirror and long mahogany sideboard that sat against one wall. Several arched doorways led off the hall, and from one of these a tiny, buxom woman came bustling forward, her blue eyes shyly meeting Fancy's.

Hurrying up to them, she dropped a swift curtsy and said, "Welcome to your new home, mistress. I am Martha, Jed's wife."

"And the best cook in the Colonies, too," Chance said with smile.

The remainder of the party entered the hall just then and more introductions were made, although Hugh needed none, as he was obviously well-known to the Thompsons. Tired from her jolting ride in the wagon, Fancy was glad when, just as soon as the initial flurry of their arrival had died down, Chance said, "Martha, if you will show Ellen and Annie to their rooms and see to their needs, and Jed, if you'll tend to Hugh's wants, I shall escort my bride to our rooms." He glanced down at Fancy and smiled crookedly. "Tomorrow will be soon enough to explore your new home. From the look of you, you are longing for your bed." To Martha he added, "Have Maryanne bring up a tray of light refreshments to our rooms after you have settled everyone."

Bidding all good night, Chance took Fancy's arm and led her up the spiral staircase. At the top of the staircase they entered another handsome hallway, and he ushered her along. Finally he stopped at a door and said with surprising diffidence, "Your rooms, madame. I hope you find them satisfactory."

Fancy smiled softly at him, her eyes shining. "I am sure that I will."

Bringing her closer to his tall length, he stared down into her face. Brushing his lips tantalizingly across hers, he murmured, "Mine are just next door. There is a connecting door between the suites. I have sworn not to make love to you during this month, but I trust you recall where you are to sleep."

Fancy half scowled at him. "As if you would let me forget."

He laughed and threw open the door. Her breath held expectantly, Fancy stepped inside, Chance following directly behind her. It was a beautiful room that met Fancy's gaze, spacious and airy. A lovely needlework carpet in soft shades of rose and cream lay in the center of the glistening pine floor; a pair of wing-back chairs in a deeper rose color sat near one of many windows, a small table of mahogany and pine between them. The four-poster bed was a delicately carved affair, and the bed hangings and curtains draping the many windows were of printed cotton in the same soft shades as the carpet. A variegated silk coverlet of cream, rose, and green lay over the feather-filled mattress, and with pleasure Fancy noted that the marble on the tables near the bed and the washstand were pale green and blended charmingly with the decor.

There were more furnishings in the room, but letting out a sigh of delight, Fancy turned a pleased face up to Chance and said, " 'Tis a lovely room, Chance. I shall spend many happy hours here, I know."

Shutting the door behind them, he murmured, "They will be exciting hours, too, once you let me join you in that bed."

A blush suffused her cheeks and she said hastily, "Does that door lead to your rooms?"

Flashing her a wry glance, he nodded. "Yes, and our dressing rooms. Would you like to see them?"

Very conscious of his warm body standing close behind her, and terrified that if he should touch her, she would forget it was her idea to wait to resume intimacies, Fancy said quickly, "Perhaps just a brief glimpse? I *am* rather tired."

The dressing rooms were comfortable and commodious; Chance's bedroom was larger than hers, the ruby-and-gold colors of the hangings and curtains as bold and masculine as he was himself. Averting her eyes from the massive mahogany bed that dominated the room, she said brightly, "It is very nice, too." She gave a little yawn and added, "Oh, my, but I did not realize how *very* tired I am. Do you mind if I retire now?"

Chance turned her gently around and she found to her excitement and alarm that she was effectively trapped by his strong arms as they settled around her waist and pulled her closer to him. Then he kissed her, a warm, lazy kiss that sent her senses spinning.

Gazing down into her suddenly desire-flushed face, he said softly, "Fancy, I do not intend to leap upon you every time we are alone. I told you that I would give you time. I will. Do not fear me."

She smiled up at him mistily, unaware of how very tempting she looked with her cat-slanted eyes golden with emotion, her mouth rosy and damp from his kiss. " 'Tis not just you I fear, husband," she breathed huskily, "but myself as well."

What could he do after that disarming admission but kiss her again? His arms tightened and his mouth found hers, his lips warm and demanding as they stood there locked together.

Drowning in his embrace, Fancy swayed in his arms for endless moments, feeling the seductive sweep of desire flowing through her. It was his hand on her breast, the fingers shaping her sweetly aching nipple, that brought her back to the present.

She gasped and stepped swiftly from his arms. "You promised."

Chance sighed. "Fool that I am." His eyes narrowed. "But tease me again as you just did and I am afraid that I shall be forced to take back my promise."

"Tease you?" Fancy flashed back, defensive and embarrassed at the same time. Had she teased him? She had not meant to. Not meeting his eyes, her color much heightened, she muttered, "I did no such thing. You simply took what you wanted."

"If I had taken what I wanted, Duchess," Chance drawled, a devilish glitter in his blue eyes, "you would be lying on that bed with your skirts tipped up and me lodged securely between your soft thighs."

Ignoring the rush of heat that went through her at his words, she brushed past him and said tightly, "You are crude, sir. I will not stand here and listen to you a moment longer."

Chance let her go, but he followed her to her room. Lounging against the doorjamb, he murmured, "And I am your husband. Remember that, sweetheart. You married me."

Remembering just how he had connived that state of affairs, Fancy bristled. "You tricked me into marriage, do not forget. That is precisely why I want some time to, to . . ."

"Grow used to my crude, barbaric ways?" he drawled.

"Exactly."

There was a gentle tap on the door and Chance strode over to answer it. A small young woman stood there, twisting her hands together nervously. Her hazel eyes brightened when Chance smiled at her. Ushering her into the room, Chance said to Fancy, "This is Martha's youngest daughter, Charity. While she cannot claim to be a fully trained lady's maid, I am sure that you will find her services adequate." Pushing Charity forward, he said, "Charity, this is my wife, Fancy, your new mistress. And you will soon see that she is not the ogress you fear."

Charity blushed hotly and sent a beseeching gaze in Fancy's direction. "Oh, mistress, I never once—"

Fancy smiled warmly at the young woman, whose bright red hair and small buxom stature would have proclaimed her Jed's and Martha's daughter even without Chance's introduction. "Do not pay him any heed," she said kindly. "I am sure that we shall deal very well together, Charity. I hope that you find helping me a pleasure and not a trial." She shot her husband a look. "As I am sure your parents have found Chance to be upon occasion."

Chance laughed. "Yes, I am sure that they have." He gave Fancy a mocking bow and said, "I will leave you in Charity's capable hands. There are things that I must see to, having been gone for much longer than I had originally planned. Her sister, Maryanne, will no doubt show up in a few minutes with some refreshments. Good night, Madame Wife."

Charity proved to be eager and helpful, and by the time Fancy was comfortably ensconced in her bed and ready for sleep, she had also met Maryanne, enough like Charity to be her twin, except that Charity, at eighteen, was five years younger than Maryanne. After having partaken of the chicken soup and thick slices of bread and butter that had accompanied the light meal, Fancy waved the two young women away, hardly able to keep her eyes open.

She was deeply asleep when Chance slid into bed beside her. Pulling her close to him, he murmured into her ear, "The bargain, sweetheart, have you forgotten it?" Fancy made some sort of sleepy protest and then proceeded to snuggle deeper into his arms. A smile on his face, Chance fell asleep.

When Fancy woke the next morning, hot bright sunlight was spilling into the room and there was only the indentation in the pillow next to hers to show where Chance had lain. Not wishing to dwell upon the situation between her husband and herself, eager for her first glimpse of her new home, she sprang out of bed and hurried to one of the windows. Pushing aside the printed cotton, she looked outside. A smile of pure pleasure lit her face as her eyes fell on the great green expanse of grass, interspersed with towering oak and magnolia trees, that lay before her. The land sloped gently downward toward the shining silver of the river in the distance, and she spied a sizable dock built out into the flowing water. A wide road that ended in a broad sweeping circle in front of the house divided the view in front of her. To her left she saw a large, rail-fenced pasture, half a dozen mares busily cropping grass while their foals gamboled about. A flower garden lay on the right, delightful walkways edged with bright blooms of pink, yellow, and purple, the faint scent of roses and spicy stocks wafting on the warm air.

Fancy had not known what to expect at Devil's Own. The memory of Chance as she had first seen him in his well-worn buckskins had always been at odds with the fine clothes and elegant manners she had observed at Walker Ridge. She had been intensely curious to see which man his home more resembled. For all she had known, the rich attire he'd worn at Walker Ridge had been the sum of his wealth, and Devil's Own could have been a dank and ramshackle log cabin set in the shadowy, sinister depths of the forest.

Turning away from the window, she admitted she was very glad that her new home was *not* the dungeonlike cabin that had occasionally flitted through her thoughts. There was much about her new husband that was a mystery to her, and she realized uneasily that she had been forced to entrust her very life into the hands of a man she knew little about—other than the disagreeable fact that his slightest smile warmed her heart and his lightest touch set her on fire. Her lips twisted. *Not* a strong foundation upon which to build a marriage. Then she shrugged. There was no use repining, and she could console herself with the knowledge that at least she had a more than adequate home in which to live—instead of that imaginary hovel.

Devil's Own was not nearly as grand, or as impressive, as Walker Ridge, but in some ways that pleased her. Having lived a number of years in the huge, palatial ancestral home of the Merrivale barons, she was looking forward to a home in which she would not get lost—as she had done several times in her early days as the new Baroness Merrivale. Devil's Own, she thought happily, seemed to be just about perfect. Smiling to herself, she rang for Charity. She could hardly wait to start exploring.

Several hours later, an extremely amiable Chance at her side, Fancy acknowledged that her initial excitement had not abated one whit; if anything, it had grown. As she had guessed, the house was not overly large. It boasted a mere six bedrooms compared to the almost twenty that Merrivale Manor had possessed. But each was spacious and as charmingly furnished as one could wish, and she found herself thinking with pleasure that the house was perfect—comfortable and more than ample in size, yet somehow retaining a beguiling coziness.

Pride evident in his voice, Chance pointed out that the original portion of the white clapboard house was two and a half stories high, with wide porches at the front and rear and a hipped roof with dormer windows and towering chimneys at either side. Four years previously, he explained, he had added the large one-story wings at each end of the first structure. The effect was now one of elegance and graciousness. There were outside blinds on all the windows, which were painted a deep green and gave the house a crisp, clean look. Lilacs and trumpet-flower vines and honeysuckle twined around the columns of the covered porches, their shiny dark green foliage contrasting pleasingly with the blinding whiteness of the house.

At the rear of the main house, the outbuildings—the kitchen, the smokehouse, the laundry, a dairy, a weaving house, and Chance's office—spread out in an ever-widening circle, and beyond those neat structures were the houses and cabins where the servants and all the other people who worked on the plantation were quartered. Since the majority of the workers at Devil's Own were either indentured servants or those, like the Thompsons, who had served out their contract, there were few slaves, and housing consisted of fewer than a half dozen small cabins in a staggered row. Beyond the outbuildings Fancy could see the stables, several large buildings and barns that Chance promised to show her another day. Beyond that area were the drying sheds for the tobacco.

The plantation was more like a small village than a lone outpost in the verdant wilderness, and as she and Chance wandered about, Fancy was struck by the comparison. There was a bustling air about the place; people hurried here and there, busy with their various tasks. Chickens clucked and crowed, the sounds of the milk cows' lowing could be heard, and the frequent calls and neighs of the many horses punctuated the air, as did snatches of conversation and laughter from the humans.

After returning to the house following a light meal they had all eaten together, Hugh disappeared in the direction of the stables, where Chance was soon to join him. The other ladies retired to their rooms for a brief nap during the hottest part of the day, and so it was that Chance and Fancy were left alone again for a few minutes. Leaving the confines of the house, they chose a cool, shady spot nearby to sit and enjoy the view of the river, and their conversation was aimless until, a twinkle in his eyes, Chance said, "I am sorry to desert you so soon after your arrival, but I have hardly had time to acquaint myself with the English horses I purchased. I have been far too busy chasing after a different spirited and lovely English filly."

Fancy choked on the lemonade she had been drinking, glad that there was no one else around to hear his outrageous comment. But, gathering her wits about her, she said tartly, "Filly? Oh, no, my dear sir, I fear that you have been misled. Surely a barren mare is more apt?"

Chance smiled lazily and, gently running a finger under her chin, leaned nearer as he lifted her face to his. "Barren? I doubt that. I believe that this particular creature has never been mated with a truly potent stallion."

Fancy flushed clear up to her hairline, but she could think of no jesting comment. Their careless teasing had hit a raw spot. Painfully she said, "I think you will find the fault is with the female, sir. The, er, first stallion had already sired three sons, but with . . ." She stopped, her eyes suddenly shimmering with unshed tears. She had longed desperately for a child when she had first been married to the baron, and since there was ample proof that *he* was fertile, as the years had passed and she had never become pregnant, she had been certain that the fault lay with her. It had been a bitter blow, and she had long ago sadly buried the idea of one day having a child of her own.

Aware of her distress, he kissed her gently on the nose. "We shall see, shan't we?" He smiled down at her, a smile that made Fancy's very bones melt. "And if your words prove true, sweetheart, then I shall still consider myself as having made an excellent bargain."

Fancy was grateful for his kindness, but it only added to her confusion about him. He had shown himself to be a crafty scoundrel in the manner in which he had gained her hand in marriage; he had almost admitted that he had done it in some mad quest to take revenge on Jonathan, and yet . . . And yet . . . Fancy sighed. Would she ever understand him?

*   *   *

The ladies were left to their own devices for the remainder of the day, and after the worst of the sticky heat had abated in the late afternoon, the three women began to explore farther afield than the confines of the house.

With an odd feeling of pride, Fancy showed Ellen and Annie many of the things and places that Chance had shown her earlier in the day, pointing out the various buildings and their purposes. Despite the waning of the day, there was still much activity going on—children playing, dogs barking, and adults hurrying around on last minute errands before dusk fell.

Her eyes sparkling as they wandered over to a large pasture to watch the antics of the foals, Fancy said, "And to think that Constance worried that I would be bored or lonely." She could have bitten her tongue as soon as the words left her mouth and she saw the flush that stained Annie's pale cheek. Hastily she added, "But it is so nice not to be thrust right into the middle of a crowd of strangers. Do you know many of these people, Annie? I certainly hope so, or Ellen and I are going to be at an utter loss." Sending the older woman a smile, she continued, "Thank goodness Constance suggested you come to stay with us for a while to help me through the first awkward days. Have you ever been to Devil's Own before?"

Utterly disarmed by Fancy's kind manner and speech, Annie relaxed somewhat and said simply, "No, I have never been here before, though I have heard talk of the place. Mister Sam had spoken of it often. He is very proud of what your husband has accomplished in such a short time. But I do know quite a few of the servants. Over the years many of them have accompanied your husband to Walker Ridge from time to time."

Despite her initial reservations about Annie's inclusion into her new household, Fancy had discovered the previous day, during their long journey to Devil's Own, that the older woman tried very hard to please and was actually an enjoyable companion, given a little encouragement. Today further confirmed Fancy's growing good opinion of Annie, but she was a little puzzled by Constance's behavior in thrusting the woman at her. Chance had already indicated that Annie always looked at him as if she expected him to sprout two heads, and since she and Ellen were utter strangers to the other woman, *something* must have made a sojourn to Chance's home seem attractive to Annie herself.

Unable to help herself, Fancy asked, "Do you usually do much traveling and visiting when Mistress Constance gives you leave to do so?"

Oh, I have never gone anywhere without Mistress Constance before," Annie admitted candidly. Realizing that her reply was going to raise questions in Fancy's mind, she muttered, "That is, I do not like to travel by myself. I usually accompany Mistress Constance most places and so have had no need to go on my own."

"I see," Fancy said slowly, a little frown between her eyes. Constance's insistence that Annie come with them had bothered her from the beginning, and now Annie's admission that she normally traveled only with Constance added to Fancy's puzzled unease. Why had Constance wanted Annie to accompany them? To spy on them? Her nose wrinkled. That did not seem very feasible; she and Chance had nothing to hide. So why had Constance insisted that her trusted servant come to Devil's Own with them?

Fancy couldn't come up with any answer that satisfied her, but since Annie was proving to be pleasant and might actually be helpful during the coming weeks, she dismissed the speculation about Annie and Constance from her mind. She had far more interesting things to consider: the baffling actions of her husband for one thing and Ellen's foundering romance with Hugh for another.

It was obvious that something was seriously amiss between the young lovers. Ellen had been ecstatic that the situation with Jonathan had been resolved, and she had been eager to explain the misunderstanding to Hugh. Unfortunately, Hugh would have nothing to do with her. At best he coolly ignored her shy requests for private conversation, and the rest of the time he merely pretended that she was not even in the same room with him.

Having observed the scene between Jonathan and Hugh the day of the wedding, Fancy was positive that she knew what lay at the root of Hugh's treatment of Ellen. But due to the circumstances, she'd had no time to talk privately with her sister to explain what she suspected. Ellen's puzzled, unhappy expression had not gone unnoticed by Fancy, and when Annie tactfully excused herself and returned to the house, Fancy turned to Ellen and asked, "Have you had no chance to talk to Hugh?"

"Oh, Fancy," Ellen said in a miserable tone. "He will not grant me a moment alone with him. He just fixes me with that icy glare of his and says that we said all that needs to be said to each other. What am I to do?"

Fancy sighed. "I do not know, dear, but I am very much afraid that Jonathan has a hand in why Hugh is acting as he is."

"What do you mean?" Ellen asked uneasily. "I know Jonathan told Hugh that there is no question of a marriage between us. I had thought that Hugh would be pleased." Her lower lip quivered. "But he has not been. He has been a beast to me, and I do not know why." Tears filled her eyes, and dabbing frantically at the dampness with her embroidered handkerchief, she sobbed, "I have never been so miserable in my whole life. I knew that Hugh's feelings were wounded when Jonathan announced the engagement, and that he was furious with me, but I thought that once he realized Jonathan had not been strictly speaking the truth, he would understand and forgive me." She turned lovely blue eyes toward Fancy. "I do not think I like being in love very much. It hurts terribly. I feel as if my heart is breaking and there is nothing I can do about it." Miserably she added, "I just do not understand men."

Fancy put an arm around Ellen's slender shoulders and said lightly, "I know, poppet, I know. I do not understand them very well, either. They are maddening, baffling, arrogant, and dictatorial and utterly fascinating at the same time."

Her head resting on Fancy's shoulder, Ellen asked in a small voice, "But what am I to do? He will not even let me explain. I am certain that if he would just listen to me, I could make him understand."

"I am afraid that Jonathan may have filled his head with more than just the news of your broken engagement," Fancy said reluctantly. When Ellen glanced up at her, she admitted unhappily, "I am as positive as I can be without having actually heard the conversation that Jonathan has told him some ugly untruths about you and your supposed betrothal."

"But what could he have told him that would make him look at me with such aversion? As if I were a poisonous toad?"

Fancy shook her head. "I do not know, darling. I only know that I saw them talking together and that whatever Jonathan was saying, from the stricken expression on his face, Hugh found it devastating."

"But what . . . ?" Ellen's face went white. Her hands clenched together, she asked in a hushed tone, "You think that he—? That he told Hugh that he and I were—? That I am . . . ruined?"

Slowly Fancy nodded her dark head. "Yes, I think that is exactly what Jonathan did. And worse, I fear that Hugh believed him."

An angry sparkle suddenly lit Ellen's blue eyes. "How dare he," Ellen said furiously. "Of all the despicable—" Words failed her, and tears forgotten, she took an agitated step toward the house. "Oh, but just you wait until I get my hands on him."

"Well, I am afraid you're going to have to wait awhile for your confrontation with Jonathan. We just left Walker Ridge yesterday, and I do not believe that we are to return there anytime soon," Fancy replied calmly, glad to see that her sister was not looking so woebegone anymore. Ellen was normally the gentlest of creatures, and a little show of temper would be good for her.

Ellen spun back to look at her. "Jonathan?" she asked sharply. "You think I am talking about Jonathan?" She shook her blond head vehemently. " 'Tis not Jonathan I am angry with. He is not the man I thought him to be, and I am not surprised that he slandered me, but for *Hugh* to believe him . . ." She took in a deep, furious breath. "I intend to tell that young man exactly what I think of him. How dare he believe me capable of such wicked and unchaste actions." Her chin lifted. "I have every intention of telling him so this very instant. How dare he believe such ugly and untrue things about me! How *dare* he!"

Before Fancy could utter another word, Ellen wheeled about and, eyes flashing with righteous indignation, fists clenched determinedly at her sides, with a stride and militancy to her slender body that would have done a Valkyrie proud, she marched swiftly toward the stables.

Chapter Eighteen

Her cheeks blooming with color, Ellen stormed into the cool, shadowy interior of the first building in the stable area that she came upon. Fortunately, she had chosen the right place: the breeding barn. Chance and Hugh were both there, admiring the new imported English stallion. The horse was cross-tied in the wide middle aisle, and from his gleaming bloodred coat and shiny black mane and tail, it was apparent that he had greatly benefited from the excellent care he had received at Devil's Own since his arrival.

At Ellen's precipitous entrance into the barn, the stallion snorted and pranced in the cross-ties. As the two men glanced in her direction, the stallion suddenly threw up his handsome head and let loose a piercing scream that reverberated in the rafters of the barn. Unused to the antics of stallions, Ellen was considerably startled by the sound, and to the amusement of both men, she gasped and took a hasty step backward.

Smiling at her, Chance said, "Do not be frightened, Ellen. He is firmly tied and cannot hurt you. Besides," he added, patting the elegantly muscled neck of the horse, "Devil's Own Promise, as we have renamed him, appears to be very much a gentleman."

Momentarily thrown off guard by the stallion's actions, Ellen quickly regrouped. Approaching the two men, she looked at Hugh and said tightly, "If my brother-in-law can spare you, I would like a private word with you . . . . *now*."

Hugh's amused smile faded and he replied stiffly, "I can think of no reason why that would be necessary. Anything you have to say to me can be said in front of Chance."

Ellen's flush deepened, and she sent a beseeching glance in Chance's direction. He cocked an eyebrow at her, noting with interest the signs of angry agitation on her face. Then he looked thoughtfully at Hugh's closed features. One would have had to be blind and deaf not to realize that something was seriously amiss between the young pair, but since Hugh had not unburdened himself to him and since he was not inclined to meddle, Chance had not dwelt upon the situation. It was obvious, though, that Ellen was prepared to have her say, and since a prudent man did not take sides in a lovers' quarrel—not if he wanted to remain on speaking terms with either party—Chance shrugged and said to no one in particular, "I believe that I shall put Promise away and go in search of my wife. She is no doubt, ah, anxiously wishing for my company." Ignoring the aghast expression in Hugh's eyes, Chance bowed to Ellen and murmured, "If you will excuse me?"

She gave him a curt nod, her gaze still fastened on Hugh's face. Ignoring the pair of them, Chance quickly unfastened Promise and led the stallion away, leaving Ellen and Hugh alone in the cool shadows of the barn.

Barely able to contain her sense of injustice, Ellen hardly waited for Chance to pass from view before she took a step forward and, poking one stiff little finger in the middle of Hugh's broad chest, said hotly, "How dare you believe such ugly things about me! How *dare* you!"

Unprepared for her attack, Hugh frowned and asked unwisely, "Pardon? What are you talking about?"

"Jonathan!" she said with loathing. "As if you did not know."

Ellen's blond curls framed her pretty face, and with her

cheeks rosy with temper and her blue eyes flashing with anger, she was vastly appealing as she stood before him. Too appealing, Hugh thought bitterly, feeling the now familiar ache in the middle of his chest intensifying. Despite all his vows to the contrary, as he stared down at her, he felt his heart-wrenching resolve to have nothing to do with her crumble. Grimly he reminded himself that in spite of how lovely she looked at the moment, she was an utterly amoral creature, a cruel young woman who ensnared the unwary heart and then, when she had sighted new prey, carelessly threw it away—as she had done to Jonathan. She was *not*, he had sworn to himself, going to have a chance to do it to him. The last thing Jonathan had done, he reminded himself painfully, was to beg him to take care and not be fooled by her air of innocence. Jonathan had warned him, too, that she might attempt to deny everything, and if he interpreted her stance and words correctly, that was precisely what she was trying to do now.

Conscious of the angry, resentful anguish that had been his constant companion since Jonathan had opened his eyes to her true nature, Hugh asked coldly, "And just what is it that my cousin Jonathan is supposed to have done?"

Ellen stamped her foot. "Oh, do not toy with me. You know very well that he told you something about me that has made you act as if I am some sort of a leper. And you are a fool if you believe a word that lying snake of a cousin of yours has said about me."

Hugh flicked a sardonic brow upward. "Am I to understand, then, that you did *not* break off your betrothal to him?"

Suppressing a most unnatural urge to slap him, she said through clenched teeth, "Of course not. I *did* request that we cry off, and since we were never officially engaged there was no disgrace in it. It was clearly understood between us before we left England that the reason for our trip to the Colonies was to see if Jonathan and I would suit. But nothing had been formally arranged—Fancy wanted us to wait and we agreed with her—thank heavens." Her eyes darkened. "For your information, Jonathan never requested my hand in marriage. He just announced our engagement in front of you and everyone else. He certainly had not asked *me* what I thought of the idea."

"I find that rather difficult to believe, and I fail to see why you think this should interest me."

For a brief second Ellen's expression was so stricken that Hugh nearly caught her up in his arms and kissed her. Then the moment passed, and, holding himself firmly in check, he stared icily back at her.

His air of utter indifference and his cool words finally pierced the hot anger that had sent her willy-nilly to confront him. She was suddenly, painfully, mortified. It was clear that nothing she could say would change his mind about her, and now, as her normally sweet nature reasserted itself, she was extremely anxious to leave behind this embarrassing scene and minister to her broken heart in private. Her eyes glittering with unshed tears, she turned away and said huskily, "Forgive me, I shall not bore you any longer. I have misunderstood the situation between us."

His face suddenly twisted with pain, Hugh muttered, "Just as Jonathan did, no doubt."

"What do you mean by that?" Ellen asked sharply, glancing back at him.

Having said that much, he could not easily retreat. Deciding to have it all out in the open, he said stiffly, "You do not have to pretend to me. I know everything. Jonathan told me how you had led him to believe that you loved him and that you were going to be wed." Not meeting her gaze, he added, "And that he never would have anticipated your marriage vows and made love to you if he had not been absolutely certain that you intended to marry him. He insisted that the only reason you had broken your promise to him was that you had grown bored with him and that you had decided that seducing me might prove more entertaining."

"And you *believed* him?" Ellen asked in angry, incredulous tones.

His jaw clenched. "Why would he lie about something

like that? He showed himself in nearly as unflattering a light as yourself."

"Why?" she cried furiously. "You mean you honestly do not know? Didn't you and Chance warn Fancy and me about him? Has his nature changed so much in the weeks we have known each other? Has Jonathan somehow become such a saintly creature that his word is above suspicion? And have you so little respect for me that you would listen to him and not give me a chance to defend myself?"

There was such passion, such pain, in her voice that Hugh's certainty that his cousin had spoken the truth began to waver. Jonathan, he reminded himself uneasily, was not noted for his integrity. How often in the past had Chance said that lying and conniving were second nature to his cousin, especially if it obtained him what he wanted? Thinking straight for the first time since that shattering afternoon, Hugh realized immediately that if Jonathan had intended to marry Ellen and she had cried off, he would not, as an honorable man would have done, have simply stood aside. No, Jonathan would have made certain that Ellen suffered. And if he suspected that her heart had chosen another, wouldn't he have done his best to destroy her chance for happiness?

An arrested expression on his face, he stared at her, the terrible suspicion suddenly writhing through his brain that Jonathan had played him for a perfect fool. Lost in his own painful jealousy, he had taken Jonathan's words as if they had been cast in stone and had believed the vilest things about Ellen. Things, he realized with bitter insight, that could not possibly be true—not of the beguiling, sweet creature he had grown to love so very much over the past several weeks.

There was nothing sweet and beguiling about Ellen at the moment as she glared up at him, anger and hurt fairly vibrating through her small frame, but Hugh felt his spirits suddenly soar. It did not matter if she was furious with him, he thought almost light-headedly. He deserved it for having believed Jonathan's spiteful words for even one second. All that mattered was that he had been a gullible dolt and that, reveling in his own misery, he had hurt one of the gentlest creatures he had ever known. He brightened instantly as a thought struck him, all of his bleak unhappiness these past days vanishing. Weren't Jonathan's actions an obvious indication that he had believed that Ellen had deep feelings for *him*? Why else would his cousin have tried to poison his mind against her? And wasn't Ellen's profound distress with the estrangement that presently existed between them indicative that she cared a great deal for him and his good opinion of her? Why else would she have been so upset with his cold manner toward her? Could it be that, perhaps, she . . . loved him . . . as he loved her? His heart began to beat swiftly.

Suddenly confident of his ground, he took a step nearer her, his features softening. He reached out and caught one of her hands in his. "I must offer you my deepest, sincerest apologies, Ellie." He smiled ruefully. "It would appear that I have been a great, silly jackanapes, and I am very sorry for it. If I had not been half-mad with jealousy that afternoon, I would have realized immediately that Jonathan was trying to keep us apart." His voice deepened. "Anyone but a blind fool like myself would have known that someone as sweet and gentle as you are would never act in the foul manner Jonathan claimed. I am indeed sorry if I caused you pain."

Ellen's tender heart fairly melted at the warmth in Hugh's gaze and tone. But reminding herself how hurtfully he had wounded her, she resisted the powerful impulse to fling herself into his arms and tell him that she had forgiven him. He was not, she decided with uncharacteristic resentment, going to charm his way into her good graces *that* easily. He *had* hurt her. Her chin held at an imperious angle, she said tartly, "But not as sorry as you are going to be, if you think that a mere apology will undo the misery you have caused me."

A smugly masculine gleam in his blue eyes, Hugh pulled her closer to him. "Have my actions truly made you miserable?" he asked huskily. "Do you care so very much what I think of you, sweetheart?"

Realizing with dismay that she was only a second away from total capitulation, Ellen jerked her hand from his grasp and said gruffly, "Do not put great store in the fact that I have not been happy with you thinking ill of me. No one wishes for their reputation to be unfairly tarnished." Putting more distance between them, she took a deep, steadying breath and said prosaically, "I am glad that we have had this moment to talk privately. We can now put this unfortunate misunderstanding behind us and be comfortable with each other." She tipped her head to the side. "We shall be dear friends once more."

Since being "comfortable" or "dear friends" with Ellen was the last thing on Hugh's mind, he wasn't best pleased by her words. Some of his satisfaction with the situation fading, he asked, "Is that all you have to say?"

Ellen opened her eyes very wide. "Why, sir, what else would there be for us to discuss?"

Hugh scowled at her, suddenly not so certain of his ground. "Ellie, I am warning you, do not toy with me."

"Oh, la, sir, I would not dare," she murmured, her eyes dropping demurely. Spinning on her heels, she gave a saucy toss of her blond curls and skipped gracefully from the shadows of the barn into the bright sunlight outside, leaving Hugh, his expression frustrated and baffled, to stare after her.

Women, he decided caustically, were the very devil! There was simply no understanding them.

When Chance found him shortly thereafter, Hugh was frowning and muttering to himself as he grimly brushed the already shiny coat of a long-legged bay mare. Having passed a sunnily smiling Ellen just a few moments previously, he had expected to see the same expression on Hugh's face, but it seemed that he had misjudged the situation.

Picking up a curry comb from the box of grooming equipment on the floor in the middle aisle, Chance entered the roomy stall where Hugh worked and, beginning to curry on the opposite side of the contented mare, asked quietly, "Is something wrong? You do not look very happy."

"I am not," Hugh answered tightly. "And I am undecided whether to strangle Ellen first and then go challenge that bastard Jonathan to a duel, or kill him first and *then* strangle Ellen."

"Would you care to explain?"

Hugh snorted. "No, I would not, but I will." He looked over the mare's back at Chance. "You have to know first that I am the biggest fool in nature. I listened to our dear cousin Jonathan tell me the blackest pack of vicious lies in creation about Ellen and then, having made the mistake of hearing him out, I *believed* him."

Chance's eyes narrowed. "He vilified Ellen?"

Suddenly wary of the dangerous glitter in Chance's gaze, Hugh glanced away. "No one else knows about it." He smiled bitterly. "In fact, I suspect that I am the only person who would have been cork brained enough to listen to him without planting him a facer then and there."

If Hugh was attempting to deflect Chance's anger, he was not successful. "What did he say?" Chance asked in ominous tones.

Hugh shook his head, a stubborn slant to his mouth. "If anyone is going to face Jonathan on the dueling field, it is going to be me. 'Tis *my* woman he insulted."

In a lightning swift change of mood, Chance grinned at him. "Oh, and does Ellen know of this fascinating fact?"

A scowl crossed Hugh's face. "No. She says we are to be 'friends.' "

There was such disgust in Hugh's voice that Chance laughed. "I would not despair, my friend. If she did not care for you, she would not have been so determined to clear her reputation with you. Knowing the feminine sex as I do, I would wager that our Ellen intends to punish you just a trifle before relenting and telling you what is really in her heart."

Hugh nodded glumly. " 'Tis what I feared."

Unaware that Fancy had entered the barn and was approaching the stall where they worked, Chance said darkly, "And as for Jonathan . . . I am afraid that you will have to wait until after I have taken my own revenge before you will be allowed to take yours."

Suddenly concentrating on the motions of his brush, Hugh said idly, "I had wondered if, after all this time, you still truly blame him for Jenny's death. Or if hating Jonathan had merely become a habit."

" 'Tis not a habit, Hugh. I do blame him," Chance said flatly. "I just have not been able to decide upon an effective way of painfully teaching him that seducing other men's wives and then leaving them to their fate cannot be done with impunity. That there is a high price, a very high price, to be paid for carelessly destroying lives."

"It happened a long time ago, Chance," Hugh murmured. "Jenny has lain moldering in her grave for over seven years now. Perhaps 'tis time for you to forget the thought of vengeance and put the past behind you. Killing Jonathan will not bring Jenny back. You have a new wife now and a new life. Why risk destroying it to take vengeance for a long-ago deed?"

Chance gave an ugly laugh. "I do not want to kill Jonathan, my friend. If it were that simple, I could have done that years ago." He shook his head. "No, I do not want to kill him. Death would be too swift and kind. I want the selfish bastard to suffer for a long time, a lifetime. I will not be satisfied until he learns what it is to lose forever something precious and irreplaceable and," Chance said grimly, "to live, as I had to live all these years, every day regretting and mourning his enormous loss."

The smile of greeting that had been on her lips vanished, and Fancy stood frozen in the center of the aisle, Chance's words ringing in her ears. All the uncertainties about her marriage to him suddenly bloomed into full flower once more, and she wished violently that she had chosen a different time to go exploring. Or that her entrance into the stables would have made enough noise to alert the two men to the fact that they were no longer alone and that their every word could be overheard with painful clarity. Of course, she thought miserably, she could slip away before she heard any more of their private conversation, but her feet seemed to have rooted to the spot where she stood and she could not move.

"And how do you plan to arrange that?" Hugh asked, his voice troubled.

"By taking away something that means a great deal to him . . . and letting him live, knowing that I hold his dearest possession firmly in my hand."

His words sank like a knife into Fancy. It had been obvious from the beginning that Chance had believed that *she* was the Merrivale sister Jonathan had intended to marry, and if she had needed confirmation that she had merely been a pawn in Chance's desire for revenge against Jonathan, he had just given it to her. All along she had tried to convince herself that she had been wrong about him and his motives for marrying her, but it seemed that she had not been wrong at all. She had been all too right, and the gently burgeoning hope in her breast that their marriage might prove to be a joy to both of them, that she had somehow misjudged him, disappeared instantly. Bitterly aware that she had *again* allowed herself to be lulled by his dark charm and her own treacherous emotions into a false feeling of happiness, she felt a dull weight settle in her chest.

Wounded and full of angry remorse that she had not followed her first inclination and faced the scandal an annulment would have caused, Fancy turned and quietly left the barn. She had been a fool. And she had no one to blame but herself—that and her equally foolish heart. Because the unpleasant fact still remained that she was married to a conniving rogue and that, unfortunately, she was hopelessly in love with him.

Alone in her bedchamber, Fancy paced the floor, wondering unhappily what she was going to do. Leaving was out of the question. She was married to the man and, despite all the reasons not to be, she was in love with him. It was a bitter, bitter admission, but she could think of no other reason to explain her incomprehensible actions. He had only to look at her, smile, and put out his hand, and like a fawning bitch at the heels of her master, she followed wherever he led. Not only was she in love with this man she had married, but he was outrageously charming and just the slightest brush of his body against hers whipped her own into a frenzy of yearning. She should have been elated to be married to a man she loved and whose mere presence gave her pleasure. But she most definitely was not.

Since the wedding, she had managed to push away many of her doubts and uncertainties. Chance, with his laughing eyes and teasing mouth, had made it fatally easy to forget that their marriage had not come about in normal circumstances. The fact remained, however, that she *didn't* know her new husband very well and that there were certain events surrounding their marriage in which he more resembled a scoundrel than an honorable gentleman. His changeability kept her confused and in a turmoil. One minute he boldly compromised her, compelling her to marry him. Then the next he agreed not to force his conjugal rights upon her . . . for a month. A tremor went through her. A month that would fly swiftly by.

She closed her eyes in anguish, her hands clenched at her sides. What was she to do? Pretend she had never overheard that damning conversation? She knew she wouldn't be able to do that—no matter how often she pushed it away, the question would rise again and again in her brain and devil her mercilessly. She had to know the truth. Though her heart quailed at what she might learn, she was determined to find out if Chance had married her only because it had been a way of taking revenge upon Jonathan or if there had been some other reason. Some other reason that would lessen this terrible pain in her breast.

The evening meal that night was not an overwhelming success. It should have been. The heat and humidity of the day had lessened somewhat; the dining room was large and elegantly appointed; the food was, no doubt, delicious; and Jed and Maryanne were expert at serving the table. But Fancy might as well have been eating weevil-filled biscuits in some cold and dank cellar for all the pleasure she took in her food. She wasn't so lost in her own misery that she didn't notice that Hugh spent most of the meal scowling across the table at Ellen or that Ellen seemed to be unusually gay and sunny, if the smiles and snippets of conversation she shared with Chance were any indication. Annie Clemmons, despite Fancy's warm manner toward her, was still feeling uncomfortable with the situation in which she found herself and kept to herself, replying politely to any conversation sent her way but for the most part keeping silent.

While enjoying Ellen's innocent flirtation with him, Chance wasn't entirely oblivious of Fancy's lack of appetite or subdued air. More than once during the meal he sent her a speculative glance. The tour of the house and grounds earlier in the day had gone rather well, he had thought, and when he had last seen his bride, she had been smiling and apparently happy with her new home. What had happened in the hours since?

It wasn't until everyone had retired for the night that Chance had an opportunity for private speech with Fancy. He and Hugh had drunk a few snifters of brandy after the ladies had gone upstairs to bed. When he entered his rooms some time later, he was surprised to find his wife still dressed as she had been at dinner, waiting for him. She was sitting in one of the maroon leather chairs, her hands folded in her lap, the expression on her lovely face hard to define. Angry? Hurt? Resigned? Perhaps all three, he thought slowly.

Shrugging out of his jacket and undoing the stock around his neck as he walked across the room toward her, he said, "I did not expect to find you here."

"Since you have ordered that I am to sleep in your bed, where else should I be?"

There was a note in her voice that was also hard to define, and the first faint chill of unease stirred within him. Giving himself time to consider the situation, he sat on the bed and swiftly removed his boots. Something had obviously disturbed her, but try as he might, he could not fathom a reason for the change in her manner toward him.

Leaving the bed and standing in front of her, his hands on his hips, he said carefully, "I am flattered that you remembered my, er, orders, but you are not garbed for bed. Unless, of course, you intend to sleep in what you are wearing right now."

Fancy looked up at him, and something in that searching topaz gaze made his feeling of unease sharpen. He leaned forward and, resting his hands on the arms of the chair, his face mere inches from hers, asked quietly, "What is it, Fancy? What has happened to make you look at me so?"

Fancy took a deep breath, her gaze locked with his. "Why did you marry me, Chance?" she asked abruptly. "Why did you create the situation that made our marriage imperative?"

Chance stiffened. Standing upright, he took a step away from her. Looking back at her over his shoulder, he said dryly, "I am sure that you have drawn your own conclusions about it."

She nodded slowly. "Yes, I have, but I would like to hear your explanation. Why?"

"Why?" he asked lightly, feeling his ground as he went. "Why else, madame, but that I found you so fetching that I could not help myself?"

"Do not jest. I deserve an answer. Why did you marry me?"

Since he didn't know that answer himself and since it was painfully apparent that much rested on his next words, he moved idly around the room, trying to figure out what was going on. Why did she want to know now? Why was she so insistent upon it? And what the hell had happened to the beguiling companion he had escorted around earlier in the day?

"Why is it so important to you? My reasons would change little. We are married and the marriage has been consummated. What difference does it make why I compromised you? The deed is done."

"Yes, and we have to live with it for the rest of our lives. But that does not change my right to know why the deed was committed in the first place." Her voice shook a little. "You deliberately compromised me. Why?"

Chance shot her a dark glance. She wasn't going to budge, and no matter how he tried to deflect her course, she came right back to the original question. Why *had* he sought out her bed that morning and allowed them to be found in such a scandalous manner? Damned if he knew! Except, he thought irritably, it had made tremendous sense to him at that time. He'd have his revenge against Jonathan and give himself something that he desperately wanted—Fancy for his own. But he could hardly tell her that. Knowing how badly he wanted her and to what enormous lengths he was willing to go to get her would give her a weapon against him. His mouth twisted. And she certainly wouldn't like learning that an emotion as base and petty as revenge had partly initiated his actions. He realized suddenly with a sinking feeling in his stomach that vengeance against Jonathan had merely been an excuse, that if Jonathan's bride had been any woman other than Fancy, he never would have hit upon the scheme that he had.

Moodily he looked away from her. Trying to explain his own ambiguity about his deepest feelings for her would only lead him to deep, dangerous water, where he was liable to lose his head and blurt out something foolish . . . such as, I am half in love with you and have been since I first laid eyes on you. I want you, that I have only to think of you, of your soft mouth and sweet body, and I am on fire for you. That when I am with you 'tis springtime even if snow o'erspreads the ground. Which, of course, was all utter nonsense. Hadn't he sworn upon Jenny's death never to let himself love again? Never to let a mere woman be the sum of his happiness?

Ignoring Fancy, Chance walked over to a long table and opened one of the many crystal decanters there. After pouring himself a snifter of brandy, he crossed to where she sat and took a chair across from her. Staring down at the swirling amber liquor, he asked suddenly, "Why is it so important to know my reasons?"

She smiled bitterly. "Must you always answer one question with another?"

He shrugged and took a sip of the brandy. "Let us just say that I am curious to know why the question has arisen now instead of some other time."

"I came to the barn this afternoon," Fancy said levelly. "I came looking for you. I wanted to see if you had time to show me around." Her eyes dropped from his intent gaze. Becoming enormously interested in pleating the fabric of her skirt, she said softly, "You were talking to Hugh about Jonathan and Jenny and revenge." Her eyes lifted and clashed with his. "I did not mean to eavesdrop, but I could not help hearing every word said between the two of you. It was a rather illuminating conversation."

Chapter Nineteen

Chance's face did not change expression, but he was silently cursing the damnable fate that had allowed Fancy to overhear that particular conversation. He had no trouble recalling the words spoken to Hugh, and after examining them, he groaned inwardly.

Fancy's name had never been mentioned, nor had his marriage to her been remotely connected to a quest for vengeance against Jonathan. But . . . His eyes narrowed. Already suspicious of his motives, already having suspected that it had been precisely to punish Jonathan that had occasioned their marriage, Fancy would have had no trouble applying his expressed sentiments to their own situation. How could she not? And he could hardly claim that revenge against Jonathan had not had *any* part in the circumstances surrounding their sudden wedding, not when his own words could be used to call him a liar. Worse, it was partially true, and there was no way he could reasonably explain to her his jumbled thoughts the night he had decided to compromise her. Not, he admitted savagely, without revealing how completely she had bewitched him.

To give himself time to think, Chance took a long swallow of the brandy. His thoughts no clearer than they had been, he frowned across at Fancy, wondering how she would react if he told her the truth, that as he looked back on that night, he had realized that taking revenge against Jonathan had only been an excuse, a reason to allow him to gain what he really wanted—her. His mouth tightened. And freely hand her a weapon with which to tear his heart from his chest?

He got up abruptly and returned the snifter to the table. Swinging back to face her, still playing for time, he asked, "And what momentous conclusions have you come to regarding what you heard?"

Fancy rose to her feet. "Still avoiding the question, Chance? Still returning question for question?"

A spot of color burned high on his cheeks as he said, " 'Tis obvious that whatever you think you overheard does not bode well for me. I think I am entitled to know what it is I am on trial for tonight."

"There is no trial," Fancy said wearily. "I merely wanted the truth from you—for once. As you said earlier, we are married and it is unlikely that the situation will change. But since you have seen fit to so cavalierly rearrange my life, I think you owe it to me to tell me why." Her eyes hard and bright, she asked for perhaps the fifth time, "Why? Why did you marry me?"

"Because I wanted you," he said bluntly, his body braced as if for a blow.

A bitter laugh came from Fancy. "And that is to satisfy me? That is all you have to say? You wanted me?"

Chance nodded curtly.

"And Jonathan? Can you swear that taking vengeance against him had nothing to do with our marriage? That you did not believe that it was me he intended to marry and that you did not do as you did in order to take me away from him? To punish him? To get your revenge?"

In one swift stride he was upon her, and digging his fingers into her arms, he jerked her next to him. His face near hers, he said tautly, "It does not make any difference why I married you. You are my wife, and by heaven, nothing will change that fact. Have done, Fancy. Forget what you over-heard this afternoon. It was a private moment between Hugh and me, and it had nothing to do with you."

Scornfully she stared up at him. "I see. I am just to forget about it and pretend it never happened? How convenient that would be for you."

Chance's jaw clenched. "Fancy, I do not want to fight with you. Let it alone—please."

Hurt and angry, Fancy shrugged out of his grasp and turned her back on him. "I do not seem to have any choice in the matter," she said stiffly, and walked toward the door that separated their rooms. It was only when she had her hand on the crystal knob that she glanced over her shoulder at him. A bitter smile curved her soft mouth. "You do real-ize that your very silence on the matter—your refusal to an-swer me—leaves me with no choice but to believe that you did think I was to be Jonathan's bride and that it was *pre-cisely* to wound him that you compromised me."

Better she think that, Chance admitted savagely, than to know how completely she had him enthralled. One hand clenched into a fist at his side, he fought the urge to snatch her into his embrace and give free rein to all the powerful emotions that preyed upon him. "I cannot control what you want to think," he said finally, when he thought he had him-self safely under control from any silly outbursts. "I can only swear to you that no matter what the circumstances of our marriage, I will be as good a husband to you as I can. I will try to make you happy."

His words warmed her, melting some of the ice around her heart and making her wonder for one treacherous second if she had been all wrong in her conclusions about him. There was such sincerity in his voice. It would be so easy, so simple, to accept the olive branch he was holding out to her. So easy to ignore all her doubts and fears and let herself be swept along in his wake. She stiffened. But that was what happened every time. He charmed her. Beguiled her. Made her forget the real situation between them—just as he had on their wedding night. Suddenly furious, she snapped, "You want to make me happy? Never let me look into your scoundrel's face again! Now, that would make me happy!"

She flung open the door, but before she could escape, his voice stopped her. "Haven't you forgotten something?" he asked grimly.

"What?" she demanded, spinning around to glare at him.

He cocked a brow. "Your bed, madame." He nodded in the direction of the massive four-poster. "You are sleeping here tonight, remember?"

Fancy took in an outraged breath. "Surely you do not mean to keep me to that ridiculous bargain we made?"

His eyes gleamed. "Of course not. If you wish to forgo your part of the agreement, then I would have no difficulty whatsoever in allowing my part to lapse."

Smothering an urge to strike his mocking face, Fancy snatched up her skirts and stalked swiftly to the high bed. After viciously kicking off her satin slippers, she bounded into bed. Petticoats and silken skirts frothing around her slim ankles, she sat bolt upright in the bed, her arms folded across her chest, and sent him a baleful look. "I am in your bed," she snarled. "Does this satisfy you?"

Chance's dark mood lifted at the sight she made, sitting there so militantly in his bed, her elegant clothing in charming disarray around her. Suppressing a dangerous urge to grin, he said, "Sweetheart, you know very well that I am not satisfied." His voice thickened. "And you damn well know exactly what it would take to make me satisfied."

Fancy's clothing suddenly felt too tight, her breathing instantly became erratic, and to her eternal mortification, she could feel the heat that flooded her lower body at his words. Damn him! She was certain that she had never hated any man as much as she did Chance Walker—or felt so gloriously alive with anyone else.

Fancy discovered during the night that followed that there were several very good reasons why one did *not* normally sleep in day wear. She could hardly move, for one thing. Her petticoats and skirts got caught time and again under her body as she twisted and squirmed, trying to get comfortable.

Her bodice seemed fashioned for the express purpose of squeezing the breath out of her, and her laced stays poked unmercifully into her waist. Her head ached, too; the pins that kept her hair in its fashionable pompadour dug into her scalp and made her miserable.

Of course, Chance slept wonderfully, and Fancy spent most of the night thinking up several extremely horrid fates for him. She did finally sleep toward dawn but woke a short time later, heavy eyed and achy headed, to find that Chance had risen and left for the day. Thank God!

Sliding from his bed, she left a trail of discarded, crumpled clothing in her wake and staggered into the next room. Wakeful just long enough to rid herself of the punishing pins in her hair and the remainder of her clothing, clad only in her embroidered shift, Fancy emitted a grateful sigh and sank into the welcoming softness of her own bed.

The next time she woke it was late afternoon, and with pleasure she spied a tray with a china pot, steam still rising from its spout, sitting on the table under the window. Stifling a mighty yawn, she slipped from the bed and sat in one of the chairs near the window, sipping her coffee appreciatively and gazing outside.

The sky was sullen with dark clouds. Faintly in the distance Fancy heard the boom of thunder. But her mind wasn't on the coming storm; she was mulling over last night's confrontation with Chance. Her lips twisted. A confrontation that had accomplished little. Except, she decided sourly, Chance now knew that she was aware of his scheme to hit back at Jonathan—and that he had used her to do so. She might have preferred to delude herself otherwise, but she didn't doubt that this was the reason why Chance had married her. That he wanted her, that she pleased him in bed, only made the revenge against Jonathan all the sweeter.

Her problem was that her knowledge about his perfidious actions did not change a thing. Not the situation, or the turmoil in her breast. In spite of everything, she loved Chance Walker. While she could agree that loving him, knowing what she did about him, was the act of a foolish, utterly besotted goose, it didn't make any difference to what was in her heart.

Sighing, she put down the china cup and gazed blankly off into space. If only Chance would be honest with her, she thought mournfully. They couldn't change the past; she couldn't change the reasons he had married her. But those reasons, painful and humiliating though they were, could be acknowledged and then put behind them. There was much to be gained from their marriage. They may have started out badly, but they could start afresh and over time build a good marriage. But not as long as Chance refused to be open and honest with her. His unwillingness to trust her with the truth opened a huge chasm between them. She vowed fiercely, as she stood up and rang for Charity, that she would make no attempt to bridge it. He had created it. Let him be the one to cross it.

As August slid into September, the heat and debilitating humidity seemed to press down upon the land, animals and humans alike moving more slowly, frequently seeking shady spots to escape the punishing force of the sun. All the while, watermelons ripened, black-eyed peas made their first appearance on the table, Indian corn was finally ready for eating, and the leaves of the tobacco plants began to droop and turn faintly yellow—sure signs that harvesttime was imminent.

Despite the discord between the newlyweds, the passing days had not been unpleasant. On the surface, in front of the others, she and Chance seemed to rub along together tolerably well, able to converse mundanely about the day's accomplishments. It was only when they were alone that the stiffness and constraint between them was obvious. They had little of a personal nature to say to one another when the doors to their rooms shut behind them each night, and Fancy grew to dread the falling of darkness. She continued to sleep in his bed, as she had agreed to do, and while there were times when his arms would unconsciously slide around her and he would pull her close, or mornings when Fancy woke to find herself snuggled confidingly against his broad chest, there were no attempts to change the terms of their bargain.

Fancy couldn't claim that it didn't disturb her to lie night after night in such intimate proximity with a man she tried to tell herself she despised. It did disturb her—a great deal—yet he was also a man she loved, a man whose very look could make her dizzy with longing. But she fought stoutly against his magnetic pull, reminding herself of his trickery whenever she was in danger of weakening.

Fortunately, Fancy's days were full and she had little time to brood over the situation between herself and Chance. Chance was gone from the house for several hours at a time, overseeing the various projects that needed his attention as everyone worked steadily in the shortening daylight hours in preparation for winter, so she was spared his mocking presence for much of the day.

Life at Devil's Own was a stunning revelation to Fancy. Until she had married Spencer, she had lived simply, often helping with ordinary tasks, picking eggs for Cook and even, upon one memorial occasion, milking their cow. But she still hadn't been quite prepared for life on a large plantation in the middle of the wilderness. Devil's Own was almost entirely self-sufficient. They did need raw supplies, sugar, salt and some spices, and other items that they did not make or grow themselves, and these were brought in sporadically from the small outlying towns. Twice yearly there were trips to Richmond or Williamsburg for major restocking. As the owner's wife, she discovered that it was up to her to oversee all things connected with the running of the domestic side of the plantation, from the sowing and harvesting of food for everyone, to the care and feeding of the chickens, pigs, and cows. As the wife of a baron in England, she had been able merely to give her orders for the day to the servants and think no more about it, but at Devil's Own she was expected to take a much more active part, from helping weed the extensive gardens to sowing the winter vegetable crop.

To her great alarm, she found herself pressed into duty as

teacher to the children of the plantation workers and, upon occasion, physician and midwife. There was very little connected with the smooth running of the various households that did not require some intervention on her part, even if she did not do all the backbreaking work involved. It was, she told Ellen one morning, rather like being responsible for the total well-being of a small, isolated village.

There was much for Fancy to absorb. With Annie's gentle guidance and ably assisted by Martha and Jed, she and Ellen quickly learned the art of making candles and soap and even a simple paint that might be needed for some hasty repair. The sisters mastered the methods for pickling and preserving the various fruits and vegetables (Fancy was especially proud of her plum brandy, though it would be six weeks before they actually tasted it) and the steps necessary for the smoking and corning of various meats, including the making of the renowned Virginia hams.

Winter was not many months away, and this was one of the busiest times of year. Fancy and Ellen both were occupied nearly every moment of every day, either helping, overseeing, or learning some new task. There were still vegetables in the garden that at the proper time would be harvested and placed in the huge root cellars: potatoes, turnips, onions, garlic, beans, pumpkins, and squashes. Martha showed them how to properly store the foods, explaining, with a twinkle in her eyes, "If things rot and you are reduced to eating nothing but cabbage and salt pork until spring, you will never again carelessly heap your harvest in some damp and moldy corner of the root cellar."

At night when she fell into bed, Fancy's head was full of what she had learned that day, including recipes for everything from preserving fresh cream to making vinegar and even cement and pink dye.

But despite the fullness of her days, she was uncomfortably aware of the swift passage of time. Her month of married chastity was approaching its end, and nothing of any importance had been resolved between herself and Chance. She couldn't pretend that she hadn't learned something more of his nature during this time. They did speak, mostly about the workings of the plantation, but she was able to observe him with the others and realized that he was an able and respected taskmaster. He was also, she admitted glumly, kind, intelligent, thoughtful, considerate, and generous—traits she would not have connected with a man who had acted so dastardly. Chance Walker was a mystery, one she was determined to solve.

Fancy was not alone in wanting to solve the mystery of Chance Walker. Sam Walker would have given everything he owned and more to know the truth about the events surrounding the night of Chance's birth. He implicitly believed Morely's story of finding the abandoned infant on the bluff. It was too outrageous a tale not to be true. And with all his wild ways as a youth, Morely had never been given to telling lies. Having a lifetime of knowledge of the man, Sam knew that if Morely said he had simply found the newborn infant squalling on the bluff overlooking the river, that's exactly what happened.

No, the mystery wasn't in Morely's incredible tale. The mystery was in what had happened *prior* to Morely's discovery of Chance.

For hours at a time, in the days and weeks that had followed Morely's confession, Sam would catch himself staring blindly off into space, his keen mind exploring ways to unravel the tangled skeins that time had woven. Constance, of course, would deny everything, even if he were mad enough to question her or dared to hint at his suspicions. Annie Clemmons was Constance's creature, and therefore whatever she said would be suspect. Besides, at the moment Annie was out of reach at Chance's plantation. The only other person who could throw light on that night was his own dear, beloved Letty.

With every fiber of his being, Sam shrank from bringing up the subject to Letty. He did not want to arouse painful memories, remembering her dangerously fragile state all those years before when he had returned home to learn the crushing news that she had been delivered of a stillborn son. It had been years before she could even return to the place where their infant child had been buried. How much worse it would be for her if he were to give her the hope that a young man she had long loved was actually her own son— only to have to snatch it away later. It could very well destroy her, and Sam was not willing to run that risk, at least not yet.

But he *had* to talk to her about that night. He had to know what she remembered. Standing in his office, staring broodingly at the glinting ribbon of river in the distance one afternoon, Sam sighed. Here it was, the middle of September, and he had been unable to discover anything that would lend credence to the wild supposition that Chance Walker was his son. Morely and Pru had remained at Walker Ridge for a week after Chance and Fancy left for Devil's Own, and every moment he and Morely had been alone, they had speculated on that decades-old night. By the time Morely and Pru had left, the two men had grimly decided that if they were to prove Chance's ancestry, they would have to take certain events as fact.

The most obvious event that they had agreed upon was that Letty had to have given birth to twins that fateful night and that one of the twins was born dead, the other alive. The next most glaringly evident occurrence had to have been that Constance had determined instantly that the surviving twin was to disappear. There was no doubt in their minds that she would have delegated that highly risky deed to Anne Clemmons.

Sam frowned, his hands clasped loosely behind his back. All that was well and good, as far as it went, but why didn't Letty realize that she had given birth to a second child? Surely a woman would know such a thing?

Those rare times she had been willing to talk with him about that night, it was obvious that she remembered clearly the birth of their stillborn son. Not only how perfect he had been, but every physical aspect of his dear little form, right down to the identifying six toes. But never a word or a hint of a twin.

Sam took an agitated step around the room, painful memories and emotions roiling within him. Was he deluding himself? Grasping wildly at straws? Was he simply being an old fool to conceive, even for a moment, that Chance was his and Letty's own flesh and blood? That Letty had unknowingly given birth to a second child, a strong and lusty one, and that Constance had swiftly attempted to get rid of it? That only Morely's chance encounter had saved the infant's life?

It was incredible, he couldn't deny it. Yet it seemed highly likely. No other explanation for Morely's finding of the infant fit the situation quite as well, he admitted as he sat down and began to leaf idly through the old ledgers on his desk. Ledgers he had combed diligently for any clue that might shed light on that event.

As much to disprove as to prove the truth of the matter, in the intervening weeks Sam had pored over any record of that time that he could lay his hands on. He had torn through the contents of dusty, long forgotten trunks in the back of the storerooms and attics to search out what letters and snippets of information he had from those painful days. Reading those accounts made his heart ache and brought back all the terrible anguish of that time. Reviewing his accounts of expenditures and receipts revealed little, except he discovered that he had made no note of any other children being born at Walker Ridge during that critical time. And he had always, he reminded himself slowly as he continued to turn the fragile, yellowed pages, been meticulous about such things. He had kept excellent records of nearly every event on the plantation, from planting and harvest dates to the weather, the births and deaths of slaves and others who worked for him, and even the birth of a litter of puppies by his favorite hunting dog. If another child had been born anywhere near the time Morely had found Chance, wouldn't he have made note of it?

Thoughtfully he stared at a notation that leaped from the page in front of him. It was dated March 21, 1740.

Missy, a sixteen-year-old slave I purchased two years ago in Williamsburg, gave birth today to a fine healthy daughter this afternoon after a long, hard labor. We feared we would lose them both, but all ended well and mother and daughter, even as I write this, are sleeping soundly. 'Tis Missy's first child and she has named her Ginnybell.

The next child to be born at Walker Ridge, God willing, will be mine and Letty's. I count the days until that joyous event.

His own words mocked him, and with a savage motion, he threw the leather-bound ledger to the floor. With his head buried in his hands, Sam cursed Morely for ever having told him about finding Chance. He had dealt with the knowledge that he and Letty would die leaving no heirs of their own bodies, and he had long ago sadly accepted that fact as God's judgment. But now! Morely's words danced dizzyingly in his brain, and joy such as he had not known since Letty had first shyly told him of their impending parenthood raced through his veins whenever he considered the stunning possibility that Chance Walker might well be his and Letty's own son.

Sam raised his head finally and with a sigh rose and picked up the offending ledger. His meticulous records had not helped him very much in his quest, he thought bitterly. All they had done was to remind him of a sad, mournful time. Again he flipped to the notation of the birth of Missy's first child. Suddenly his gaze narrowed as the full import of his words hit him. If Letty's child was to have been the next one born . . . Quickly he scanned the following pages, his heart beginning to pound. No births. None. Not until after he and Letty had left for England and Morely had taken over keeping the records and had noted that Patience Ragsdale, the wife of his overseer, had given birth to a daughter on

April 30 of that fateful year. Ignoring the excitement building within him, Sam swiftly forged ahead to the following year. It had always been the practice to record the first birthday of all children born at Walker Ridge, since so many never lived that long. Sam found the entry where Ginnybell's first birthday was recorded in Morely's spidery handwriting.

Telling himself that in his grief surrounding the loss of their child he might not have recorded any unexpected births in those few days before they left for England, Sam carefully examined all of Morely's entries for late March and early April of 1741, looking specifically for mention of *any* child's first birthday. Except for Ginnybell's, there were none. Quickly scanning backward, he found Morely's entry of November 3, 1740, revealing that, sadly, the Ragsdales' daughter, born in late April, had died of a fever on that date. There were other notations of deaths on the plantation during that year, but not of any infants less than a year old.

So. It was reasonable to assume that except for Ginnybell and the Ragsdale child, no other births had been recorded during the period that interested him. Except for the stillborn birth of his own son. Yet, according to Morely, Chance had been found with the birthing blood still on him that same night.

Sam slowly closed the ledger. He had to talk to Letty. He had to find out what she remembered of that night.

It proved to be easier than he had expected. Late the next afternoon, when the blistering heat of the day had faded somewhat, Sam, hoping to broach the subject gently, had suggested a stroll. He'd had no particular destination in mind, but he had unconsciously brought them to the family burial plot, a charming spot to which they had often strolled. Situated on a small knoll, well behind the outbuildings of the plantation, the wrought-iron fence that surrounded the area was festooned with honeysuckle and scarlet-trumpet vine. Old sprawling oaks and china-berry trees cast welcome patches of shade over the various headstones, some going back a hundred years.

Letty did not appear to think that there was anything odd about the path their walk had taken them, and she was not the least hesitant as Sam pushed open the gate and they entered the graveyard. Stopping a short distance inside the area, she took in a deep breath and, turning to Sam, said, "Isn't the scent of the honeysuckle absolutely intoxicating this time of day?"

Sam nodded. "I am glad that you suggested planting it after my father died. I think it would have pleased him."

Instinctively Letty began to walk toward the area where their child's small grave was situated. Her face soft, she stared at the weeping pair of gray marble angels that marked where the infant was buried. "He would have been a fine man, Sam."

Tenderly Sam put his arm around her frail shoulders. "I know, sweetheart. I know."

They stood in silence for several moments, then Sam asked hesitantly, "Do you remember very much of the night he was delivered?"

Letty shook her head. "No. It is all very hazy to me. I remember wishing that you were there with me and being afraid, at one point, that both the child and I might die and that you would be left all alone."

"You would not have lain in your grave very long without me," Sam said huskily, his arm tightening. "I do not think I could have gone on living if I had lost you. Losing the boy was terrible enough, but losing you . . ."

Misty eyed, she turned and kissed him on the cheek. "After all these years, Sam Walker, you are still the most romantic man I have ever known."

They smiled tenderly at each other. Sam glanced back at the small, neatly tended grave. A frown between his eyes, he asked slowly, "Letty, is there nothing about that night that struck you as strange? Did anything happen that made you wonder . . . ?"

She touched the side of his face, and he looked at her. Questions in her eyes, she demanded softly, "What is it, dear? Why are you so curious about that night after all these years?"

Not meeting her gaze, he cleared his throat uneasily. "I, er, we, ah, never talked about it a great deal. It was Constance who broke the news to me when I returned home and related all that had happened. You never said very much to me about it at all. For months after we were in England, you did not want to admit to anyone, even to me, what had occurred."

"I know," Letty said with a sigh. "It just hurt too much. I simply wanted to forget and not think at all about what we had lost." She smiled forlornly. "It was very foolish of me, was it not? I should have shared my grief with you." Staring off at the woods in the distance, she said quietly, "The truth is, my dear, that I do not remember very much of that night. There was a terrible storm, I know that. And I remember that Annie handed him to me and that I held his dear little body in my arms and refused to believe that he was dead." She shook herself, as if coming awake from a bad dream. "I am afraid that after that, my memory is even more hazy. I think I was hysterical, and as I recall, Constance gave me some laudanum to make me sleep." She frowned. "The pain had lessened somewhat for a while after I had brought him forth—but then it started in again, hard. I remember Annie reassuring me that it was merely the afterbirth, but to me it felt as if I were still struggling to have the baby."

Chapter Twenty

-----◆-----

Sam gave no indication of the fierce jolt that went through him at her words. An unconscious note of accusation in his voice, he demanded, "They gave you *laudanum* immediately afterward?"

Letty looked at him, puzzled. "Well, perhaps not immediately, but not long after the baby was born. Sam, I was hurting prodigiously. They were only trying to be kind."

"Were they?" Sam muttered, his fists clenched at his sides. "I wonder." Letty's earlier words had banished any lingering doubt he'd had about Chance's parentage. In all his searching he had not been able to find one piece of proof that Chance was *not* his son. To the contrary, everything pointed to that young man very definitely being a twin to the child who had been born dead. Even Letty's own words, that it had felt as though she were still having a baby, added to the growing circumstantial corroboration. For a moment, a wave of such joy went through him that Sam was dizzy. Chance was *his* son! He knew it! Felt it in the very depths of his soul. And yet he could not prove it.

"What in the world is wrong with you?" Letty asked, her forehead wrinkled in a frown at his odd expression. "You have been acting almost as if Constance and Annie had done something wrong, instead of trying very kindly to lessen my pain and to let me sleep and escape for a little while from my grief."

There had never been any secrets between Sam and Letty, from the day he had asked her to marry him until the day Morely had told him about finding Chance. In the intervening time, Sam had found it extremely difficult not to relate Morely's conversation with him to her—or to explain why these past weeks he had been digging around so frantically in all those old, dusty ledgers and trunks. Sam had been desperate to share with her his discoveries and beliefs, hungry for her opinion on the entire situation.

Now he was hungry to see the ecstatic light blaze in her eyes when she realized the truth. It was time, he thought slowly, that Letty knew, past time to tell her what he and Morely had suspected and what he now firmly believed. *Chance Walker was their son.*

It would bring him such indescribable joy to share his knowledge with the one other person most closely related to the tale, but still he hesitated. Letty was no dissembler. If she came to believe, as he did, that Chance was their son and that Constance had tried to get rid of him at birth, would she be able to maintain a normal facade in front of the other woman? And how would she feel about Morely's years of silence? Would she understand? Or hate him for what he had done? Sam himself, while understanding Morely's delay, could not help the occasional spurt of angry resentment against his old friend. But he had been able to put aside most of his ill feelings, too delighted that Morely had *finally* spoken to dwell overmuch on the past. But would Letty be as forgiving? Perhaps. The real problem, however, would be Letty's reaction to Constance.

Suspecting what he did about his stepmother, Sam had found it difficult enough these past weeks to smile and converse casually with Constance, but how much more difficult would it be for Letty? And Chance? How would Letty act around him? She had always been very fond of the boy, but how would she behave around him now, believing that he was actually her own son? Sam didn't even know how *he*, who was the less emotional of the pair of them, was going to react the first time he was face-to-face with the young man he was now convinced was his very own son. Would Letty be able to control her emotions? Would he?

Sam had no answers, but he knew what he was going to do. Taking Letty's wrinkled hand in his, he led her over to a sheltered spot beneath one of the spreading oak trees, where there was an old stone bench. After seating her gently on it, he joined her. Clasping her hands between his, he said softly, "I have something to tell you . . . something you might at first find unbelievable, but something that I know, with every beat of my heart, is true."

It took him a while to tell the tale as they sat there beneath the oak tree, an elderly couple who had long believed that their dearest wish had been denied them. Letty's eyes never left Sam's face, never wavered, as gruffly he revealed all that he had learned and why he so strongly believed that she had given birth to not one child, but two, on that long-ago night.

Beyond the gradual paling of her delicate features and the ever-increasing tightness of the grip she kept on his hands, Letty showed very little reaction to his words. A small silence fell when he finally finished speaking.

For several moments Letty did not move, her eyes fastened almost beseechingly on his, her fingers digging painfully into his hands. Then a shudder went through her small body, and releasing Sam's hands, she stared blankly into space.

"I always wondered," she murmured, half to herself.

"What do you mean?" Sam demanded sharply. "You had some idea that you had given birth to twins and that Constance had tried to dispose of our child? And you never said anything to me?" His voice rose accusingly on the last words.

Letty shook her white head and smiled tenderly at him. "No, dear. Nothing as cruel and terrible as that. But Chance always reminded me so *very* much of you . . . always. I think that is why I have loved him since the moment I first laid eyes on him, and why I have been so grateful that Morely seemed so willing to leave so much of his care to us."

There was a stunned, affronted expression on Sam's handsome, craggy features. "You thought he was *mine*? That I had betrayed you?" At Letty's slow nod, he said stiffly, "Well, I cannot thank you, madame, for your low opinion of me."

In spite of the tenseness of the situation, the gurgle of laughter that had charmed him for decades suddenly came from Letty. "Oh, Sam, darling, do not be so pompous. What else could I have thought? To me, you and Chance are as alike as two peas in a pod. And Morely's refusal to acknowledge him, and the way he was forever pushing Chance at us, certainly seemed to lend credence to my suspicions."

Still looking rather ruffled, Sam admitted grudgingly, "I suppose you are right, but *dammit*, Letty. You have to have known that you have always been the only woman in my heart and in my arms."

Misty eyed, she bent forward and kissed him at the corner of his mouth. "Indeed, I always hoped it was so and have told myself dozens of times over the years that there had to have been some sort of extraordinary situation that would have resulted in you fathering a child on another woman." She looked away. "Even believing that Chance was your bastard, I never blamed you, you know. Every man wants a child of his own, and I had failed you."

Sam pulled her close. "You never failed me. *Never*. Not even when we thought that we would be forever childless."

She rested her soft white head against his shoulder, the enormity of what Sam had revealed these past several moments only just now sinking in. Her voice full of wonder, she murmured, "We have a son. A strong, fine, healthy boy."

"Chance is no boy," Sam muttered huskily, "but he is a son any man would be proud to call his own."

Her face suddenly alight with an incandescent joy, Letty bounded to her feet with the lithe movement of a young girl.

Tugging excitedly at his hands, she cried, "Oh, Sam. We must go to him. I cannot wait to look into his dear face and know that he is ours. Oh, do come! 'Tis too late to leave this afternoon, but by dawn we could be on our to way to see our son."

"That is precisely what we cannot do," Sam said heavily. "Have you forgotten that it is only by the merest chance that he still lives, that someone wanted him to die badly enough to abandon him to the elements when he was only minutes old?"

A fierce glitter in her gray-blue eyes, Letty said, "No, I have not forgotten. We will deal with Constance and her per- fidious actions later. Right now, I want to see my son! Be- cause Morely was such a dithering, cretinous fool, I have waited thirty-four years to do so, and I do not intend to be deterred."

"Not even if your actions put Chance in danger?" Sam asked quietly.

The fierceness faded from her eyes, and she made a face. "You know that I would never do anything to harm him," she said softly.

Sam rose to his feet and pulled her against him. "I know, sweetheart, I know. But we must use our heads, not our hearts. We must not reveal to anyone even a hint of what we believe." He glanced down at her. "You have no doubts that Chance is our son? That you did give birth to twins that night?"

Letty nodded slowly. "It is such an obvious explanation for so many things—not only Chance's likeness to you, but the pain I experienced before the laudanum took over. Knowing, as we do now, Morely's part in it all, I do not see what other conclusion we can make. You have not been able to find any proof to the contrary. In fact, what you have found only bolsters the premise that Chance is our son. I be- lieve that old fool Morely when he says that he found Chance on the bluff. And that belief coupled with everything else we know makes our conclusions inescapable. I *did* give birth to twins, one dead and one alive, and Constance . . ."

Her gentle eyes grew fierce again. "Well, Constance saw an opportunity to advance Jonathan and she took it."

"We are going to have to be very careful in the coming days," Sam said. "You must not act any differently around her. Remember, she tried to get rid of him once, she very likely would try again. And you must not act differently around Chance, either. Remember, too," he added gravely, "that I have no solid proof, nothing that would stand before the law. *We* know that Chance is our son. But if we want him to take his rightful place, as our son and heir, we must try to find something more compelling than Morely's tale and the fact that I cannot find any notation in my records to disprove Chance's parentage. Jonathan would fight us every step of the way. He stands to lose a great deal—my personal fortune, which is the largest portion of the Walker wealth. Certainly he would contest, and he would stand a good likelihood of overturning any will of mine that left Chance my fortune." Sam sighed heavily. "I do not want my son to spend the rest of his life trying to prove his legitimacy and his right to my fortune. There is going to be scandal and gossip aplenty as it is. Without proof, overwhelming proof, we would be doing him an injustice, and we would be leaving him open to malicious speculation and scorn by many if, based on what we have now, we were to declare him our son."

As Letty nodded in agreement, he sent her a speaking glance. "Above all else, remember that we cannot, *dare* not, alert Constance to what we believe. She is a dangerous woman. I know that it is going to be difficult for you, but we cannot let anyone know what we have learned. Especially not Constance . . . or Jonathan."

"You do not think . . . ?" Letty began fearfully.

"Jonathan and Chance have always been at daggers' drawing. You know that Jonathan has always displayed an unwarranted dislike of Chance, and if he were to learn that Chance is our son . . ." Sam sighed deeply. "Jonathan is, after all, his mother's son."

Jonathan was definitely his mother's son. Even as Letty

and Sam were discussing the situation and coming to grips with the enormity of the problem that lay before them, Jonathan was very busy, happily plotting Chance's demise.

Only two days previously Simmons had reported to him the pleasing information that the Thackers had received his message and were awaiting further word. Gratified that the two ruffians had not yet departed for a winter of trading with the Indians and had been found so swiftly, Jonathan had waved Simmons aside and spent the intervening time considering how best to bring about Chance's death—with no suspicion falling upon himself. Naturally.

Having had time to consider it, Jonathan had completely given up any idea of pursuing Chance's soon-to-be widow, but he hadn't quite made up his mind whether or not he wanted Fancy dead. She was, after all, a delightful piece of baggage, and while he might not be interested in marriage any longer, he wouldn't, he conceded slowly, be at all averse to making her his mistress. He smiled. In fact, he rather liked that notion.

He rubbed his hands together gleefully. Events were moving just as they ought, and as soon as he decided upon the best method of ridding himself of the problem Chance represented, he would meet with the Thackers. He smiled. And that, he thought with satisfaction, would be that.

Jonathan hadn't been, at first, quite as pleased about Annie's presence at Devil's Own. He had been furious with his mother when he learned, too late to prevent it, of Annie's departure along with the others. He knew very well what Constance had been up to, and it worried him almost as much as it enraged him. He trusted his mother implicitly, but he was rather shaken that with so much at stake, she had boldly defied him and managed to put Annie out of his immediate grasp. They had had a terrible argument about Constance's actions and her obstinate refusal to agree to Annie's murder. Her lack of consent to Annie's demise didn't deter him from plotting, but it did irritate him. Imagine! Going against his express wishes in order to save the life of a servant who had outlived her usefulness. Bah! His mother was a fool.

His Walker blue eyes cold and hard, Jonathan glared out the window of his study at Foxfield, his mood decidedly sour. While Constance had returned to Walker Ridge, he had elected to continue to reside at the smaller plantation house, discovering that he liked having his own establishment. Constance had been clearly uneasy about his decision, but as had been the case for most of his life, he had simply pleased himself. Aside from everything else, there was another, more pressing reason for him to be living alone at Foxfield. It made it so much easier to come and go without notice or comment from any of his relatives.

Broodingly he stared at the wide expanse of river in the distance; nearly all plantation houses were built with a river view, and Foxfield was no exception. His fists clenched at his sides, he mentally turned over various means of killing Annie and Chance. A faint smile suddenly curved his mouth when a method occurred to him: an Indian attack. If white men could disguise themselves to steal aboard ships in Boston Harbor to toss over tea, why couldn't the Thackers and some of their wretched cronies disguise themselves as Indians and launch a swift attack against Devil's Own?

His smile grew. Chance and Annie would be the specific targets, but of course, if anyone else got in the way, that would just be . . . *un*fortunate. Only the Thackers would be aware of the purpose behind the raid: the cold-blooded murder of Chance Walker and Annie Clemmons.

Jonathan's sour mood had vanished entirely, and he felt *very* pleased with himself. It would be so tidy. Two of his problems would be eliminated in one fell swoop. And those stupid Thackers would be none the wiser for the reasons behind it. Besides, they would be so happy to lay their hands on Chance that killing one old woman would almost be a pleasure for them. His smile deepened. They would almost be willing, he suspected, to pay *him* for arranging everything so neatly for them. Best of all, no one would ever connect *him* to the tragedy. It would all be blamed on those heartless, murdering savages. Perfect.

He crossed to the bell rope and gave two sharp yanks—the summons for Simmons. Waiting impatiently for his valet, he continued to think about the situation. Killing Chance and Annie was the simplest solution. With those two safely dead, there wasn't even an urgent need to kill Morely. And the fewer deaths, the better. He wanted no suspicions to suddenly arise, about why so many people connected to the Walker family had met a tragic end in a short period of time. And if Morely had kept his suspicions to himself all these years—and surely the dolt must suspect what had happened—after Chance was dead, there was no reason for Morely to speak. Jonathan smiled wolfishly. No reason at all.

Simmons's knock upon the door jerked Jonathan from the delightful contemplation of his cleverness. Looking across at his valet, he said briskly, "Make arrangements for the Thackers to be at that old hunting cabin near the south boundary one evening before the end of the month. Once a date has been agreed upon, let me know it." He looked thoughtful. "I shall give them their orders myself. Your presence will not be necessary. I want them to arrive just at dusk. My horse will be well hidden and I will await them inside the cabin." He frowned at Simmons. "My identity is to be kept totally secret. You can warn them that they are not to be anywhere near the cabin until it is time for me to meet with them. The cabin will be in darkness, and they are *not* to attempt to light a candle or lantern. They are to enter the cabin, hear my proposition, and leave. They are not to linger. I am depending upon you to make certain those cretins understand the instructions." Jonathan's voice hardened. "If they deviate in any manner, the entire project will be abandoned—and they will be out a sizable reward of gold. As for you, be successful in this endeavor and I shall see that you are handsomely served. Fail me . . ."

Simmons bowed low, his face impassive at the implied threat. Inwardly he was burning with rampant curiosity, but there was no sign of it in his voice as he murmured, "As you wish, sir. I shall see to it immediately."

Unaware of the momentous, and equally menacing, events that were swirling on the horizon, Chance, like many planters in Virginia at this time of year, preoccupied with the harvesting of the tobacco crop—and the ever-widening chasm that existed between him and his wife. The month that he had agreed to give her before demanding his conjugal rights had come and gone, and he was conscious that his patience and temper were beginning to fray rather badly.

He had thought that the month-long abstinence from following the dictates of his eager body and taking his fill of Fancy's many charms would be agony, and he had not been wrong. But that time, torture though it had been, was nothing to what he was experiencing now. The month was over. The truce, or whatever one wanted to call the silly situation—and Chance could think of several decidedly nasty names—had ended and there was, ostensibly, nothing to prevent him from finally claiming his wife in every possible way. Except . . .

On this particular afternoon in the last week of September, Chance was seated astride a restive chestnut gelding, overseeing the gathering of the tobacco crop. He was only half paying attention as the highly valued tobacco plants were cut down and loaded into carts for transportation to the drying sheds behind the stable area; his thoughts centered mainly on his confoundedly aloof and elusive wife. While she still kept stonily to her part of the original bargain, even though it was technically no longer necessary, and slept in his bed each night, that was the only time he was alone with her.

Granted this was a busy time of year, and he was aware that her days were as full as his, but his wife seemed to disappear into thin air at first light. She was no longer even present at meals, and while no one seemed to find it strange, Chance was certain that she was avoiding him. And he didn't like it one damn bit, he thought sourly.

As a matter of fact, he didn't even like it that she was still sleeping in his bed. Not that he wanted her to sleep somewhere else, but he was growing damned tired of her chilly manner toward him. When she climbed warily into his bed at night, she neither greeted nor acknowledged him. She simply blew out her candle, turned her back to him, and pulled the covers over her shoulders. And he'd had about all of *that* treatment that he was going to take. She was his wife, dammit. He had given her long enough, far longer than most men in his position would have, he reminded himself virtuously, to get over her displeasure with the way he had brought about their marriage. She was just going to have to accept the fact that they were married and that he didn't intend to spend the rest of his life living in this increasingly difficult chaste state. He wanted her—desperately. He wanted to taste that soft mouth again and feel her sweet body clench around his.

Yet, for all his growing impatience and frustration, and the belief that he had right on his side, Chance also had the distinctly uneasy feeling that if he attempted anything so ridiculous as to make love with Fancy, it would prove exceedingly disastrous. He cursed himself a dozen times a day for agreeing to her damned, silly bargain in the first place.

His face set in grim, forbidding lines, he turned his horse away from the busy scene in front of him and began to ride toward the house. It was time he settled this situation with her. It could not and would not go on any longer. He was going to find his cat-eyed little witch, wherever she was hiding today, and tell her precisely how things were going to be from this moment on. She might be in his bed tonight, but she had better be prepared for scant sleep.

It took him a while, and several increasingly sharp inquiries, before he finally found her wandering through the fruit orchard with Ellen, Annie, and Martha. The four women were inspecting the apple and quince trees, assessing the ripeness of the red and yellow globes that hung from the trees, some already having fallen on the ground.

Unaware of Chance's steady regard, Fancy was laughing

at something Ellen had said, her expression carefree and cheerful, and Chance felt something twist painfully in his chest. Damn her. She had no right to look so lovely, so appealing, as she stood there garbed in a homespun dark green skirt and a simple yellow spotted bodice and cotton blouse. Like many a plantation wife, she wore a linen apron tied round her slender waist and a beribboned mobcap. A shallow wicker basket in which lay a few apples was carried across her arm. Scowling at her, Chance stared, noting enviously the way the sun brushed a tawny glow across her cheeks and kissed the curls of her hair as they fell in careless splendor around her shoulders.

As Chance swung out of the saddle and threw his reins around the top rail of the wooden fence that enclosed the orchard, Fancy laughed again, this time at some comment from Annie. His mouth thinned. His wife sure as hell didn't laugh very much in his presence, he thought grimly. Nor was her expression as open and sunny as it was right now. No, for him, he admitted irritably, her usual look was an infuriating mixture of wariness and militancy. And he was damned tired of that, too.

Though his approach was silent and the women were preoccupied with their own affairs, Fancy must have sensed his presence, because she suddenly glanced in his direction and her smile faded; that wary, militant expression crept over her face, and Chance swore under his breath. Not bothering to hide his displeasure, he walked up to the women. He barely acknowledged the greetings of the others as he stopped in front of Fancy. Hands on his hips, his blue eyes boring into hers, he said coolly, "I am sorry to take you away from the others, but I would like a word with you."

"Now?" Fancy asked, all sign of her earlier cheerfulness gone. "Could it not wait? We are very busy right now."

"Oh, we are not that busy," Martha said with the familiarity of one comfortable and secure in her position. " 'Tis too late in the day to start any new project anyway. We will go to the house and leave you and the master with some privacy."

Chance and Fancy might not have been in a state of open warfare, but the fact that there was something seriously amiss in the marriage hadn't escaped Martha's eagle eye. Sending Chance a speaking glance, and before Fancy could protest, she quickly hustled Ellen and Annie toward the house. "Now," she said placidly to Ellen, "I shall show you how to make a flummery. When paired with my chocolate cream 'tis young Hugh's favorite dessert."

Ellen needed to hear no more. An eager look upon her pretty little face, she quickly fell in with Martha's suggestion, and with Annie following behind, the three women left the orchard.

Fancy watched them go with acute misgiving—and, to her intense shame, a wildly beating heart. She was not exactly positive why Chance had sought her out in such a blunt manner, but she had a fairly good idea. Her cool attitude toward him had finally gotten under even *his* thick skin, and he was determined to bring an end to it. Her lips twisted. And no doubt, to their chaste marriage bed.

When the other women reached the house and disappeared inside, Fancy brought her eyes reluctantly back to him. She wasn't looking forward to this confrontation, and she had realized some days ago the wisdom of that age-old advice—never go to bed angry at one's spouse. The anger and hurt she had felt had not lessened; it had only festered and oozed like an unclean wound. Her month-long bargain, especially after the night they had argued about his reasons for marrying her, had accomplished little. But having thrown down the gauntlet between them, she wasn't certain how to retrieve the situation . . . especially without causing herself embarrassment.

Fancy sighed. She did not really mind if she was embarrassed, but it hurt her deeply to realize that Chance had married her, had totally disrupted and destroyed her life, simply to strike back at Jonathan. Revenge was a poor foundation upon which to build a life together. While she had admitted that she loved Chance, she didn't think that her love alone would be enough—for either of them . . . or for the child she suspected was growing in her belly.

It had not been only to avoid Chance that she had taken to arising at first light and had forsaken joining the others at mealtimes. The very smell of food these days was likely to send her into a fit of retching, and it was worst in the mornings. She had been keeping her increasingly queasy stomach easy with plenty of hot tea and dried bread—which helped but didn't entirely alleviate all symptoms.

The first time she had gotten sick, she had put it down to something she had eaten. But when the sickness became a regular part of her morning ritual, the stunning possibility that she might be breeding had suddenly occurred to her. With a sinking feeling, she had realized that she had not had her "woman's time" since before she had married Chance. There was every likelihood that she had conceived that day on the bluff.

Fancy did not know how she felt about the prospect of a child. Once, it had been her dearest wish, but believing she was barren, she had put away all thought of having a child. To discover that Chance was right, that it was the *stallion* and not necessarily the mare that had led to the lack of children in her first marriage, was galling. Trust him to be right about that, she thought waspishly. Yet despite all her uncertainties about her future with Chance, she was filled with awe and a sense of wonder that together they had made a child, that come spring she would give birth.

An odd, secretive smile curved her mouth, and seeing it, Chance growled, "Something amuses you, Madame Wife?"

Fancy sighed and, reaching up, took off her mob cap and shook her hair loose. Dropping the cap carelessly into the basket that she still carried on her arm, she said, "No, I find nothing amusing in this situation."

Chance stared transfixed at her hair as the sun wooed a glint of fire here and there in the dark mass. His mouth went dry, and he was conscious of an urge to drag her into his arms and bury his face in the shining mass. His voice husky, he said, "Perhaps 'tis time we did something about it."

Her eyes wide, Fancy stared up at his dark face. Something in the cast of his mouth, something in the expression of his blue eyes, held her nearly spellbound. But ignoring the sudden leap in her pulse, she asked, "What do you suggest?"

"A cessation of hostilities? A truce, mayhap?"

"Our present truce, if you can call it that, has not accomplished very much. Why do you think another one would change things?"

"Because we cannot go on this way," Chance muttered. "I did not marry you to spend my nights as chastely as I have. Nor did I ever envision my marriage as one of polite tolerance."

Fancy's jaw hardened. "When you marry a woman who does not want you and for the spiteful reason of revenge, you should not be surprised if the marriage is not as you envisioned or to your liking."

Chance suddenly grinned. "Now, I never said that the marriage was not to my liking. And you are only playing a game with yourself if you think that you don't want me."

Fancy took in an outraged breath, her eyes blazing with golden lights. "Of all the conceited, arrogant—!"

Chance laughed and dragged the basket from her arm, then tossed it aside as he pulled her struggling form into his embrace. Swinging her around, a teasing glint in his blue eyes, he said, "Ah, Duchess, you do not know how much I have missed that fire in your eye and the lash of that sweet tongue of yours."

To her dismay, Fancy felt herself responding to his teasing, her heaviness of spirit vanishing magically, a bubble of irrepressible laughter surging up through her. How could she think of laughing when she was furious with him? But it was true. She did not want to be furious with him, she wanted to laugh, to fling her arms around his neck and let him sweep aside all her doubts and fears. She fought frantically against his powerful appeal, afraid of losing the very essence of herself if she gave in to the unfair promptings of her heart. Terrified that she would lose her head—as she always did where he was concerned—with a great effort, she suddenly hurled herself out of his arms. Picking up her skirts, she began to run; but, having lost her sense of direction from his whirling her about, instead of running toward the house, she ran into the nearby woodland.

Fancy realized her mistake almost at once and swerved to change her course, but Chance caught her about the waist and they both fell to the ground. His body was half on hers, and at the sudden, carnal curve to his lips, as he stared down at her, she felt breathless, a breathlessness that had nothing to do with her exertions.

Determined not to give in to the shocking surge of desire that flowed through her, Fancy glared up at him, her eyes daring him to give in to the primitive urge that was clearly revealed upon his dark face. Chance smiled twistedly at her expression. "Sweetheart, if you did not want this to happen, you should not have run away."

Chapter Twenty-one

Fancy's lips parted to angrily refute his words, but his mouth caught hers in a fierce kiss, his hard body pressing hungrily against hers. Sweet fire exploded deep inside of her as the feel of him, the taste of him, the virile scent of him, overpowered her senses. She was vaguely aware of the soft grass against her back and the warmth of the dappled sunlight on her skin, but mostly it was Chance, the longed-for pleasure of his weight on her, the intoxicating magic of his mouth moving on hers, that flooded her mind. For an instant she gave herself up to the elemental emotions his embrace aroused, letting her lips soften and cling to his, letting her arms creep around his neck.

Chance kissed her like a starving man, his lips, tongue, and teeth all tasting and exploring her willing mouth. Desire, kept so long in check, suddenly ran rampant through him, and his manhood instantly became hard and aching, the urgent need to mate with her nearly driving any thought but that one act from his mind. Gripped by powerful passion, Chance fought to keep from falling upon her like a ravening beast, every fiber and sinew of his body urging him to rip aside her clothing and his own and make them one.

Breathing in harsh gasps, he was finally able to lift his mouth from hers, and his eyes black with naked need, he said thickly, "Fancy, sweetheart . . ." He groaned and kissed her again, deeply, passionately, before flinging himself to the ground beside her, his hand tightly clasping one of hers.

They lay there side by side on the sun-warmed ground, sheltered from sight by a slight rise in the grassy terrain between them and the houses, as well as the spreading branches of a huge oak tree, its green leaves showing the faintest trace of gold. Birdsong drifted through the hot, humid air; the whistling call of a quail could be heard in the distance, and the drone of the bees and insects was a drowsy concert all around them.

His breathing slowing, Chance turned and propped himself up on one elbow. Staring down into Fancy's flushed face, he said quietly, "I want you. I always have, and these past weeks have been very difficult for me." Softly he added, "I do not want to force you, but if you continue to deny me, I fear . . ."

"Threats?" Fancy asked, her eyes daring him to deny it.

He smiled bitterly and shook his head. "No. I would never threaten you, but I find myself in an untenable position. You are my wife. You married me. If not of your own free will, you certainly agreed to the marriage and all that it entailed." His gaze hardened. "If you meant for us to live our lives as celibates, if my touch is so repugnant to you, why did you not simply damn me to hell and go back to England . . . instead of chaining us to a situation that, if not resolved, is going to make both of us live a life of misery?"

Fancy looked away and bit her lip. Damn him! He was being so reasonable and, worse, had put his finger on the crux of the matter. Despite the scandal it would have caused, she could have left the Colonies. She'd known that and had even considered it. But she hadn't left. She had chosen to stay—and to become his wife.

"What do you propose? A divorce?" she asked tightly.

His eyes narrowed. "Is that what you want?"

"Would you allow it?"

"I cannot stop you from leaving me," he growled. "If you wish to return to England and seek a divorce, there is nothing I can do to prevent it."

"You would let me go?" she demanded incredulously. "After you went to such deplorable lengths to marry me?"

He hesitated. Looking away, he spoke as if the words were torn from him. "If you cannot find it in your heart to forgive me for the way I coerced you into marriage and you intend to deny me my rights as your husband, I think that perhaps it would be the best solution for us."

His words shocked him nearly as much as they did Fancy. In all his dwelling on the situation between them, until this very moment Chance had never considered either a divorce or the possibility that his wife would leave him. But he realized with sudden, painful insight that they could *not* continue as they were, that though he had kept his promise to her these many weeks, he did not trust his control if she were to remain close at hand. And if he were to give in to his baser instincts and force his body upon her . . . He sighed. He would hate himself and grow to hate her, and whatever tender feelings she had for him would surely wither and die.

Fancy fairly gaped at him, hardly daring to believe she had heard him correctly. When he said nothing more, but continued to stare blankly off into the woodland, she jerked upright and, angrier than she had ever been in her life, spat, "Well, I like that! You seduce me; force me to marry you; force me to share your bed; and now, at the first little obstacle in your path, you decide to throw up your hands in despair and turn me loose." Her eyes glittering furiously, she startled both of them when she suddenly slapped him. "How dare you! How dare you marry me and then toss me aside. How *dare* you."

His cheek tingling from her slap, Chance turned his head and looked at her, a dangerous smile curving his lips. His eyes alight, he grabbed her hand as she started to her feet and jerked her back down beside him. Despite her struggles, he brought her hand to his lips and dropped a warm kiss on the back of it. A hint of laughter in his voice, he said, "Forgive me, Madame, I'm afraid that I have misread the situation." He turned her hand over and gently pressed another kiss on her wrist, feeling the pulse suddenly begin to race beneath his lips. "You must put my lack of understanding of the situation down to being a mere colonial and not used to the ways of the, er, fancy."

"Oh, no, you don't," she said breathlessly, aware of a sweet languor creeping over her as his mouth continued its soft, oh so seductive exploration of her lower arm. "You are not going to escape the blame that easily."

"I throw myself on your mercy, Duchess," Chance murmured, half-teasing, half-serious. "I have greatly wronged you, and I am sorry for it."

Her uncertainty clear, she asked huskily, "Chance, are you really sorry? Sorry that you married me?"

His light mood vanished and, his eyes steadily meeting hers, he said gently, "Sorry for the way I gained your hand? Yes. Sorry that I married you?" His voice thickened. *"Never."*

"But why?" she nearly wailed. "Why did you force me to marry you in such an underhanded way?" Almost accusingly she added, "It was not worthy of you."

Chance had come a long way to understanding quite a lot about himself in these few moments with her, but he was not quite ready to make that final confession—not even to himself. His eyes once more on the woodland behind them, he said simply, "I wanted you. I did not want you to marry Jonathan." His gaze swung back to her. "I have always wanted you—from the first moment I spied you leaning on the ship's rail in Richmond. I just never knew how much until I feared that you would be lost to me if I did not stop you from marrying Jonathan." His lips thinned. "And arranging that little scene in your bedroom at Walker Ridge, disgraceful though it was, seemed a simple solution."

"It—it was not just to take revenge against Jonathan?"

Chance sighed and threw himself back full length on the

ground, dragging Fancy with him. Positioning her next to him, her head on his shoulder, his arm around her waist, he stared at the canopy of leaves overhead and asked abruptly, "What do you know about my . . . first wife, Jenny?"

Fancy tensed. Chance's previous marriage wasn't something she wanted to think about, and she was surprised by the burst of plain old green-eyed jealousy that knifed through her at the soft note in his voice when he said the other woman's name. Forcing herself to relax, she said casually, "Only that she was a local heiress whom you swept off her feet and married—despite her family's protestations—and that she died tragically. A suicide."

Chance laughed mirthlessly. "I suppose I do not need to inquire who told you the 'heiress' part. I see Jonathan's fine hand there."

"He did mention it, yes."

"Did he also mention that while I was away in England on business, he seduced my wife? That he got her with child? And abandoned her? That he left her to face me alone—her belly already showing signs of the babe who grew there? A babe who could not possibly be mine?"

Fancy rose up to look at him, her face showing her shock. "No, he did not." She smiled bitterly. "Jonathan is very careful in what he chooses to divulge."

Chance cocked a brow. "Learned that, have you?"

"Yes—unfortunately." A little frown crossed her features. "But if you knew what he had done, why didn't you . . ."

"Challenge him to a duel?" Chance asked dryly. At her nod, he added, "I thought of it—especially the day I finally discovered who her lover had been. I could have killed him. Easily. But, conveniently for him, Jonathan was away on business in Boston at the time, and it was several weeks before he returned to the area. By then I'd had time to consider the situation more coolly and had realized that, while killing him would have given me immense, immediate satisfaction, it would have hurt Sam and Letty a great deal. They have always been very good to me, and I would not willingly cause them grief." His voice hardened. "And I realized that by merely killing him, that Jonathan would have escaped too lightly. I wanted him to suffer. I wanted him to feel as I had felt when I discovered that my wife had betrayed me." He stopped and looked away. "I wanted him to feel all the pain of losing someone beloved and to suffer as I did those months and years following Jenny's death."

"And so, thinking I was to be his bride, you decided to punish him by forcing me to marry you," Fancy said harshly, bitterly aware that she was uncharacteristically jealous of a dead woman.

Chance looked at her, the expression in his eyes enigmatic. "No," he said slowly, "that was the excuse I used to take what I wanted . . . you."

A flush stained Fancy's cheeks. She glanced away from him. Stiffly she said, "It does not seem like a very good reason to me."

Gently Chance pulled her to him. "It wasn't," he said huskily, "but I wanted you so desperately that I was not thinking straight. I never have where you are concerned. All I could think of was having you." Softly he kissed her cheek. "And of holding you in my arms," he murmured as his arms slipped around her. "And kissing you," he breathed against her lips the second before his mouth claimed hers.

His words didn't answer all her questions, nor did they remove all the hurt. But they did fill her with warmth and hope, and, loving him as she did, she realized dimly, as the familiar sweep of passion rose up inside of her, that for now it would have to do. Wanting was not love—she had no illusions about that—but perhaps from such an emotion, love could grow.

Her mouth opened willingly for him, her hands clasping the back of his head, pulling him closer to her. Her actions told him as clearly as words that he had won the day, and with a smothered groan, he bore her back into the grass, his hands moving urgently over her.

Desire erupted through them both, and heedless of their

surroundings, between hungry kisses and increasingly explicit caresses, their clothing was hastily discarded and provided a bed for their naked bodies. It was like the first time they had made love and yet so very different.

This time Fancy knew the pleasure his hard body could give her; this time Chance knew the sweet completion he would find in her yielding flesh. This time Fancy had no doubts that this was where she wanted to be, that this one man was the only man she had ever loved. And Chance? Well, Chance had not come that far, but he knew that no other woman, not even Jenny, had made him feel the way Fancy did, that no other woman set him on fire as she did, that he wanted no other woman in his arms.

There was tenderness in his touch, a lazy sensuality in the way his mouth traveled from her lips down her throat to her waiting breasts. The warm wetness of his tongue gently laving her nipples, the scrape of his teeth, sent a fiery arrow of need streaking to the throbbing ache between her legs, and Fancy's fingers dug into his shoulders.

His mouth tugging hungrily at her breasts, Chance caressed her, his fingers drifting over her slender form, kneading and exploring, wooing and pulling her deeper into their own secret, sensual heaven. Her flesh was silky and warm beneath his touch, and the shape of her shoulders, the narrow back, the gentle curve of her hips, were enchanting. He lingered there awhile, his hands cupping and fondling her firm little fanny, marveling at the soft texture of her skin, reveling in the tantalizing brush of her body against his.

The lure of her mouth proved too much for him, and he left off his suckling to kiss her lips, to drink deeply of her. His tongue met hers, tangling and twining with hers, and he groaned his delight as the fire between them leaped higher.

Dizzy and wild with passion for him, her breasts aching for the return of his mouth, the demanding hunger between her thighs becoming urgent, Fancy purred like a cat as she moved beneath him. Her fingers caressed his warm chest, seeking his small, hard nipples, pleased when he moaned his pleasure at her touch. Tauntingly her hand moved lower to his belly, his gasp and the sudden tightening of his body revealing clearly that he was as helpless against her caresses as she was against his. Made bold by his reaction, she slid one shapely thigh over his, pushing up against the hard length of his member.

Chance groaned and reluctantly lifted his mouth from hers. A lock of black hair falling across his forehead, his blue eyes glittering with desire, he said thickly, "Madame, continue as you are and you may get a great deal more than you expect—and considerably swifter than either of us had planned."

Fancy looked innocent. "Oh, am I disturbing you?" she asked archly as her fingers played across his groin. It was a new and heady experience for her, this intimate teasing, made all the more so by the satisfying reactions of Chance's body to her lightest touch.

Chance sucked in his breath at the sensations that rippled through him at her gentle explorations. A crooked smile lifted his lips. "I think, Madame Wife, that you know *exactly* what you are doing to me." His eyes darkened with an emotion that made Fancy's already fast-beating heart race. "You have always known," he breathed against her mouth. "Always."

He kissed her, and while it was as passionate and hungry as any kiss they had ever shared, there was some new emotion in it, some indefinable emotion that made Fancy's body shudder with longing. Feeling her response, Chance moaned and his mouth bit more hungrily into hers, his long fingers sliding tormentingly along the inside of her thigh, traveling slowly toward the aching center of her. When he touched her, when he parted that tender flesh between her legs and gently stroked and probed, Fancy's whole body jumped, a spasm of utter pleasure roiling through her.

She was warm and wet, his fingers sinking deeply inside of her, and Fancy twisted up frantically under his knowing caresses, the fire in her belly consuming everything in its path, until all feeling, all sensation, seemed to be centered beneath his driving fingers.

Instinctively she reached for him, her hand closing firmly around his swollen shaft. Chance jerked at her touch, and as she explored him, her fingers sliding along the silken length of him, he dropped his lips to her breast, his teeth nipping at her stiff nipples.

Engulfed by the most basic of emotions, Chance pushed her thighs apart and fitted himself between them. His mouth found hers again, and holding her hips to his liking, he lifted her and plunged deeply into her welcoming heat.

Nearly delirious with pleasure, Fancy eagerly accepted his invasion, her body rejoicing at the feel of being one with him. His chest crushed against her tingling breasts, his warm hands clenched her buttocks and urged her to meet his heavy thrusts, demanded her to join him in the intoxicating race for fulfillment. It was a race she was eager to run, the sweet sensations of his body moving fiercely on hers, the texture of his sun-dappled skin beneath her caressing fingers and the heady taste and scent of him all assailing her in the most elemental way.

Her body singing its burgeoning delight, she tightened her arms around him and her hips rose and fell rapidly, matching his increasingly deeper, more urgent thrusts. The feelings that rippled through her were sweet and powerful, the hunger to reach completion growing with every vigorous movement of his body upon hers. Time and time again he plunged avidly into her, stroking the honeyed ache, making her twist and writhe beneath his powerful onslaught. A frantic tension built within her, her body clenching as she was suddenly forced to surrender to the primitive madness, pleasure, hot and intense, shuddering wildly through her, making her cry out.

Fancy's cry was smothered beneath Chance's mouth, his own heaven already on the horizon. Compulsively he drove into her, his hands gripping her hips almost painfully, holding her to his demanding rhythm. The convulsions of her body around him, the slick heat and sweet friction, were more than he could bear, and raw ecstasy enveloped him as helplessly he emptied himself into her.

Only dimly did he become aware of his surroundings, of the sounds of the plantation in the distance, the humid heat of the afternoon. Chance knew he should move, but he was unable to, so he held still with Fancy in his arms, his kiss gentling as he savored the delicious aftermath of their coupling.

Too spent and languid to make any attempt to change their positions, Fancy, too, was thoroughly enjoying this gentle descent from the scarlet heights. She returned his kisses, her hands resting lightly on his buttocks, realizing giddily that there was much pleasure to be gained from such a leisurely interlude.

But it was only an interlude. Soon enough, Chance kissed her once more and slid slowly from her body. Lying beside her, he propped himself up on one elbow and stared down at the slender length of her body. Silky smooth flesh met his gaze, flesh the color of cream, the entrancing expanse broken only by the rosy tips of her breasts and the ebony curls nestled at the junction of her thighs. Her breasts were small and high, the nipples still temptingly engorged, her waist narrow, and her hips and thighs lithe and oh so seductively shaped.

"You are," he said huskily, as one hand fondled her breast, "undoubtedly the loveliest creature that God ever created—and I am most thankful that you are mine."

Pleased, but embarrassed, too, Fancy flushed rosily and made some inarticulate reply. It must have satisfied him, for he laughed softly and dropped a kiss on her nose. Suddenly very conscious of their naked state now that passion had fled, she brushed aside his lazily exploring hand and sat up. Pushing back a tangle of hair that fell across her temple, she said hastily, "Shouldn't we dress? What if someone were to find us like this?"

Chance sighed. "I suppose that we should, although I doubt we are in any danger of discovery." A teasing note in his voice, he added, "The next time I want to make love to my wife in the open, I shall carry her deeper into the forests where no one would dare interrupt us." A decidedly carnal smile lit his face. "I know just the place—a green glade with a small, crystal-clear pond. Once our first passion was slaked, it would be, ah, invigorating to bathe in the pond." A devilish glint in his eyes, he murmured, "I think that I should definitely enjoy washing you, every delectable inch of you—and of course, I would expect you to return the favor."

Despite their recent activities, Fancy felt a wicked tingle low in her loins. Embarrassed by her body's instant reaction to his words, she blushed and scrambled to her feet, grabbing one of her petticoats as she rose. Unbearably aware of his bold gaze upon her, she flung it hastily over her head.

Chance smiled at her antics but said nothing more to disturb her, although the lasciviously teasing manner in which he helped her dress did nothing for her temper. Attempting to push her wildly tangled hair into some semblance of order, she said vexedly, "It is all very well for you to find this so humorous, but I assure you that it has not been my want to—er, frolic in the woods. I do not know how I am to face the others looking as I do. I am sure that they will take one look at me and know *precisely* what I have been doing with you."

By now fully clothed himself, Chance grinned at her, thinking she looked utterly adorable with her hair all tumbled about and her cheeks rosy. Certainly nothing like a haughty baroness. But then, he reminded himself with immense gratification, she wasn't a baroness any longer, she was his own sweet wife. Gently swatting aside her fumbling fingers, he swiftly brought her locks under control, and, hiding the worst of the damage under her mob cap, he kissed her thoroughly. "You look," he said with open satisfaction when he finally lifted his mouth from hers, "just as a recently married wife should—and well loved."

Fortunately for Fancy's peace of mind, teasingly assisted by her infuriatingly smug husband, she was able to enter the house without anyone seeing her. At the base of the stairs, Chance kissed her again—he seemed to like doing that a great deal, she thought dizzily, any worries of being discovered vanishing from her mind the instant his mouth found hers.

A moment later he reluctantly broke off kissing her. A warm gleam in his blue eyes, he brushed his fingers against her cheek and murmured, "You best run along, sweetheart. I think I hear Martha coming."

Fancy blinked drowsily up at him as she drifted back to reality and his words sank in. Hearing the sounds of voices approaching them, she made a small, mortified noise and, picking up her skirts and petticoats, fled upstairs to her rooms.

Chance watched her go, an incredibly tender expression on his lean face. Whistling merrily to himself, he turned and left the house, his step jaunty and his mind full of the pleasures that he would be his . . . tonight.

Jonathan, wearing old clothes and a broad-brimmed hat that he kept pulled low across his face, had arrived quite some time ahead of the scheduled hour for the meeting with the Thackers. He had carefully concealed his mount behind a thicket of brush a goodish walk from the hunting shack and had proceeded to the wooden building on foot. He had trod carefully, checking the rampant undergrowth and encroaching forests constantly, making certain that there was no one about to observe his approach.

The shack was just one bare room with a minimum of rough furnishings and a small fireplace. It had been built with a mind to providing a modicum of shelter for any luckless hunter caught in inclement weather or overtaken by night far from home. The only amenities were a scarred, rickety table, a candle stub in a cracked pottery holder, and four mismatched chairs of uncertain vintage. A tidy stack of dry firewood lay near the hearth, and a battered iron pot hung from a hook over the old pile of ashes in the fireplace. Other than that, the room was empty.

Closing the solid door behind him, Jonathan viewed the resulting suffocating darkness with satisfaction. Smiling to himself, he reopened the door for some light and checked to make certain that no unwelcome inhabitants had taken up residence. Then he pushed the table near the hearth and shut the door once more. Selecting the sturdiest of the chairs, he placed it in the far corner from the table, out of the view of anyone entering the shack, and settled himself to wait.

He had chosen dusk as the time of the meeting, and as the hour approached, he finished his preparations, bringing forth a black silk half-mask, which he swiftly put on, and a long-barreled black pistol, which he laid across his lap. He was ready.

The Thackers appeared to have followed his instructions exactly; there was no sign or sound of them, until the shadows of dusk began to fall. Hearing the noise of approaching horses, Jonathan stiffened and gripped the pistol.

The low murmur of voices could be barely heard through the walls of the shack, and a few minutes later, the door was opened cautiously, admitting a swath of feeble light from outside.

From his place of concealment, Jonathan could barely make out the shapes of the two men as they entered warily. "Stay where you are and do not turn around," he commanded once they were far enough into the room for his liking. "I should warn you," he added with soft menace, "that I have a pistol leveled at your backs and will not hesitate to shoot if you do not follow my orders."

Both men stiffened, obeying his commands instantly. Udell said sharply, "We did not come to cause no trouble. We was tole to be here at this time. Supposed to meet a fellow . . . to discuss a, er, business arrangement. You that fellow?"

"Indeed I am," Jonathan said, "but you are still not to turn around. You *are* to do precisely as I say, is that clearly understood?" A resentful grumble of assent came from the pair, and Jonathan said, "Excellent. Now then, ah, Udell, approach that table and light the candle. Clem, remain just where you are."

The candle lit, Jonathan said, "Clem, you may now shut the door, and do not even think of looking in my direction. When you are done, go stand by your brother. Both of you keep your hands where I can see them. No tricks or sudden moves, if you please."

Those tasks accomplished, Jonathan relaxed slightly. Eyeing the two hulking figures as they stood obediently with their backs to him, he congratulated himself. "Now then, gentlemen," he began heartily, "I will lay out my proposition for you. It is my understanding that you have good reason to hate Chance Walker. Is that correct?"

"What if it is? What difference is it to you?" Udell asked sourly, clearly unhappy with this situation.

"That is none of your concern, but suppose," Jonathan said, "I could arrange it for you to be able to catch Chance Walker by surprise and kill him. I would be willing to pay you a goodly sum for your trouble. Would something like that interest you?"

Udell grunted. "It might. 'Cept everyone knows that Chance and I ain't exactly friends. His murder might make folks think I done it. Me and Clem ain't fools—we do not want to have our necks stretched, not even to kill thet bastard, Chance."

"But suppose I have a plan that will ensure that no blame falls upon you?"

"I am listening," Udell said grimly.

Wishing he could see the expressions on their faces and more accurately gauge their reactions, Jonathan swiftly explained his plan to kill Chance Walker and an old woman named Annie Clemmons in a supposed "Indian" attack.

"Passing ourselves off as savages is a good notion, and I know a fellow or two who would not mind joining us— especially if you is goin' to be as generous as my cousin says," Udell said thoughtfully when Jonathan had finished speaking, "but Devil's Own ain't just some pore dirt farmer's cabin. Chance has a whole passel of men there, well-armed men. Because of thet, it ain't likely thet those murderin' savages *would* attack them."

Jonathan smiled to himself. "That is true," he agreed easily, "but I happen to know that during the first week of October, Chance routinely sends a large contingent of his people to Richmond and Williamsburg to replenish their supplies. Devil's Own will be virtually deserted for several weeks." He paused before adding sweetly, "I am sure that a pair of enterprising fellows like yourselves should be able to secretly observe the happenings at Devil's Own and discover for yourselves precisely when this occurrence takes place."

"Suppose Chance and thet ol' woman you want us to kill goes with 'em? What then?" Clem asked suspiciously.

"Chance is a new bridegroom, and it is unlikely that after the events of the exhausting past weeks his new bride would wish to go to Richmond or that he would go off and leave her." A malicious note entered his voice. "I believe that Chance has learned how unwise it is to abandon one's bride for any length of time. And as for the old woman . . . I do not believe that she will go to Richmond. If she does, we shall have to consider another plan for her, er, disposal."

There was silence as the Thackers mentally considered the plan. "You jest want Chance and the old woman killed? Anything we steal is ours to keep? I hear thet he has got some real fine horses and such. There ought to be pretty good pickings. Do you take a share?" Udell asked.

Disdainfully Jonathan replied, "A share in your ill-gotten goods does not interest me. Do we have an agreement, gentlemen?"

"You will pay us the gold thet our cousin mentioned? Half now and the rest when the deed is done?"

Affronted by this haggling, Jonathan reached inside his coat and brought out a small leather bag of gold. He stood up and contemptuously tossed the bag onto one edge of the table. "There is half the gold, as promised. Do we have a bargain?"

Udell opened the bag and lifted out one of the gold coins. He bit it and then carefully examined the marks. To Clem he muttered, "It is real."

"Of course it is real, you fool. Are you going to do it?" Jonathan asked impatiently.

Clem shrugged and Udell slowly nodded. "Don't see why not," he said casually, one hand lightly rubbing his scar. "I have been wanting to kill Chance Walker a long time."

Chapter Twenty-two

The October trip to Richmond for the semiannual replenishment of supplies for Devil's Own came up that same evening in conversation. Dinner had been eaten some time ago, and the ladies had retreated to the front parlor to enjoy a glass of ratafia before retiring to their rooms. The gentlemen had stepped outside to enjoy a clay pipe of Virginia's fine tobacco.

Chance and Hugh were seated comfortably in a pair of pine rockers on the broad front porch of the house, the pleasing scent of tobacco from their pipes wafting in the air—and helping to keep at bay the many voracious insects.

Eager to join Fancy and the delights of the marriage bed, Chance had not planned on lingering, but there was an air about Hugh that brought his thoughts back from decidedly carnal realms and made him ask quietly, "Is something amiss, Hugh? You have been uncommonly quiet of late, and it seems that I have not heard your ready laugh very much. What is wrong?"

In the darkness Hugh made a face. "A woman, what else?" he asked bitterly.

"Ah," Chance murmured understandingly. "Ellen still has not forgiven you."

"Forgiven me!" Hugh burst out indignantly. "She will not even talk to me. I tell you I am at my wits' end. I have tried to explain—countless times. But all she will do is look down that saucy little nose of hers at me and then stalk off. I have begged her to forgive me, to give me another chance, but to no avail." He paused, then said heavily, "I am leaving next week when Jed and the others do. I shall accompany them part of the way before turning off for Fairview. There is nothing here for me now." He sighed. "Perhaps absence will make Ellen more amenable."

Chance puffed thoughtfully on his pipe. "I think that you are probably right," he finally said. "And I also think that you have been letting that little madame lead you around like a bull with a ring in its nose. 'Tis high time that you stood up to her and stopped allowing her to punish you. Your mistake was an honest one. After all, Jonathan can be most persuasive, and while I see nothing wrong in her punishing you a trifle for her pride's sake, I think it has gone on long enough. If you are gone from her presence, 'tis possible that she will discover she is not quite as angry with you as she pretends. Unfortunately, if her heart remains hard against you, I am afraid that you will have to forget about her."

Chance's levelheaded words were not what Hugh wanted to hear, but he understood the wisdom in them. His jaw tightened. "You are right, of course. There is no use repining over a woman who has no use for one."

Silence fell as both men smoked their pipes and considered the situation. Abruptly Hugh asked, "When exactly is Jed leaving for Richmond?"

Standing, Chance stepped off the porch and, after knocking his pipe clean and crushing out on any remaining embers with his boot heel, said, "Probably Wednesday. It is the first of October and seems as good a day as any. Jed and Martha are already making the lists of supplies we will need for the winter and looking forward to visiting some relatives who live in the vicinity of the city."

Glumly Hugh said, "I am glad 'tis so soon. At least I will have only a few more days to be scorned by Ellen."

Chance chuckled and clapped the younger man on the shoulder. "Who knows, she might have a change of heart when she hears that you are leaving."

Hugh snorted and shook his head. "She is far more likely to volunteer to help pack my belongings and speed me on my way."

Of the two of them, Chance's assessment proved the more accurate, although it wasn't until the next day that Ellen learned of Hugh's planned departure. She had been in the kitchen with Martha, learning how to make a tomato marmalade, which Martha had explained was excellent for seasoning gravies and such, when Hugh had come to deliver a message from Jed to his wife.

He stopped abruptly when he saw Ellen. After sending him a disdainful glance, Ellen turned back with renewed vigor to her task of pounding the cloves for the marmalade. Hugh could not take his eyes off her slim form; one of Martha's large aprons was tied snugly around her narrow waist, making her look at once very adult and yet absurdly young. Her features were fiercely intent as she ignored him and worked with the spices. Hugh had no doubt that she was imagining it was his head she was pounding with the stone pestle, and his heart ached.

Martha greeted him with a warm smile. "Good morrow to you, young Hugh. I hear that you are going to come with us, at least part of the way, when we leave for Richmond on Wednesday."

With an effort Hugh dragged his gaze from Ellen's enchanting form and, forcing a smile, said quietly, "Yes, I am. 'Tis time I returned to Fairview."

Ellen stiffened at his words, her eyes flying to his. A stricken expression on her pretty face, she cried, "You are leaving?"

Hugh met her gaze squarely. Levelly he said, "On Wednesday. There is no reason for me to remain here—and

I do have other duties. I have been away from Fairview for far too long. 'Tis time I returned."

The pestle dropped nervelessly from her hand, and she took a step toward him. "Oh . . . but," she began helplessly, hardly aware of Martha's highly interested presence. "But you *cannot*."

Hugh looked very haughty. "Indeed? And why not?" His voice grew hard. "Why should I stay? I repeat, there is no reason for me to remain—is there?"

A sparkle of tears shimmered in Ellen's fine blue eyes and she very nearly stamped her foot in vexation. He was such a dolt! How *could* he think of leaving her when she absolutely adored him? She knew she had treated him rather shabbily lately, but he had deserved it for believing Jonathan's lies about her. Besides, she thought indignantly, he was not supposed to have accepted her rebuffs so lightly; he was *supposed* to have cajoled and wooed his way into her good graces once more. If he cared at all for her, how could he so tamely accept her rejection? How could he *leave* her?

Looking at his forbidding, tight-lipped features, Ellen realized miserably that she had badly misjudged him. He was not, it dauntingly occurred to her, one of her many light-hearted London beaus who were well versed in playing a flirtatious game and happily brought to heel by her charmingly coquettish manner. It was suddenly clear to her that she had played the game a trifle too long and that she had brought this disaster on herself. It was not, she thought frantically, supposed to be this way!

"Well?" Hugh demanded coldly when Ellen remained silent. "Can you give me one reason why I should stay?"

Her eyes fixed firmly on his dusty boots, she slowly nodded her fair head. Her heart thumping madly in her breast, almost inaudibly she said, "I—I—I am here."

Martha, deciding that this fascinating scene would play out much more satisfactorily without observation, murmured something about hearing Jed calling her and swiftly departed. Neither of the two principals was aware of

Martha's tactful disappearance. They were aware of nothing but each other.

Ellen's hands were pressed nervously together in front of her, her head still downbent as she stood in front of Hugh, and it was all Hugh could do to prevent himself from sweeping her into his arms. Her quiet words had filled him with a wild exultation, and his heart began to race. His eyes boring into her blond head, he asked carefully, "And should that make a difference to me?"

Already mortified that through her own capricious actions she had found herself in this position, and just a little angry that he seemed to be so thickheaded, Ellen snapped her head up and cried out, "If you love me as I love you, it should make all the difference in the world." Appalled at what she had just revealed, but unable to help herself, she stamped her foot and said fiercely, "You great lout! I love you. How can you go off and leave me?"

Hugh let out a whoop and, eyes gleaming with laughter, swept Ellen's small form into his arms. "I do not know that I could, but I was certainly going to try. You have," he said in loving accents, "treated me most shamefully, minx."

Ellen's arms had instinctively gone around his neck, and throwing whatever maidenly restraint she still possessed to the winds, eager to make amends, she admitted huskily, "I know. I am a wicked, *wicked* creature. I would deserve it if you hated me."

Smiling idiotically down at her, Hugh murmured, "Hate you? Sweetheart, I adore you."

"Do you truly?" Ellen stammered delightedly, stars beginning to peep into her blue eyes.

"Truly," Hugh said firmly the instant before his mouth closed over hers.

Lost in the sweetest dream imaginable, Ellen tightened her arms around him and gave herself up to the sheer bliss of finally being where she belonged—in Hugh's strong arms. When Hugh eventually lifted his head some minutes later, they were both breathing heavily and there was a glitter in his eyes that made her suddenly shy. Toying with the point of his shirt collar, Ellen asked softly, "And what do we do now?"

Gently lifting her chin, his eyes full of tenderness as they roamed over her flushed features, he said, "And now we tell the world that you have agreed to become my bride and that I am taking you back to Fairview with me on Wednesday. We shall marry at Christmas."

Her eyes got very big. "R-r-really?"

Hugh smiled. "R-r-really," he mimicked tenderly the moment before his warm mouth found hers again. It was several delirious minutes later that a discreet cough brought them floating dreamily back to reality.

Hugh looked over his shoulder to meet Chance's amused gaze. "I take it," Chance murmured, "that congratulations are in order? Or am I to be forced to defend Ellen's honor?"

Ellen blushed rosily and buried her head in Hugh's chest, feeling his arms tighten instinctively around her. "Congratulations," Hugh said happily, a huge, almost dazed smile breaking across his handsome face. "Ellen has just agreed to become my bride."

Dinner that evening was most festive. After all the signs of the meal had been cleared, Chance stood and, raising his glass of claret, glanced from Ellen to Hugh. "A toast to the engaged pair," he said. "May you enjoy many happy years together." His gaze traveled to the other end of the table where Fancy sat, and staring intently at her, he added softly, "May you find the joy in your own marriage that I have found in mine."

Fancy felt a rush of warmth through her entire body. He had not said that he loved her, but if the passion they had shared last night and the look in his eyes was anything to go by, he must care deeply for her. He *must*. She could not bear it if he did not.

After they had all adjourned to the front parlor, the conversation was given over entirely to the plans of the newly engaged pair. There was some discussion about whether Hugh should return to Fairview and inform his parents of his decision to marry before presenting Ellen to them or if, as he and Ellen wanted, he should leave on Wednesday for Fairview, taking Ellen with him.

Her expression troubled, Fancy murmured, "I cannot like Ellen traveling alone with you, even if she is your betrothed. Nor, I might add, do I believe it proper for you to just thrust her into the bosom of your family in such a hurly-burly fashion. It is all so unseemly." She flushed slightly. "After the way Chance and I were so hastily married, I should like Ellen's engagement and marriage to be more conventional. Surely you should tell your parents first."

Hugh and Chance exchanged a look. Grinning, Hugh said, "I *have* informed them. This afternoon, Chance very kindly sent a servant on one of his fastest horses to Fairview with a letter from me explaining all to my parents." He smiled reassuringly at Fancy. "The news that I am to marry your sister will not come any surprise to them. My parents are well aware that my affections have been fixed upon Ellen for some time."

Fancy sent her husband a look. "I wish," she said wryly, "that you had discussed this with me before doing anything. After all, I *am* Ellen's guardian."

Her eyes glowing joyfully, Ellen crossed the room from where she had been seated by Hugh and, her blue silk skirts billowing out around her, sank gracefully onto her knees in front of her sister. "Oh, Fancy," she said fondly, "do not be so stuffy. Since the moment we landed here, we have been doing the most unconventional things imaginable. This is not London. No one will think it odd that Hugh and I travel to Fairview together." She smiled winningly up at Fancy. "We want to be married from Fairview, and Hugh wants me to stay with his family until the wedding at Christmas. Tell me, best and most beloved sister, that you are happy for me and that I have your blessing."

Brushing back a lock of fair hair from Ellen's brow, Fancy said ruefully, "You know that I can deny you nothing. If this is what you want . . . ?"

"Oh, 'tis," Ellen breathed rapturously, her hands grasping

Fancy's where they had lain in her lap. "More than anything I have ever wanted in my life."

Hugh had approached them and now stood in front of Fancy, one hand lying possessively on Ellen's shoulder. "I will always take care of her," he said simply. "No harm shall come to her."

Fancy gave a laugh. "Oh, very well. I cannot withstand both of you. Do as you wish. With my blessing."

Fancy still had some misgivings. She was very conscious of the whiff of scandal that had surrounded her own wedding, and she wanted none of that for Ellen. She said honestly, "Ellen, I know I have given you my blessing, but darling, will you not consider waiting here while Hugh sees his parents and arranges a proper escort for you to his home? I cannot like just the two of you haring off like a pair of Gypsies."

"I think you are repining over the formalities too much, Duchess," Chance murmured. "Fairview is not above a hard day's ride from here. And while I am certain that Ellen could travel that distance without mishap, Hugh has already planned for them to spend the night at Walker Ridge, where they will be most adequately chaperoned by Sam and Letty. The next day they will ride on to Fairview." A mocking gleam lit his blue eyes as he added, "What are you afraid of, that he will ravish her in the woods?"

Fancy felt her cheeks pinken and she could have boxed her husband's ears. But before she could think of a suitable reply, help came from an unexpected quarter. Annie Clemmons had been, as was her wont, sitting quietly near the fireplace, knitting placidly. Diffidently she entered the conversation by saying, "Mistress Fancy, I could go with them, if that would set your mind at ease." When Fancy turned and stared at her uncertainly, she added, "I do not believe that it was ever the intention for me to remain with you forever. You have been most kind to me, but I feel a perfect fraud. You have no need of me any longer, if you ever did. I think 'tis time for me to return to Walker Ridge."

Astonishing all of them, Annie had fitted easily into the

small family circle at Devil's Own; she had proven herself a pleasant companion with a gentle, encouraging way about her, and she was always cheerfully ready to help with whatever task was necessary. During the weeks they had been together at Devil's Own, Fancy had grown fond of her and looked upon her much like a distant member of the family. And while it was true that, with Martha having a firm rein on the mundane daily chores, Annie hadn't been technically needed, she had somehow made herself a welcome addition to the household. Even Chance remarked once to Fancy that he had been mistaken in her character. To her surprise, Fancy discovered that she would be sorry to see her go. The house would seem very quiet without Ellen and Hugh and with Annie gone, too.

"Are you certain?" Fancy asked gently. "We would be very happy for you to remain with us."

"You have been *most* kind to me," Annie said, her eyes on her knitting. "Kinder than you know. You have made me part of your family and treated me with great consideration and respect, and I thank you for it. But I should return." Her eyes lifted, and staring thoughtfully at Chance, she added, "There is a pressing matter that I must see to." A strained smile crossed her worn features. "I cannot tell you what these weeks here at Devil's Own have meant to me, and no matter what happens in the future, I shall always remember this time with great fondness. But it is best that I go."

The matter was settled and the conversation became more general. But that evening as Fancy slipped into bed beside her husband, she asked, "What can Annie's 'pressing matter' be?"

Chance, his thoughts more on getting his wife out of her demure cotton gown and feasting on all the sweet flesh he knew lay under it, murmured, "There probably is not any such matter at all. She has shown herself to be a kind soul, and I suspect she simply wants to go home."

His hands were already sliding Fancy's gown upward, his skin warm against hers, and as she felt the first flicker of desire stir within her, Annie and her pressing matters vanished from her mind. Last night had been like nothing she had ever experienced, and she shivered with anticipation as her gown was thrown on the floor and Chance's mouth caught hers, one of his hands fondling and stroking her breasts. Tonight proved to be just as thrilling, his explicitly carnal lovemaking taking her once again to that scarlet heaven they shared together.

Only when they were both sated and lying together in lazy exhaustion did the subject of Ellen's marriage to Hugh come up again. His fingers leisurely tracing an aimless pattern on her arm and shoulder, Chance said quietly, "I know that it will be a wrench for you to let Ellen go, but you shall still be able to see her frequently. We shall go and visit them several times a year, and Hugh will, no doubt, bring her here often enough."

Fancy nodded, saying softly, "It is just that she is so young and I have had the care of her for so many years. We have always been together. It will be an adjustment, but one I will gladly make." She rose up to look down into his face, the faint light of the moon outlining his chiseled features. "She *is* happy, isn't she? And Hugh will make her an excellent husband, won't he?"

"Indeed, he will. Almost as excellent a husband as I have made you," Chance said teasingly.

"If that were the case," Fancy retorted tartly, "I should forbid the banns."

Chance chuckled and pulled her onto his naked chest. He kissed her with great relish, his lips warm and knowing against hers. "I think," he said eventually, his breathing somewhat erratic, "that we shall deal very well together, sweetheart—despite our unpropitious beginning."

A soft little smile curved Fancy's mouth as she thought of all her foolish fears and silly misgivings. Chance had not said he loved her, but he had proved himself to be a most exceptional husband so far. There was still rough water ahead of them, but they *had* managed to deal very well with each other indeed.

Fancy was aware that she was looking forward to their future together, that she had no regrets at the hand fate had dealt her. And there was the joy of knowing of the babe that was already growing within her. She had never thought she would have a child, and the wonder of it was too new and sweet and overwhelming to speak of. At present it was still her secret, and she clutched it to her, relishing the private knowledge and yet taking delight in imagining Chance's face when she finally told him that he was going to be a father. Next spring, she mused dreamily, we shall have a child . . . a boy, she decided sleepily, with his father's brilliant blue eyes.

The first of October dawned cool and clear, a hint of frost in the air. Standing on the wide porch of the house, just as the first rays of the rising sun kissed the treetops, Fancy watched teary eyed as Hugh and Ellen, followed by Annie, rode slowly away from Devil's Own. Jed and Martha and the rest of the Richmond party had departed just a few minutes previously, and Fancy was feeling a little dejected and lonely. She *was,* she told herself repeatedly, happy—no, delighted—about Ellen's engagement to Hugh. It was what she always wanted for her sister, a true love-match. Hugh was a fine young man, and there was no doubting that the pair of them were deeply in love. But, oh, I *am* going to miss her, she thought wryly, surreptitiously wiping away a tear.

Chance, standing by her side, noticed the furtive little movement and put his arm around her shoulder. "Perhaps we can find time to visit at Fairview in early November," he said softly, "if the weather is not too inclement."

"No, that will not be necessary. I know that we have much to do to prepare for winter, and with Martha and Jed gone, we shall be very busy," she said tremulously. "I can wait until the wedding to see her again. 'Tis just that I am a little emotional at seeing her leave. This is the first time that we have ever been separated."

She flashed him a misty smile, her lovely topaz eyes shimmering with unshed tears, and Chance felt something shift painfully in his chest. She was garbed simply in a green-and-russet-striped bodice worn over a white cotton blouse; her skirt was made of green merino wool. Due to their early rising, her hair was loose, a dark cloud that tumbled charmingly around her pale face to her shoulders; her cheeks were pink from the chill morning air; and her lips were a soft, rosy temptation. Completely riveted by her, Chance decided that he had never seen her appear lovelier than she did at that very moment. He was unutterably thankful that she was his wife—no matter the means he had used to marry her. Which reluctantly caused him to admit something else, something he had been denying for weeks. He had never felt about anyone the way he did Fancy—not even Jenny. The fierceness and strength of the emotion he experienced every time he looked into Fancy's sweet face frightened him, and he was baffled at the way just one sad look from her could make him willing to do the most foolish things. He stared down at her intently, trying to understand what had happened to him. *I love her*, he thought suddenly, dazedly.

Becoming uncomfortable by his fixed stare, Fancy moved restively. "I wish," she said with a touch of acerbity in her voice, "that you would not stare at me in that fashion. If you are trying to put me out of countenance, you have done so."

Chance shook himself as if coming out of a stupor. A slow, incredibly tender smile crossed his handsome face. "Out of countenance, Duchess? Never. I was merely congratulating myself on my good luck in marrying you."

Fancy flushed and shot him an uncertain glance. The look in his blue eyes made her heart flutter, and almost shyly she asked, "Were you really?"

He pulled her into his arms and kissed her very, *very* thoroughly. "Indeed I was," he said huskily when he finally lifted his mouth from hers. "And you? How do you feel about our marriage?"

Her flush deepened, and keeping her gaze fixed firmly on the middle of his chest, she murmured, " 'Tis not too terrible a fate, I think."

Chance laughed, his eyes dancing. He was, he admitted,

utterly besotted—even her tart tongue delighted him. It was all he could do not to sweep her up in his arms and declare himself to her—and the world—and demand that she love him as much as he loved her. She was not indifferent to him, of that he was convinced. But would she ever love him? Trust him?

He sent her a calculating glance. Winning Fancy's love, he realized, meant more to him than anything else on earth, and he was not about to be denied it. She *will* love me, he vowed. I shall woo her, court her, and snare her heart before she is even aware of what I am doing. Her heart, he swore softly, will be mine for the taking. And only mine.

If Fancy noticed a difference about Chance that day, she put it down to the departure of the others. It was true that they were both extremely busy during the daylight hours, and not much in each other's company, but there was an intimate dinner that evening with just the two of them. Neither was aware of the servants hovering in the background as they talked and teased and unknowingly fell deeper in love with each other. And afterward, when they were alone in Chance's big bed, there were the long, leisurely hours in which he made exquisitely sweet love to her and brought her completely under his spell. That night as she lay in his arms, Fancy was blissfully certain that she had never been happier in her entire life, and she blessed the fate that had brought her and Chance together.

If there was any cloud on her horizon, it was the fact that Chance had not yet mentioned those three magic words she most wanted to hear—I love you. Aware of his baby growing stronger within her, she longed to hear him admit that he loved her. It would, she thought sleepily, allow her to look forward to a cloudless future.

Udell and Clem had been watching the comings and goings at Devil's Own for only two days when Jed, Martha, Hugh, and the others had departed. They were elated at their luck, having thought they would have to spend several more days lurking about in the underbrush before the party for Richmond had left. Fancy's presence as well as Ellen's had come as a pleasant shock, and they were both looking forward to renewing their acquaintance with the two Englishwomen who had escaped them. The fate they had planned for the sisters was not at all promising. That it appeared that Fancy was Chance's wife made Udell's eyes gleam with an ugly expression. He swore that he'd keep Chance alive just long enough to see his wife defiled and gutted in front of him.

Make the bastard suffer first, Udell thought savagely, unconsciously touching the scar on his cheek. Make him listen to his woman scream and plead for mercy—*then* I will kill 'im.

Neither Thacker had been pleased to see Ellen and Annie leave with the main party. They had recognized Annie from the detailed description they had been given, and it presented them with a quandary. The man who had hired them had said *both* Chance and the old woman were to be killed in the Indian raid. But Udell didn't see how it could be accomplished, now that Annie had left Devil's Own. Clem was all for sloping off after the departing party and attempting to get rid of Annie and waylaying Ellen before coming back to Devil's Own to finish up their chore. Udell thought it over and finally convinced him to wait, unaware that their quarry was not going to Richmond.

"There will be time enough for thet, once we git Mister Chance Walker taken care of," Udell had insisted. "Think of all thet gold. We will finish up here tomorrow morning and overtake 'em. With them wagons and such, they will travel slower than us. Richmond is a fair ways off. There will be chances along the trail for us to git our hands on thet yallar-haired gal and take care of the old woman."

With much grumbling Clem had agreed. "But you jest remember, the yallar hair is mine. I owe the little bitch a thing or two."

Udell had nodded, and in perfect accord the two men went back to studying Devil's Own. Udell figured from their earlier reconnoitering that there weren't more than three or four able-bodied men, including Chance, left on the place.

There were several women and children, as well as the slaves, but he did not think they'd give them much trouble.

Clem grunted his agreement. "And if we do it at first light," he said thoughtfully, "everyone is likely to be still abed. We should be able to git inside the main house and take care of Chance and the woman afore anyone else even knows what is happening. Besides, they will all be busy with them"—he snickered—"other Indians."

Udell rubbed his bearded chin. Peering at the house from their hiding place in a clump of tall grass at the edge of the forest, he said softly, "I been thinking some about them other Indians. I shore do hate the idea of us having to share thet gold with anyone else."

Clem looked surprised. "You figgering we do it alone? Jest the two of us?" He swallowed. "Won't thet be kinda risky?"

"Might. But then again . . ." Udell grinned wolfishly at him. "If just us do it, thet gold will be all ours."

Clem considered it. Cautiously he said, "If we wuz to slip in and pick off as many of the other men as we could, quiet like . . ."

"There would be," Udell said with satisfaction, "nobody to trouble us when we go after Chance and his woman." He grinned craftily at Clem. "Nobody to share any gold with, either."

A grin as greedy and ugly as the one on Udell's face broke across Clem's dirty, bearded features. "Don't have to worry none about anyone mebbe talkin' about it sometime, either. Be jest between the two of us—gold and all."

The two brothers nodded to each other, and a moment later, after one last calculating look at Devil's Own, they silently slunk off into the forest. Tomorrow, Udell promised himself savagely, tomorrow a lot of debts would be settled with Mr. Chance Walker and that uppity English bitch.

Chapter Twenty-three

Chance never knew what woke him. One second he was sleeping soundly, the next he was alert and wide awake. A swift glance at Fancy, sleeping by his side, told him that it had not been his wife who had disturbed him, and another glance at the purple-gray murk outside the windows that bespoke those moments before dawn informed him that it was not yet time to rise.

So what had wakened him from a deep slumber? Something had, and he lay there, listening intently. All seemed normal, but a tightening in his gut, the compelling sensation that all was *not* normal, had him rising silently from bed and quickly dragging on a pair of breeches.

Every sense alert, the feeling growing second by second that something was seriously amiss, that there was danger in the air, he laid his hand on the wide-bladed knife that was seldom far from his side. A loaded musket stood ready in the corner, a seemingly curious oddity in the elegant surroundings, but a grim reminder that for all its serene, civilized air, Devil's Own *was* a lone outpost in the midst of wilderness. Indian attacks were rare these days in this area, but the war with Corn Stalker and his allies had not yet been settled, and while Corn Stalker's raids were farther west, it didn't preclude *other* Indians from striking out on their own. And Indian attacks were not the only danger a place like Devil's Own faced—there were always ruthless men who preyed upon the weak and vulnerable.

Normally Chance would not have been alarmed, but with the major portion of the inhabitants of Devil's Own on their way to Richmond, the plantation was not up to its usual fighting force. Considering the situation, he realized that he had grown too confident these last years, a little too secure. The semiannual trips to Richmond for replenishment of supplies were common knowledge, and he concluded grimly that if someone were planning to attack Devil's Own, now would be a very good time.

As the seconds passed and he heard nothing more, he began to feel a bit silly. Whatever had awakened him had probably been nothing out of the ordinary, and he was letting his imagination run wild. At least that's what he told himself, but he didn't believe it. He had lived too long by his wits alone, and the gut feeling that he was experiencing now, gut feeling that something was seriously amiss, had saved his life too many times in the past for him to totally discount it now. But as more time passed and he heard nothing else, he decided that he must have been mistaken.

He was about to return to bed, somewhat disgusted with himself, when there came a furtive creak from the direction of the main staircase leading to this floor. Chance froze. He was familiar with every nuance of his surroundings, and he knew that creak. It was the sixth stair from the top.

Wasting no time, he silently crossed the room to wake Fancy. He shook her slightly and whispered urgently against her ear, "Fancy, sweetheart, wake up."

She stirred, her eyes flying open a second later as she realized that Chance was no longer at her side, that he was standing over her. She started to speak, but his fingers against her lips and his low, "Shush. Quiet," stilled her movements instantly. Her gaze full of anxious questions, she looked up at him as he loomed over her in the shadowy murk.

Softly Chance said, "I believe that someone is in the house. *Not* someone who should be. Do you understand?"

Fancy's breath caught and she paled. Visions of hordes of painted, screaming savages bursting through the bedroom door flashed through her brain. She swallowed painfully, but meeting Chance's intent look, she nodded.

"Good," he said simply, and briefly flicking a finger down her cheek, he turned away to face the source of the danger.

As Chance edged nearer the door leading to the main hall, Fancy slipped naked from the bed and frantically grabbed various articles of her clothing that were scattered haphazardly about the room—her demanding husband had been so eager to claim her last night that he had not allowed her to disrobe properly before taking her to bed and making exquisitely sweet love to her. At the moment, as she ignored undergarments and petticoats and scrambled into the simple mulberry-colored bombazine gown she had worn to dinner the previous evening, she was inordinately thankful Chance's ardor had forced her to leave all her clothes at hand. Facing a possible Indian attack was frightful enough; facing one stark naked or in her night attire didn't bear thinking about.

Her heart banging painfully against her ribs, Fancy glanced about for a weapon. Her gaze fell upon the musket in the corner. She hesitated. There had been talk of teaching both her and Ellen how to load and fire various weapons, but so far the promised lessons had not taken place. She bit her lip. Hadn't someone said it was simply a matter of cocking the hammer and pulling the trigger? Deciding that if she couldn't shoot it she could use it as a club, she snatched up the musket.

Her fingers had barely clenched around the musket barrel when she watched with growing horror as the main door to the bedroom stealthily swung inward. Unaware of anything but that ever-widening gap in the doorway, unaware of the way Chance's body shifted imperceptibly into a menacing stance, the knife held ready for battle, she was suddenly filled with righteous indignation. How dare some murdering heathen creep into their bedroom!

That thought had hardly crossed her mind when the intruder was fully revealed as the door finished its opening arc and she stared numbly at the fearsome apparition who stood there. The figure garbed in stained, filthy buckskins was truly a thing of nightmares, from the long greasy braided hair festooned with feathers, to the terrifying streaks of vermilion and black that had been painted on its face. A tomahawk was held in one hand and in the other was a knife, an almost identical twin to the one clasped so lethally in Chance's hand.

That the intruder had planned to catch them asleep in their bed was apparent from his expression of dismay when he found himself confronted with two very wide-awake, armed inhabitants. There was a moment of tense silence, and then the man in the doorway smiled, nastily, and Fancy's breath caught in her throat. Beneath the Indian disguise, she recognized that yellow-toothed grin, and a smothered gasp escaped her. *Udell Thacker.*

"Well, damn me for a sinner," Udell said almost jovially as he stepped into the room. Keeping a wary eye on the blade in Chance's hand, he added, "You never did act like I expected you to. I do not know why I figured this time would be any different."

Chance smiled grimly. "I do not either, my friend." Seemingly oblivious of the fact that he was half-dressed and confronting a deadly enemy, he asked with deceptive politeness, "Might one inquire what brings you to my bedroom at this hour of the morning?"

Udell's grin widened. "Seems thet I ain't the only feller who would like to see your liver on a skewer."

Chance cocked a brow. "Oh? And what might that mean?"

"Means thet I met with a feller who does not bear you any love, and we put our heads together and decided to get rid of you." Udell snickered. "This morning's work is going to be a real pleasure for me—I get to kill you and my new, er, partner, is going to pay me a tidy sum of gold to do it."

"Who would dare do such a dastardly thing?" Fancy burst out, shock and anger apparent in her pretty face.

In spite of herself, even with Chance between her and Udell, she flinched when Udell's frankly lascivious gaze slid slowly over her slim form, the memory of her time as his captive rushing through her. Her revulsion was plain to see, and some of Udell's satisfaction faded.

"Don't matter," he said nastily. "If I were you, mistress, I would worry more about myself. When I get through with you this time, you ain't going to run off nowhere."

"If I were you," Chance drawled dangerously, "I would not make promises that you have no hope in hell of keeping."

"Is thet so? And what makes you think thet I ain't going to keep thet one?"

"Because I will kill you before you lay a hand on her," Chance replied levelly. One part of his mind was on the situation at hand, but his racing brain was also turning over the astonishing information that someone had actually sent Udell Thacker to his home to kill him. There was only one person Chance could think of who hated him that much and who would stoop to such treachery—Jonathan.

Udell chortled merrily at Chance's warning. "Think so?" he taunted, obviously enjoying himself.

Chance's gaze narrowed. Something was wrong. Udell was too confident, too certain of himself—and he shouldn't be, not having lost the element of surprise and finding himself faced with two armed individuals. So why was Udell standing there grinning at them when he should be running?

The answer exploded across his mind, but it was too late. From behind him, Chance heard a soft gasp from Fancy, followed almost immediately by Clem's voice saying, "I will take thet musket, little lady."

Cursing himself, Chance pivoted slightly so that, while not losing sight of Udell, he could see what was happening with Fancy. It was not a reassuring scene that met his gaze, and he cursed himself again. Approaching from the rear, Clem had caught her by surprise and had grabbed the musket from her grasp and tossed it aside. Holding Fancy firmly captive in his massive paws, he grinned at Chance. An icy thrill of fury went through Chance at his own stupidity. He should have remembered, he thought savagely, that where Udell was, Clem wasn't far behind. It was obvious that while he and Fancy had been occupied with Udell, Clem had entered the bedroom through the connecting doorway from Fancy's room and had slipped up behind her. Intent as she had been on Udell, it had been easy work for Clem to disarm her, and by doing so, he had changed the situation drastically.

Fighting the feral urge to spring across the room and free his wife from Clem's brutal grip, Chance asked, "What do you intend to do now?"

Udell grinned. "Well, I think thet it would be a good idea if we put some distance between us and here. Our business is with you two." Magnanimously he explained, "We had planned to kill anyone who might be inclined to prevent us from finding you, but me and Clem decided not to waste time and we came directly for you two. Thet's what we are getting paid for. And if you do not want any of your friends to die, I suggest you do *exactly* what we tell you to. It don't matter to me how many people I kill. But you follow my orders and your own skin is the only one you have to worry about." He grinned nastily. "And thet of your purty little wife."

Chance ignored the provocation and nodded curtly, ideas for getting Fancy out of Clem's grasp speeding through his brain. It looked as if there was little hope of saving himself, but there was the possibility, faint though it was, that he might be able to get Fancy free—if only he were clever enough. Despite his outward calm, Chance was frantic, knowing very well what fate Fancy would suffer if he were fool enough to allow her to be taken away by Udell and Clem. His gaze flicking swiftly over Fancy's angry, terrified features, he swore to himself that he would die before he would let that happen.

But Fancy had plans of her own, and they didn't include having her husband and herself kidnapped and murdered by a pair of scoundrels like Udell and Clem. She had given up twisting in Clem's hold. Deciding to do the only thing left to her, she suddenly bent her head and bit his wrist as hard as she could.

Clem let out a yowl and tried to jerk his hand away from her sharp little teeth, but Fancy held on like a tigress, biting even deeper. No longer holding her prisoner, Clem was actively trying to get away from her, dancing wildly about the room, beating her about the head and shoulders with his free hand and yelling for Udell to help him.

It was the opportunity that Chance had been waiting for, and like an arrow released on its lethal errand, he launched himself at Udell. Udell had been staring astonished at the bizarre sight his brother presented as Clem careened violently from one direction to another, trying desperately to free his arm from Fancy's teeth. Before Udell had time to collect himself, Chance was slamming into him with such force and fury that the tomahawk was knocked from his hand and they fell to the floor, locked in a deadly struggle. The blades of their knives gleamed dully in the ever-growing brightness of dawn as they rolled and twisted on the floor; a chair and a small table went flying as their writhing bodies smashed into them, each man trying to find a vital opening in which to strike the telling blow. Unbearably aware of the frantic need to go to Fancy's aid, Chance fought with a cold, deadly concentration, grimly intent on ending the fight swiftly.

They were well matched. Neither man had been able to bring his knife into position for a fatal strike, each one holding the other's knife at bay. Icily determined, Chance sought to rip his wrist from Udell's crushing fingers, as well as keep his own brutal grip on Udell's knife hand. Both were breathing harshly, their eyes full of fury and hatred as they continued to thrash across the floor, each man fiercely seeking an advantage. It came suddenly. One minute Udell's fingers were digging into his flesh, and the next Chance's knife hand swung free. A savage smile on his face, Chance thrust his blade deeply into Udell, driving it inward and upward, striking for the heart.

Udell groaned, stiffened, and then lay still. Chance leaped upright and twisted the knife out of Udell's limp grasp. A deadly expression on his face, he swung around to confront Clem.

The fight between Udell and Chance had taken mere minutes, but for Fancy, valiantly hanging on to Clem by her teeth as he yowled and struck her and scrambled for escape, it had seemed to last for hours. Her heart had told her that Chance would win, but as the minutes had passed, her certainty of the outcome had wavered. All her attention had been focused on Clem and the damage she was doing to him, but suddenly the room seemed abnormally silent and she knew her fate was sealed. Any moment now she would be safe in her husband's arms, or condemned to suffer a fate truly worse than death. She had been using both her hands to keep Clem's wrist in contact with her teeth, and the struggle was costing her dearly. Clem was much larger and stronger, the blows he rained upon her punishing, but Fancy had grimly hung on, knowing that Chance's life and her own depended upon it. When Clem had discovered that he could not easily dislodge her, with his free hand he had grasped a large chunk of her hair and was attempting, it felt to her, to tear her hair from her scalp.

Just as Chance's gaze had fallen upon them, Clem suddenly managed to free his savaged wrist from Fancy's teeth. With a muttered curse, before Chance could move, Clem jerked her head backward and hit her cruelly with his badly bitten fist. Fancy didn't make a sound. She simply folded and slid unconscious to the floor.

Panting heavily, Clem glanced in Chance's direction, the incipient smile of satisfaction beneath the Indian war paint instantly gone when he realized that it was Udell lying dead on the floor and not Chance Walker. For a long, ugly second they regarded each other, Chance's eyes a fierce, burning blue. Clem cursed and reached for his own knife, but Chance's blade was already in the air.

Just as Chance planned, the knife sank to the hilt in Clem's throat. There was an odd gurgle from Clem, and he sank to his knees, clawing at the weapon protruding from his throat. A moment later, like his brother, he lay dead.

Chance had little sympathy for either man. They had dared to invade his home with evil on their minds and had attacked not only him, but his woman. They had died too easily, Chance thought savagely. The dangerous flame in his eyes unabated, he stalked over to Clem and, putting his foot against the other man's chest, jerked out the blade.

Ignoring the bodies, Chance took a deep, steadying breath and turned to Fancy. The sight of her slender form lying so still on the floor sent a spear of stark fear through him. He flew to her side and sank to one knee, laying down the knife before lifting her gently into his arms.

A large bruise on Fancy's cheek was already beginning to make itself apparent where Clem's fist had hit her, and Chance felt a surge of fierce satisfaction that Clem would never hit another woman again. Fancy groaned in his arms and Chance crooned softly to her.

She did not respond, and, an anxious frown furrowing his forehead, Chance murmured, "Fancy, sweetheart, wake up. You are safe now. 'Tis over—we have vanquished them."

But as the minutes passed and Fancy remained silent and unmoving, Chance's anxiety grew. Terrible thoughts began to crowd his mind. It had been a powerful blow she had suffered, but surely not . . . He swallowed, his throat suddenly very dry. Surely there was nothing *vitally* wrong with her? Raw fear gripped him. What if Clem's blow proved to be more dangerous than he had first thought? An icy claw ripped through his heart. He had seen men die from a blow to the head.

He could not complete the terrifying thought, and almost crushing her to him, he muttered, "Sweetheart, wake up. You must! I love you. I could not bear life without you."

The knowledge that he had never said those words aloud before smote him. The agonizing awareness that Fancy could die without ever knowing that he loved, *adored*, her filled him with despair and angry remorse. She had to live. She *had* to.

With Fancy's slim body in his arms, Chance stood and carried her to their bed. She remained frighteningly still as he carefully arranged the blankets and sheets around her, only the even rise and fall of her breast revealing that she was still breathing. Seating himself on the edge of the bed beside her, he tenderly brushed back a swath of thick, curly hair that fell across her cheek, his eyes hardening when they fell upon the spot where Clem's fist had struck her. The mark was clear, and by the morrow he had no doubt that the delicate skin would be marred by a painful area of virulent green and purple.

Chance sat there for several seconds, his gaze fixed keenly on Fancy's face, remorse and anxiety gnawing at him, even as his fury against the Thackers—and Jonathan— grew. Thoughts of revenge, instant and deadly, against Jonathan filled him with a savage glee, but there was Fancy to see to first. Fancy, his sweet little wife, who had no idea how much he loved her, how much she meant to him. She was, he realized, everything a man could ever want in a woman—lovely, spirited, passionate. Brave and valiant, too, he thought slowly, recalling the way she had fought Clem.

A faint smile creased one cheek. What a fierce little vixen she had been. Her actions had probably saved both their lives, giving him the time he had needed to dispose of Udell before coming to her aid. But at what cost to herself? he wondered bitterly. Had she saved his life only to lose her own? His gaze ran over her slender form once more. She seemed so small and vulnerable lying there—so young and lovely, her long lashes dark against the paleness of her skin, her lips faintly pink and softly curved.

He bent his head, assailed by guilt and regret for having forced her to marry him, for *not* having told her of his love. It will be different now, he swore fiercely. From this moment on, she would know that she was treasured and adored and that his life wouldn't be worth living if she wasn't at his side.

Half lying, half sitting beside her, he rained delicate, desperate kisses across her pale face. "Fancy, you must wake up," he demanded huskily. "You cannot die—not now, when we have our entire future in front of us. I love you—I have always loved you—from the moment I first laid eyes on you, only I was too damned stubborn to admit it."

His impassioned words seemed to evoke no response. But just when he was on the point of going in search of help, Fancy's lids fluttered. She gave a soft moan and opened her eyes. Gazing into Chance's anxious features, she asked dazedly, "What happened?"

Chance laughed, a joyous, exultant sound in the quiet room. "We sent the Thackers to visit Satan in hell, Duchess, that is what happened."

A half-horrified, half-satisfied smile spread across her face. "They are dead? Both of them?"

Chance nodded, his face grim. "Indeed they are, quite, quite dead. You need never fear them again."

A shadow lingered in her fine eyes. "But what about the man who hired them? Who could be such a villain to hire someone to kill you?" she asked with a catch in her throat. "And why? Why would anyone want to kill you?" The instant the words left her mouth, the answer occurred to her. Her eyes wide and filled with horror, she whispered, "Jonathan!"

"I suspect that you are correct," he admitted calmly, "and I intend to pay my esteemed cousin a visit to discover for myself the truth of the matter."

"Oh, Chance, you cannot confront him by yourself. He is evil incarnate. Promise me you will not," Fancy begged vehemently, her hands clutching his arms. "I could not bear it if something were to happen to—" She stopped abruptly, embarrassingly aware of what she had almost revealed.

Far more interested in the latter part of Fancy's words, Chance instantly forgot about Jonathan. Brushing his lips against hers, his eyes very tender, he asked gently, "Would it bother you very much if something were to happen to me, sweetheart?"

Fancy bit her lip and glanced away. There was no use pretending any longer, she thought bitterly, that she didn't care a great deal, a very great deal, about what happened to him. She loved him. For pride's sake she might attempt to hide how completely he had enslaved her, but at this moment, after what had nearly happened to them this morning, it suddenly didn't seem all that important any longer. Besides, she admitted acidly, after the disgraceful way she seemed to always fall into his arms and bed, he had to know she was in love with him. What difference did it make if he knew, anyway. He held her heart firmly in the palm of his hand and always would. Still not looking at him, she said gruffly, "Yes, you wretched beast, it would."

Chance smiled wryly. "Must you always fight me, Duchess? Do you not know that you have won? That I love you more than life itself and that I shall all the days of my life?"

Fancy's head jerked around at his words, and she stared at him. At the sight of the incredibly tender expression on his hard face and the warm light in his eyes, her heart began to beat so hard and fast that she was certain it was going to leap right out of her breast. "What did you say?" she asked cautiously, still not believing that she had heard him correctly.

"I said," he murmured, "that I adore you. That I have adored you since I first glanced up and saw you standing on the deck of that ship in Richmond. And *that*," he added in thickened accents, his eyes very dark and blue, "is no doubt the reason I was willing to go to *any* lengths, honorable or not, to make you my wife. *I love you.*"

Joy sang in her veins, and tears of happiness glittering in her eyes, she flung her arms around his neck. "Oh, Chance," she said breathlessly. "You are a wicked, wicked rogue, and after the way you have treated me, you do not deserve that I should love you, but heaven help me—I do."

"Sweetheart."

There was very little coherent conversation between them for several minutes, both eager to confess their deepest emotions and revel in the sweetness of knowing that their heart's choice had been won. In between passionate kisses and soft murmurings, all the misunderstandings and hurts of the past became mere trifles, something to laugh about and smile at now that their love had them wrapped warmly in its powerful embrace.

A knock on the door brought them slowly back to the present. Sliding off the bed where he had been lying next to Fancy, Chance grimaced as his gaze fell upon the two bodies. He had completely forgotten the Thackers and Jonathan, and his lips tightened as he walked over to the door and opened it.

Orval Hewitt, a cousin of Jed's and the man in charge of the brood mares, stood there, an embarrassed, worried look on his lined, sun-darkened face. Seeing Chance standing there half-dressed, Orval flushed and muttered, "I am sorry to bother you, sir, but I think you should know that young Robert found some horses and a couple of pack mules hidden in the woods behind the main barn. He called and called, but no one answered. We thought you should know about it, in case it meant trouble."

Chance nodded. "I do know about it, and it did mean trouble—trouble my wife and I have managed to handle to our satisfaction." Stepping aside, he opened the door wider and indicated the two bodies.

Orval gasped, and after ascertaining that the master and mistress were unharmed, a torrent of questions poured from him. Keeping to himself his suspicions of Jonathan's part in the near tragedy, Chance answered Orval's inquiries easily. When the worst of Orval's curiosity had been satisfied, Chance asked that the bodies be removed as soon as possible. He and his wife would use her rooms for the time being.

Shutting the door behind Orval, Chance glanced back to his wife. "Well, madame," he drawled, "shall we retire to the, er, less crowded accommodation of your rooms?"

Fancy smiled dreamily at him; not even the knowledge

that two dead men lay in her husband's bedroom could dent the warm, golden glow that surrounded her. "Hmm, if you think we should."

Chance laughed. His eyes gleaming with loving possession, he plucked her from the bed and carried her along the passageway that separated their rooms. Kissing her soundly as he set her slowly on her feet, he murmured, "Does this mean that you shall always obey me in all things?"

Fancy wrinkled her nose at him. "It means," she replied spiritedly, "that when you show good common sense for doing something, I shall approve. Otherwise . . ."

Holding her firmly against him, Chance caught her mouth in a deep, hungry kiss. "Otherwise?" he asked thickly several moments later.

"Hmm?" Fancy asked, utterly bemused, her senses reeling.

Chance smiled to himself, his lips very busy teasing and tasting the corners of hers. "Nothing of any importance, sweetheart. I am resigned to my fate. You shall, no doubt, lead me around like a bull with a ring in his nose. And I am so in love with you, so utterly besotted by you, that I shall be quite content that this is so."

"Oh, *Chance*."

There was no serious conversation between them for several minutes, but eventually reality intruded. The bodies were removed, and Chance and Fancy had dressed and eaten a light repast in the morning room downstairs before Jonathan's name was mentioned again.

Setting down his cup of coffee, Chance looked across at Fancy and said quietly, "I am going to Walker Ridge to see Jonathan. Until I settle this with him, no one here will be safe. The next time—and we both know there will be a next time—who knows what he might plan? We might not be so fortunate." Seeing the storm of protest gathering in Fancy's eyes, he went on grimly, "I will not have you in danger, and as long as he lives, your own life is threatened simply because you are my wife. Someone striking at me might harm you by mistake. I leave tomorrow morning for Walker Ridge."

Filled with dismay, Fancy stared back at him, recognizing the determined jut of his chin and the fierce light in his eyes. She could not persuade him differently, she realized with a sinking heart. He had decided upon a course, and he would see Jonathan whether she agreed or not.

Putting down her fork carefully, she met his steady gaze. "Very well, then," she said softly, hiding her fear, "since you have obviously already made up your mind about this, we shall both go to Walker Ridge. And Chance," she added firmly when she saw that he was about to argue with her, "you cannot change my mind, nor deny me. And short of trussing me up like a chicken for market and locking me in the cellar, you cannot stop me. I *will* go with you."

Chapter Twenty-four

The argument did not end there, and though Chance protested vociferously, Fancy would not be swayed. She was, he decided half-angrily, half-admiringly, some hours later as they lay together in bed, as beautiful as she was stubborn—and he would have her no other way. Even if, at the moment, he was strongly inclined to wring her neck.

They had, more or less, resolved their difference by the time they had retired for the night, and by unspoken consent, the disagreement was not allowed in their bed. Their lovemaking that night was especially tender and satisfying, the morning's near brush with death adding a delicious urgency. The knowledge that it was love that bound them together made their joining even sweeter.

Her head resting comfortably on Chance's shoulder, her body still tingling from his possession, Fancy considered telling him about the baby. All through the day the words had trembled on her lips, and a dozen times she had nearly blurted it out, wanting to share this last secret between them. But the right moment had never presented itself; she had hoped to tell him this evening when they were alone in their rooms, but his vehement denouncement of her plan to accompany him tomorrow to Walker Ridge had given her pause.

In the darkness she made a face. If he knew that she was pregnant with their child, he *would* truss her up like a chicken and leave her under guard in the cellar. She sighed. It wouldn't, she admitted regretfully, be a good idea to mention the coming child just now. She would have to wait until the situation with Jonathan had been resolved.

The next morning Chance made one last attempt to dissuade her from accompanying him, but seeing the obstinate slant to her mouth, he gave up and ordered a pair of horses saddled. Just an hour after dawn on that Friday morning, they set off for Walker Ridge.

The trip passed swiftly, and to Fancy's surprise it seemed no time at all, instead of several hours, when they eventually left the forest behind and rode into the openness of the cleared fields on the outskirts of Walker Ridge. The sun was high in the sky by now, and Fancy had long ago taken off the blue woolen cloak with which she had started the journey. She had never been much of a horsewoman, and as the main house of Walker Ridge came into view, she admitted to herself that it was a most welcome sight.

Lifting her down from the sidesaddle in which she had ridden, Chance smiled slightly and caught her when she half stumbled as her feet touched the ground. "Not used to so many hours in the saddle, are you, Duchess?"

"No, but I shall soon be a most superior horsewoman, you shall see," Fancy said loftily, her eyes gleaming with laughter.

Chance bussed her on the nose, wondering how he could have been so lucky to have found her—and to have her love him.

Walking up the broad steps of the house, Chance murmured, "They are going to be quite surprised to see us."

Fancy nodded. "I know. Which is why I think 'tis such a good notion that we tell as much of the truth as we can."

On that point he and Fancy had been in total agreement.

They would tell everything about the previous morning's attack by the Thackers, even the fact that Udell had admitted to being hired by someone to kill Chance. The only detail they would omit would be their suspicions about Jonathan's part in the murderous attempt.

Upon their entrance into the house, they had been ushered immediately into the small, comfortable parlor at the rear of the house, where Sam and Letty had been sitting. Greeting them with a wide smile and a fierce, bear-like hug that caught Chance by surprise, Sam seemed especially pleased to see them. Startled by Sam's unexpectedly affectionate hug, after the first flurry of greetings and exclamations had died down, Chance instantly became aware of an odd feeling in the air. There was something definitely peculiar about the way Sam and Letty were acting.

Some minutes later, once he and Fancy had both been seated and offered some refreshments, Chance was further nonplussed when he happened to glance over at Letty and caught her staring at him with an expression of such bemused delight and deep emotion that he was thoroughly mystified. What the devil was going on here?

Sam could have explained it to him, but he was still reeling from the ecstatic knowledge that Chance Walker was truly his and Letty's only child. And he would be forever grateful to Annie Clemmons for finally telling the truth about the tragic night Chance had been born. When she had arrived on Wednesday with Hugh and Ellen, Annie had barely stepped into the house before she had sought out a private interview with Sam. That interview had confirmed all that he had suspected. Annie's quiet, hesitant words had filled him with such happiness, such blinding joy, that he found himself feeling pity for her rather than anger.

His emotions toward his stepmother were not so generous. In the forty-eight hours that had passed since Sam had learned the truth, he could hardly bring himself to look at Constance, much less converse politely with her. Letty, upon being told by Sam what Annie had revealed, had been torn between dizzying rapture at Chance's identity and utter fury at the black crime Constance had committed. Like her husband, she had avoided her stepmother-in-law, not certain she could be in the same room with Constance without attacking her. The aloofness of the elder Walkers had not been so noticeable while Hugh and Ellen had been there, but they had left early Thursday for Hugh's home, and since then a definite chill had permeated the house.

Constance was not a stupid woman. She had sensed the change in Letty and Sam almost immediately. Discovering that Annie had returned home without warning and was currently ensconced in one of the suites in the house, she quickly surmised what had transpired. She had beat a strategic retreat to her quarters. Constance had hoped that she was being unduly apprehensive, but when her attempts to talk privately with Annie were firmly rebuffed, she knew that her worst fears had been realized. A frantic note to Jonathan had brought the return message from his secretary that Mr. Jonathan had gone to visit friends for a few days and wasn't expected back until Sunday or Monday.

The atmosphere since Annie's return had been a curious mixture of tenseness and quiet joy. Sam and Letty were delightedly hugging to themselves the knowledge that Chance was their son, eagerly contemplating the time when not only they but the whole world would know his parentage.

Constance's fate presented them with hardly any concern. She would likely return to England to live out her days once the scandal became public. There was no way, they both admitted, that the truth could be wrapped in clean linen—or that she could remain at Walker Ridge. It was Chance and how he would be affected by the revelations that consumed all their energies.

Once Annie's tale had been told, it had been almost impossible for Sam and Letty not to leave immediately for Devil's Own, but they had restrained themselves. They believed Annie's words implicitly, but would Chance? And how would he feel to discover that they were his parents? Would he be pleased? Dismayed? They viewed his unexpected arrival at Walker Ridge as a wonderful stroke of good fortune, and their joy at seeing him was nearly palpable.

Even Fancy noticed the unusual degree of warmth that seemed to emanate from Sam and Letty, but she convinced herself it was because she was so in love with Chance that she just naturally assumed everyone else found him so utterly charming. She was, she decided with a dreamy little smile on her lips, absolutely besotted with the wicked and oh so dear blue-eyed wretch.

The conversation among the four of them was desultory for several minutes before Chance was able to bring up the reason for their sudden arrival. Sam and Letty heard him out as he explained the attack by the Thackers, Letty's face paling, Sam's fists clenching at his sides.

When Chance finished speaking, Sam asked abruptly, "They did not name the man who hired them?"

Chance shook his dark head. "No, sir, but I believe I know who it may have been."

Sam nodded grimly. "Jonathan, of course."

Chance and Fancy both looked startled. A frown between his brows, Chance asked, "I know why Jonathan is my choice, but why is he yours, sir?"

Sam and Letty exchanged glances. A tremulous little smile on her lips, Letty said, "We must tell him, Sam. I want him to know." She gave a surprisingly girlish laugh. "In fact, I cannot *wait* for him to know."

Sam was seated next to Letty on a straw satin-covered settee, and he picked up her slim, wrinkled hand and kissed it lightly. "As you wish, madame," he murmured. "When have I ever been able to deny you anything?"

Letty tapped him smartly on the sleeve. "None of that now—*tell* him."

Chance and Fancy were on the opposite side of the small room from the older couple, Chance standing behind Fancy's chair, one sun-browned hand lying possessively on her shoulder. They both looked mystified by the exchange, and seeing their expressions, Sam smiled faintly. "I am sure you are wondering why we are acting so strangely. If you will bear with me, I have a tale to tell you that will explain all," he began slowly. "A tale that begins over thirty years ago. In fact," he said carefully, his gaze boring into Chance's blue eyes, "it begins on the night of your birth."

Chance and Fancy listened spellbound as Sam revealed all that he and Letty had so recently learned. Everything from Morely's years of silence, to Sam's perusal of the old account books, to Annie's confession just two days ago.

When Sam's voice died away and silence fell, Chance looked dazed. "Are you saying," he finally got out as he looked from one to the other, "that I am *your son*? Your legitimate child? A twin?"

Smiling mistily at him, Letty nodded vigorously. "Yes. Oh, Chance, is it not wonderful? You are our *son*."

A multitude of emotions exploded in Chance's chest. Amazement, anger, regret, wariness, hope. And last, a burgeoning joy. "Are you positive?" he said at last. "Certain that I am indeed your son?"

Sam nodded slowly. "I tried as much to disprove your identity as I did to prove it. And do not forget, we have two people, Morely and Annie, whose stories, when combined, mesh completely." A twinkle lit his eyes. "And of course, there are the toes!" His voice hardening, he added, "There is no doubt that Constance tried that night to get rid of Letty's living twin—you. And only"—Sam smiled wryly—"because of *chance* you are alive today. If Annie had followed Constance's orders, or if Morely had not come along—this story would have a very different ending."

Her face full of yearning and sudden uncertainty, Letty gazed at Chance. "Does it displease you," she asked almost timidly, "to discover that we are your parents?"

Chance stared at her. "Displease me?" he repeated in a strangled tone. "I am overwhelmed. I do not know whether to find Morely and knock his teeth down his throat or pick you up in my arms and dance around the room with joy."

Letty's eyes glowed. "I know which one I would prefer . . . son."

In one stride Chance was across the room, and dropping

lithely to one knee, he bent his head and kissed his mother's hands. In a choked voice, he managed, "I always wondered who my mother might be and why she never wanted me. Now I can only thank God that we are together at last."

Letty nodded slowly and lifted a trembling hand to caress his dark, tumbled hair. "At last," she said softly, tears coursing down her cheeks. "At long last."

It was a deeply emotional moment, and Fancy felt a lump grow in her throat. When Chance stood and his father embraced him, she had to blink furiously to keep her happy tears at bay. Holding Chance tightly to him, Sam murmured over and over again, "My son. My son. *My son.*"

Several minutes passed before anyone in the room was capable of coherent conversation. Then, as if a dam had broken, there was a torrent of words as the four of them sought to assimilate and understand the wonderful event that had just transpired. There were questions aplenty, but there were answers, too, answers that explained so many things.

Shaking his dark head, Chance said for perhaps the hundredth time, "That Morely! Keeping such a secret to himself all these years. I may still knock his teeth down his throat."

"Well, I for one," Sam said easily, "am willing to forgive him much for finally having spoken. It took courage to admit what he had done after all this time." He shot Chance a look. "He could have kept his tongue between his teeth, you know."

Chance grimaced. "I know. It is just . . ." He shook his head. "I just find it hard to believe that I am your son and that Morely knew, or at least suspected it, right from the beginning and yet said nothing."

Thinking of her own babe growing in her womb, Fancy added tartly, "I think your wrath should be directed at Constance. She is the one who set the situation in motion, *not* Morely. To my eyes, he is a hero." She looked speakingly at Chance. "He saved your life. And he did his best to ensure that you were with your parents, even if none of you realized it."

"I stand corrected, Duchess," Chance replied lightly. "Morely is a saint."

"Not a saint, perhaps," Letty said fairly, "but certainly not a villain."

"No, not a villain," Chance muttered. "That title we can save for Jonathan and his mother." From beneath his brows he glanced across at his father. "Does Jonathan know the truth?"

Sam nodded slowly. "From what Annie said, indeed he does." He sighed heavily. "I have been worried about you since Annie admitted that Jonathan knew the truth. But until you told me about the attack by the Thackers, I never really believed that he would stoop to naked murder. Otherwise, I would have warned you of the danger."

"But what do we do now?" Fancy demanded. "We have no proof that he hired the Thackers."

"We do not need proof," said Sam. "Once Chance's identity is made public, Jonathan's reasons for wishing him dead are gone."

Chance snorted. "Jonathan has hated me for years, and that was *before* he learned who I really am."

Letty's lovely blue-gray eyes full of fear, she asked agitatedly, "What are we going to do? We cannot let him harm Chance."

A smile flitted across Chance's dark face. "Mother," he said slowly, savoring the word, "I think you should worry more of what I might do to Jonathan than what he might do to me."

Letty flushed with pleasure at hearing the word "Mother" for the first time from her son's lips, but she insisted worriedly, "Jonathan is not to be trifled with. If he did hire the Thackers—and there is no doubt in our minds that he did— who knows what sort of wicked villainy he might undertake?"

"The only real protection for Chance is for the truth to be made public as soon as possible," Sam said quietly. "Jonathan is not stupid. Once the world knows that Chance is our son, he would be aware that if anything untoward were to happen to Chance, he would be the first and primary suspect."

"Short of putting a sign around my neck and parading me through the colony, I do not see how that can be swiftly accomplished, sir," Chance replied dryly.

Sam smiled whimsically at him. "Could you not call me Father?"

Chance grinned. "Indeed I can . . . Father. And it gives me great pleasure to do so."

"Our son is right, you know," Letty said softly. "We know the truth, but how are we to let the world know?"

"I have already taken some steps to do just that," Sam admitted. "I had Annie write down precisely what happened the night Chance was born. Before Hugh left, I had him and my secretary witness her signature on the document. Neither of them knows what was contained therein, but that document, along with a letter from me, revealing all that I have learned, is currently on its way to Williamsburg and our family attorney." He looked a little guilty. "I did not swear him to silence."

"Sam, you didn't," Letty exclaimed. "When we had not even told Chance?"

"I know, I know. It was hasty of me, but I wanted the truth to come out as soon as possible, and I assumed that before any word could trickle back here, we would have seen Chance and explained." He glanced over at Chance. "Do you mind?"

Chance shook his head. "Indeed not. It is precisely what I would have done."

Fancy smiled across at Letty. "They are very alike, are they not?"

"I have always thought so," Letty said, her eyes traveling caressingly from one man to the other.

Dinner that evening was a merry occasion, a joyous celebration, and while they all knew that there was going to be one almighty scandal and unpleasant days ahead when the truth came out, for the moment they simply treasured this intimate time together. After they had eaten, the ladies, both of them exhausted by the events of the day, sought out their own rooms, while Sam eagerly led Chance off to his office to discuss how they were going to handle the affair and the more practical business of Chance taking his place as the rightful heir to Walker Ridge and the vast, far-flung Walker fortune. It was easily decided between them that Jonathan's portion, which had come to him from his father, would be immediately and completely split off from Sam's estates. As Sam's son, Chance would one day be the master of Walker Ridge and in control of the majority of the Walker wealth.

It was a rather dazed and bemused Chance who eventually joined Fancy in their rooms. She was waiting for him in bed, and he shed his clothes and joined her. After settling her comfortably in the crook of his arm, he muttered, "Well, Duchess, it would seem that you made a much better marriage than you ever knew."

Demurely Fancy said, "Perhaps now that you have discovered that you are the heir to the Walker fortune, it is you who regrets our marriage. After all, what is a mere baroness to a Walker of Walker Ridge? Just think: if you had waited, you might have been able to marry a true Duchess."

Shifting her so that he was looking down into her smiling face, he said huskily, "You are the *only* Duchess I shall ever want. You are my life, and fortune or no, I would still want you for my wife. Only you, my own sweet, tart-tongued little Duchess." He kissed her, and Fancy promptly forgot about everything but the delight of her husband's ardent embrace.

The interview the next morning with Constance in Sam's office was most unpleasant. She tried to deny everything, casting vile aspersions on both Morely and Annie. But in the end, staring into Sam's and Chance's implacable features, she realized that she was beaten, that she had lost. The truth was already on its way to Williamsburg, and there was nothing she could do about it but accept defeat and retire from the field.

But she refused to be completely cowed. Her lips tight

and grim, she demanded, "And what do you intend to do with me? Lock me in my room? Pretend I do not exist? You cannot bring charges against me—you have your precious son. All I did was deny you his whining youth."

"I believe," Sam said levelly, hiding his distaste, "that you should immediately consider taking a trip to England. I am sure that you can find some pleasant village in which to settle. I shall, of course, make certain that you receive all the monies that you are entitled to under my father's will."

Her face went white. "You are banishing me? Sending me away from Walker Ridge?"

Gently Sam said, "Would you prefer to stay and face the scandal? Have your former friends stare at you in horror when they learn what you did?"

She closed her eyes in anguish. No. Of course not. That was unthinkable. Sam's suggestion was the only solution. In a colorless voice she said, "Very well. I shall go to England. Immediately." Glaring at Sam, she asked, "What about Jonathan?"

"You need not worry about your son. He shall have all that he is entitled to under our father's will." Sam smiled coolly. "Everything else shall go to my own son, Chance."

Her hands clenching in impotent fury, Constance shot a venomous look at Chance, who stood silently beside his father. Her lip curled. "Do you really think that this backwoods jackanapes will be able to usurp my son's position here in the Colonies?"

"I think you forget," Sam said softly. "This backwoods jackanapes, as you call him, is *my* son. He is the rightful heir to Walker Ridge."

Her face twisted with hatred, she swung around and fled the room.

Chance let out a low whistle as the door banged behind her. "The lady," he murmured, "has no love of us, I think."

"Do you know," Sam replied with mock astonishment, "I believe you are right."

Both men chuckled, relieved that the ugly scene was behind them. After a few minutes' more conversation, they went in search of their wives. Since the morning was fine, they found the ladies strolling contentedly in the rose gardens, a few hardy blooms still showing their brightly petaled heads.

Both looked up expectantly, and after greeting his mother and wife, Chance said quietly, "She is leaving for England."

"Thank goodness," Fancy exclaimed. "Now if Jonathan will only prove to be as accommodating."

Unaware of the calamity that had befallen him, Jonathan returned home to Foxfield Monday evening in a rather smug frame of mind. He had gone visiting to a friend's plantation, a good day's ride from Foxfield, and had thoroughly enjoyed himself. The trip had proved timely. His friend had been entertaining relatives from Philadelphia, rich, influential relatives who just happened to have their charming daughter with them. Their charming daughter who was their only child. Jonathan had been much taken with the young heiress, thinking she would do very well as a bride for him, and it was apparent that she found him equally attractive.

Striding up the steps to Foxfield, he had been whistling to himself, happily contemplating the future with his lovely bride at his side. She didn't have a title, it was true, but she was close at hand, and her family was well connected. Before she returned with her parents to Philadelphia, Jonathan intended to have won her hand.

Entering his study, he tossed his hat and gloves on a nearby table, then poured himself a glass of port. Seated behind his desk, his boots propped upon the shiny surface, he slowly drank his wine, savoring the future. The Thackers would take care of Chance for him; he was going to marry a delightfully naive young heiress; and soon enough Sam would die and he would be in complete control of all the Walker wealth. He was very pleased with himself.

He noticed the missive from his mother lying on a silver salver on the corner of his desk, and recognizing her handwriting, he sighed. Now what the devil did she want?

His contented mood vanished when he read the news contained in his mother's note. He swore viciously as he flung the note down. *Annie returned.* Constance had not gone into detail, but from her jumbled words it was obvious that the worst had happened.

Jonathan frowned blackly, his mind racing. But all was not lost, he thought suddenly, relaxing slightly. It was Constance who had committed the crime, not he. It was his mother who had ordered Annie to dispose of the baby; he'd been a mere child himself and utterly blameless. And as for learning the truth and not saying anything . . . His agile brain quickly came up with a likely reason for his silence: he had been stunned and appalled by what he had learned, and while he'd had every intention of telling Sam and Letty, he had naturally wanted to protect his mother. He had only been holding his tongue until he could get her safely away and shielded from the worst of the scandal. He smiled. That should take care of anything Annie might have said concerning his knowledge of the affair. And as for Chance . . . He smiled nastily. The Thackers were going to take care of Chance for him. With Chance dead, he would still be the heir.

He rang for Simmons. Perhaps his valet had heard from the Thackers and Chance was already dead. Wonderful thought, that.

Simmons entered a moment later. Bowing, he asked, "Yes, master? Is there something you wanted?"

There was a note in Simmons's voice that made Jonathan look at him sharply, but seeing nothing except bland politeness on the man's face, he demanded, "Have you heard any word from those rascally cousins of yours?"

Simmons looked suitably saddened, although there was a gleam in his eyes that was at variance with the expression on his sallow features. "You have not heard, master? Everyone has been talking about it." With relish, he added, "It seems that my poor misguided cousins attacked Master Chance and his bride at their plantation some days ago and were both killed. Such a tragedy."

Jonathan's eyes narrowed. He didn't like Simmons's attitude at all. And the news he had imparted was devastating. Thackers dead. Chance alive.

A malicious glitter in his eyes, Simmons said softly, "While you have been gone, there has been great excitement, sir. Master Chance and his bride arrived on Friday with news of their narrow escape, but that was nothing to the news that Master Sam announced just yesterday to all of us connected with Walker Ridge: apparently information has come to light proving that Master Chance is Master Sam and Mistress Letty's only child." The malice more open, he continued pleasantly, "It seems your mother tried to get rid of the child at birth. Who would have suspected her of such a dastardly act? Everyone is quite stunned—no one can talk of anything else." Complacently, he ended with, "Master Sam has written to the Walker relatives, explaining all to them, and has notified his attorney in Williamsburg. I believe that your mother left for Richmond to catch a ship for England only this morning. Such a pity that you could not be with her in her hour of need."

Jonathan's face was white by the time Simmons finished speaking. Good God! That bastard Chance had moved swiftly. The news was no doubt already spreading like wildfire through the colony, and before the end of the month everyone would know. There was no way to conceal Chance's real identity now. Jonathan swore and slammed his fist upon the desk.

Glaring at Simmons, he snapped, "I know that I should not have trusted those worthless cousins of yours. I should have taken care of things myself."

Simmons looked innocent. "Oh? Were the Thackers working for you?" He smiled. Wolfishly. "That is not something that you would want for public knowledge, is it?"

"And what do you mean by that?"

"Oh, just that I think that I have worked for you long enough and that I would like to try my hand at something new. Of course," he added lightly, "I would need a stake . . . um, something like double the amount you were going to pay my cousins to kill Chance Walker for you."

"Are you trying to blackmail me?" Jonathan thundered, his eyes bright with rage.

Simmons rubbed his chin thoughtfully. "Ah, no. I am simply looking out for my own future. And since yours has changed so dramatically during these past few days, I think it behooves me to watch out for myself. I mean, after all, you are no longer in line to inherit much, are you? And as for speaking of my, er, disposal of my former employer . . . I am afraid that if you were to mention it, why, I would just have to mention your little arrangement with my cousins." Letting his satisfaction show, he smiled and added sweetly, "Quite a change in circumstances, is it not?"

"By God, you are not going to get away with this. I will see you dead before I pay you one penny."

Simmons shrugged. "Whatever you say . . . but I would like my money within the hour. My bags are already packed and I plan to be gone from here before dark."

Jonathan stared at him, knowing that he was trapped. So angry he couldn't think straight, he bounded up from behind his desk and stalked over to the large hunting print that hung on the wall and concealed the safe where he kept a large of supply of gold. "I will pay you this time, you damned blackmailer, but never again." After pushing aside the picture, he swiftly opened the safe and, reaching inside, extracted a small bag of gold from the several that lay stacked together. His back to Simmons as he started to shut the safe, he growled, "You will take what I give you, and if I ever see your murderous face again—"

Simmons had stealthily closed the distance between them, and as Jonathan started to turn around, he suddenly felt the other man's presence . . . and the sharp bite of a knife at his throat.

"No," Simmons said softly as he kept the blade of his knife against Jonathan's neck, "I will take exactly what I want."

A swift, vicious slash and Jonathan fell to the floor, his throat cut nearly to the bone. His life blood pouring out, he dimly heard Simmons say, "So thoughtful of you to keep so much gold on hand. I am certain that it will take me a long way from here."

Coolly stepping over Jonathan's dead body, Simmons helped himself liberally to all the bags of gold. Smiling, he quickly exited the study, locking the door behind him. It would be hours before Jonathan's body would be discovered. Ten minutes later Simmons was on a horse, riding swiftly away. Now where, he wondered, would he go? Spanish territory? He had heard New Orleans was a most sinful city. He smiled. It sounded like just the place for a fellow like him.

Epilogue

Fair Horizons

Late Spring 1775

Look, how my ring encompasseth thy finger,
Even so thy breast encloseth my poor heart;
Wear both of them, for both of them are thine.

William Shakespeare,
King Richard III

Epilogue

Fair Horizons

Late Spring 1779

Chapter Twenty-five

The storm, Letty thought uneasily, reminded her a little too vividly of the terrible storm that had raged the night that Chance had been born. The wind was howling and the rain pounding fiercely against the house, and her gaze slid worriedly to Fancy. Fancy had been in labor since yesterday afternoon, and as Letty watched her, the young woman groaned softly on the big bed as another contraction hit her. Please, Letty prayed fervently, please let this birthing be normal. Please let nothing go wrong.

Her glance met Ellen's, and seeing the girl's anxious features, Letty pushed aside her own fears and memories and said softly, "Do not fret, dear. Having a baby takes time."

"I know," Ellen said quickly, "and Fancy has not been in labor overly long. It is just that the baby is very early, is it not? I thought it was not due for weeks yet."

Letty smiled. "Babies decide when they arrive, and I am very much afraid that they do not look at calendars."

The contraction having passed, Fancy muttered, "Early or not, I just wish affairs would move more swiftly. It seems that I have been lying here struggling for days, and so far I have nothing to show for it."

Letty chuckled, and after wringing out a cloth where it lay

in a bowl of cool water, she tenderly wiped the signs of perspiration from Fancy's temples. "I know it seems like a long time, dear, but it is just twenty-fours ago that your water broke. You young people are just so impatient."

There was no sting in Letty's words, and despite her great discomfort, Fancy smiled at her. In the months that had passed since Chance's parentage had been revealed, Fancy and her in-laws had become very close, and she had decided some time ago that she could not have wished for a kinder or more understanding mother-in-law.

It had been a tumultuous several months that they had endured together, the news of Chance's true identity and the events surrounding the night of his birth rocking the society in which the Walkers moved. Of course, the family stood firm, but there were those who whispered that Sam was merely attempting to foist off his bastard on them and that Letty was a fool for condoning it. But those people were few, and most believed Sam's version of what had happened. The fact that Constance was *not* universally liked made it easier for everyone to accept that she was quite capable of such a wicked act. Of course, there would always be those who were firmly convinced that the Walkers were pulling the wool over everyone's eyes, but for the most part, Chance had been warmly received as Sam and Letty's legitimate son.

Jonathan's shocking murder tended to cloud the issue, and there was a great deal of speculation all that winter about the coincidence of Jonathan's death and the revelation of Chance's parentage. The pity felt for Constance upon the murder of her only son helped temper some of the public disgust with her ugly deed, but it was felt by all to be a good thing that she had decided to live quietly in England.

There was no mystery about who had murdered Jonathan; the open safe, the missing gold, and the disappearance of his valet, Simmons, made it obvious what must have occurred.

Sam had offered a huge reward for his capture, but Simmons seemed to have vanished into thin air. Privately

Chance thought that the fellow had done them all a favor, but he kept that opinion to himself.

Not surprisingly, being acknowledged as the Walker heir had caused a huge upheaval in Chance's and Fancy's lives. There was no question of them continuing to live at Devil's Own; Chance was now the Walker of Walker Ridge. With a certain amount of regret, in November they had bade their first home good-bye and had moved into the elegant house they now shared with Sam and Letty.

It had been a wise move; there was much that Chance had to learn as the man who would one day control the Walker fortune. With Jonathan gone, it was necessary for him to quickly grasp the reins of the immense Walker empire. As the months passed, more and more Sam relied upon his son to handle the family affairs.

Devil's Own had not been abandoned. Hugh and Ellen had married at Christmas and eagerly accepted Chance's offer to run the plantation and the horse-breeding operation until such time as Hugh would take over his own father's estates, an event they all hoped would be a long time in the future.

The news that Fancy was to have a child had delighted Chance and thrilled the prospective grandparents. Fancy found herself coddled and cosseted by her husband and his parents to the extent that she was hardly allowed to lift a finger to help herself. And despite her laughing protests that they were all spoiling her, the loving trio simply ignored her and continued to do just that.

The past several months had proved to be a turbulent time not only for Chance and Fancy, but for all of the British colonies. The scent of war permeated the air everywhere. In March of this year, the firebrand Patrick Henry, at St. John's Church in Richmond, had declared, "Give me liberty or give me death." Four weeks later the British had fired upon the Minutemen at Lexington in Massachusetts. Virginia's governor, Lord Dunmore, fearful of the hotheaded young rebels, had fled, leaving the Virginians in charge of their own fate. The Continental Congress was to meet in Philadelphia in the summer, and there was no doubt in anyone's mind that war with England was imminent.

At Walker Ridge they were insulated somewhat from the furor, but no one could be unaware of what was happening. As Fancy's time neared, the coming baby pushed the momentous events taking place in Williamsburg, Boston, and other parts of the Colonies into the background.

That the baby had decided to come several weeks ahead of schedule had alarmed Chance and Sam, but smiling serenely, Letty had pushed them from the room and told them, as she had Ellen, "Babies come when they are ready."

She was not feeling quite so serene now. Watching as another contraction ripped through Fancy, she bit her lip. Had she been overconfident? Was something wrong? She thought not. The pregnancy had progressed normally, and Fancy was young and strong; despite all their scoldings, she had continued to walk at least a mile every day, even with her hugely swollen belly and equally swollen feet.

Everything should go just fine, Letty told herself firmly. And the storm was just a coincidence. *Not* an omen.

Just then Fancy gave a sharp gasp, and leaning over to check the progress, Letty exclaimed with as much relief as excitement, "Oh, push, dear. The head is there. Push!"

Ellen rushed to the door and flung it wide, motioning to Chance, who had been pacing anxiously up and down the long hallway. Smiling at him, she said, "The baby is coming."

Chance had not liked being banished from the birthing room, and only Fancy's promise that she would have Ellen bring him in when the baby was finally ready to make its appearance had placated him. Sam, his expression worried, yet full of anticipation, stood uncertainly in the doorway, yearning to enter but not wanting to intrude at this most intimate time.

Sam might have remained there indefinitely, but Fancy suddenly gave a powerful push, and with a loud, heartfelt groan, her child was born. Scooping up the squalling bundle, Letty cried, "Oh, Sam, 'tis a boy! Come see!"

Sam needed no further urging, and as Letty laid the new-born babe in Fancy's outstretched arms, Sam was hovering just behind Chance's shoulder. After staring wonderingly at the baby, Sam met Letty's eyes. "Our grandson," he murmured reverently, hardly daring to believe the miracle.

"And our son," Chance said proudly, his eyes resting caressingly on Fancy's tired features.

Fancy stared in bemusement at the tiny, wrinkled face. Her son. She and Chance had created a new life, this wonderful, wonderful child she held in her arms. Her heart blossomed with fierce emotion. She had thought that she could love no other person as strongly as she did Chance, but she realized that she had been wrong; this small bit of humanity engendered a love as lasting and as powerful as the emotion she shared with her husband.

Almost hesitantly Chance asked, "May I hold him?"

Watching the extreme tenderness with which Chance lifted his son, Fancy smiled. Chance would be a good father.

With the parents' permission, the newborn was eventually passed into the eager, trembling arms of his grandparents, and as she watched the elderly couple marvel at his perfect form, Fancy's eyes stung. They had missed so very much, but if God was kind, they would be allowed to gain much of what they had lost because of Constance's greed.

Happy that the birth was over, Fancy was simply enjoying the aftermath, watching Chance as he stared at his son, who once more lay in her arms, and then staring in wonderment herself at the miracle they had made.

A cramp made her frown, and seeing her expression, Letty said calmly, "No doubt it is the afterbirth."

Fancy nodded, but when she experienced another one, harder and stronger, her eyes widened. "I do not think so," she muttered, hurriedly passing the baby to Chance. A third wave of pain clawed through her, making her body arch.

The next minutes were confused and frantic as Fancy strained and pushed, the pain washing savagely through her.

"Bless the Lord," Letty suddenly exclaimed. "There is another one. 'Tis *twins*."

And indeed it was. Less than twenty minutes after his brother had been born, Fancy brought forth her second child, a boy as strong and perfect as the first—and just as loud, his indignant wails ringing through the room.

When the excitement had died down and her two sons were lying in her arms, Fancy stared in complete bemusement at the two bundles. "Twins," she said slowly, her disbelief evident in her tone. "Who could have imagined it?"

"Well, dear," Letty said proudly, "twins do run in Chance's family. I suppose we should have considered the possibility."

That Sam and Letty were overjoyed with having not one but two healthy grandsons was evident, and watching the way they hovered over them, Fancy suspected it was a good thing that there were two of them; one would have been *impossibly* spoiled, while two just might manage to be *merely* spoiled. Her eyes met Chance's, and seeing the twinkle in those dark blue depths, she knew he was thinking much the same thing.

"What are you going to name them?" Letty asked.

A wicked smile on his lips, Chance murmured, "Considering my name, and my skill at gambling, I think that something on the order of 'Lucky' and 'Ace' or"—and the wicked sparkle in his gaze grew more pronounced—" 'Ace' and 'Deuce.' "

The ladies looked scandalized, and hugging her children tighter to her, Fancy said firmly, "Absolutely not. They shall have normal, sensible names." Fixing her grinning husband with a stern glance, she said, "We had already decided upon 'Andrew' if a boy, and that is what our firstborn shall be called." She dropped a kiss on the newly named Andrew's downy head. Smiling at her second son, she thought a moment and then said, "And you, sweetheart, shall be named Samuel." She looked challengingly over at her husband. "Do you object?"

Chance shook his head. "No. Those are fine names, I just think that Luck—" He stopped, the expression on his wife's face making him laugh. "Duchess, if you could see yourself! You look like an enraged tigress defending her young."

"I *am* defending my young," Fancy replied spiritedly. "From their father. Lucky and Ace! What sorts of names are those?"

Three weeks later, on a fine May day in the rose garden at Walker Ridge, Andrew and Samuel were duly baptized by a traveling preacher. Watching as her two sons were carried away to the house by their doting grandparents, Fancy knew that while she may have won the battle, she had lost the war. Both Sam and Chance continually referred to the boys as Lucky and Ace, and she had even caught herself occasionally thinking of them with those names. She sighed. Chance could be very determined about some things. At least, she consoled herself, their *legal* names were respectable.

Hearing her sigh, Chance, who had been walking beside her, looked down at her and asked, "Something the matter, sweetheart?"

She smiled ruefully up at him. "I have decided that you are a determined man. Devious, too."

"Where you are concerned I am indeed determined, *very* determined," he admitted, his mouth a little grim.

She pinched him lightly on the arm. "I was not referring to me, you wretched creature. I was referring to the under-handed manner in which you have gotten your own way in the matter of our children's names."

"I had much rather talk about you," he murmured, pulling her into his arms, "and how much I adore you."

At his words and the touch of his mouth at the corner of her lips, Fancy promptly forgot about her sons and their vexing names. Melting into Chance's possessive arms, she gave herself up to the joy of loving and being loved by him.

It was several minutes later before Fancy emerged flushed and breathless from her husband's passionate embrace. "Oh, Chance," she said softly, "I do love you—even when you are being utterly impossible."

His face suddenly very serious, he stared down at her. Huskily he said, "I love you, Fancy. More than life itself. I have loved and wanted you since the moment I first laid eyes on you, but I have never given you much choice in what happened between us, have I?"

She shook her head, but there was a tender smile on her lips. "No. You simply decided you wanted me, and my fate was sealed, no matter my opinion of the situation." She kissed him lightly on the mouth. "You are fortunate that I had the good sense to fall in love with you."

"No regrets?" he asked, a faint question in his gaze.

Staring at his dark, intent features, aware of the hint of uncertainty about this always most certain man, she felt her heart swell with love for him. Flinging herself into his arms, she said earnestly, "My heart is yours. It has always been yours. Yours for the taking."

With infinite tenderness, Chance enveloped her in his embrace, his mouth warm and worshiping on hers. And then, arm in arm, they turned and walked toward the house and the love-filled future that awaited them there.

Please turn the page for a
bonus excerpt from

And Love Remains

by
Shirlee Busbee

Coming soon
from
WARNER BOOKS

Chapter One

———— ◆◆◆ ————

"*Mercy!* What do you mean, he is moving *here*! Surely you have misread the letter, maman?"

Lisette Dupree frowned at her daughter. "I assure you, petite, that I did not make a mistake. Hugh Lancaster states quite clearly that he is moving to the New Orleans area just as soon as he is able to put his business affairs in Natchez in order. Here, read the letter yourself."

Somewhat gingerly, almost as if she expected it to bite her, Micaela Dupree took the letter from her mother. There was silence as she read the offending document. She sighed heavily. "It is true," she said in a voice of deep gloom. "He is moving here."

The two women, who appeared more like sisters than mother and daughter, were seated side by side on a delicate settee covered in worn blue velvet in a small room at the rear of the Duprees' New Orleans townhouse. It was midmorning on a cool, wet Monday in late February 1804, and the two ladies had been enjoying a cup of chicory-laden coffee when the letter from Hugh Lancaster had been delivered.

The arrival of a letter had been unusual enough to add some excitement to a dull day, but the news it brought had totally destroyed the pleasant mood they had been enjoying.

Micaela's lovely but troubled dark eyes looked at her mother. "Francois," she said slowly, referring to her brother, a year younger than herself, "is going to be most disturbed by this news."

Lisette nodded. "And your uncle Jean, too."

The two women sighed almost simultaneously, their resemblance to each other even more obvious. Only a few weeks away from her twenty-first birthday, Micaela was in the full bloom of her undeniable beauty, while Lisette, having turned thirty-eight just the previous month, was a fetchingly mature version of her only daughter. They did not look precisely alike; Micaela's nose was longer than her mother's charmingly retroussé affair, her brows thicker and more noticeably arched, and her mouth more lavishly formed, with a decidedly saucy curve to it. Both women were small boned; Micaela, however, much to her chagrin, stood three inches taller than her petite mother. The shapes under their simple muslin gowns were curvaceous with full bosoms, narrow waists and generously rounded hips. The celebrated creamy matte complexion which each possessed contrasted enchantingly with their gleaming blue-black hair and long-lashed midnight black eyes. With lips as red as cherries, pale lovely skin and flashing ebony glances, their proud Creole blood was very evident.

"What are we going to do?" Micaela asked eventually, as she handed the letter back to Lisette.

Lisette shrugged. "There is nothing that we *can* do. The American is coming to live in New Orleans—whether we like it or not."

Micaela stood up and took agitated steps around the pleasantly shabby little room. Stopping to look out at the rain-splattered courtyard at the rear of the house, she said moodily, "If only that arrogant creature Napoleon had not seen fit to sell us to the Americans like a cartload of old fish! I still cannot believe that it is done—that we are now to call ourselves Americans! Unthinkable! We are French! Creoles!"

Though it had been over seven months since the inhabitants of New Orleans had heard of the sale of the entire Louisiana Territory to the fledgling United States, the actual exchange had taken place barely two months ago in the waning days of 1803. It had been raining that day, too, Micaela thought unhappily. It was not fair! To be sold to those rude, overbearing Americans on the whim of an upstart Corsican general who now had plans to name himself Emperor of the French!

The Americans had been jubilant at the sale; they had long desired free use of the mighty Mississippi River and the Port of New Orleans, the gateway to the ocean and European ports. The Creoles had been stunned, despising the Americans on principle, thinking them loud, vulgar and brash.

The Creole population almost unanimously resented the presence of the new owners of the Territory, many unwilling to even speak to one of those cursed *Americains,* their wives refusing to have them in their homes. Of course, the Americans reciprocated the feeling in full measure, convinced that the Creoles were lazy, vain, and frivolous. Each faction regarded the other with loathing, suspicion, and mistrust.

Micaela's mouth twisted. And the arrival of Hugh Lancaster, one of those despised *Americains,* was going to make the Dupree family painfully aware of just how much had changed since the Territory had become American. Her brother and her uncle were going to be livid.

"I wonder," Micaela said softly, "why Monsieur Lancaster wrote to you and not Uncle Jean? Should not *mon oncle* have been notified first?"

Lisette looked uncomfortable. "Your uncle has not been very, er, pleasant to Monsieur Lancaster when he has come to the city on business. I assume he thought that I would view his intentions more kindly."

Micaela glanced at her mother in astonishment. "Do you?"

Lisette became extremely interested in the fabric of her

gown. "Not exactly . . ." A rosy hue blooming in her cheeks, she murmured, "I—I—I have never held the Americans in quite the aversion that everyone else does." Meeting her daughter's stunned gaze, she added firmly, "I actually liked young Hugh the few times I have met him—he . . . he seems a personable young man."

"But maman! He will ruin us! You know that he believes that someone is stealing from the partnership. You know that the last time he was here, he almost as good as accused *mon oncle* of outright thievery—Francois, too—do not forget that!"

"I have not forgotten; I think that Hugh is simply mistaken, but I do not blame him for being concerned. Something is obviously amiss. The profits of Galland, Lancaster and Dupree have been falling for the past eighteen months, and the report that we received in September, when Hugh was last here, makes it clear that *someone* has been very careless in making proper records of our various sales and expenditures. In all the years that we have been in partnership with Hugh's stepfather, John, we have never suffered a decline in profits like we have recently."

"You mean since papa and grandpere died and Jean and Francois have been overseeing the firm, do you not?" Micaela demanded tightly.

"Your grandfather died over two years ago," Lisette gently reminded Micaela. "Your father has been dead for five and Jean has been handling Renault's share of the business for you and Francois since that time. Do you suspect your uncle of doing something to harm his own fortune as well as yours and Francois'?" She arched a brow and then went on calmly. "As for your brother . . ." An indulgent smile crossed her face. "I know he is young and spoiled, but he will grow up into a fine man; he only needs time. Do you really think that Francois would do anything to harm the firm his own father and grandfather founded? He will, as you will, eventually own fifteen percent of the business. Do you truly think that he would steal from himself?"

Micaela made a face, trying to think of a tactful way to tell her mother that Francois was more than just spoiled. He was, Micaela thought unhappily, *extremely* spoiled. His father's only son and heir, and presently his uncle's heir, too, from birth Francois had been pampered and doted upon by everyone. Her charming, handsome brother was not selfish by nature, Micaela admitted fairly. He could be quite generous and thoughtful—when the whim struck him. But . . . She sighed. Unfortunately, in Creole society, the males were the light of their fathers' eyes, the joy of their mothers'; gods to their wives and indulgent, generous fathers to their children. Was she merely being jealous that Francois had been born a male while she was only a lowly female? Not liking to think she could be that petty, she wrinkled her nose and tried to think more charitably of her sometimes infuriating younger brother. Perhaps maman was right—he was simply young and in time would be more responsible than he appeared to be now.

As if her thoughts had conjured him up, Francois, a merry smile upon his delicately handsome features, strolled into the room. He was a slim, elegant young man, not more than an inch taller than his sister and fashionably garbed in a form-fitting jacket of Spanish blue cloth with a striped marseilles waistcoat above his nankeen breeches and boots. His black hair gleamed in the light of the candles that had been lit because of the gray day, and his dark, speaking eyes were warm as they fell upon the two women. Approaching Lisette with his quick light stride, he bent down and exuberantly kissed her on both cheeks. "Ah, maman! You grow lovelier every day. I am a fortunate son, to have such a beautiful and charming maman!"

Lisette smiled with pleasure and caressed his cheek. "Such gallantry, so early in the morning, *mon amour!* I suspect that there is a fine new horse that you simply *must* have—or is it a new carriage?" The fondness of her expression took any sting out of the words.

Francois laughed without embarrassment. "Ah, maman—

you know me too well! Which does not mean that I do not truly think you beautiful and charming."

Glancing across to Micaela, he said, *"Bonjour,* Caela, you are also looking extremely becoming today."

Micaela cocked a brow at his fulsome manner and wasn't the least surprised at the hint of color that leaped into his cheeks at her expression. Turning hurriedly back to Lisette, he sat down gracefully beside her and, taking one of her hands in his, he said in a coaxing voice, "Maman, there is a horse, a most handsome animal I assure you, and the cost will not be too dear."

Involuntarily Micaela made a vexed sound. "Have you run through this quarter's allowance already—gambled it away?" she asked quietly.

"It is none of your affair," he said grandly, then spoiled the effect by demanding, "What difference is it to you? I am a man now and my money is mine to spend as I see fit."

"Perhaps if you would spend it more wisely, you wouldn't have to come begging to maman to buy you a new horse just halfway into the new quarter," Micaela snapped before she could stop herself.

A scowl marred Francois' handsome features and a hot retort hovered on his lips.

"Children!" Lisette said hastily. "That is enough! The day is unpleasant enough without the two of you squabbling."

Micaela made a face and turned away to stare out the window once more. It was senseless to try to convince Francois that the Duprees were not as wealthy as they once had been. They were not poor, *merci, non!* but they no longer commanded a fortune that was so large that it seemed endless. Her father's and her grandfather's gambling habits had seen to that! It was because of her grandfather Christophe's gaming losses that a pair of outsiders, Jasper De Marco and Alain Husson, now possessed an interest in the family firm. It appeared that Francois had also inherited the fatal trait.

The once great wealth of the Galland and Dupree families had been reduced to a comfortable size rather than the impressive amount it had been just a decade or two ago. In fact the major source of their income came these days from Galland, Lancaster, and Dupree, although the plantations that remained did contribute a small amount to their wealth. Micaela sighed. Regrettably, Francois could not seem to be brought to understand that he could not game away a small fortune night after night and still be able to live in the grand manner in which they had in the past. And maman, she thought half-annoyed, half-tenderly, cannot seem to understand that it is doing Francois no good for her to continue to buy him whatever strikes his fancy as has been done since he was a child! Another horse! Why, there must be a dozen or so eating their heads off in the Dupree stables at this very moment—and those were only the horses in the city!

Closing her ears to Francois' wheedling voice, Micaela stared unseeing down at the wet courtyard. She already knew how this little tête-à-tête was going to end—Francois would get his horse. A rueful smile suddenly curved her mouth. She didn't know why she resented Francois' actions so very much; maman would do the same for her if she expressed a yearning for a new gown, or even a new horse, no matter how outrageously expensive. Perhaps it was because Francois did it so regularly and took maman's generosity as his right?

Telling herself that there was nothing she could do about Francois' spendthrift habits, she turned her thoughts to the disturbing letter announcing Hugh Lancaster's imminent arrival in the city. Lisette had met him a few times over the years, but Micaela had only met him this past September, when Jean had reluctantly invited Lancaster to dine and stay the night at the Dupree plantation, some miles below New Orleans. Even now, several months later, she could still feel the powerful jolt of awareness that had gone through her when Hugh Lancaster, a tall, powerfully built young man of thirty, had politely bent over her hand and brushed his lips across her suddenly sensitized flesh, his cool gray-eyed glance moving indifferently over her.

Micaela, though unmarried at an age when most Creole daughters were already wives of many years and mothers of hopeful families, was not used to handsome young men looking at her in that particularly dismissing manner. Almost without fail, there was a glint of admiration in their eyes when they met her and, without being vain, she had expected no less from Hugh Lancaster. That he had seemed utterly indifferent to her had been something of a shock, especially when she saw the charming manner with which he had greeted and conversed with Lisette. Of course, Lisette had been clearly pleased to see him, while the remainder of the family and been stiff and icily polite.

Micaela had told herself repeatedly that it did not matter that Hugh Lancaster did not hold her in high esteem—after all, he was an *Americain*. What did she care for his opinion of her?

Only to herself would she admit that the tall, broad-shouldered American had, despite her will to the contrary, piqued her interest. He was very different from the Creole gentlemen whom she had known all her life, although with his black hair and olive complexion, he had the look of the Creole—especially those of Spanish blood. Whether it was his commanding height—at six feet he towered over all of the Duprees—or the startling impact of those thickly lashed gray eyes in that dark face, or the cool, precise way he talked as opposed to the excited volubility of her uncle and Francois, she couldn't tell. But something about him awoke an odd feeling deep within her—a feeling that none of her many Creole suitors had ever aroused—and it frightened her. She scowled, suddenly angry at herself. She did *not* want to think about Hugh Lancaster!

Micaela had not been paying attention to the conversation between Lisette and Francois, but the moment she heard him exclaim, "*Mon Dieu!* You are not serious!" she knew exactly what caused his outburst—maman had obviously told him of Hugh's plan to move to New Orleans.

Micaela swung around and watched his face as he finished reading the letter, all signs of his merry smile and light mood vanishing. His face pale with anger, he glanced toward Lisette. "Why did he write to you? Does the swine have no manners? It is to *mon oncle* that he should have imparted this news."

Seeing that her mother was groping for a tactful way to explain the probable reasons for Hugh's actions, Micaela said swiftly, "It does not matter to whom he has written. All that matters is that he is determined to move to New Orleans within the next few months."

Francois jumped up from the settee. "I will not have that overbearing *Americain* snooping in our business! From the very beginning the Duprees and Gallands have always controlled this end of the partnership—without interference from the Lancasters. I will not have it! *Sacre bleu!* To have him looking over my shoulder all the time. It is insupportable!"

Micaela said nothing, merely watching as her brother raged about the room, his handsome features tight with fury. She did not blame him—there was a certain amount of truth in what he said.

In the very early 1780s when Christophe Galland, John Lancaster, and Renault and Jean Dupree had formed Galland, Lancaster and Dupree, it had been decided, as Francois had said, that the Galland and Dupree partners would handle all the affairs in New Orleans. This had been agreed upon simply because they were residents and could deal with the local officials, the overtly suspicious Spaniards—something that John Lancaster, as an American, could not.

John Lancaster might have owned fifty-five percent of the new partnership, but without Christophe Galland and the Dupree brothers he would not have been able to freely do business in New Orleans and so he had wisely given the Creole partners carte blanche there. But it was Lancaster, headquartered upriver in Natchez, who procured the majority of the raw products that were barged down the Mississippi River to New Orleans and that were loaded onto the ships for export. It was Lancaster, too, who dispersed most of the goods that were carried in the holds of the ships on their return journey to New Orleans to eager American buyers. For nearly twenty years, it had been a very profitable partnership and it had worked exceedingly well, because Lancaster astutely stayed in Natchez and, with scant interference, let the Creole faction run the New Orleans end. But apparently, that was about to change.

Three years ago John Lancaster, thinking to retire, had sold Hugh a forty-five-percent interest in the partnership, retaining only a ten-percent interest for himself. Hugh had acted as his stepfather's agent for a number of years and already had a keen understanding of the business, at least the Natchez end of things, but since then with increasing frequency he had been asking many pointed questions about the affairs of the New Orleans portion of the business. Considering that Hugh was now the largest single shareholder, his deepening interest was justified, but both Micaela's grandfather and uncle had been highly affronted by the situation. And while she had listened to them rail against what they claimed to be Hugh's unwarranted intervention in affairs that were none of his business, she had privately thought his visits and queries not exactly *un*reasonable—annoying and irritating perhaps, but not totally without justification.

Her grandfather's death, however, seemed to have engendered in Hugh Lancaster an acute concern about the future of the partnership. Micaela suspected that it was because of the long-existing hostility that existed between Hugh and her uncle Jean. Christophe Galland had acted as a buffer between the two younger men, but his death had forced them to deal directly with each other.

As his only child, Lisette had inherited Christophe's remaining shares and, not inclined toward business herself, she had, not unnaturally, asked her brother-in-law to handle her shares, just as he did his brother's for Francois and Micaela. With John Lancaster preferring these days to let Hugh run things, Hugh and Jean, as the two active principals, were almost continually at odds—the shares owned by De Marco and Husson were nominal and their dabbling in the business was perfunctory. The situation between Hugh and Jean, however, was most unpleasant, especially when coupled with the general animosity most Creoles felt toward Americans, which was now further exacerbated by the sale of the Louisiana Territory to those same despised Americans.

Growing weary of Francois' increasingly tiresome tirade against the American, she glanced back at him and commented, "Francois, you are beginning to repeat yourself. I think that you have made your feelings about Monsieur Lancaster quite clear to both maman and me. Obviously, you are not happy at the prospect of Monsieur Lancaster living in the area, but there is nothing that maman and I can do about it. I suggest that you take your views to Monsieur Lancaster."

"Micaela!" exclaimed Lisette sharply. "Do not even suggest such a thing! It would be rude and uncalled for . . . and . . . and just not wise."

Micaela was instantly ashamed of herself, knowing what her mother had left unsaid. Francois' hot temper was notorious and though he had just turned twenty at the beginning of the month, he had already fought two duels. Fortunately, they had both been with high-spirited young men his own age over trifling matters and no one had been seriously hurt. Hugh Lancaster's skill with both pistol and sword, however, was well known up and down the Mississippi. If Francois were to provoke the older man to a duel . . . Micaela's mouth went dry and she cursed her unruly tongue.

Francois looked from one woman to the other. He drew himself up stiffly. "You think that I would deign to challenge Hugh Lancaster to a duel, *oui*?" Fierce pride glittering in his dark eyes, he spat, "You have nothing to fear—I would not sully my hands fighting with an *Americain*!"

"That is very high minded of you," Lisette said gently, "but if you do not wish to inadvertently provoke a quarrel with him, I would suggest that you, if not graciously, at least politely, accept the fact that he is moving to New Orleans."

Francois grimaced, silently acknowledging the wisdom of her words. Sending a sheepish grin to both women, he muttered, "I have been acting rather a fool, haven't I?"

Micaela smiled warmly back at him. Francois' mercurial moods were one of his charms. A teasing twinkle in her eyes, she said lightly, "Since I do not intend to risk another display such as we have just seen, I shall not answer that question."

Francois laughed and, bowing to first one and then the other, he said, "Forgive me! I let my vile temper rule me."

"There is nothing to forgive, *mon fils*," Lisette said fondly. "It is understandable that you would be upset by the news, but we must accept the fact that Hugh Lancaster will be living in the city and that he will, no doubt, be taking an even more active interest in the business."

Francois sat down once more by his mother. Shaking his head, he said wryly, "Well, if you think that I took the news badly, *mon Dieu*! I do not even want to consider how *mon oncle* will take it when he finds out! We should be grateful that he is out of the city until tomorrow. At least we will not have to face his rage today."

It happened that the family had more of a respite before facing Jean's expected displeasure at the news than they had thought. He had been due back from the Dupree plantation the next day, but that very afternoon a servant had appeared with a note from him, informing Francois that it would be three days hence, on Thursday, before he returned. By tacit agreement no one sent a return message to him revealing Hugh Lancaster's intentions.

On Friday morning they were still at breakfast, seated around a small table, considering how to break the news, when the door to the pleasant room was suddenly flung open. His dark eyes blazing, his normally even features twisted with outrage, Jean Dupree burst into the room. "Do you know," he demanded in savage accents, "who just walked up to me on Chartres Street? *Hugh Lancaster!*"